DEADLY
CHARADE

FBI NEW RECRUITS #1

DEADLY CHARADE

LYNETTE EASON &
KELLY UNDERWOOD

Revell
a division of Baker Publishing Group
Grand Rapids, Michigan

Published by Revell
a division of Baker Publishing Group
Grand Rapids, Michigan
RevellBooks.com

Printed in the United States of America

Library of Congress Cataloging-in-Publication Data
Names: Eason, Lynette author | Underwood, Kelly author
Title: Deadly charade / Lynette Eason and Kelly Underwood.
Description: Grand Rapids, Michigan : Revell, a division of Baker Publishing Group, 2026. | Series: FBI new recruits ; 1
Identifiers: LCCN 2026001972 | ISBN 9780800747640 paperback | ISBN 9781493455539 ebook
Subjects: LCGFT: Romance fiction | Christian fiction | Detective and mystery fiction | Novels
Classification: LCC PS3605.A79 D43 2026
LC record available at https://lccn.loc.gov/2026001972

Cover design by Mumtaz Mustafa

Baker Publishing Group publications use paper produced from sustainable forestry practices and postconsumer waste whenever possible.

26 27 28 29 30 31 32 7 6 5 4 3 2 1

LYNETTE:

I love the dedication page. An author puts a LOT of thought into who she wants to dedicate a story to. It's not done lightly. On that note, this book is dedicated to my good friend, Dru Wells—or her official title, FBI Supervisory Special Agent (Ret.) Drucilla L. Wells, BAU/CIRG (Behavioral Analysis Unit, Critical Incident Response Group). Dru is so generous with the amount of time she gives for *free* to read the books and offer her expertise in the law enforcement arena. She gave a ton of feedback for this story, and we worked hard to make sure it reflected that. If we got something wrong, that's on us, not her! So, thank you very much, Dru! Love you bunches.

KELLY:

Dedicated to the memory of a good friend and fellow writer, Wesley "Dave" Crowder. We're all grieved by the sudden loss, and I just hope heaven has an endless supply of Dr Pepper for you.

1

FBI SPECIAL AGENT KIRA MILLER circled the glass case housing a long-forgotten piece of history. Six cameras, four infrared lasers, and pressure plates built into the tile floor might be overkill. But no one would get near the art gallery's prized possession—an ugly marble rabbit statue.

"I will never understand the hype of this piece," Kira whispered to the empty room.

She leaned over the gold velvet ropes that cordoned off the priceless Russian artifact display and stared at the figure perched on top of a steel pedestal.

People were talking about this statue on the dark web, and that had caught Kira's attention, enough for her to visit District Gallery in the heart of Washington, DC, on a Saturday evening.

A gallery attendant walked into the exhibit area, adjusted his blue blazer, and approached her, looking down his nose at her casual appearance—jeans, a white T-shirt with a Harley-Davidson logo, and a leather jacket. Apparently her staple outfit violated the art gallery's dress code, but she'd made the trip on impulse on her day off. So, she'd work with what she had.

Time to play infatuated art student. Kira shot the well-built man a smile. "Do you have more information about this piece?"

She pointed to the statue, then pulled out a notepad from her crossbody bag.

The man—his name tag read Vince Palmer—checked his watch and smirked. “I suppose. But we close in fifteen minutes.” His haughty attitude had faded somewhat with her interest, and he began his spiel. She pegged the man to be in his late thirties, with silver peeking around the edges of thick dark hair. He droned on about Russian artifacts while Kira inspected the display. His stare irritated her, but she feigned interest in his rehearsed speech. She’d already studied the piece and likely knew more than he did, even though his main role was to answer questions about the artwork.

“One fortunate person purchased this particular statue at an estate sale.” The man’s nasally voice scraped over her nerves, but she needed to glean some new insight so her supervisor would open an official investigation. “After authentication, this statue has been confirmed to be part of a Russian art collection thought to be lost during World War II. We have a few other pieces you might be interested in . . .” He started toward a different exhibit, but Kira didn’t follow.

“Could I have a minute, please?” She stood in front of the slender eight-inch marble statue of a rabbit with a placard that read “Зайка (Zaika).”

“The little bunny,” she said, her voice low, reverent.

“That’s right.” Vince sidled up next to her, his eyes narrowed behind glasses with lenses thicker than the case enclosing Zaika. “Do you speak Russian?”

“A little bit.”

That was an understatement. Kira grew up in a Russian orphanage until an American family adopted her at age ten. She spoke fluent Russian. It was one reason she now had a desk job with the FBI instead of working in the field. The other? Kira rolled her shoulders and heaved an inward sigh of relief at the very minimal twinge. During her last defensive tactics training at Quantico, she tore her rotator cuff. She had surgery the day after graduation, and the FBI assigned her to the linguistics team until she healed.

At least she was able to graduate, but a boring desk job wasn't why she signed up to be a Special Agent. She had to endure only one more week, as long as her doctor cleared her as fit for duty. For now her reality consisted of translating snippets of conversations and emails from Russian into English while counting down the seconds until she could be assigned a field position.

"I don't understand why a hunk of rock is so important," she said. Playing dumb wasn't exactly something she enjoyed, but she did it well. "Why all the security?"

He raised a brow and grunted. "This is a very rare find. The piece dates to the seventeenth century, but a lot of Russian art disappeared in the early twentieth century and scattered. This finding proves . . ."

She already knew that. If only she could examine the statue. What was so important about a statue of a bunny that two Russians would reference it in a conversation?

Zaika moy. My little bunny.

None of the higher-ups at the FBI bought her theory—that the Russians were talking about this particular artifact.

But there *had* to be something here. Her gut instinct rarely steered her wrong. As a former New York Police Department detective before joining the FBI, she had a knack for spotting the signs that a crime was imminent.

It couldn't be a coincidence that the Russians referenced Zaika with this exhibit in town.

"Excuse me a moment, please," her guide said.

"Of course."

Vince greeted another patron but kept glancing back at her as if to say, *You don't belong here.* Was he afraid she'd steal something? Probably.

A security guard entered the room, followed by a well-dressed older man. The pair hovered in the corner of the exhibit room and whispered. Intensity laced their hushed tones. An argument? In Russian? She was across the room, too far away to eavesdrop, and she couldn't get any closer without drawing suspicion. Could she?

She returned her attention to the plain statue that had an estimated market value in the millions. The piece was nondescript—a shiny white-and-gray hunk of marble chiseled into the shape of a rabbit. Nondescript was Kira's best adjective to describe the long-lost piece of art. The rabbit sat with its front paws on its long torso, poised to hop off its pedestal. But the ears were the biggest feature—long and pointing straight up, with a small gap between the two oblong shapes. She expected some bling or ornate carvings, but other than the sparkly amber-colored gems for eyes, nothing stood out on the piece.

How could a piece of rock hold that much value? Imagine what that kind of money would do for starving children in orphanages. Instead, the overpriced estate-sale find of the century sat behind thick glass panels while tourists gawked at it. One man had paid ten dollars for the statue, and the art gallery bought it for an undisclosed amount. That lucky man became an instant millionaire.

A loud family with four children passed through the room, and Kira fell into step with them as the two men in the corner fell silent. The din of excited voices bounced off the barren beige walls of the square room. When they exited through an archway leading to the next exhibit, she feigned interest in a nearby exhibit, planting herself in front of it so she could see the men in her peripheral vision.

With the family gone, the two men resumed their heated discussion. The security guard's face turned red. The man in the black suit and tie pointed a finger at the guard, accusing him of . . . something. She kept her focus on the painting in front of her while scoping them out.

Her gut reaction reaffirmed her suspicions—these men were up to no good. A sheen of sweat dotted the security guard's forehead. The bigger guy's voice grated with agitation, and the security guard waved his hands in front of him as if in surrender.

"I don't have it," the guard said in Russian, his panicked voice raised enough for Kira to translate. "I need more time."

So, this was a shakedown? Money? Art? And who were these guys anyway?

Kira frowned. Should she get involved? It might be nothing. After all, she had just wanted to check out the statue and the gallery security. She took out a notebook and pretended to jot notes about the painting. But she couldn't escape the image of the security guard's pale face and shaky hands.

The voices fell away, and she checked over her shoulder. The men had disappeared and the door marked Staff Only clicked shut. The gallery attendant had also left the room, probably ushering other patrons toward the exit for closing time.

Why were her instincts screaming at her to follow the men? The heated argument and angry voice of the older man had given her goose bumps. Something was off.

This wasn't an active investigation, but the security guard could be in danger. She walked to the staff door and listened. Raised voices caught her attention. The men were still arguing. Making a split-second decision, she cracked open the door and scanned the hallway.

No one.

She stepped into the back rooms of the gallery to confirm the guard's safety. Then she'd hightail it out of the gallery.

The area resembled a ghost town. She started walking past the paintings stacked along the hallway, and multiple rooms contained portraits, sculptures, and display cases. Not very well organized for an art gallery. Then again, the public didn't see this part.

The voices reached her from the end of the hall, so she headed in the direction of the red exit sign. If they were leaving, the guard might be good, but she needed to make sure he wasn't being targeted or in trouble.

Another door slammed, and Kira followed the source of the noise into a stairwell. To her left, stairs led to the second floor. To her right, she faced a door, its exit sign plastered across the peeling white paint. Which way?

She hit the metal bar and pushed the door open. Cold rain pelted her in the face. She hugged the inside wall, checking her surroundings before stepping outside. Fluorescent lights lit the service alleyway behind the gallery. The smell of the dumpster sent her gag reflexes into overdrive.

She took a few more steps and stopped. Her gaze focused on the narrow alleyway between two buildings that led to the main road. Had the security guard or the man run out the back door? What were they up to?

As if to answer her question, the man in the suit stepped out from behind the trash bin and swung a piece of a frame like a baseball bat. Kira tried to duck, but it connected with her forehead in a glancing blow. The nausea hit before the throbbing pain registered. Spots danced in front of her eyes. She lost her balance but caught herself and staggered back. Her hand went to the empty area where her gun should be. And wasn't.

The attacker ran, his steps echoing through the alley. Buildings surrounded them on either side. Blood flecks speckled her white T-shirt from the cut on her forehead. She stanched the bleeding with her sleeve, and it appeared to be minor.

She checked the area for anything she could use as a weapon. If only she had brought her gun. By law, she could carry the weapon anywhere, but she'd expected to spend her off-duty evening touring a gallery, not defending herself from a bad guy in some dark back alley. So, she had decided not to tangle with the gallery security screeners in hopes of flying under the radar. Lesson learned.

She reached into the dumpster and pulled out a broken chair leg. At least it was something heavy she could use as a makeshift weapon. Adrenaline took over, and she sprinted and caught up with the guy. He stopped to take another swing with his improvised bat, but Kira deflected it with the wooden chair leg and countered with a roundhouse kick to the man's side.

He staggered, his dark eyes full of rage. "You don't know who you are messing with." The man spat out the words in Russian, but Kira pretended not to understand.

The guy had to be in his late fifties—pretty fit for an older guy—with dark hair peppered with gray around his temples and a goatee. He gave off godfather vibes. Russian mafia? What had she stumbled into?

And here she was.

They stared each other down, until the man whipped out a knife from inside his jacket and flung it at Kira. She hit the ground, the blade passing over her head and clanging off a dumpster.

He bolted toward the main road. She jumped up to go after him, but he threw himself into the passenger seat of a waiting car. She stumbled to a stop at the curb, trying to grab the license plate number while he waved his ring-clad stubby fingers to her from the window. But the plate had been covered up. Just great.

Kira backtracked to the gallery's exit. If the suit was bad news, what had happened to the security guard?

She reentered the building through the back door and stopped short at a noise.

"Help." A voice rasped and then coughed.

Kira turned toward the stairwell and walked around to the alcove behind the stairs.

A man lay slumped over. A pool of blood coated the gray concrete floor.

She gasped. "No, no, no." The security guard lay against the wall under the stairs, his hand clutching his chest.

She raced to the victim on the ground. Where had he come

from? The area had been empty when she came out of the building. Kira's head swiveled around to check for trouble.

Blood seeped through the guard's fingers. A dagger like the one the Russian guy had flung at her lay next to the man. Kira dropped to her knees next to him. So much blood.

He wheezed. "Closer." He coughed.

She took off her leather jacket and pressed it against the wound. He wrapped his bloody hand around her T-shirt and tugged her down next to his moving lips. But she still couldn't make out words.

"What is it?" she asked.

"Zaika."

"What?"

"Follow the rabbits." The man's breathless voice made it hard to hear. His eyes closed, and Kira checked his pulse.

Nothing.

The man was gone.

"Hold it right there, ma'am."

Two DC Metropolitan police officers and four armed security guards surrounded her.

"I'm FBI," she said. "I'm going to reach for my badge."

"Don't move." One of the officers trained a gun on Kira.

"This isn't what it looks like." Why did she say *that*?

She was hovering over a body in the back of an art gallery, covered in the victim's blood, next to the murder weapon on the ground. If she were a police officer, she wouldn't buy her story.

She could kiss her job goodbye. Because after this stunt, she'd be lucky if she even kept her job in linguistics.

THE TRILL OF A CELL PHONE kicked FBI Special Agent Bryce Lambert into action, and he swiped at the nightstand to answer the call. In the dark, he missed the iPhone and sent his lamp flying off the edge. The crash helped push the fog of sleep away. He opened his eyes, located the phone, and connected to the call from his supervisor.

"I have news you'll want to hear." No introduction, no pleasantries. His boss, Assistant Special Agent in Charge Leon Soto, cut straight to the point.

Bryce rolled out of bed, put the phone on speaker, and began to dress. Getting a call at 1:30 in the morning meant he needed to be somewhere ten minutes ago, making him already late. "I'm listening."

"I got a call from the Supervisory Special Agent in our DC Field Office. Jeremiah Turner has a rookie agent that may have stumbled into your active case. His team looked into her discovery and validated Agent Miller's findings, which led them to contact us. They have credible evidence that suggests a Russian artifact might be a target for the art smuggling ring you've been investigating."

Interesting. "What'd she discover?"

"She's been working in linguistics and translated a conversation. A Russian attorney is very interested in a piece called Zaika."

Bryce had heard of it. The bunny. "It's allegedly the first piece that has surfaced from a crate of looted art that went missing from Germany. A gallery in DC has it on display. But why call in the middle of the night?"

"I figured you'd want to talk to Agent Miller, who is currently in Metro Police's custody. Apparently a security guard at the gallery was murdered, and Agent Miller happened to be in the wrong place at the wrong time. Supervisory Special Agent Turner from the Washington Field Office wants our offices to work together on this one. We're not investigating the murder, but having a dead body at the art gallery tells me there may be eyes on this statue."

"I'm on my way."

He stifled a groan. A rookie in police custody? Not a great

way to start her career. But if his supervisor thought she had information that advanced his case, he'd make the two-hour trek from Richmond, Virginia, to DC without complaint. Or much anyway.

He grabbed his company-issued windbreaker and headed out the door.

Who was Special Agent Kira Miller and what had she gotten herself into? He wished he'd asked a few more questions, but he wasn't going to call Soto back now.

After a pit stop at a twenty-four-hour gas station for some caffeine, Bryce had made the trip in record time and now sat across from Agent Miller in the cold, gray, sterile police conference room.

"I didn't kill that security guard," she said.

He said nothing. She held his gaze, with her arms folded over her bloodstained T-shirt. Her long black hair spilled curls across her shoulders. The woman had a "don't mess with me" attitude etched across her face, but something about her intrigued Bryce.

"The place has a million cameras, and my prints aren't on the knife. How do I know that? Because I'm smart enough to not touch an obvious murder weapon." She issued her defense as if he were the judge.

She never broke eye contact with him, her warm brown eyes challenging him.

He leaned back in his chair, the metal groaning. Bryce flipped through his hastily scribbled notes that he'd jotted down when ASAC Soto had rattled off information at a rapid-fire pace. Too bad the agency didn't provide handwriting analysis classes to interpret his own early morning scrawl.

"Let me get this straight," he said. "On your day off, you follow a hunch about a translation that no one deemed important enough to investigate and somehow manage to chase a possible Russian mobster down an alley. Then you're caught kneeling over a dead body, with blood on your clothes. Am I leaving anything out?"

"That's a pretty accurate assessment." She blew out a breath. "I wasn't expecting anything to go down. I just wanted to check out the security. For my troubles, the Russian guy hit me with the side of a painting frame." She pointed to the bandaged spot on her forehead. "And threw a dagger at me. Then I ran him down until he hopped into a waiting car. And before you ask, no, I didn't get the plate. It was covered up. Once I lost him, I went back and found the security guard. And the others found me. That's about it."

Could this be a connection to his case? Maybe, but he needed more information. His first impression of the calm, cool, collected rookie? She was beautiful and smart, yet took unnecessary risks. His mind screamed at him to keep his distance, but curiosity was getting the best of him.

He leaned forward and placed his hands on the table. "I'll let the police know you'll cooperate and give a full statement. Plus, you'll need to sit with a sketch artist. You're on administrative duty, not in the field until you're medically cleared. What were you thinking?"

The metal chair scraped the floor when she shifted. "The same thing you're thinking. Why else would the higher-ups send you to bail me out? We've never met, so I must be onto something. Possibly this situation intersects with one of your active cases?"

He tried not to smile at her spot-on intuition. He waved his hand. "Please, enlighten me. Why did I get out of bed at one thirty and drive two hours to bail a total stranger out of the Metro Police station?"

She leaned across the table and lowered her voice. "I translated a conversation from the dark web, and it led me to the gallery to do a little research and see if my theory panned out."

"And what is your theory?"

She smiled. "That the Russians are a little too interested in Zaika."

His adrenaline spiked at the mention of the rabbit statue. His team had suspected it originated from treasure looted in World War II and couldn't help wondering if, since it was found in West Virginia, there would be more pieces going up for sale.

This had the smuggling ring's fingerprints all over it. A priceless piece like that? They'd sell it, and a part of history would disappear forever.

Along with the auctioneer he'd been trying to stop. His team worked hard, but they'd never found the locations for the illegal auctions until after the smugglers skipped town with their cash from the sale of stolen art pieces.

Still, Agent Miller needed more solid evidence for him to be able to follow these new leads. "Zaika might be the pet name for a loved one. The man may have been talking about his wife." He made a mental note to review the transcripts.

"You don't believe me." Agent Miller shook her head and sank back in her chair, arms folded again. "Just because I'm a new agent that's been assigned to desk duty doesn't mean I don't have strong instincts."

Bryce leaned forward, not taking his eyes off Kira. "I wouldn't have driven two hours in the middle of the night if I didn't intend to hear you out. I'm not questioning your instincts. I'm just trying to wrap my mind around your claims and see what I can do about them."

She glanced up at the camera mounted in the corner of the room. "Is that recording?"

"No. I asked an officer to turn off the cameras so we could speak freely."

She relaxed. "The security guard wasn't dead when I found him. One of his last words to me was 'Zaika.'"

Okay then. She was definitely onto something.

She stood, placing her hands on the table. "The dead security guard and the other man were speaking in the exhibit room directly across from the statue, Agent Lambert. I tried to get close enough to them to hear their conversation but only managed to pick up a few words. However, I could tell they were speaking fluent Russian. I heard the security guard saying 'I don't have it' and 'I need more time.'"

Interesting. If the Russians were after the rabbit statue, the piece had value—more than just a hefty asking price. "Let's debrief first thing on Monday. I still don't understand why you were there, and I'd like to hear more about your theories."

And maybe score an opportunity to meet this interesting woman again.

Bryce shook his head to dislodge the unruly thought. He'd given up on relationships a long time ago. He knew better than to let those thoughts linger, not when he had a case to close.

She tapped the metal tabletop with her dark red fingernails. Interesting color choice for a Special Agent. It was bold, almost daring. He stared at her until she looked away first.

She ran her fingers through her curls. "I honestly just wanted to see the piece, find out what the fuss was about. Okay, and check the gallery security."

Bryce studied the woman in front of him. "Regardless of what you translated or overheard at the gallery, we don't have definitive proof that anyone is going to steal the statue."

Agent Miller walked to the back corner of the room and leaned against the concrete brick wall, never taking her eyes off him. "I can see it on your face. You believe my hunch that something is going down. Some shady people have their eyes on this particular piece of history. They think it's important. Don't you agree?"

"I do."

She moved back to the table and sank back into the chair. "Then put in a good word with SSA Turner and let me help with the investigation into the statue."

"That's above my pay grade. And you're still on medical

restrictions. From what I can tell, you're doing amazing work in linguistics. Your translation skills far surpass everyone else's." He suspected most translators wouldn't have connected the dots that Agent Miller had, not to mention follow up with a mini off-the-books investigation of their own. He stood and moved toward the door. "I'll get this cleared up with the officers. You need to lie low. Like I said, let's meet on Monday and we can talk some more. I need time to do a little digging."

Bryce found the officer in charge and explained why Agent Miller had been at the gallery. He left out the part where her investigation wasn't sanctioned. The officer relented. They'd checked the security footage and had caught an image of the man she had described, corroborating her story. Bryce asked for copies of the videos and still footage of the suspect.

He walked back into the room where Agent Miller waited, impatience written all over her face, and sat across from her. "I've vouched for you and explained your presence at the gallery. They're releasing you after you give your statement. And we'd like you to review some recent photos of known Russian mobsters to see if you can match them to the suspect at the gallery."

She nodded. "Okay. I will do that. Thanks."

The police detective entered, and Bryce took the chance to leave. "I'll see you on Monday, Agent Miller. We will meet with your boss at the downtown office."

"Please, call me Kira. And I'll be there."

"We can drop the formalities then. Call me Bryce."

A ripple of excitement pulsed through his veins. His fascination with Kira trumped the logical part of his brain, and he'd like to see more of her. What was he getting himself into? She was so clearly an impulsive woman. Bryce didn't have a spontaneous bone in his body. Slow and steady, armed with tons of research before he made any kind of decision or acted. That's how he operated.

Plus, he wasn't interested in a relationship, not after his marriage had crashed and burned. That ship had sailed . . . and sunk. But Kira Miller might be a solid asset in his investigation. She seemed unstoppable, like the type that might kick down the door until she got what she wanted.

And that made him like her more.

2

KIRA SAT ON THE CAFÉ PATIO, a free woman. After countless interviews and working with the sketch artist, the police finally released her. And she did what any newly released prisoner would do. She got a few hours of sleep, then rallied support and headed for food.

She and her roommates Violet Bancroft and Everly Harlowe had a standing Sunday lunch meetup. They'd all met in Quantico and formed their own team as friends and agents who watched out for each other.

"I can't believe Bryce Lambert had to pick you up from the police station." Violet Bancroft's Southern accent made that statement sound even more dramatic. "Although, if I wound up in jail, I'd want a hunky man coming to my rescue. It could have been worse."

Kira couldn't argue that the agent was handsome. Any woman in a twenty-mile radius would notice his rugged jawline, the close-shaven beard, forest-green eyes, and wavy—although a tad too long—brown hair with some hints of silver around the hairline. His attitude and posture screamed *by the book,* but his hair suggested a hint of rebellion, which she liked. A lot. He was probably a little older than her age of thirty-three. She'd guess mid-thirties.

"I wasn't in jail, Vi. I just got detained for being in the wrong place at the wrong time. And I never even heard of Bryce Lambert until this morning."

Violet dipped her chip in the thick, chunky salsa, blond curls swaying around her shoulders. "I met Agent Lambert once. The guy is as straitlaced and by the book as they come. The complete opposite of you. But he's one of the most eligible FBI bachelors. All the ladies adore him, but he's perpetually single for some reason."

"He's so not my type." Memories of her ex-boyfriend popped up unbidden, and she shoved the thoughts aside. It's not like she was interested in the man, not after her last failed relationship with a coworker. Work and romance were a volatile mixture.

But why did she feel the need to justify that she didn't like Bryce Lambert? The man might be good-looking, but her assignment took precedence over the equivalent of a fleeting middle school crush.

Everly cut into her oversized burrito and took a bite, closing her eyes, savoring the flavors. The three took their Mexican food as seriously as they took their friendship. Violet attended church on Sundays, and Kira and Everly always met her afterward for lunch, despite Violet's open-ended invitation to join her for the service.

"Why were you there anyway?" Everly asked. "That doesn't sound like your thing. I see you more at a Harley museum than a pretentious art gallery." Everly's straight black shoulder-length hair contrasted with her light blue eyes. The oversized, burgundy-rimmed glasses added to her nerdy vibe. At least she'd lost the purple-striped hair from last month.

"I thought I had a lead on something big. Something that everyone seemed to ignore."

"Well, you found it." Violet took a bite of her chicken and spinach enchilada. "You walked right into a murder scene."

Kira frowned. "At least Agent Lambert believes me. That's

one good thing he has going for him. He didn't reject my theory. Something is going down and it involves that rabbit statue. I just hope there's some evidence that backs up my hunch and I can be part of the investigation. I can't handle another day chained to a desk, listening to recorded conversations. It's important work, but I just . . . ugh."

"Believe me, fieldwork isn't all it's cracked up to be." Violet might be the definition of a fish out of water as a rookie Special Agent. People underestimated the woman because of her petite size, blond hair, and thick Southern accent, but she was an excellent agent. "I have a temporary partner. Joe Brindleman."

"Brindleman? Why does that name sound familiar?" Everly's eyes darted left and right as she ran the name through the database in her head. The twenty-five-year-old was off-the-chart genius, with an eidetic memory and a knack for all things high tech. The woman had more of a social life online than in real life and rarely left their apartment other than to go to the office and meet for lunch once a week. Even in the office, she kept to herself.

"Got it," Everly said. "Is Brindleman the old New Yorker that smells like a deli? I met him once."

"That's the one. His car has a distinct salami and cheese smell. Because that's what his wife packs him for lunch. Every single day! My favorite had to be the mustard stain down the front of his white shirt, smudged across his ample belly. We interviewed a suspect on my first day, and the man kept staring at the yellow glob. It was quite distracting."

The three dissolved into giggles. Prim and proper Violet never left the house without her outfit pressed and her makeup flawlessly in place. Rumor had it that she was a former model, but Violet spoke little about her past even with them. Other than wanting to leave her old life behind when she joined the Bureau.

"I can't believe they paired you with a slob," Everly said in between bursts of laughter.

Kira took a bite of her enchilada. "My favorite memory of Vi at Quantico is when you shot 100 on range day and they posted your score. Only one other man shot that high in the qualification run. We might be living in the age of equality, but it wasn't hard to see the men were livid to be outperformed by you."

Vi smirked. "I think that's the same day you threatened everyone that if they called me Barbie one more time, you'd level them."

"Hey, I take care of my friends." Kira was the oldest of the group and no one messed with her inner circle.

"How did we all become such great friends?" Everly studied the women. "I mean, Violet is so girlie-girlie. And Kira is the exact opposite. And I don't make friends easily."

"But you keep us grounded, Everly." Violet reached across the table and squeezed Everly's hand. "And you help Kira and me with any technical problem thrown our way. We work well together because we each bring our own unique skills."

"Well, that and we all share the same obsession with queso." Kira picked up the empty cheese dip bowl. "We need to pick a healthier option for lunch next week."

"No way am I giving up my enchiladas." Violet took another bite of her favorite dish. She was lean and fit yet ate cheese with every meal.

The women at the table held a special place in Kira's heart. They'd become the sisters she'd never had. After being adopted by Glen and Jenna Miller when she was ten, Kira experienced a warm and loving home for the first time. But the Millers never had children of their own, and Kira had desperately wanted a sister. Now it felt like she had two.

Kira's phone buzzed on the table. Any work call on a Sunday couldn't be good. She punched the screen. "Hello?"

"Agent Miller, I'd like to talk with you more about your adventures yesterday. We have a situation that's come up and needs immediate attention. How fast can you get to the office?" Her supervisor, SSA Turner, never bothered with pleasantries like a greeting. The man jumped straight to the point, which Kira appreciated.

"I'm on my way."

She ended the call and tucked some bills under her plate. "I'll have to skip dessert. I've got to head to the office. I'll see you back at the loft later." The three of them shared a loft apartment in an up-and-coming part of DC, close enough to the train station so they could easily get to the FBI headquarters. Violet's father was a senator and insisted she live somewhere safe, and Violet needed two roommates to help with the cost. Even then, it was still expensive.

But they'd managed to get assigned to the WFO—Washington Field Office—and all remain in the same city, an unheard-of feat. Typically, new agents had to relocate. It helped that they had different skill sets, so they weren't in the same squads. While they were still in their probationary period, Violet wanted to investigate white-collar crimes while Everly focused on cybercrimes. With Kira's language skills, she hoped to work on organized crime cases.

Kira headed out of the café to her motorcycle parked in front. If only she could enjoy the light-traffic drive through DC, but her mind replayed recent events on a never-ending loop.

She'd completely blown things before she'd officially been in the field.

The last thing she wanted was to be left behind. She'd have to double down on her efforts and show her superiors that she was more than capable of her earned position as a Special Agent. Maybe she'd made a poor choice by visiting the gallery on her own, but her need to prove herself drove that decision.

Twenty minutes later, she parked her bike in the WFO garage and took the elevator to the fourth floor.

She opened the door to Turner's office and stopped short. Bryce Lambert occupied the chair opposite her boss, looking like he just stepped off the cover of a fashion magazine. She ran her fingers through her windblown locks.

Well, her dreary day just found a ray of sunshine. Violet's comments rang true—*hunky* was a good description of the man. Not that she needed to be noticing that. She nodded to Bryce, then focused on her boss. "You wanted to see me, sir?"

"Have a seat." The fluorescent office light bounced off Turner's shiny scalp. The Black man was in his early fifties and lived and breathed his job. His intense dark eyes with fine lines at the corners scrutinized her.

Kira dropped into the fake leather chair next to Bryce. She glanced at him, wondering if he knew why they were summoned. As though he read her mind, he shrugged his shoulders like he had no idea.

Turner cleared his throat and sank farther into the swivel chair, crossing his thick, muscular arms across his chest. If Kira googled the definition of intimidation, she'd find a picture of this man.

"While I'm not condoning your stunt at the museum earlier," he said, "I've reviewed the transcripts you translated. Not the most riveting material, but you have some good instincts for picking out key words."

He pulled two files from a drawer and dropped them in front of him on the desk. "We've had our eyes on a Russian attorney, Alexandr Dominik, for some time. Analysts have confirmed he was one of the two individuals in the online conversation you translated. We believe he has connections with the Russian mafia—the Bratva. Alex's client list is less than stellar. I spoke with Agent Lambert and he explained the situation. You heard the guard and a man speaking in Russian?"

"Yes, but I was too far away to make out their conversation and didn't want to approach and seem like . . . you know . . . a rookie." Might as well accept that he held the power to make or break her career. All she wanted was an opportunity to prove herself.

Her boss's tight facial features relaxed a fraction. "I do love a good Special Agent who follows her instincts. Next time, give me a heads-up, please. No more going rogue. Don't need you adding to my gray hairs." He ran a hand over his smooth head and she grinned.

At least he wasn't mad.

"I've decided to open an investigation into the threat against Zaika," he said. "If the Russians are interested in the piece, so are we. And now that it's center stage to a murder, our job is to collect more intel." He stood. "Lambert, ASAC Soto has given you a temporary assignment here in the WFO with me. And meet your new temporary partner, Agent Kira Miller."

She blinked back the surprise. If they were partners, this meant—

"Congratulations, Miller. You are cleared to be in the field. I contacted your doctor, and he agreed to lift the restrictions based on your progress. You only had a few days left anyway, and this is now a joint operation between our two offices. Our case intersects with Bryce's investigation into an art smuggling ring. We believe the statue will be sold in an underground auction."

Kira bit her lip to keep her professional demeanor intact, while inwardly she threw a party. She was released to be in the field.

She stared at Turner. The man's grin spread across his face. He passed an envelope to each of them. "Congratulations, Agents Lambert and Miller. You two are going undercover and moving in next door to Alexandr and Sophia Dominik."

"We are?" she asked.

"Yep. As a married couple."

"Wait," Bryce said. "You mean . . ."

"I mean," Turner said with a hint of a smile, "congratulations on your recent nuptials."

BRYCE'S MIND SPUN, and his mouth refused to form coherent words. Undercover? Kira? Married? What?

Marriage wasn't a road he wanted to travel down again, even

if it was strictly business. The last thing he wanted was to be reminded of his own failed marriage. While it was seven years since things had ended, he didn't need to relive those days. Not when Adelaide walked out of his life two months after they walked down the aisle.

The opportunity to work with Kira was intriguing, but he'd never been undercover a day in his life. Most art crimes didn't involve clandestine operations. Not to mention that he preferred things by the book and needed a predictable partner. In no way did that word seem to apply to Kira.

He snuck a peek at her and shut down the unprofessional thoughts that poked through his mind regarding the attractive woman. At least the shock registering on her face matched his own.

Details. He needed more information. Right. Time to get his head together and take control of the situation. "What is the assignment again? We're going to . . . uh . . . be . . . what?"

"I think the word you're looking for, Lambert, is *married*."

"Right. Of course. But why?"

Kira said nothing. Now would be a good time for that impulsivity to show up. Couldn't she go off the rails, rebel, get mad? Instead she sat stone-faced and resigned. Should this even be his assignment? And Kira was barely day one in the field. But SSA Turner marched on with his instructions, not leaving any room to object.

"Alexandr and Sophia Dominik are in the US on a temporary work visa, and they've rented a brownstone for a few months. This is where the statue intersects with Lambert's investigation." Turner motioned for Bryce to brief Kira.

"My team has been investigating the sale of illegal or stolen artwork," he told her. "A network of art smugglers will host underground auctions in various cities, and before we can move in, they're gone. Along with priceless works of art." He turned his focus to Turner. "Are you assuming Zaika will be auctioned off?"

Turner nodded. "Another translation project revealed there's a secret auction coming in the next few weeks, here in DC, and we might just be ahead of things for once. I need you two to score an invitation to that auction." Turner pointed at Bryce, then Kira, as if that would help get the message across. He sat back in his chair with a creak and folded his muscular arms. "As luck would have it, the brownstone next door to theirs is also for rent."

When Turner mentioned the address, Bryce bit his lip to keep from letting out a long whistle. That ritzy neighborhood had real estate price tags starting in the millions. Not his style at all.

Time to slow this train down. "Sir, with all due respect, agents usually have months of training and assessments before going undercover. Agent Miller is new to the role and I don't have—"

Turner raised a hand. "Objection noted. In an ideal scenario, we'd follow standard procedures, but we don't have time. You've spent a lot of man hours on this case and have the knowledge. Miller has the language skills, and if there is an underground auction happening in DC, it's here and gone before we know it. We need to act fast. The Dominiks have plane tickets back to Russia in a week and a half. This shrinks our time frame."

Turner cleared his throat, closing the door on any more comments from Bryce. "Miller, you'll befriend Sophia while the two of you try to get intel about what Alexandr is doing in town—and an invitation."

Kira still sat silent. Why didn't she say something?

"Your cover story will be that you work for a private art collector. We've got our tech experts creating fake profiles online. Miller, though you work with Lambert, mostly your role will be a money-spending socialite, just like Sophia."

Bryce switched tactics. "Will they recognize Agent Miller? She had a run-in with the Russian man at the art gallery. If the guy is connected to Alexandr, they might identify her."

Turner scratched his chin. "Good point, but I've got it covered." He turned to Kira. "Would you be willing to change your appearance, maybe dye your hair a lighter color?"

Kira gave an imperceptible nod but remained still. She wasn't putting up any kind of a fight. This was going to happen. He and Kira would be "married."

He really had to get out of this assignment. "Sir, are you sure there aren't other agents who've handled this kind of undercover work before? Kira is new and I've never gone undercover. It will take too long for us to get up to speed—"

"I'll do it."

Oh, now she speaks.

Bryce's and Turner's attention snapped to Kira. "I want to be in the field. And while I'm grateful to work in linguistics while I was healing, I don't want to be there forever."

Turner leaned back in his chair. "I have no doubt you'll make a fine field agent, Miller. I wouldn't have tapped you for this assignment if I didn't think you could handle it. I saw in your file that you did some short-term undercover work when you were with the NYPD. That helps me approve you for an assignment like this, since you're still in your probationary period. Just don't go rogue and chase Russian men in back alleys, please."

Bryce's mind spun in a thousand directions. He might finally catch a break on his case. So why was he hating so hard on this whole thing? The minor inconvenience of a fake undercover marriage would be worth it in the end if he closed his case. Wouldn't it?

Turner stood. "Open your packets. All the information you need is in there. And one more thing. You start tomorrow."

Bryce snapped his lips shut and opened the manila envelope. The contents included a floor plan of a house, information on Alexandr and his wife, and a dossier for their new identities.

Brian Beckett, married to Katrina Beckett, living in Manhattan. Both worked for a billionaire private art collector rumored to have a stolen painting in his collection valued at over $200 million.

The pictures of the three-story brownstone mansion resembled something out of a magazine. Lush landscaping and a patch of green lawn created the postcard-worthy appearance. Just what he needed—to move into a pretentious neighborhood with his "wife" and pretend like he belonged. A far cry from growing up as a kid in the backwoods of West Virginia. At least he'd lost the accent.

He shook his head to dislodge the thoughts of his broken and broke upbringing. "This is where we're staying?" He turned to Kira. If he was out of his element in this kind of place, she'd never make it in her leather jacket and black jeans.

Turner nodded. "We lucked out. It's a short-term rental that is fully furnished. I've expedited the paperwork, but we have the green light for this assignment. The undercover unit is working overtime right now to get you set up with what you need." He pulled a grocery store bag from his drawer and slid it across the desk to Kira. She took out a box of hair dye and held it like it might poison her. "I wasn't kidding about the hair, Miller," he said. "You need a disguise. And a new wardrobe."

She pulled out an envelope of cash from the package, and Bryce noted he had one also. At least the FBI would spring for new clothes.

Turner ushered them out of his office. "I've got work to do. And so do you." He shut the door, and Bryce stood there a moment trying to process.

Kira started for the elevator and he hurried after her. "Well," she said, "I guess we should get to know each other since we'll be in close quarters for a while."

Bryce smirked. What had he gotten himself into? He'd gone from finding Kira interesting to being "married" to her in less than twenty-four hours. He punched the elevator button. "Let's read through the information and we can quiz each other about our aliases on our ride out to the house." His private life was off-limits as far as he was concerned. But—maybe spending time with Kira wouldn't be the worst assignment in the world.

They rode the elevator in silence so thick he could cut it with a knife. He walked toward his car with Kira at his side. "How about I pick you up first thing in the morning? Does nine a.m. give you enough time to get ready?"

Kira's eyes narrowed, and she flicked her gaze at the Harley parked two spots over from his own Honda Civic. "I guess I can't show up riding my Harley."

"Yeah, you may need to dial back the bad-girl vibe a bit. You saw the pictures of the house. This is high society."

She groaned. "Right. I'll have to play the part. At least it's just for a few weeks."

Bryce took out his phone and sent an email to the undercover unit to see if they had a luxury car in the FBI fleet. They might be able to score a fancy ride from the cars the FBI seized from illegal activities. They needed to arrive in style, right? "Why don't you go home, get ready, and I'll pick you up in the morning. Says here the surveillance equipment will arrive tomorrow in a moving van, and they'll be the official movers."

"Of course."

Her dazed look from earlier had faded and determination now shone in her eyes, silently communicating that despite her displeasure with the assignment, she'd give it 100 percent. And that was all the confirmation he needed.

He placed a hand on her shoulder, a move that took him by surprise, as if his hand had a mind of its own. "This isn't ideal, but we'll make the best of it. But for now, maybe stop at some high-end store and pick up fancy clothes? I'll do the same."

The warmth emanating from her sent his pulse pounding, and he dropped his hand to his side. What had him all flustered? The assignment or spending time in close proximity with Kira? She wasn't his type, but the thought of being trapped with her for the foreseeable future intrigued him. It wouldn't hurt to get to know her a little better.

And maybe, somehow, in the midst of everything, he'd find the break he needed in his case.

Yes, he could do this.

A fake wife with black—or blond—hair. A house he'd never afford in his lifetime. Mingling with wealthy elitists. Protecting an ugly rabbit statue. A smuggling ring to bring down. And a new rookie partner to protect.

What could possibly go wrong?

3

KIRA HAD POCKETED THE CASH, shoved her emotions to the side, and gone on a shopping spree in her roommate's closet. She'd save the FBI funds for later expenses.

"Ready for your close-proximity assignment next to a hunky FBI agent?" Violet asked. She tossed an all-too-slinky black dress on the queen bed near Kira, along with three similar options but different colors. Violet was prepared for any and every occasion.

"Relationships, fake or otherwise, aren't your thing." *Thing* became *thang* with Violet's accent.

Kira pinched the lace of the frilly pink comforter gracing Violet's bed. "Do you really think I'm going to fit in your fancy long black dress?"

Violet cleared her throat and tapped her foot, her hands on her hips. "I will not let you change the subject. Yes, we're about the same size. But are you prepared to play housewife with the FBI's most eligible bachelor?"

Kira rolled her eyes. "This is my chance to prove myself as a Special Agent. It gets me into the field. I don't want to be stuck behind a desk in linguistics. This is a huge opportunity for a rookie agent. Turner probably had to get a million approvals to offer me this role."

Violet rummaged through her closet, flinging shoes, pants, and dresses onto the bed. When Violet received a task, she went all in. Apparently the SSA's choice of box dye wasn't up to her rigorous beauty standards, so she'd ordered a delivery from a store that offered a higher-quality—and much more expensive—product. It had arrived just in time for Kira to dye her hair last night. That's what she got for letting a former Miss America contestant dress her like some sort of Barbie doll. But Violet never talked about her pageant days. Ever. And Kira respected not dredging up the past—for herself or others.

"Still didn't answer the question. Can you pull it off?" Violet's voice held warmth and concern. "You'll have to make people think you're in love, as if you're a genuine couple—create your own magic."

"Oh, please. I was born an actress. Bryce and I will be just fine."

"*Bryce*? Well, you got personal awfully fast with *Agent Lambert*."

Kira huffed. "He told me I could call him by his first name, and I think we've moved past the formal names if we're going to pretend to be married."

"True. Just be careful, Kira."

This mission had to go well. She needed to earn her position. Sure, she'd graduated from Quantico, but the ultimate test as a rookie—she despised that term—stared her in the face. She'd do everything in her power to ensure her first assignment succeeded, even if it meant pretending to be someone else for a little while.

Which wasn't too much to ask. She knew how to blend in, go unnoticed. Her days in the orphanage taught her how to adapt to any situation. So this mission wasn't that big of a stretch. She'd just have to play a role until the bad guys were put in jail.

But Violet had a point. How much did she know about Bryce? Having him that close for the duration of the undercover operation might pose a challenge. How were they ever going to pull off the kind of relationship a newlywed couple had? Surely everyone would see right through them.

Violet flung some sort of spandex-covered medieval torture device at Kira. "It's not you I'm worried about. Does Agent Lambert know what he's signed up for? I've seen how grumpy you can be in the mornings."

"I'm supposed to wear this?" Kira stretched the fabric as far as it would go and rethought her undercover assignment. She wasn't ready to play the role of socialite. Violet made it seem so easy, but with that much spandex, how was she going to breathe?

"Have you never seen Spanx before?"

"Apparently not." She tossed the item in the open suitcase, silently vowing not to wear Spanx as long as she lived.

Violet tsked. "It's how you'll fit in my formal black dress. Which will knock Agent Lambert's socks off for sure."

Kira stretched on the bed and refluffed the pillows behind her. "I'm not interested in knocking his socks off." Liar. "Nothing's going to happen between Agent Lambert and myself. I mean, Bryce. Or maybe I should start calling him Brian. The bottom line is we're both professionals. This assignment is temporary." Who was she trying to convince?

Violet smirked and moved on to her makeup table, tossing tubes, brushes, sponges, containers into a different pink bag. "I just think you both will be in for some culture shock. Not only having to pretend to be married but sell it to the couple next door. They'll need to believe it's genuine if you expect to receive an invitation to the art auction."

"Not telling me anything I don't know," Kira said.

Violet added a few remaining items into the suitcase and zipped it up. "Okay. Time for your hair. Do you trust me? I used to do hair and makeup for a few of my friends. But I'm better with a gun than a curling iron these days, so my skills might be a bit rusty."

Kira snorted and stood. "Let's do this. Make me look like a million bucks."

Two torturous hours later, Kira had her eyebrows waxed, her hair cut—which now was a shade called light auburn—and her lips stained a deep shade of red. She donned the outfit Violet had left on the bed for her.

Kira emerged from the bedroom, trying not to stumble in the high heels. Everly's jaw practically hit the floor. "Kira? Is that really you?"

Her friend's awestruck words tickled her, but she didn't dare laugh or she might fall over. She strode across the main room of the open loft, concentrating on staying upright. Even if she avoided a bullet during this assignment, the shoes might kill her. "Of course it's me."

"You look amazing." Everly gave an approving gaze, and Violet grinned.

Kira stopped in front of the mirror that hung over the sectional sofa and stifled a gasp. She ran her hands through her chin-length hair. Light reddish-brown ringlet curls had replaced her long black wavy locks. With makeup and hazel-colored contacts brightening her naturally dark brown eyes, she'd transformed into someone else entirely. The outfit of black pants and a shimmery pale blue sweater made her *feel* like a new person. For a moment, she could only gape at the person staring back at her.

Hello, Katrina Beckett. "It's amazing, Violet. You outdid yourself."

Violet added lipstick and more makeup to Kira's purse—another borrowed item from Vi's closet. "Thank you. It helps to have a lot to work with." She tossed Kira a cheeky grin, then sobered. "Just know that Everly and I have your back. No matter what."

Kira's eyes watered, her throat suddenly tight. Some days her lack of blood family hurt, left her feeling down. But today, having Violet and Everly in her corner was all the family she needed.

Violet circled Kira. "You'll have to make sure Mr. Lambert keeps his hands to himself."

Kira and Everly laughed. "He'd be insane to try anything," Everly said.

Kira had some time to kill before Bryce arrived. Not much, though. She hadn't had a moment to breathe, let alone to fully prep herself for this mission. She headed to the balcony and sat at the bistro-style table. The chill in the air reminded her that winter was around the corner. But she'd relish the final days of autumn temperatures while she still had them.

Time to get this over with. She pulled the materials from the manila envelope and began to read.

Katrina Beckett. Age thirty-five. She paused. "What?" They couldn't have made her younger, like her actual age of thirty-three? She rolled her eyes and kept reading.

Art buyer from Manhattan. Married to Brian Beckett. Too bad Kira hadn't paid attention in art history classes in college. She'd need a crash course from Bryce with his knowledge in this area. She couldn't risk coming off as a giant fraud.

Everly joined her on the balcony and set two mugs of coffee on the table. "I've been assigned to help you on this mission. My team lead has created your fake online presence. Dropping breadcrumbs in the dark corners of the web that you and Agent Lambert—I mean *Brian Beckett*—are interested in acquiring some particularly rare Russian art pieces for your billionaire boss."

"Glad I have you in my corner."

Everly nodded. "Just be careful. I know you're not used to working with a partner."

"I don't think getting along with Bryce will be my biggest problem."

Everly froze, her gaze intense. Kira followed her stare. "Is that—"

"Yes. That is definitely a man hiding behind a tree, taking pictures in front of our building."

Kira and Everly picked up their mugs and calmly moved inside. Violet joined them as they flanked either side of the sliding glass door. Kira peeked through the slats and watched the man adjust his telescopic camera lens and point it straight at their apartment once more.

BRYCE PULLED UP, parallel parked in front of a Chinese restaurant, and glanced up to Kira's loft apartment. This area of DC combined restaurants and shops with high-rise apartments. Kira's building took up the entire block, with offices, businesses, and restaurants under the apartments. He questioned how she could afford a nice place, but he'd heard she had two roommates. He'd met Violet Bancroft once, and she came from money. Her father was a senator from Georgia.

And here they were. Partners. Soon to be "spouses." He couldn't unravel the knot forming in the pit of his stomach. His and Kira's inexperience bothered him on many levels. They had no idea what they were walking into. So the goal was to get in, find intel, and hightail it out of there. Too much room for error. If anyone suspected that he and Kira were anything other than newlyweds . . .

He'd have no way of protecting her.

The knot tightened.

Movement caught his attention. A man dressed in black pointed a telephoto lens in the direction of Kira's apartment.

What in the world?

Bryce eased the door to the Mercedes open and moved toward the cameraman. Before he got within ten feet, the guy bolted. Bryce gave chase, dodging walkers, dog leashes, and tourists milling around the area. At least the obstacle course of the DC suburban sidewalk slowed the dude down.

Bryce didn't get a good view of the man's face but ran down a checklist in his mind to ID him later. About six foot. Muscular, like the guy lived in a gym. He had dark features and jet-black hair.

The suspect tripped over a chair from a restaurant's outdoor seating. Bryce picked up the pace, but as he raced across the entrance to the underground parking lot for the building, something hard and metal walloped him in the face.

"Ah!" Pain radiated through his skull and he staggered backward, hand to his head. He opened his eyes to find a blurry woman holding a trash can lid like a shield. He blinked, bringing her into focus. Tall, gorgeous reddish-brown curls, warm golden-colored eyes. He rubbed his aching temple.

"Bryce? I'm so sorry. I saw the man running and assumed he had a partner. I can't believe I whacked you with the lid."

"Kira?" Wow. Like . . . wow.

She lowered the lid. "I'm so sorry. Are you okay?"

"Yeah. Nothing some ibuprofen won't take care of."

"I meant to hit the other guy."

"I gathered."

"But Violet will probably snag him around the corner. I tried to drive him toward her. I cut through the building into the garage in case he crossed here."

He blinked and stared at her, and she noticed. Red bloomed across her cheeks. "Well, I guess my makeover worked if you don't recognize me."

"You . . . you look . . ." No way could he say the words that flitted through his mind. Beautiful. Stunning. Gorgeous. Strong.

Rein it in, Lambert.

"Adequate."

Of all the words in the English language, that's what came out of his mouth? He snapped his lips shut.

"Great. I was going for boring or sensible, so I guess adequate works." Kira rolled her eyes, and they walked back to the apartment.

Violet sat on the stairs leading to the lobby, waiting for them. He peeked through the double glass doors to see an ornate area with post office boxes along the back wall and elevators for residents who lived above the retail space. The smell of garlic and spice from the first-floor Chinese restaurant still clung to the air from the night before.

"He got away," Violet said, her eyes bouncing between him and her roommate. "He had a car waiting for him on a side street just before he got to me."

Kira introduced them. "I caught the wrong guy and accidentally hit Bryce instead."

Way to wound his pride even more. Time to deflect. "Who was that guy?" Bryce asked.

Kira squinted and surveyed the area. "It might have been someone from any of our cases. Or related to our new one. But there's no way of telling now."

"Our roommate, Everly, has been working on some pretty top-level stuff." Violet stood and headed up the stairs. At the door, she turned and gave Bryce a quick once-over. "How is your head?"

"I'm good. I don't even think it left a mark." He touched his temple and didn't feel a bump. At least he wasn't going to show up for this assignment with a black eye.

Violet looked like she didn't believe him but pulled out her phone from her jeans pocket. "Maybe you two should head out to the brownstone. I'll call this in and take care of things here. I got a good description of the cameraman."

Or maybe they called the whole assignment off? Could the mystery photographer be linked to the Russian from the art gallery?

"I only glimpsed him before I caught the wrong suspect." Kira flexed her index finger at Bryce.

Heat rose up his neck. Was he blushing or swelling from where she'd clocked him in the face? He turned to her. "Should we pull the plug on this mission? What if they tracked you here?"

Violet turned and squinted at Bryce like he'd said something wrong.

Kira put her hands on her hips. "Did you recognize me?"

"No. Not at first anyway."

Violet snorted. "Well, there you go. You're good. I'll hold down the fort here." She headed inside.

Kira surveyed the bustling street in front of the stores and turned back to Bryce. Her gaze flicked to his forehead and remorse filled those gorgeous eyes. "I really am sorry. Let me run upstairs and get you some ice."

"No need. It doesn't hurt and I don't think it's swelling." His pride was wounded more than his face.

She reached up to touch his forehead but then must have thought better of it. "It's barely a red mark. You should be good." She dropped her hand and backed toward the steps. "I'll grab my things. Once we're on the way to the brownstone, I'll report this to Turner. If he wants to pull the plug, that's his call. I'll be right back."

He opened his mouth to reply, but she'd already marched up the stairs while he stood on the sidewalk sweating in his designer suit. He chuckled under his breath. Never a dull moment with her. He moved back toward the car parked on the street to wait. How long would it take her to gather her things—

Kira walked out the lobby door with a light pink designer bag draped across her arm that might as well have had the word *expensive* written all over it. She also carried a small suitcase.

"That was fast," he said.

She glanced at her watch. "I'm ready to get going."

All Bryce could muster was a nod. He opened the car door for Kira, and she raised a brow at him. "Get used to me opening doors for you," he said, "and all the stuff that couples do. We have to sell our relationship."

She smirked. "It's not the door opening. I'm good with that. It's the car. Does Turner know you sprung for this?"

He shrugged. "We need to show our wealth. This beauty came from our impound lot where the FBI seized some very nice cars. We can't drive up in my old Honda." The jet-black Mercedes SUV sparkled in the morning sunlight.

"As long as Turner knows you got the car, I'm good." Kira sank into the passenger seat, and Bryce walked around to the driver's side. "You drive an old Honda? That I can see. Very sensible and straitlaced."

She wasn't wrong, so why did it bother him that her impression of him included words like sensible and straitlaced? "Since I'm an art buyer for the uberwealthy Levi Solinger, I figured I needed to commit to the part." He was overexplaining and snapped off the words. "Let's hit the road and enjoy the luxury car while we have it."

The engine purred and Bryce pulled away from Kira's apartment. But he couldn't get past the other part of her comment. "What gives you the impression that I'm some straitlaced, uptight, by-the-book agent?"

Kira glanced at him. "I asked around. Those words may have come up."

"Violet? That's your source? I met her once. Briefly. Also, note that my first impression of you happened in a police holding cell. And your second impression smashed me in the face with a trash can lid. So let's push past impressions and learn our new roles."

"At least I know you're direct and to the point." Kira's phone chimed. "It's Turner." She put the phone on speaker and gave him a rundown of the loitering man with a camera.

Turner cleared his throat. "It appears that Violet's father wanted to document the safety features of your new apartment. He sent someone to check out the area around the place. He was told not to get caught. That's why he ran."

"Ohhh, how did Violet take the news?"

"You might say she's not too happy about this. But continue to watch your backs for anything suspicious or out of the ordinary."

The man hung up.

"Well, I guess that answers a few questions." Kira stashed her phone in the front pocket of the designer bag. He caught the slight wince, as though the bag might turn to lava the moment she touched it. Interesting. "Turner's description of Violet is probably an understatement. I imagine she's pretty livid. You haven't seen Violet get mad," she said. "It's not pretty."

"I'm sure it's not. I made a mental note when I met her. *Don't cross Violet Bancroft.*" He'd checked up on Kira's roommates. Violet might be petite and Southern, but she held one of the best shooting records coming out of Quantico.

Kira pulled out the envelope Turner had given them. She cleared her throat, an audible clue that she had the same awkward emotions about this undercover operation that plagued him. "How did we meet?" she asked. "I haven't had a chance to give the paperwork a thorough read-through. I spent my time playing dress-up."

"Let's start with some introductions. I'm Brian Beckett, art buyer and connoisseur of the finer things in life."

She twisted in her seat to face him. He kept his eyes on the road after a quick glance. "I'm Katrina Beckett. Wife and art buyer for Levi Solinger."

Gone was her low, deeper voice, replaced with a fast-paced, high-pitched nasal whine in a perfect New York accent.

Bryce laughed. "What was that?"

"It says we're born and raised New Yorkers. Specifically, Upper East Side. Why wouldn't I have an accent?" She kept the thick intonation in place while she talked.

"It's spot-on, I'll give you that."

"Are you sure it won't draw too much attention? Should I go with something more nondescript?"

"No, I think it lends credibility to our story. How did you learn to do that?"

"I've spent a lot of time in my life playing various roles,

pretending to be people I'm not. Plus, I worked hard as a kid to lose my Russian accent so I didn't have to explain to people where I came from." Her authentic voice, the one he preferred, resurfaced. Rich, melodic, and maybe even a bit sexy.

He immediately rerouted his wayward thoughts back to the conversation, and while he wanted to explore her last statement, professionalism reigned as king in his life. "We met at an art auction in New York." He tried to suck the emotion out of his voice. Dry as toast. That's what his colleagues called him when they assumed he wasn't listening. Not that it hurt his feelings. He did thrive on predictability and routine. "We met when we were bidding on the same piece. Six months ago. Solinger hired you shortly after. We married within three months. We're still newlyweds, so people might forgive us for not knowing everything about each other."

"That works."

And just like that, they were an old married couple who slipped into silent mode. She seemed lost in thought—probably pondering her first assignment in the field. Yet he couldn't wrap his mind around mysterious Kira . . . or Katrina. He'd better get used to her new name.

He'd read her file. Questions settled on the edge of his tongue, but he didn't dare voice them. How old was Kira when she came to the United States to be adopted? Her file held no details prior to this. What was it like growing up in an orphanage in Russia?

This is business. Don't get personal.

The warning message blared through his brain like a high-pitched train whistle—loud and irritating. He'd spent countless hours tracking stolen art and the smuggling ring and wouldn't let anything hinder his investigation. Especially the intriguing stranger with black-now-auburn hair whom he had to pretend to be in love with.

4

KIRA FELT LIKE SHE'D DOVE headfirst into the deep end without a life vest for her new role as an undercover Special Agent. She pressed her feet into the floorboards to keep her legs from bouncing, refusing to expose any hint of nervousness to Bryce. *Brian.*

After perusing the paperwork, she still needed more information. What was Bryce like? What made the man tick? In order to understand Brian, she required a few more details about the man driving her to their new home. "Quick question. What is your favorite food?"

Bryce glanced her way at the abrupt question before returning his eyes to the road. "What?"

"I just want to get to know you a little better, and these tidbits might come into play."

Bryce nodded. "I love a good Italian meal. Breaded chicken, pasta, with a rich garlicky sauce. But shellfish doesn't agree with me, so no seafood. What about you?"

"Anything smothered in cheese. But mainly tacos or any kind of Mexican food."

"Lots of cheese. Got it. My turn. Are you nervous at all about this assignment?"

She shifted in her seat. Not the kind of information she

wanted to share, but she'd play along. "A bit. Everything happened so fast I just haven't had time to process." She waved her hand toward the neighborhood outside the window. "This place is way out of my comfort zone. Check out the size of these houses."

They rounded a hill that led to a gated subdivision. Rows of townhomes drifted by as they drove down the immaculate, oak-lined street leading to their temporary residence.

"I feel the same way. But we're both professionals. We'll get the job done."

The property sparkled. Hedges were neatly trimmed and uniform, separating the stairs that led to each unit. There wasn't so much as a stray leaf on the cobblestone sidewalk that ran in front of the houses.

"These homes are massive," Kira said, twisting in her seat to take in a three-sixty view of the area. The street was lined with buildings of four three-story homes each. Not a blade of grass was out of place on the well-manicured yet small front yards. Kira gave a pleasant nod to a man walking a well-behaved golden retriever.

The road ended at a park, with a cross street connecting to other homes. The Dominiks' was the end unit on the left.

Bryce made a U-turn and pulled up to the curb in front of their new home, next to the Dominiks'. "Welcome to the lifestyles of the ultrawealthy. I've met a few millionaires when I worked at an art gallery but never had a firsthand view into their homes. It's so—"

"I think the word you're searching for is *adequate*." Kira shot him a mischievous wink, grabbed her pink designer bag and suitcase, and exited the car. No way was she letting him live down his goofy choice of words. And she needed to get him to lighten up a little.

"This place is definitely way more than adequate." Bryce rounded the car, grabbed his bags from the back seat, and stood with her in front of the walkway that led to the front door. "Ready?"

"Ready."

They walked up the stairs to the front stoop, and her gaze slid over the ornate archway above the door that set the tone for the whole place—excess and opulence. "These dark brown bricks give me haunted house vibes," Kira said, her head on a swivel, eyes scanning the area. "There are way too many hiding places in these tall hedges, not to mention the people living in the brownstones that surround us. I wonder why our new neighbors chose this neighborhood."

"Because it's in the right zip code and costs more money than I'll make in a lifetime. It's all for show."

Bryce used the key Turner had provided and pushed open the heavy wood door.

Kira shoved a hand in her pocket and palmed the portable RFI detector that she'd pulled out of her bag earlier. She leaned in close to Bryce and whispered, "Don't say anything until I've swept the place."

The entryway on the first floor opened up to a spacious living room, with high ceilings, white crown molding around the edges, and an electric fireplace. The open concept allowed them to see the entire area—the living room opening up to the dining room and kitchen in the back. Stairs in front of them led to the second and third floors as well as to the basement.

Kira wasted no time. She scanned every inch of the four floors, starting in the basement, which was used for storage. Bryce had put their bags in the dining room, and by the time she returned, he'd set up his laptop at the countertop bar that separated the dining area and kitchen.

She approached Bryce, and the device lit up, close to where he had dropped her small bag behind him. His eyes widened.

And then she remembered. "False alarm. The entire place is free from all bugs, both electronic and the creepy crawlies."

She reached into the borrowed bag and pulled out an AirTag. "Violet puts these on just about everything she owns. She's got at least twenty, and we can always find Violet if she ever goes missing. I think she may have invested stock in the company. Or she's just quirky." She pointed to the bag. "That's hers."

The fine lines around Bryce's eyes returned to a normal, relaxed position. "I'm glad we're all clear, but . . ."

"Why the AirTags?"

"Dying to know."

She laughed. "In college, Violet had a roommate who 'borrowed' her things without asking. As an only child, she never had to share before and this horrified her."

"I'll back up Violet on this one. Not asking is stealing."

"Agreed, but still . . . Anyway, when AirTags became a thing, she went a little overboard buying them and attaching them to anything that had sentimental value."

"Interesting."

"She is."

"So, give me a rundown of the place. I poked around a bit but want your opinion. Any security concerns?"

She liked the way he got down to business. "The main floor has this nice open concept, giving us an entire view of the front and back doors at any point. The basement has an entryway, but it's got a nice deadbolt. The second and third floors have two bedrooms each."

She walked to the back French doors that opened onto a glass terrace. "The balcony area is above a two-car garage, which has a doorway to the basement stairs. Again, deadbolted. Stairs off the outdoor space lead to the brick driveway. A thick brick wall separates the units. They built this place with privacy in mind."

"I don't like how big this community is." Bryce tapped on his keyboard. "I'm on their website, and they have eighty units in this subdivision. Behind the woods out back is another row of homes. The nature adds some nice privacy for the residents but could be a security spot we need to cover."

"I'll make sure we tell the other agents our concerns." Kira moved back to Bryce and glanced around the spacious home. "I might be able to get used to a place like this. Even if it is temporary."

Bryce walked to the refrigerator and opened it. "Your loft apartment seemed pretty fancy."

She rolled her eyes. "I share the place with two other women. I definitely couldn't afford a place like that without roommates, and even that's stretching my budget. We each have a bedroom, but I share a bathroom with Everly. I could fit my entire apartment in this one room and have space to build a swimming pool." She waved her arms for dramatic effect.

"At least the kitchen is fully stocked. We have plenty of food in the refrigerator and pantry for a week."

"Quick question. Are you a coffee drinker or a tea drinker?"

He smiled. "Coffee drinker. I need that jolt of caffeine to keep me going."

"I think we'll get along fine, then. I can't live without my coffee either, so there'd better be a coffee maker or I quit."

"Would you settle for an espresso bar?" He pointed to the counter along the back wall, next to the immense refrigerator.

"This kitchen is a dream." The amenities in this place were incredible, and she gaped at the fancy latte maker that easily cost a thousand dollars.

Bryce raised a brow at her. "It might be high-end, but I don't really cook, so I have no idea."

She stood on the opposite side of the bar from Bryce, his laptop, papers, and pens all neatly lined up. "Don't worry. We won't starve. I like to cook."

He stared at her with those intense green eyes. "I wouldn't have expected that, but you continue to surprise me."

Good. She planned to keep the man on his toes. "I'm going to bring my bags upstairs and take a better look around," Kira said, already heading toward the stairwell.

"Sounds good. I'm going to log on and check some emails and will be right behind you."

His voice faded on the last couple of words. She probably should get used to waiting for a reply from Bryce before taking off. She smirked. But he also needed to keep up with her.

She'd already picked out her bedroom on the second floor, facing the front. The expansive layout would give each of them plenty of space, and each room had its own en suite bathroom. She tossed her bags on the queen bed, staking her claim. The picture window faced the front, giving her a nice overview of the entrance. She reminded herself not to get too comfortable, but the place oozed indulgence at every turn.

Bryce rounded the corner. He pointed to the master bedroom, complete with Jacuzzi hot tub in the oversized attached bathroom. "I guess I'll be taking the back room. It's a lot of space but has a great view of the back of the house. It also shares a wall with the Dominiks. The two other agents can set up surveillance equipment on the top floor. That gives them the largest view of the area. They'll be posing as our staff and take the night watches. It's not like we don't have plenty of bedrooms for everyone."

Did this man have an off switch, or was he just all about work? She wanted to pry into his personal life but at the same time didn't want to intrude. It wasn't her business, and as someone who valued privacy more than most, she kept her questions to herself.

They headed back to the kitchen.

Bryce sat back at the bar. Kira had to admit it was a good spot to work. He could be outside through the balcony door in an instant, but he was close enough to the living room window in the front so he could watch for signs of trouble on both sides of the house.

He tapped a few keys to bring his laptop to life. "I can set up a secure network for us. I'm sure the Dominiks have their Wi-Fi locked down."

Bryce busied himself with work. But Kira itched to explore their surroundings. "I'm going to check out the back and walk around outside."

She backtracked to her room to grab several pairs of gloves from her bag before exploring the back of the brownstone, just in case she found evidence—and she'd need them for where she planned to look.

The glassed-in terrace area extended across the back of the townhome and created an extra room. Two plush white couches turned an ordinary balcony into an elegant seating area, perfect for hosting parties. Kira crossed the beige travertine tile floor and headed down the wooden-plank steps.

The fancy entertaining space sat above the two-car garage. Bryce would need to move the Mercedes back here later. A brick wall separated the neighbor's narrow cobblestone driveway from theirs, and from her vantage point, the Dominiks' layout appeared to mirror theirs. Behind the row houses ran an access road to the driveways, and across the street a wooded area gave the place a sense of privacy.

The next-door unit had the blinds down in every window. It was a Monday afternoon. Maybe they were working? Did people who lived in these homes work?

The access road allowed the city to discreetly empty the trash bins at the end of the driveways. The two units shared a fenced enclosure with a lidded, boxlike cover for their garbage receptacles. Kira walked down the driveway. At the end, her head swiveled left, then right, to make sure no one was around as she lifted the lid to find two trash buckets for regular garbage, two for recycling.

She stopped and listened. Birds chirped, but that was it. She pulled on the gloves, then opened the plastic lid to the first bucket. "Ew. Great. Trash stink." She willed her gag reflexes to stop being overly dramatic and peered into the container. Empty.

Except . . . was that a piece of paper or a napkin stuck to the side? As if she'd be so lucky to find some earth-shattering clue forgotten in the sludge of a trash bin.

She leaned over the edge of the container and grasped the wadded-up napkin, which had adhered itself to the side via a layer of gunk.

Gross. Even with the gloves on, she did not want to know what she was touching. But she refused to contaminate potential evidence, even if in this case it might already be destroyed by disgusting muck.

She might be picking up actual garbage. But once she saw Russian writing on the scrap, she thanked her instincts. A noise behind her stopped her heart for a second. She shoved the napkin into her pocket and turned.

A man rounded the raised lid of the trash enclosure and pointed a gun at Kira.

BRYCE TRIED TO CHECK EMAILS, but instinct drove him to watch Kira out the back window. He moved to the balcony just in time to see a man with a gun aimed at her.

He grabbed the wedding ring from his briefcase on his way out the door and threw on his suit jacket to hide his Glock 17.

"I will ask you one more time. What are you doing?" Bryce heard the guy's distinct Russian accent. The dude was thick—muscular arms, wide shoulders, complete with a neck that resembled a tree trunk. If he had to guess, this man was part of the security team for the Dominiks. Earlier surveillance notes in the file indicated the unit next door had heavily armed guards patrolling the area.

Kira let out a whiny, nervous laugh. "Um, I really don't think the gun is necessary. I—I live here. I—please. Put the weapon away." She sounded scared out of her mind, and he wasn't sure if it was part of her act or not. "I'm Katrina. You must live next door. I was just—"

"There you are, honey," Bryce called out. The man turned his bald head and lasered Bryce with a glare.

Kira hurried to his side and hugged him. "He . . . he's got a gun. Why is he armed? I thought this was a safe neighborhood." Her voice quavered and her words came out almost as sobs.

Bryce kept an eye on the gun and its owner and pulled Kira slightly behind him, putting himself between her and the weapon. "No gun necessary, sir. She was just searching for her wedding ring."

Kira coughed, then cleared her throat. "Yes. I—yes."

"Good news," Bryce said, "I found it." He pulled the ring out of his pocket—the one he had forgotten to give her earlier. Mainly because he didn't want to be married—even fake married—and a ring gave a finality to their predicament.

He hugged Kira and turned to the meathead security guard. "Are you out of your mind pulling a gun on an innocent woman?" He let anger tinge his tone. It wasn't hard. "My wife lost her ring and thought she'd maybe thrown it out. But I found it in the bathroom. Now seriously, can you put that away before someone gets hurt?"

Kira's hand covered her heart. "I'm so relieved. Thank you, sweetheart." She turned to the muscleman. "And now your first impression of me is digging through the trash. I'm sorry."

Her fake accent came naturally to her. Gone was Kira the Special Agent. Katrina now stood before him, the somewhat ditzy socialite from Manhattan.

The man winced and narrowed his eyes as if trying to decide whether or not to believe them. But he holstered his weapon. "Sorry, ma'am. We didn't realize anyone had moved into the house next door. I am Peter, head of security for the Dominiks."

"Security? My, my. I thought this area had low crime?" Kira patted her heart and swayed a bit. Bryce tightened his grip to steady her.

The man blanched. "Oh no, this is a quiet area where people keep to themselves. We've had no problems, but the Dominiks have always traveled with extra protection due to threats back home. It's nothing for you to worry about."

Bryce offered a handshake, but the man didn't reciprocate, so Bryce gave him a wave. "Well, I feel better having you watching the place. I'm Brian Beckett and this is my wife, Katrina."

The man nodded. "Take care, Mr. and Mrs. Beckett. Sorry about the mix-up. I hope we can keep this between the three of us?"

"Of course," Bryce said.

Peter gave a slight bow and made a beeline for the other side of the brick wall separating the driveways.

"Thanks," Kira whispered as they walked toward the house. Once the door closed, she took in a breath. "That was a close one. Thanks for the assist."

"I've got your back. We're in this together."

Bryce grabbed a bottle of water from the fridge, while Kira washed her hands with at least ten pumps from the soap dispenser.

"Does trouble just follow you around?" he asked.

"Apparently it does, based on the last few days." She pulled out a barstool and sat next to Bryce at the bar.

"Next time a heads-up might be nice. Just let me know what you're planning to do. It's hard to back you up if I'm caught off guard."

She looked him in the eyes and lifted her chin. "I'll admit, I tend to rush in based on my instincts. But maybe it paid off." She donned another pair of gloves, then pulled a wadded-up napkin from her slacks. "I found this. It's a random list of names or possibly places. With lines drawn through them. It's in Russian, so I'll need to fully translate it to see if it's anything important."

"I don't want you to think I intervened because you weren't doing a good job or that I expect you to run every decision by me. I know you have fantastic instincts. But you need to be safe."

"Thank you. Can you put that in an evidence bag for now?" She stood and moved to the refrigerator. "I'm going to make a sandwich for lunch and then get cleaned up after my dumpster-diving incident. But I'll make us dinner later. Then we can talk strategy, and I can decipher the napkin. Pieces are missing, but maybe we'll catch a break."

"Sounds like a plan. I'll wait for the other agents to arrive and will try to get some work done in the meantime."

An hour later, two agents dressed in moving company uniforms complete with logo stitched across the back arrived and unloaded the boxes that contained their equipment. Two agents, Special Agents Lisa Hudson and Carrie Kaup, were to pose as staff for the Becketts. They introduced themselves and then got busy setting up a surveillance system in the bedrooms on the top floor. He'd never met the agents, but Kira knew Agent Kaup since they worked out of the same office.

Bryce headed upstairs to his room and spent some time doing research online. He wanted more information about the Russian statue. Had someone really found a piece of history that was thought to be lost? And if so, were there more treasures from the missing crate to be found?

The smell of garlic and fresh herbs disrupted his focus. He checked his watch. Six thirty already? He followed his nose downstairs. When he walked into the kitchen, he stopped short.

Kira, decked out in a pale blue T-shirt, jeans, and an apron, had the area set up like she was on a reality cook-off show. Pasta boiled on the stove, while a sauce simmered on another burner. And mouthwatering garlic bread toasted in the oven.

Chicken parm. She remembered his favorite dish.

"Dinner is almost ready," she said, tossing him a smile. "Feel free to have a seat in the dining room." She had two place settings displayed, with a spinach salad bowl in the middle of the table along with butter, salt, and freshly grated parmesan cheese. How long had he been upstairs?

Long enough, apparently.

He sat while Kira floated around the kitchen like a ballerina in a recital. He could tell she loved cooking. And this shocked him.

The rough, biker-girl exterior had morphed into some sort of domestic queen. Interesting. The woman was a chameleon, and he enjoyed seeing her different colors. Quantico wasn't easy by anyone's standards, but Kira had completed her training with stellar performance reviews. Then she whipped up a gourmet meal like it was no big deal. He watched her remove a chocolate cake from the oven, and the scent made his stomach rumble.

He sat at the head of the table. She brought in two fully loaded plates and placed one in front of Bryce.

And he couldn't take his eyes off her.

"What?" Kira took the chair next to him. "The FBI set us up nicely with these groceries. We couldn't waste good food. I made enough so we can have this for lunch tomorrow too. But it's just us. Agent Kaup and Agent Hudson fixed a to-go plate as they wanted to get a jump start on surveillance, so it's a working dinner for them."

Throughout the afternoon, she'd settled in with the ease of someone who'd lived there forever. "Okay if I say a blessing?" He usually blessed his food and didn't intend to stop now.

Kira nodded. "Violet doesn't skip a blessing, so I'm used to it. Plus, my parents are Christians, and I grew up going to church every Sunday."

Interesting. She didn't claim faith as her own but tolerated her roommate's and parents' beliefs.

He said a quick but heartfelt prayer and then took his first bite. The flavors melted in his mouth and his mind went rogue.

What would it be like to have someone to come home to every day after work? A person who cooked and cared for him?

Not that he would *expect* it, but he could get used to it. Once again he found himself having to slam the brakes on that kind of thought. He'd tried that and it hadn't gone so well. Never again.

"Where did you learn to cook?" he asked between bites.

She shrugged. "I just picked it up over the years, I guess. It's one of my many hobbies. I like to cook."

"Well, I like to eat, so I make an excellent fake husband."

Conversation ceased as they ate. Bryce was too busy savoring every bite of the exquisite meal. When was the last time someone cooked for him like this? "Hobby" was an understatement.

Kira placed her fork on the plate. "Before dessert, would you bring me up to speed on your case? I've read some of the notes but would like your take on where you are in the investigation."

"There isn't much to tell. Things have stalled like an old Chevy going up a mountain. My team has been investigating a smuggling ring. Rare art pieces resurface and then disappear again without a trace. We've narrowed down that this group is hosting underground art auctions—mainly to rich, private collectors who want those elusive artifacts. We're seeing an uptick in Russian paintings and sculptures being smuggled. And, like Zaika, they are being discovered on the East Coast of the United States."

"That's an unlikely place for rare artifacts to resurface after so much time has passed."

He nodded. "What makes Zaika of particular interest is that it came from the same time period as the famous Amber Room. During World War II, Nazis dismantled the treasure room and boxed it up in crates. If this piece came from the Amber Room, it's a significant find, since the treasure disappeared without a trace."

Kira squinted, as if concentrating on his every word. "So, if a regular bargain shopper bought Zaika at an estate sale in the middle of nowhere, West Virginia, it could mean there's more treasure out there."

"It's possible. In this case, the statue originated from a man named Derek Young. He found the statue while clearing out his father's house after his passing. He sold most of his father's belongings in an estate sale. We have agents meeting with him to see if there were other items of value in his father's collection."

Kira began to clear the dishes from the table, and Bryce helped.

"What is your gut telling you about the smuggling ring and their involvement with this?" she asked.

He added the dirty plates to the counter by the sink. "My gut? I go by facts and evidence. Not hunches."

"Well then, tell me another story. If you had to write the ending to this case, what would it look like? Who are the players? Who wins and who loses?"

He thought, then blew out a breath. "If I did have a *hunch*, it would be that the Russian Bratva is involved. They steal the piece, host the auction, sell it to the highest bidder, turn a profit, and use the money for their own criminal enterprise. They don't care about cultural significance."

She elbowed him in the ribs. "See, not a bad gut reaction. Now, how are we going to get an invitation to this secret auction? I went to the gallery, and there was no mention of Zaika being for sale, although they advertised the exhibit as a limited time. Is Zaika going to be one of the pieces that just disappears without a trace?"

"Possibly. I think tomorrow we take the direct approach. Walk over to the neighbors' house and introduce ourselves. People do that, right?"

A knock at the door startled them both. They weren't expecting anyone.

"Or maybe, they're coming to us first," Kira whispered.

Their adventure as a married couple was about to begin, and Bryce didn't know nearly enough about his new wife.

5

KIRA'S INSTINCTS kicked into overdrive, and within seconds, she and Bryce flanked either side of the front door. Agent Hudson and Agent Kaup rushed downstairs and hid in the living room, guns ready.

Bryce opened the door, with Kira tucked behind it, weapon ready just in case.

"Can I help you?"

"Hello. My name is Natalia. I am Alexandr and Sophia Dominik's housekeeper."

Kira heard the thick Russian accent from the woman. "Who is it, darling?" Kira tucked her pistol behind her back as she moved into the opened doorway and snaked her hand around Bryce's waist. She winced at her attire. Her comfy T-shirt and jeans she'd changed into before cooking dinner didn't communicate wealth, but to be fair, they weren't expecting company.

The petite blond woman stared at Kira's attire with wide eyes. "My apologies for the time. I didn't realize you might be ready for bed."

"Oh, we were just getting comfortable, that's all."

Natalia nodded. "Alex and Sophia sent me to apologize for the incident earlier with Peter."

Kira waved a hand. “Oh, we’re already over it.”

Natalia tried to peer around Bryce to get a peek inside the house. She wasn’t being too subtle about it. “The Dominiks would like to invite you to dinner tomorrow evening if you are available. To make up for the unfortunate events of today, but also to welcome you to the community. Would six p.m. work? If not, I’m sure the chef could push dinner back—”

“Six is perfect.” Kira added a squeal at the end to show her enthusiasm. “We’d love to meet the new neighbors.” She tried not to wince at her accent. The high-pitched nasally sound coming out of her mouth grated on her own nerves.

Natalia smiled. “Then please arrive at five thirty for appetizers and drinks. I will inform the Dominiks that you accept their invitation.”

The woman’s formal tone denoted her place in the household. She served the Dominiks. Despite appearing to be young—maybe late twenties—Natalia’s demeanor conveyed her age as much older. She had a hard look to her dark eyes, which were in stark contrast to her light blond hair. The woman might be beautiful on the outside, but Kira sensed the housekeeper had seen her fair share of life’s struggles that had dulled some of her shine.

Kira could relate.

Natalia turned and left. Bryce closed the door. “I guess we don’t have to invite ourselves over after all.”

“And we get to scope out their place.”

They returned to finish cleaning up the kitchen. Kira sliced the cake while Bryce finished loading the dishwasher. She loved that he helped clean up.

Kira took the plates of cake to the table with the added ice cream on the side. She texted Agents Hudson and Kaup that dessert was ready, and the pair took their cake and ice cream to their station near the living room window.

“Just an FYI, my favorite ice cream is Moose Tracks,” she said once Bryce sat down at the table. She dove into her dessert, wondering if the FBI had a dossier with her favorites listed for moments like this.

"I like plain ole vanilla."

"Really? Somehow, that doesn't surprise me."

He devoured the cake. "You really are an amazing cook, Kira."

Heat filled her cheeks. Apparently she cared what he thought of her cooking. Of her. "I'm just glad to have someone to cook for. My roommates and I don't always have the same schedules, and I hate cooking for one." She took another bite of dessert. "Enough about cooking. Tell me about your last relationship. It might give me a sense of what kind of couple we might be."

He winced.

She'd struck a nerve.

"What about you?" he asked. "Are you willing to share with me the ins and outs of your past relationships?"

He'd deflected. She'd allow it. For now. But she mentally noted he'd hit some rough patches when it came to his love life.

Hadn't they all?

If she wanted him to share, she might need to go first. "I'm not saying divulge all your personal secrets. But I want to know our relationship dynamic. If there's a disagreement, do we argue and hash it out in an epic blowup? Or are we the kiss-and-make-up kind who sweep everything under the rug?" She took another bite of her ice cream. "Are we touchy-feely in public, or stoic and separate?" She pointed her spoon at him. "Because if you try to kiss me, I put enough garlic in that chicken dish to kill a vampire. Consider yourself warned."

He laughed, and it was the first time she'd seen the man loosen up since she'd met him. Maybe he did have a sense of humor after all. If not, this was going to be a long assignment, with her sarcasm lacking a shutoff valve.

"I see us arguing a bit," he said. "You've got that fiery New York don't-mess-with-me vibe going on. We might be rich in our undercover lives, but that doesn't mean I give you everything you want. And I think we have the appropriate amount of touching without being obnoxious about it and making people feel uncomfortable."

"Noted. But I need more. Was it love at first sight? Our stories have to match."

"Really? You need that level of detail?"

She crossed her arms. "If I'm supposed to work over Sophia Dominik and become her friend, I want more than a piece of paper's worth of information."

He groaned. "Fine. But, for the record, I don't believe in love at first sight."

Neither did she. Well, until recently. And it wasn't *love*, merely a magnetically strong attraction to Special Agent Bryce Lambert. Tall, dark, and handsome apparently was her thing. Just because he made her heart skip a beat here and there didn't mean anything would happen other than they'd do their jobs and move on when this was over.

"We met at the art auction," he said. "You kept bidding on a piece I wanted. And I let you have it in the end so I could strike up a conversation with you. I asked you for coffee, and we started seeing each other. And then three months later we got engaged."

"Well, that was fast."

He paused. "Have you been engaged before?"

"I thought we weren't going to get personal."

He smirked. "I need to know 'what kind of couple' we are." He had tossed her words back at her.

Okay, fine. She'd give him a little more. "I was engaged once. It didn't work out in the end. And he wanted to keep it a secret, because we worked together, so not a lot of people knew. Sadly, it ended as quietly as it began."

Well, it really wasn't quiet when it ended with her throwing things at his cheating head. But Bryce didn't need all the dirty details.

"I'm sorry to hear that."

She expected him to pry, ask what had happened and dig for more. Instead, he ate his dessert in silence. Probably because he figured if he asked for more information, he'd have to reciprocate. This man would be tougher to crack than a safe at Fort Knox.

He cleared his throat. "I don't like my food to touch. So, thank you for not putting the ice cream on the cake. That would ruin everything."

"You're welcome." A pause. "I like to mix things together. What's wrong with a little chaos now and then?"

Bryce groaned. "Like that's ever going to come up in a conversation."

"It will when I bring it up. And the more facts I have, the less I have to improvise. Trust me, you don't want me to make things up on the spot. Like what if at dinner I tell everyone how you collect creepy antique dolls. You know, the ones with the eyes that follow you everywhere? Then everyone will request to see your collection."

"Please don't do that."

"Well, then make sure I'm well-informed."

"Noted."

Kira cleared the dessert plates away and Bryce grabbed his laptop. She retrieved her notebook and pen from her bag and rejoined him at the table. "I think that at some point, I should excuse myself from dinner and use the bathroom. That might let me have the opportunity to snoop a bit."

Bryce shook his head. "No. Too dangerous. What if you get caught?"

Was this man going to step in and try to shield her from danger the entire mission? She sat back in the chair and smirked. "Is this our first fight? See? I need to be prepared for these things."

"It's not that I can't . . . don't think you're a capable agent." He took a breath. "I'm concerned about all the things that could go wrong. We need to control the situation as much as possible." He swung his laptop around so she could see the schematics of the neighboring house. "According to the layout of the brownstones, it looks like Alexandr may have an office upstairs. Let me be the one to do the snooping. I've studied the layout. You'll make a better distraction at dinner than I will. I can slip away and snap a few pictures of the interior while I get lost on the way to the bathroom."

Kira crossed her arms. "But I'm the risk-taker. You're so by the book."

He tapped his fingers on the table. "I have a bad feeling about tomorrow night. We have to be on guard at all times. What if it's an ambush? It seems highly unlikely they just want to meet us to be neighborly. All the research says they're not that type. We don't know what we're walking into, so I don't think we should take too many chances tomorrow night. We need to play it safe."

Kira conceded. He was right. "Fine. Maybe we wait and feel things out tomorrow night. See if there is an opportunity for one of us to be alone to do some reconnaissance. But if I see an opening, I want to take it." She just realized that she hadn't shown Bryce her translation of the napkin found in the trash can. "Hold on. I need to show you something."

Bryce watched her with interest while she flipped through the pages of her notebook to the piece she'd translated. "What did you find?"

"I was able to translate the Russian letters, but it's a list of names." Kira slid the paper to Bryce. "I have no idea who these people are and why all the names are crossed out but one. Is it a hit list?"

~~Davis~~
~~Thomas~~
~~Madison~~
~~Riley~~
~~Harper~~
~~Mason~~
Sawyer

Bryce stared at the paper, the color draining from his face. "These aren't names of people. They're mountain towns in West Virginia. Maybe they searched these places for something and came up empty. Derek Young, who accidentally sold Zaika, lives in the town called Riley, a few towns over from Sawyer's Peak. The place I swore I'd never go again."

"Why?"

"It's where I grew up."

AS SOON AS THE WORDS LEFT his lips, he wanted to grab them back. But this rattled him. This case had taken a turn for the worse and now pointed in a direction Bryce had no intention of heading.

Back to his hometown.

They'd just received the information regarding Derek Young, but why hadn't he seen the connection sooner? He grew up near the town where the statue was found.

He tried to wrap his mind around his past colliding with the present. "If this is a list of towns and not names, why are they crossed off? What are our neighbors searching for?"

"I'm not sure. What do you think?" Kira stared at him with expectation in her eyes, probing for information she knew all too well he had. He didn't want her—or anyone—to know where he'd come from. The poverty, abuse, and squalor of growing up with his alcoholic and gambling-addicted father. After his grandfather had passed away, Bryce had assumed the role of the adult in the household, until his father threw him out into the cold at age seventeen.

He cleared his throat. "It seems like we both have a past that we'd like to leave behind in a trail of dust. I was born and raised in Sawyer's Peak."

"That's a weird coincidence." Kira walked to the kitchen and poured them both another cup of coffee.

He accepted the steaming mug from her. "Growing up in the area, I'd heard the legends, so I'm not surprised. Tales of buried treasure, and a secret society that guarded the hidden location. The stories grew more epic with each generation. My grandfather had a metal detector and often took me out hunting for hidden treasures."

"Ever find anything?"

"We did. Once we found some old coins. Another time it was a Civil War–era bullet. We usually came up empty-handed, but I've always wondered if there was more to his stories."

"And your family still lives in Sawyer's Peak?"

He nodded. "My father does." And he'd leave it at that. "I need to study this new lead."

"What's your gut reaction, Bryce?"

He bit back a smile. "You and your *hunches*. If I have to guess, I think the Dominiks are searching for something. Maybe more artifacts. They're checking small-town antique shops in the vicinity where the original statue surfaced."

She paused for a moment, clicking her pen as if it helped her process. "Before the security guard died, he said, 'Follow the rabbits.' I'm pretty sure he used the plural. What if there's another statue out there?"

"I'll do some research on the original. If there were more than one statue, that would make sense. Someone is scouting for more lost art from the estate sale. And if there's more than one statue, where did the others go?"

THE NEXT DAY RUSHED BY in a blur of activity. Bryce spent much of it catching up on emails and research. He'd hardly seen Kira as she used her time to study art history for her cover story. Before he knew it, he had to get ready for dinner with the Dominiks.

After getting showered and changed into his business suit,

Bryce headed toward the stairs to wait for Kira, but she was already at the bottom of the steps, standing near the front door.

She wore a silky blue long-sleeved knee-length dress, complete with spiky high heels and a sparkly necklace. He loved her jet-black hair, but this auburn color had grown on him. The light bounced off her accessories, including her diamond wedding ring.

And then, like a buffoon, he stumbled, tripped on the last step. He grasped the handrail to keep from face-planting and somehow managed to stay upright.

"Are you okay?" she asked, rushing toward him with her hand extended.

"Yeah, I just missed a step." He stared and had flashbacks to the last time he had complimented—or rather, insulted—her. "You look nice" was all he could muster. Better than his "adequate" comment, but he had some work to do in the complimenting-a-woman department.

She smiled, a radiant and genuine grin that warmed his heart. "You clean up nicely as well." She reached out and felt the lapel of his charcoal-gray jacket. "The suit is amazing, and I like the burgundy tie."

"Thank you." Why did he care so much about her thoughts on his outfit? But her comment gave him an extra jolt of confidence that he'd carry through the evening. "Are you ready?"

She nodded, and he offered his arm to her as they walked to the neighbors' house. Bryce knocked on the heavy oak door. They were two minutes early.

The housekeeper, Natalia, answered. "Please, come in." She wore a traditional black shirt and skirt with a white apron. They followed her to a formal living room area. Unlike their unit, this one had separate rooms instead of an open concept. It gave off a dark, cold vibe.

"I like our place better," Kira whispered, never taking her hand off his arm.

A gentleman who acted like he'd just stepped off the set of filming *Downton Abbey* in his finest butler attire offered them a drink.

They each took a glass and the man disappeared. Bryce swirled the white creamy liquid in the glass. "White Russian?"

Kira took a sip and scrunched up her nose. "Yep, it's a White Russian." She placed the glass on a coaster on the end table of an ornate cream-colored couch.

He set his glass next to hers. After growing up with an alcoholic father, he steered clear of any kind of booze. Paintings lined the wall of the formal living room, across from the expensive couch and love seat. One piece caught his eye. A painting with a hefty price tag of at least a million dollars if it was genuine. As if the Dominiks would own anything less than an original. He leaned toward Kira. "I think this is a Cézanne."

"It is." The feminine voice startled him. He turned to see a woman standing in the doorway. "It's one of my most prized paintings in our collection." She smiled. "Hello, I'm Sophia Dominik. And I am so sorry about the incident with Peter, our head of security. That must have been quite a scare." Her white satin pantsuit made her appear older than she probably was. Bryce guessed her age to be late twenties. She had long, straight black hair, and her dark eyes sized up her guests.

Sophia strode into the room and shook hands with both Bryce and Kira. She let her hand linger a little too long in Bryce's. "Sorry for the delay," she said. "Alex will be here in a moment. He's just finishing up a phone call."

The light hit her necklace and splattered sparkly shimmers across the low ceiling. Bryce didn't question whether all of her diamonds were genuine. They easily cost half of his annual salary per stone. And her bracelet had ten meteor-sized ones.

Kira transformed into Katrina, accent and all. "Brian and I were just admiring your paintings. Quite a collection."

Sophia took a drink from the butler—where did he come

from?—and sat on the chair next to the couch. "Please, sit and let's catch up before the other guest arrives."

Other guest? A knot formed in Bryce's stomach. He didn't like unknown variables popping into the equation. He caught Kira's eye, and she gave an imperceptible shrug.

Sophia downed her White Russian, and the butler had a fresh one in her hand before she could blink. The smell of alcohol fumes made Bryce's nose itch. Her drink must be extra strong. "So tell me all about yourselves," she said. "Why are you in town? How long have you been married? I must know all the details about your love story. You look like newlyweds. Have you ever played pickleball before? You'll have to try it . . ."

Bryce tuned out the chatty woman, who asked questions but didn't wait for an answer, sneaking a peek at the other impressive paintings in the room while searching for the exits should things go sideways tonight.

Kira's high-pitched laugh brought him back to the conversation. "Pickleball sounds so fun. We'll have to set something up. We're in town for work for a few months. Brian and I both work for a private collector. We've only been married since August. Can you believe it?"

Kira spoke Sophia's language. Money, high society, fake social politeness, and off-the-charts expensive and unattainable art pieces. They chatted until a man entered the room. He was probably twenty years older than Sophia, with his brown hair thinning around the hairline.

"Hello, my friends." The man spoke with a thick Russian accent. "I'm Alex Dominik. I'm so sorry for the unfortunate incident yesterday with my security guard. It is a pleasure to meet you."

Bryce stood to shake hands with the man. "Don't mention it. We're just glad to move into such a secure area. I travel a lot, so it's nice to know my wife will be safe if she stays behind."

"Ah, so you are a businessman?" The man's dark eyes scrutinized Bryce, as if trying to detect any deception in his story.

"I'm an art buyer. I work for a private collector."

Alex nodded. "Very nice. My wife and I love fine art."

Bryce walked over to the Cézanne. "Yes. In fact, I was admiring your collection. It's incredible."

Kira placed a hand over her heart. "What I wouldn't give for an original portrait like this. But Brian seems more interested in period pieces these days."

Alex's gaze lingered a little too long on Kira. "And which period is your favorite, Katrina?"

Bryce's muscles tensed. Her background wasn't art history. Why had she baited Alex?

"I'm a fan of neoclassical eighteenth-century works myself," she said, "but I do love the baroque style from the same time period. Brian's employer is especially interested in lost Russian antiquities. I keep hearing of people finding priceless works of art in flea markets and garage sales and wonder why we can't be so lucky as to stumble upon such rare finds."

Bryce did his best not to choke on his surprise. Of course she was prepared.

"You'd have to go to a garage sale," Sophia said, scrunching up her nose. "I'm sure there are plenty of treasure hunters out there rummaging through discount racks to find that one-of-a-kind piece, but I prefer to obtain my art the old-fashioned way."

"Which is?" Kira leaned closer to Sophia, as if sharing a secret.

Sophia waved a well-manicured hand in front of her. "Money. Lots of it." Both women laughed. Sophia's words had started to slur, but she accepted another drink from the butler.

Kira shot Sophia a conspiratorial wink. "Well, that works just as well. And Brian works on commission, so . . ." She shrugged as if everyone knew what she meant.

And from the look in Alex's eyes, the man smelled opportunity.

Kira's comments landed, hopefully setting the stage for an invitation to the illicit auction. Bryce might have the art history knowledge, but Kira understood people, a skill he hadn't fully mastered. Maybe they were a better team than he first thought.

A heavy knock on the front door thundered through the living room.

"Our last guest has finally arrived," Alex announced. "Time for dinner. I'm starving."

The butler ushered in a man in a tailored suit, his fingers weighted down by oversized gold rings. Kira gasped—soft, almost imperceptible, yet he caught it.

Okay then.

The man had spooked her, and he didn't think Kira scared easily. Who was this guy?

"Sorry for my tardiness," the newcomer said. "DC traffic is a nightmare." The accent hinted at Russian. His dark eyes and broad shoulders gave him an imposing stature.

Alex waved his guests toward the dining room. "The chef has made my favorite, beef stroganoff. Let's eat."

Bryce offered his arm to Kira and leaned in, enough to whisper in her ear. "What is it?" An intimate gesture for a couple and necessary for him to figure out what had thrown her off. They followed their host into the main hallway, toward the back of the brownstone, into a windowless formal dining room area.

"Gallery guy," she said and kissed his cheek.

Gallery guy? Bryce replayed her visit to the gallery. There was the attendant Vince, the security guard, and—

No. It couldn't be. The man she chased down an alley? The one who had hit her in the head with a frame? The murder suspect?

And why was his cheek burning?

6

KIRA DID HER BEST to keep her game face on and reassure herself that if Bryce hadn't recognized her disguised identity at first glance, the man she'd chased from the gallery wouldn't either. Right?

They gathered around the table. Kira loosened her grip on Bryce's arm while the Russian man sat across from her. Alex and Sophia claimed the seats at either end of the table. Kira tallied every possible escape, didn't like her chances, and chose to strike first. She matched the man's gaze, hoping nothing in hers gave her away. "Hi. I don't believe we've met. I'm Katrina and this is my husband, Brian. We're new to the area. Do you live in the neighborhood too?"

He held her gaze beyond the point of comfort before responding. "We've not been formally introduced before, but you seem familiar. Maybe our paths crossed in the past. I am Ivan Sokolov. It's a pleasure to meet you both."

Oh boy. Was that a hint that he recognized her?

The man was tall and thick. She guessed his age to be late fifties, based on the gray hair peeking around his temple and his salt-and-pepper goatee.

The server placed a bowl of soup in front of Kira.

"Brian is in town to acquire new pieces for a private collector," Sophia said. The two exchanged a look—Kira couldn't quite interpret it, but she suspected Sophia wanted the man to inquire more about Brian's employer.

Ivan smiled and maintained eye contact with Kira. "Well, you're in luck. The Dominiks are the quintessential connoisseurs of fine art. I'm sure Sophia can give you some great tips and places to visit. Have you visited District Gallery yet? I've heard they have a fascinating new exhibit."

Kira's pulse pounded in her ears. Was the guy baiting her? To see if she recognized him? "That one is on my list. Great tip."

Alex stood. The white creamy liquid in his glass sloshed as he raised it. "I'd like to say a few words." Their host made eye contact with Kira, and she resisted the urge to look away. If Ivan remembered Kira from the gallery, she was toast, because it would be only a matter of time before Alex discovered her identity. Maybe he'd wait until dessert was served before revealing there was a traitor in their midst.

"It's always nice to meet new friends and old acquaintances. I trust we will be seeing more of each other in the coming days as we welcome the Becketts to the neighborhood. It will be nice to have fellow art lovers nearby. Za vashe zdorovye. To your health."

Everyone raised glasses in a toast.

Ivan's gaze landed on Kira. "Yes, welcome. Are you sure we've never met?" He raised his eyebrows.

Alex took his seat but looked between Ivan and Kira, as if expecting an answer.

Kira huffed. "Please. Don't all New Yorkers look alike? I come from a large family and am related to half of Manhattan and a few of the other boroughs."

"Ah yes," Ivan said. "I've spent a lot of time in New York. I guess you just have one of those familiar faces then."

Alex and Ivan exchanged a glance. This couldn't be good.

Once their host and hostess took a bite of the soup, they all began eating.

"Wow, this soup is amazing." Bryce dipped his spoon in the bowl for another bite. "Ivan, did you say you lived in the area?"

"I did not say." Ivan paused, as if finding the question disdainful. He ate a few more spoonfuls of soup. "Alex and I are business partners," he finally said. His Russian accent saturated his words with a harsh, staccato tone.

Bryce's gaze bounced between Alex and Ivan. "And what type of industry are you both in?"

Despite the stress of the moment, Kira's stomach rumbled. Eating gave her something to do with her hands. Etiquette dictated that she not dip her roll and sop up the amazing soup, so she substituted her desire with dainty bites. Was it rude to ask millionaires for a recipe? She stared at her plate to avoid eye contact with Ivan.

Alex handed his empty bowl to the server. "I am an attorney, and Ivan is my private investigator."

Interesting and potentially true. Kira assumed these men wouldn't give any information to two strangers that wasn't shrouded in lies. They may have sent Ivan to scout the statue.

Or kill off the competition.

"But I'm also a patron of the arts." Ivan turned his attention to Kira. Again. And this irritated her more than nails on a chalkboard. Did he recognize her or not? The uncertainty was killing her.

The scent of the main course hit Kira before she received the plate from the server. Beef stroganoff with potatoes in a cream sauce. Her mouth watered.

Ivan steepled his fingers together in front of him. "What pieces are you interested in?"

"I work for a private collector," Bryce said. "His name is Levi Solinger. A hedge-fund manager by day, but a gallery owner in his spare time. It's an exclusive place, and he owns an exquisite collection. Private showings only. I've curated Rembrandts, Velázquez, and even a Caravaggio. The rarer the find, the better. Right now he's going through a bit of a Russian phase, trying to track down some of the prized art pieces that went missing during the war. I'm hoping to score a prime piece and earn a nice commission."

Name drop completed. If anyone at the table googled *Levi Solinger*, they'd find a fake profile of the elusive, eccentric billionaire art collector from Manhattan.

Sophia not so discreetly checked her phone, hopefully verifying the bait they'd dangled.

Ivan cleared his throat and locked his laser-focused gaze on Kira. "So, Katrina. Tell me. Since your boss is interested in Russian art, you must have a theory or opinion as to what happened to the mysterious and elusive Amber Room? So many art lovers have speculated, but everyone comes up empty-handed."

Bryce scoffed. "Well, that's a loaded question." He glanced at Kira as if to offer a lifeline in the conversation, but she'd read up on the subject earlier, at least enough to bluff her way through it.

"Yes, it *is* one of the world's most elusive treasures," she said. "It's a shame that the Nazis dismantled the room and tried to ship it out of the country. Most historians think the treasure sank at sea."

"I'd like to hear your theory on the missing treasure," Bryce said, watching Ivan across the table.

Alex scowled. "Ivan and his theories. Such nonsense."

The man leaned back in his chair and stroked his goatee. "Ah, I just love a good conspiracy theory conversation now and then."

"Ivan always likes to start a debate," Alex said with a roll of his eyes. "Just ignore him."

"Oh, but I'd be interested to hear Mr. Sokolov's conspiracy theories on the Amber Room." Kira leaned toward Ivan. "I love a mystery, especially an unsolved one. An entire room of missing treasure, probably worth hundreds of millions of dollars today, just disappeared off the face of the earth. Without a trace. What do you think happened?"

Ivan paused and steepled his fingers in front of his mouth. "Like you said, it probably sank at sea. But the Nazis had packed the treasure in multiple crates. Twenty-seven in total, I believe."

"I guess it would be hard to keep track of all the crates," Kira said.

"Yes." Ivan took a sip of his White Russian—his third, based on Kira's count. "Imagine, if you will, what would have happened if one crate were sold, or stolen? I've heard a few art dealers speculate about secret art galleries, hoarding stolen art in the name of preserving it."

Bryce scoffed. "Like some sort of vigilante Robin Hood of the art world? Is there proof?"

Ivan smiled. "Mainly rumors and speculation. But if someone were sitting on a repository of missing treasures, it would be the biggest find of the century." He shot Kira what appeared to be a quick wink. Had anyone else noticed or was she imagining things?

Bryce seemed enthralled by the conversation. "If a stockpile of treasure like that existed, someone would have leaked the information. There would be evidence to indicate a missing crate."

"You of all people know what a collector will do to secure their private possessions." Ivan kept his gaze on Kira, and she fought the urge to squirm. He definitely recognized her.

Alex huffed and stood. "Let's move this discussion of dark tales of the art underworld to the sitting room for some after-dinner drinks. Ivan has many theories that almost never pan out."

Everyone stood and followed their host to the living room area. Bryce escorted Kira and then asked Alex for directions to the restroom. Their host whispered to the butler to show him the way.

Kira blinked. He picked now to snoop around? She smothered a snort. Probably not a bad idea. Their cover would most likely be blown after this disastrous dinner party, so why not get as much information as he could?

She refrained from rubbing her head. Barely. If this mission went south, it was all her fault. Kira entered the living room where Sophia and Alex discussed something in whispers in the corner. She sat on the couch and smoothed out the nonexistent wrinkles in her dress. While she missed her denim and leather, she enjoyed the way Bryce snuck peeks at her when he thought she wasn't looking.

Kira set her untouched original drink on the end table, a little too close to the edge.

Ivan plunked down in the chair next to her. She willed her adrenaline to slow while she scanned the room, as if searching for her husband.

She bit back a smile. Her *husband*? Man, this role was messing with her head.

Kira grabbed for her drink and knocked it off the table. The glass tipped directly into Ivan's lap before rolling onto the floor and shattering, sending a thousand shards of glass scattering.

"Ah!" Ivan jumped up, wiping his soaked pants.

"I'm so sorry!" Kira clasped her hands to her mouth. "I can't believe how clumsy I am. I'm just . . . goodness. I'm so sorry."

"It's not a problem," Sophia said. "Please, it was an accident." She called for the butler and soon had a team of three people armed with dustpans, towels, and sprays to tackle the mess.

When they were done, it was like nothing had happened. Kira sat back on the couch and now Ivan sat next to her—too close for her comfort. Ivan remained quiet and sipped a drink that contained enough alcohol fumes to burn the house down if ignited.

Alex crossed the room while Sophia stood by the doorway, giving instructions to the butler. "Ivan, I forgot to give you the invoice you asked for. Come to my office, and I will get it to you before I forget."

Kira stiffened. Office? Not good. They'd find Bryce snooping.

Alex marched from the room and Ivan started to rise. She couldn't stall Alex, but maybe she could distract Ivan to buy Bryce some time. "Are you sure you have to do work now? I was hoping to hear more about your conspiracy theories."

Ivan leaned toward Kira. His breath smelled like a mixture of stroganoff and vodka. She willed herself not to shrink back, because while Kira despised people invading her personal space, Katrina might be less neurotic about it.

"Now, now, Special Agent Kira Miller," he whispered. "We'll have plenty of time to talk about things when I return."

THE SOUND OF SHATTERING GLASS had been his cue. He had no doubt that was Kira buying him time. But how much?

Once the butler had rushed off to the source of the commotion in the living room, Bryce had ducked out of the bathroom and taken a rushed inventory of the hallway with two other closed doors lining the second floor. The layout mirrored their unit next door, and he was thankful the butler had bypassed the half bath on the first floor and led him to the stairs.

He tried one doorknob. Locked.

He moved down the hallway and snapped a video of the surroundings. The area had a claustrophobic atmosphere with closed doors and no natural lighting. All his efforts to snoop around might be a bust. Until he noticed the last door hadn't fully latched.

Who puts a security keypad on a bedroom door unless they are protecting something? He gave the door a soft push and found himself in Alex's office. The door closed behind him, this time latching.

It took a few seconds for his eyes to adjust to the darkness while his nose detected the scent of cigars. He'd found Alex's space for sure. Between dark brown furniture and gray walls, the place felt like a cave. A bar along the back wall of the square windowless room was fully stocked and dimly lit.

Bryce desperately wanted to search the drawers of the oversized mahogany desk, but time was not on his side. He snapped a few photos of the papers on the man's desk, wishing he could sneak a peek at the contents.

He remembered the dinner conversation and Ivan's dissertation on the secrets of the Amber Room. Where had that come from? Had Ivan been fishing for information?

Unless, of course, the rumors were true, and someone was stockpiling artwork in the mountains of West Virginia. As a child, Bryce would spend every moment he wasn't at school hanging out at his grandfather's place. He'd listen to the stories for hours as they used his metal detector to find all kinds of historical artifacts, including coins, bullets, and even a well-preserved Civil War–era shotgun buried under some rocks. Whenever they found a discovery, Grandpa would hand the piece over to the authorities so it could be returned to its owner or added to a museum collection.

Grandpa wasn't trying to make a fast buck. The man enjoyed the hunt, the thrill of finding a rare gem. But his grandfather's tales were just that—stories filled with hopes and dreams of buried treasures that never amounted to anything.

Bryce's watch vibrated with the *out of time* signal. He had to get back to Kira before anyone noticed his extensive absence. One last picture and he'd leave.

Voices filtered through the office door.

He froze for a second while his heart picked up speed. His hiding options were limited. He ruled out under the desk for fear of being trapped. The only spot, although not ideal, was behind the door. When opened, it might conceal him.

Might.

He flattened himself against the wall. The keypad beeped and the door swung inward. Bryce pushed himself into the corner between the open door and the wall. At least his gray suit blended well with the walls of the office.

Two men entered, and although Bryce couldn't see, he assumed it was Alex and Ivan based on their voices. They spoke fast and in Russian.

Bryce slipped his cell phone out of his pocket, navigated with one hand to the voice recorder app, and hit Record. Their conversation grew louder. An argument? Or was that just how Russian sounded to him?

Sweat trickled down Bryce's back, despite the cool temperature of the room. He texted Kira one word. *Stuck.*

No response. But it wasn't like he or Kira could do anything, other than burn the place down to get everyone to evacuate. And he'd consider doing this if it secured his freedom. But the FBI probably wouldn't appreciate the hefty bill for rebuilding an entire brownstone neighborhood.

Someone slammed something onto the desk, and Alex said in English, "We better return to our guests. And you need to find Isaac."

Footsteps pounded and the door closed behind the men. Bryce counted to thirty. He exited the office, satisfied that the coast was clear.

He rushed toward the living room and nearly collided with Natalia. She gaped at him, then snapped her lips shut. "What are you doing here?" she whispered.

He swiveled his head around and realized he was caught at the wrong end of the hallway. Had she seen him duck out of the office? "I got lost coming out of the restroom and took a wrong turn. I'm heading back to the living room."

Her brows lifted in an arch, doubt flickering in her eyes.

"I promise, Natalia. I simply got lost and now I'm embarrassed."

The maid nodded. "Hurry. You'd better return or they will wonder what happened."

"Thank you."

She smiled, and he raced down the hall to rejoin the party in the living room.

The second he turned the corner, Kira stared daggers at him, clearly communicating that they had to get out of the house. Alex raised a brow at Bryce.

"I'm so sorry," Bryce said. "I took a wrong turn coming out of the bathroom. Your house is beautiful, but it's a maze." All true enough.

"Ah, yes," Ivan said. The man leaned a little too close to Kira on the couch, while Sophia sandwiched her in on the other side. "I told Alex to choose a different unit with an open concept. Too many closed-off rooms give the place a dungeonous feel."

Kira jumped to her feet. "We really need to be going. I didn't realize how late it's gotten. But maybe we can do this again sometime."

Bryce shook hands with Alex. "Yes. I appreciate your hospitality tonight and wonderful food and drinks. We will have to reciprocate by having you over soon."

He'd be happy to make it out of the Dominiks' home with their cover still intact.

They rushed toward the door, but Ivan stepped in the way. He extended his hand to Kira and pulled her into a hug. The man whispered loud enough for Bryce to hear. "Nice to see you again."

His stomach dropped to his feet. *Again?*

This confirmed that Ivan had identified her from the gallery. They walked out of the brownstone and down the front steps. Bryce checked over his shoulder and noted Natalia standing in the living room window, watching them walk away. The woman's dark eyes made him shiver.

7

KIRA CLUTCHED BRYCE'S ARM until they closed the front door of their brownstone.

Agent Hudson had staked out next to the living room picture window. "All clear here. Glad you two are back. We'll set up a call with SSA Turner so we can all debrief."

Kira nodded, her fingers curled around the business card Ivan had placed in her palm when she and Bryce were heading out the door. The awkward handshake and hug had rattled her, not to mention the whispered "Nice to see you again."

"Ivan knows who you are," Bryce said as if reading her mind.

"You think?" Kira sank onto the plush couch, thankful to be out of that house. Her adrenaline and racing heart began to steady. "When you left," she said, "Ivan called me Special Agent Kira Miller. How did he find that information out?"

Bryce sat next to her and rubbed his forehead. "We are going to be up all night debriefing from that awkward dinner party."

She wanted him to grasp her hand, comfort her, give her a shoulder to lean on, but the walls of professionalism remained intact. He couldn't . . . wouldn't . . . do that in front of the other agents.

Kira dismissed her wayward thoughts and got down to business. "As much as I'm dying to know what you found and how you managed to get out when Alex and Ivan headed for his office, I'll go first."

"Perfect. Tell me everything he said."

"When you were gone, Ivan returned to the living room, and we were alone for a brief moment. Alex and Sophia stepped out to discuss with the chef the dessert and drink pairings. Ivan whispered to me that he didn't kill the security guard. I'm not sure I believe him. He said, 'I'm on your side. We're after the same thing.' And then you came back and he slipped me this." Kira opened her hand and showed Bryce the card.

The front of the white business card stated the name and address of a mechanic.

"'Young Mechanic,'" she read. "With an address in Riley, West Virginia."

Bryce went to the kitchen and came back with a ziplock plastic bag. She placed the card in the bag, and Bryce turned it over to examine it. "Your prints will be on this, but our team can run it for Ivan's. Look what's on the back."

"What?"

"'Follow the rabbits,'" he read.

Kira sucked in a breath. "I don't know what to make of this. Ivan knows my name, but did he tell Alex and Sophia our true identities?"

Bryce squinted at the writing. "Is it possible he's Russian intelligence? As in, he's undercover too? Because I would think he'd already sell us out if he had any loyalties to the Dominiks."

The theory sounded absurd, but this case had thrown them for a few loops already.

She snapped a few pictures of the evidence and texted it to Everly. "It's plausible. Everly can research both this mechanic and Ivan Sokolov. She might get a hit on the name without fingerprints." She headed to the kitchen and made a pot of coffee. "I guess we wait for Turner to decide if our covers are blown." It was going to be a long night. She dished out two bowls of Moose Tracks and placed one in front of Bryce, who sat at the dining room table with his laptop open.

"You never even asked me if I wanted any," Bryce said, taking a bite of the ice cream. "Did you see how much food I ate? It was good. Let's hope they didn't poison us, because I ate every bite."

"The Dominiks' Michelin-Star chef is to die for." She put on her best snobby accent, and Bryce laughed. "But we need the sugar and caffeine combination to unlock our superpowers to put this puzzle together. Your turn. What did you find out?"

She grabbed her notebook and sat next to Bryce at the table.

He didn't answer right away but sipped his coffee. "I took some pictures of the office and I got busted."

"Busted?" Great. Both of them now had compromised identities. What a way to start an undercover operation. "How?"

"I heard Ivan and Alex come upstairs. The only place to hide was behind the door, and it worked. Until I exited and got caught by Natalia. I don't think she saw me exit the office, but I was definitely not where I was supposed to be."

Kira scrunched up her nose. "Not good. Do you think she'll rat you out that you were wandering around?"

He shook his head. "I don't know, but she watched us walk down the sidewalk to our house. Odd and definitely gave me a bad vibe." He sighed. "I feel like I came up empty-handed, except I did record Ivan and Alex arguing in Russian. I was behind the door, so I'm hoping it came through."

He cued up the recording. Kira leaned in to listen. The muffled sound might make it hard to hear, but she'd give it her best shot. She flipped to a blank page in her notebook and jotted notes.

Bryce watched her work.

"Can you play it again?" she asked. When the recording ended for the second time, she looked up. "Apparently Ivan invited himself to dinner, which Alex wasn't too keen on. He also didn't like Ivan's dinner discussion—tells Ivan to tone it down. Alex then lights into Ivan about paying him way too much for no results, and Ivan claims he needs more time. That he's getting closer."

Bryce ran a hand through his hair. "So, basically nothing specific other than to indicate that they're searching for something and there's a lot of money involved."

"It gets more interesting. Ivan recommends us as candidates for the auction. So, our intel is right that Alex is involved in the illegal smuggling ring."

"It also means Sophia and Alex bought our covers. Until Ivan or Natalia gives them reason to question it."

Kira clicked her ballpoint pen a few times. "Who's Isaac?"

Bryce drummed his fingers on the table. "I'm not sure. Another lead to follow."

Kira studied the man, noting his smooth good looks once more. She really needed to get past that. But the truth was, she liked watching him. But more than that, she found she liked *him*. In the span of a few days, she'd gone from a lonely desk job to having a partner who had her back. Someone she could bounce ideas off and dig into the case details with.

And she liked that too. Apparently she was liking a lot of things related to Bryce.

Agent Kaup came into the dining room. "Turner's ready when you are."

"Thanks. We'll set up for the video call at the table," Kira said. Agent Hudson joined them, taking a seat.

The four of them positioned themselves around the laptop, and Turner's face filled the screen. "Based on not getting to finish the red velvet cake my wife made for my birthday dessert to take this call, I'm assuming it didn't go so well," he said with his typical direct gruffness.

Kira and Bryce gave a rundown of the events, including Ivan and the encounter with Natalia.

Turner blew out a breath. "I don't like that the maid saw you sneaking around. But as far as Ivan Sokolov is concerned, we have confirmed with Russian authorities that he's deep cover with the Federal Security Service. The FSB didn't contact us until five minutes before your dinner party, so we couldn't warn you. But your cover is actually intact, assuming the maid didn't see you in the office. And Ivan pledged to protect your identities if we work with him."

Kira leaned closer to the monitor. "If he's on our side, why did he attack me at the gallery?"

Turner rubbed his chin. "I thought the same thing. He claims he didn't know who you were and intentionally missed you when he threw the knife. He just wanted to distract you enough to get away."

She rubbed her temple. "It's plausible since he could have knocked me unconscious with that blow."

"I'm keeping this investigation open," Turner said. "I don't trust Ivan. He could be working both sides for all I know, but so far, we believe the Russians want to work with us to bring down the smuggling ring. And while I don't trust them, I do want to see how this plays out. And I want your cover intact. Report back to me if you suspect he's double-crossing us. We'll keep watch on the maid and the Dominiks."

The screen split and two people joined the call. "I've had Everly Harlowe and her team lead working on your covers, and I've pulled Daria Nevsky to assist you in your operation," Turner said. "They're going to help Hudson and Kaup with the live feeds we've set up, and they also can help with online research."

"Hi, Kira, Bryce, Carrie, and Lisa." Daria waved. "Or I guess I should say Katrina and Brian? Remember me?"

"Of course, Daria. You taught a class at Quantico."

"I wondered if you'd recall meeting me."

How could Kira forget the young hacker? The Bureau only pulled Daria in for high-profile cases—so that must mean their case had caught the attention of some higher-ups. As if the pressure wasn't on before.

"Anyway, we looked into the list of names you found on the napkin and the card from Ivan, and you're definitely onto something. I'll send you the full background check on Derek Young."

"Riley is probably a forty-five-minute drive from Sawyer's Peak." Bryce showed Kira and the other two agents the map on his phone. "It's at the base of the mountains, in the valley. And it's where the estate sale was held where Zaika was bought."

Daria clicked on her keyboard. "It went for pennies in the estate sale and is worth millions. Derek must be kicking himself."

"We also believe there are two other rabbit statues." Everly clicked a few keys on her laptop. "They were part of a set. We had an agent question Derek, but he wasn't very forthcoming with information according to the report."

Kira stared at the statue picture on her iPhone. She double-tapped the screen to enlarge the details. The rabbit's eye caught her attention. She'd noted the color at the museum when she'd first seen the ugly little thing, but now it hit her. The yellow and brown colors sent a chill down her spine. They reminded her of . . . "Amber."

"What was that, Agent Miller?" Turner asked.

Had Ivan dropped hints during dinner? "Sir, I'd like permission for Bryce and me to interview Derek. He probably won't talk to the FBI, but he might entertain two art buyers offering to pay him for any additional items from his father's estate. What if there's something bigger going on than just a rare statue? What if this is a lead to recovering stolen or missing art that's worth much more?"

Turner stroked his chin. "Well, with the Russian interest, there could be something to this theory of yours. People will kill for that kind of money, so watch your backs. We also need proof. How about you two take a road trip to Riley, West Virginia, tomorrow and see how Derek Young connects to this case?"

Kira nodded. "I think it's time to *follow the rabbits*."

BRYCE'S PAST CAME FLASHING BACK to him with every mile that took them closer to the West Virginia border. He and Kira had set out early and were now eating the breakfast his new partner had insisted on bringing for the car ride. Egg and English muffin sandwiches, something Kira referred to as "walking bacon," and an ample supply of coffee.

"Seriously, what is walking bacon?" Bryce took a piece of the crispy yumminess she offered him.

"It's just extra bacon. Restaurants sometimes give patrons an extra side of bacon with to-go orders as a bonus to be eaten on the way home."

"Well, that's a winning idea."

"Do you think Derek may have more art pieces he held back from his father's estate?" Kira asked.

"It sounds like Derek and his father didn't get along. Derek hired an estate company, so I'm assuming they sold it all, but guess we'll find out soon enough."

Kira took out her notebook and began jotting notes, with her signature incessant clicking of her pen. This was going to be a long ride. He might have to buy her a new pen—one that didn't make noise.

"I was wondering," she said, shifting in her seat to face him, "what got you interested in art history? You said your grandfather used to take you treasure hunting. But how did you wind up working art crimes with the FBI?"

That was a loaded question—one that would take him back to his pitiful childhood if he wasn't careful with his answer. At least they weren't going to Sawyer's Peak. "My grandpa *did* inspire my love of art. I told you I used to go with him and watch him find hidden treasures under rocks and dirt. He'd get so excited, but he always gave his finds to a local museum or gallery. He wanted history to be appreciated by everyone, not sold to the highest bidder."

He kept one eye on the rearview mirror, checking for anyone who might be following them. "I wound up getting a full ride to Harvard and double majored in art history and business. After I graduated, a gallery hired me to be a curator. I spotted a couple of forgeries that some creep was trying to pass off as originals, and I called the FBI. The second time I called, they recruited me."

"That's impressive."

He tapped on the steering wheel. "I guess. But once I started working with the Bureau, I found my passion in stolen art. I think that's the legacy Grandpa left behind. His love of art and history resonated with me, and I hate to see paintings, sculptures, or anything of cultural significance sold on the black market, never to be seen again. Nothing makes me happier than restoring smuggled artifacts to their home and reuniting countries with their proper possessions."

"Do you believe there's a treasure trove of artifacts that somehow made its way to the mountain towns of West Virginia? Seems implausible, but what's your gut reaction?"

Bryce racked his brain for an answer. When was the last time he made a decision based on instinct alone? "Gut reaction again, huh? I prefer evidence. I've never found any proof of buried treasure where I came from. Just drunken bar gossip from some of the locals."

"Then tell me about the stories, the legends. We have a long car ride and I'm already bored."

He glanced at Kira. The sunlight shone through the window, making her auburn hair sparkle with hues of red. His fingers itched to touch it. To see if it was as soft as it looked. He cleared his throat and returned his gaze to the road. "A few locals started a rumor about a hidden bunker in the mountains full of lost art. Dating back to the Civil War. My grandpa spoke of it a few times. Claimed a man at the bar told him all about some family that kept the art on lockdown to preserve it. Allegedly, it started with someone taking paintings from a mansion during the Civil War before the home burned to the ground. And over the years, they supposedly amassed an extensive collection."

Kira jotted a few notes. The woman was old-school with her pen and paper, but he appreciated her meticulous documentation and attention to detail. Just not the pen clicking.

"Sounds like you had a great time with your grandfather growing up. But what about your parents?"

Danger warnings pumped a steady beat through his head. He did not talk about his childhood with anyone. Because talking about that would lead him to thinking about one of his biggest regrets. All he'd wanted to do was take care of his father, get the man sober, and help him find a job. But his father had refused and had thrown Bryce out the door when he'd turned seventeen.

He'd left and refused to look back. Until now. But only because she was forcing him to. "Grandpa saved my childhood—he was my hero. I lost my best friend when he died."

"And your parents?"

She would *not* let it go. But he wanted to know more about her past, so he'd throw her a bone. "My mom left when I was eight, and I remember everything that led up to her leaving. The fights, the accusations. My father wasn't a nice person. He had issues with gambling and alcohol, and his obsessions left us perpetually penniless."

"Trailer park trash . . . Hillbilly . . . Beggar Bryce."

The names whispered through his mind, as did the remembered shame, hurt—and anger. And it wasn't his fellow classmates. He'd once overheard his second-grade teacher call him a "hoodrat" and refer to William Lambert as "worthless." Just the gossip of a small town, but it left a permanent scar on his heart.

"I'm so glad your grandfather was there for you," she said.

He studied her for a brief second before turning his eyes back to the road. She'd grown up in an orphanage. At least he'd had a family with Grandpa. "I stayed at his place most of the time.

I was so blessed to have him in my life. He passed away from a heart attack when I was fourteen."

Kira gave a soft gasp. "That's rough. Did you live with your dad after that?"

"I had no other options. He wasn't abusive in the physical sense. Just in the neglectful one. I wound up becoming the parent and taking care of him. Making sure we ate and so on."

"How long has it been since you've seen him?"

Bryce wanted to change the subject but steeled his courage and pressed on. "I haven't been back since I was seventeen. The day I got accepted to college was the day my dad kicked me to the curb. Refused my help. Told me I'd betrayed him by applying to school." He clenched the wheel. "What kind of dad says that when his son gets accepted to Harvard? Later, I couldn't bring myself to return." He had kept tabs on the man through a local friend who'd let Bryce know William Lambert hadn't changed and wouldn't welcome a visit from him. So that was that.

Kira took a sip of her coffee. "I can understand why this trip is difficult for you. But I'm sure you've changed over the years, and your past has certainly shaped who you are today—for the better. I even noticed you lost any trace of a West Virginian accent."

This woman understood him in ways no one else ever came close to. It was interesting. And . . . disturbing. "I wanted to put some distance between my past and future. And you'd think I'd want to go into social services to help kids like me, but I wanted to honor my grandfather, his passion and all that he loved. Everything Grandpa found when treasure hunting with his metal detector is on display at the town historical center. Because of his passion and beliefs that those items should be for everyone, I chose fighting for art rights. It honors his legacy, and people shouldn't profit off looted history."

Bryce's father had always been waiting for the next get-rich-quick scheme that never panned out. Thankfully, his grandfather had stepped in to teach Bryce to value what truly mattered—faith, integrity, and a relationship with Jesus. That foundation carried Bryce through the hardest seasons of his life, including the day his father had betrayed him by draining Bryce's savings account and leaving him penniless. Bryce had worked two and sometimes three jobs to pay for rent and books in college.

After a few pit stops and a visit to a quaint coffee shop for a quick caffeine fix, they arrived in Riley, West Virginia. Kira craned her neck to take in the scenery as they drove down the town's main street. "I can see why people love it here. It's beautiful."

Bryce nodded. Well, some people loved it. Not everyone. Not him. But after being gone so long and seeing the place through distanced eyes, he could see the attraction.

Nestled in the valley of the Appalachian Mountains, the town had stunning mountain views on all sides. They drove through the heart of Riley, past rows of antique shops, touristy stores that sold magnets and T-shirts, and a smattering of mom-and-pop restaurants. No chains here.

Bryce's heart thawed at the sight of small-town life. People walked their dogs and socialized on the sidewalks. Banners advertised a winter carnival. In some ways, he missed the charm and beauty of these mountains. It was the memories of his father that ruined the idyllic setting and robbed him of childhood reflections filled with family, friends, cookouts, and community.

The mechanic's shop sat at the far north end of town. Bryce pulled onto the gravel driveway and parked by the main garage. A man walked out to their car before they'd even gotten out. "Can I help you?" he said with a thick West Virginian drawl. The guy was probably in his fifties but appeared much older with tanned skin and gray hair.

Kira jumped out of the car and extended a hand. "Hi, I'm Katrina Beckett and this is my husband, Brian. We're here to see Derek Young." Kira had softened her accent—still New York, just muted enough not to clash with someone so far removed from the rush of city life.

"I'm Derek." The man squinted at Kira. "Your car is too new to need work. I'm guessing you're not here for maintenance. If you're one of them city reporters, I have nothing to say about that rabbit statue—"

"Not reporters." Kira put her hand up. "Just art lovers trying to get some more information. Possibly inquire if your father's estate has any other art pieces for sale?"

The man snorted in disgust. "You and every other art collector up and down the East Coast. Believe me, if I had more, I wouldn't be up to my elbows in motor oil day in and day out." He wore greasy jeans and a worn bomber jacket. The coat, cracked with age, had a vintage military look, complete with patches on the chest and sleeve. Maybe it had once belonged to his father—or even his grandfather.

He waved a grimy hand at them and marched inside. They took that as an invitation to follow. Derek led them into a cramped office space at the back of the garage. In the larger area, two ancient, rusty cars were up on the hydraulic lifts, but no other mechanics were in sight.

"You work alone?" Bryce asked.

"I've got an assistant, but I do most of the work. I own this fairy tale." He waved his arms around the glass window separating his office from the garage.

A space heater kicked on, blowing a steady warm breeze across the square musty room that contained a desk, three mismatched chairs, stacks of invoices, and miscellaneous nuts and bolts.

Several invoices spread across the desk had red OVERDUE stamps across the top.

The man offered them a seat, and Bryce sat in a plastic lawn chair, hoping it would hold up. "We're interested in the rabbit statue and would love to hear how it came into your possession."

The man winced. "Like I've told others, my father and I never got along. I hadn't spoken to my old man in years, even though we lived in the same area. He was a hoarder—junk piles from floor to ceiling. And the Youngs collected junk for a century. It was my grandfather and great-grandfather's boxes as well. I had no time to go through it all. Nobody has that kind of time. So I hired an estate company to clean it up and sell everything."

"Why didn't you and your father get along?" Kira asked. She'd chosen to stand, over sitting in the flimsy chairs.

Derek ran a hand through his shaggy hair. "He wanted me to take over the family business as town historian. But I love working with my hands and wanted to have my own business, not sit in some stuffy library maintaining records. My old man didn't like it, but he didn't like much about me. Never good enough for him. But"—he paused as if to compose himself—"I've come to accept it and move on."

Bryce had the urge to reach over and hug the guy. He knew too well the hollow ache of never being enough for a father. His own had made sure of it—every word, every look a reminder that Bryce was a disappointment. The criticism hadn't just stung, it had carved itself into him, staying with him long after the moment had passed. And the cruelest part? Even after he'd been the one who shouldered the burden, working to keep a roof over their heads and food on the table, it still hadn't been enough. It never was. He kept his mental grimace off his face. He hoped.

"What happened to your father's will?" Bryce wanted to keep the man talking but also recognized the emotional toll it was taking on him. "He never mentioned anything about owning priceless antiques?"

Derek's face hardened. "No. I didn't have any siblings, and he left me his house and whatever money he had. I'm kicking myself for not listening to him. He tried to reach out multiple times over the past few years, but after a childhood of being told I wasn't enough, I wrote it off as the ramblings of a crazy man."

"So there's nothing remaining from your father's possessions?" Kira's question brought Bryce back to the present.

Derek held up his hands, palms up in defeat. "Nope. The house is empty. A few people—treasure hunters probably—bought any remaining boxes from me. But the only thing of value so far was those dumb rabbit statues."

Statues? This was confirmation that more than one rabbit existed.

Kira stared at Derek. "How many statues were there?"

"Three."

8

THREE STATUES?

Kira blinked. This had to be what Alex was after, with the list of towns crossed off. He was searching for the remaining statues.

"I'm sorry," she said, "you said there were three statues sold?" The existence of three complicated their investigation. If one was worth a fortune, the complete set would be priceless.

Derek nodded. "All three were up for sale in the estate auction. They all looked the same, but each had their ears pointing in different directions. I assumed they were knickknacks. Most of the items my father owned appraised for little to no value. The estate company even deemed them worthless when they sold them. You'd think a reputable estate company would have done a quick Google search before shipping them off like they were junk. I have a lawyer reviewing my case against them."

Kira sat in a lawn chair and leaned over the paper-and-grime-filled desk. "Where did the other statues wind up?"

The man flexed his fingers into a fist, and his face flushed red. "A curator for an antique shop bought two. But when I called his store, they said the statues were either sold or *misplaced*." Derek air quoted the last word.

"I'm so sorry about that," Kira murmured.

"My father was sitting on a fortune and never told me." Regret and grief were etched across his face. "He tried to give me the statues. They were in a box with my name on it, along with a note. But I was broke and trusted the estate company to manage my father's belongings."

The man had to be devastated at the mix-up. Not only had he lost his father, but those pieces may also have been a gift.

Derek opened a desk drawer and pulled out an envelope. He slid it across the desk to Kira. She opened it, pulled out a note card, and read it aloud.

"'Derek—I know we didn't always see eye to eye, but if something happens to me, you need to continue my work. These rabbits are the key.'"

Kira couldn't hide her interest in the note but tried to focus on Derek. Questions flooded her mind. What work was Fenton Young doing besides being the town historian? And what did he mean that the rabbits were the key?

Did Derek have a sentimental bone in his body? He'd kept the note but gotten rid of the one thing his father meant for him to have.

Derek took a sip from his cola can. "The Young men were hoarders through and through, and I wanted none of it. Plus, my father was incredibly eccentric. My place is too small to store all the boxes my dad had crammed in his house. But I assumed my estate company was appraising everything before they sold it."

A bell dinged and Derek stood. "I've got a customer picking up a car now. But good luck with everything. Wish I could help you more."

He escorted them through the garage toward the exit. Their time was almost up, but Kira had one more question. "If you don't mind me asking a personal question, how did your father die?"

Derek stopped and turned. "It's common knowledge." He gestured to the car on the lift. "He took a curve too fast coming down the mountain in the rain and wrapped his car around a tree."

"Where was he headed?" Bryce asked.

"I'm not really sure. It happened in the evening. He might have even been coming to see me for all I know, but I hadn't heard from him in months. If only he'd told me the value of those statues." The man blinked, as if to hold back tears. Whether he was distraught about his father's passing or losing out on a secret fortune, the man had a right to grieve both.

They thanked Derek for his time and headed outside, where Kira gulped a deep breath of fresh air. "That office smelled like cigarettes and those Christmas tree air fresheners."

"That's an accurate description. But at least it was a productive trip," Bryce said, pulling the keys out of his pocket.

"Where to next?" Kira jumped into the passenger's seat and pulled out her phone to check out the GPS map.

Bryce sat for a moment drumming his fingers on the steering wheel. "Since we're here, why don't we check out a few of the antique shops around the area? See what the local gossip is about the three statues and who's been asking for them."

Kira researched several of the antique shops within a thirty-mile radius. "There's one a few towns over called Copper Creek Collectibles. Let's start there. If the Russians are searching the area, they may have already found the other two rabbits."

Bryce navigated onto the main street that cut through town. His eyes shifted from the road to his rearview mirror. Kira caught him looking and craned her neck to see out the back.

"That pickup truck pulled out behind us when we left the auto body shop," Bryce said. "And I just made two turns. The truck hung back, but I think it's following us."

"I see it."

The drive out of town morphed into a two-lane mountain passage, with winding curves and narrow shoulders. The truck kept its distance but continued on the same path.

"We're one hundred percent being followed, Bryce."

A sign with a white arrow pointed toward Copper Creek,

and Bryce took the turn to head down the mountain they'd just crested. "I'm going to shake him off." Trees lined both sides of the road. "Hold on." Bryce swung the SUV around and turned onto a narrow dirt path that Kira hadn't noticed.

She chewed her lip.

Who knew they were coming to see Derek? Had they been followed from DC? She frowned and discarded that idea. They'd been watching too close to have missed that. She braced herself as the car rocked from potholes and placed her hand over the butt of her weapon.

Bryce made a three-point turn so the car was facing the road but was hidden under the wild canopy of trees and shrubs on an overgrown plot of land.

"I can tell you grew up in this area," she said. "You've got some great navigational skills."

He shot her a small smile. "This is probably someone's driveway or an abandoned lot, but it should give us enough distance off the road to let this guy pass."

From her position under the overgrown vegetation, Kira could make out a fence, and behind them she could see the roof of a forgotten structure.

The sound of an engine reached her, then the truck rumbled by their hidden car. It was going slow—searching?—but didn't stop.

Kira tried to take a picture of the passing license plate, but the foliage blocked her view. "Do you think Alex or maybe even Ivan sent someone to trail us?"

"I'm not sure. I feel like it may be a local. I didn't see that truck until we left Young's repair shop. Maybe someone was watching his place and didn't like us coming to town and asking questions?"

Bryce eased the car over the uneven terrain, and Kira held the dashboard and door handrest, bracing herself against the bumps and jolts again. Finally, they were back on paved road.

A few minutes later, another cute downtown area came into view. A banner hung across the road reading WELCOME TO

COPPER CREEK. And right under that stood a construction sign: DETOUR. ROAD CLOSED FOR FOUNDERS DAY PARADE.

Bryce turned left at the dead end. On both sides of the main street, people, kids, dogs, and lawn chairs lined up to wait for the parade.

"What in the Mayberry did we stumble upon?" Bryce muttered as he navigated the traffic and found a parking space in a jam-packed dirt lot.

Kira made note of their surroundings. Security would be an issue with so many people heading to the parade. And then she saw it. "Check out that truck in the row of parked cars in front of us to the right."

Bryce craned his neck to the spot Kira pointed. "I think it's the same vehicle that followed us here."

A man stepped out of the truck cab. The thirtysomething guy had a long beard and a myriad of tattoos running up and down his meaty arms. But what caught Kira's attention was the gun holstered on his hip. He pulled his heavy coat from the back seat, slid his inked arms into the sleeves, and zipped up. He snagged a beanie from the coat pocket and tugged it over his head.

"I say we follow him," Kira said and was halfway out of the car before she heard Bryce agree.

The man headed toward the main street but looked over his shoulder and made eye contact with Kira. Then bolted down a side street and into the crowd of people.

"Well, that's not suspicious at all," she said. She picked up the pace and Bryce stayed with her.

The parade had started, with floats, cars, and marching bands from five different high schools in the area. Everyone was decked out in patriotic flair for the town's anniversary.

A dog leash tripped Kira, and she stopped long enough to detangle herself from an unhappy poodle with an owner who apologized multiple times and offered her a hot chocolate. She politely declined and raced to catch up with Bryce.

Bryce stopped and pointed. Their suspect was cutting through the parade route, weaving through a high school band marching their way down the street.

"Should we cross in front of the floats?" Kira asked, out of breath from dodging people parked in their lawn chairs. "Or there?" She pointed to a break in the parade behind the band but before an American bald eagle float, complete with a moving head and a halo filled with sparklers.

Bryce nodded and they raced in front of the eagle. Kira saw the man weave through the crowds on the sidewalk and duck into a store named Treasure Trails.

"Travel agency." She pointed to the brochure in the window, then pushed open the door.

The bell dinged, announcing their arrival. The cramped place reminded her of a department store shopping aisle. A counter with a register lined the back wall, and racks of brochures highlighting a variety of tourist destinations and tours lined the two side walls.

Kira approached the young man behind the counter, who had thick black glasses and wore a commemorative T-shirt from the city celebration. His name tag read Adam.

"We'd like to speak with the guy that just came in. Tall, brown coat, black beanie?"

The kid blanched. "Don't know who that is. I'm alone."

Kira placed her hands on her hips. "Adam, is it? You wouldn't mind if we have a look in that back room then?"

The kid froze and his eyes darted back and forth like he might make a run for it.

The door swung open. "I'll take it from here, Adam."

The tattooed man emerged. He shed his coat and the beanie, crossed his arms over his broad chest, and smiled. "So you two have been following me? What can I help you city slickers with? Are you hunting for buried treasure? We've got some great tours coming up."

"Why were you following us?" Kira asked.

The man leaned over the counter and lowered his voice. "Why were you talking with Derek Young?"

BRYCE NARROWED HIS EYES, keenly aware of the weapon on the guy's hip. "Why do you care?" Bryce mirrored Kira's stance but left one hand resting close to his pistol concealed under his jacket. "You followed us through the mountain pass."

Kira scowled. "Who are you?"

The man held up his hands in mock surrender. "Fine. You win." He turned to the store attendant. "Adam, why don't you go outside and enjoy the rest of the parade. And bring me back a sweet tea." He handed the kid some cash, then leaned his tattooed arms on the counter. "I'm Theodore Durham. My friends call me Theo. I own this place."

"So, we're friends?" Bryce raised a brow.

"No. Not yet. But I hope we can both help each other out. See, I know the only reason anyone drops by Derek's place driving a vehicle like yours is if they want information about his father's estate. And grandfather's."

"Derek give you a heads-up we were there?"

"Hmm. He's a good guy despite his bitterness with his family. And he needs money. He lets me know things."

"You're a treasure hunter." Kira let her guard down a bit, with her arms falling to her sides.

Bryce wasn't backing down just yet. This man had some explaining to do. And he was still armed.

Theo nodded. "I take city slickers like yourself out into the wilderness in search of buried treasure. We play up the local folklore and tell a few ghost stories to give tourists an adventure while camping. Throw in a few s'mores, and people shell out big bucks for one of our tours. But we mainly do white water rafting and *glamping*, if you can believe that."

He huffed. Despite the man's rough exterior, his Southern accent somehow softened his appearance.

Bryce still wasn't ready to trust him, though. "What does any of this have to do with us?"

"I know one of the rabbit statues was on display in a fancy museum. If you're searching for the other two, I might be able to help."

Now they were getting somewhere.

Bryce snorted. "For a price, I'm sure."

"I've got to earn a living somehow."

"I'm Katrina and this is my husband Brian," Kira said. "We work for a private collector who pays top dollar for one-of-a-kind finds."

Bryce nodded but stayed silent, waiting to see where Kira was going with this.

Theo leaned forward, interest sparking in his blue eyes. "I can tell you what I know. All I ask is you pay me a finder's fee. Shall we say fifteen percent?"

Kira glanced at Bryce, and he gave her a look that said *Let's do it.*

"I think that's a fair price," Bryce said. Of course, the FBI wouldn't be paying this guy a dime. He struck Bryce as the type who played both sides, throwing out shady offers to anyone who might bite. But was he all talk?

Theo leaned back, a glint of satisfaction in his eyes, and Bryce sensed he enjoyed spinning tales as much as chasing treasure.

"Ever heard of the Collector?" Theo asked.

Bryce shook his head.

"No," Kira said.

"The legend of the Collector dates back to the Civil War." Theo lowered his voice, as if the walls might overhear. "According to the story, one man set out to protect valuable artwork during the war. As Union troops moved across the area, he gathered expensive paintings to keep them safe. When a mansion reputed to have several valuable pieces caught fire, this guy risked his life and darted into the flames and saved them."

If what this guy said was true, Bryce's theories of someone sitting on a stockpile of art might hold water.

"The man built a bunker for the paintings in some remote and secure place where he could guard the collection," Theo continued, pausing every so often for dramatic effect. "When he passed away, his son took over. It's said that each generation took the reins and became the new Collector. At some point, they added climate control and maintained high standards to preserve history. They guarded the art and the secret."

He paused once more, and Bryce smothered a smile. Theo had so much showmanship that he could see why people would go on treasure hunts with him.

"What does this have to do with rabbit statues?" Bryce asked.

Theo waved his hands as if he were about to pull a rabbit statue out of a hat in some epic magic show. The theatrics were starting to wear on Bryce's nerves. "I've been researching this for years. I believe the man had a grandson who became a soldier in World War II. My theory is that he added to the collection. The family mission was to save art—by stealing it. It's possible this guy retrieved art looted by the Nazis and got it out of Germany."

"So, let me get this straight. You think that missing and stolen artifacts from the Civil War through World War II have been secretly housed in some small town in West Virginia?" Bryce leaned across the counter, his brain working, comparing what he knew to be fact to this new information from a questionable source.

Theo smiled, obviously loving the spotlight. "If that man passed the role of Collector to his son, that soldier could be Derek Young's grandfather, Daniel Young. Derek's father Fenton had been town historian his entire life, taking on the role from his father. What if Fenton was the last Collector?"

"That still doesn't make sense," Bryce said. "Why wouldn't they have found someone else to take over? If they'd been that meticulous for five generations to keep this secret, they'd have a contingency plan in case something happened."

Theo crossed his arms across his muscular chest. "Fenton was eccentric. People discarded his crazy ramblings. Maybe he didn't trust anyone, including Derek. Fenton died in a car accident about a month and a half ago. It was unexpected. My theory is Fenton was hoping Derek would come around but died before they could reconcile. Derek had no idea the family legacy he had rejected. His only thought was to make a quick buck by selling everything."

"And you have proof of this?" Kira asked. "It seems a little too far-fetched that one family could have kept this kind of secret for over a hundred and fifty years."

"Of course I have proof," Theo said. "But that will cost you."

Bryce stared at the man. "How much is Alex Dominik paying you to locate the statues?"

Theo frowned. "I'm not sure who that is."

"You haven't had anyone else inquire about the artifacts?" Kira asked.

Theo unfolded his arms and placed his hands on the counter. "Just one man. Some Russian guy by the name of Victor."

Victor was a new name.

"And you didn't make a deal with Victor?" Kira asked.

Theo hesitated, then his face paled. "Okay, I'll be honest. I'm a rough guy, but Victor had me quaking in my boots. I didn't offer to help him and lied about having any knowledge. That kind of guy would kill to get what he wants. And if I were you two, I'd watch my back. Don't talk to strangers is a good motto when it comes to inquiring about stolen art."

Bryce pursed his lips. The advice seemed sound. Yet they were expected to believe his tales of centuries-old treasure, a hidden trove of priceless art, and murderous Russians?

Theo pulled a card from his jeans pocket. "I've given you enough freebies for now. When I see the cash, you'll get the proof. Let's keep in touch."

Bryce's mind churned with the information after they left the tour shop and walked back to the car. The parade was over and the crowd had thinned.

Had his own grandfather been searching for the hidden collection? Could that have been the reason for all his treasure hunting?

"Well, that was a productive meeting," Kira said when they arrived at the car. "I'll put in a request for a background check on Theo."

Bryce started the car and turned on the AC. Sweat beaded at the back of his neck, despite the cool November mountain air. "Part of me believes him. Not the part where he wants to work with us. The guy has ulterior motives, and for all we know, he has the other two statues. But the legend might be true."

"What next?" Kira asked, since they were still sitting in the parking lot.

Did he have what it took to face his past head-on? Bryce let out a deep breath. "I have an idea. It's a long shot, but . . ."

This was lunacy and he might be wrong.

But what if . . .

"I think we should head to Sawyer's Peak. To pay a visit to my father."

9

"I KNOW THAT COMING BACK to West Virginia dredges up some painful memories for you," she said, her captivating eyes communicating an understanding Bryce hadn't experienced in a long time. "But if you want to visit your father, I'm on board. It's up to you."

She gave him the out he desperately desired. Which gave him a burst of courage to proceed. "As much as I don't want to, I think we should head to my childhood home."

Kira nodded, a slow and deliberate movement. "What would we gain from visiting Sawyer's Peak? Theo didn't give us any information on the location of the other two statues, other than we know it was on the list—and not crossed off. Do you think the other statues might be there?"

Bryce shifted in his seat to face Kira. Might as well rip the Band-Aid off. "I told you that my grandfather used to take me on all kinds of treasure hunts as a child. He knew these mountains backward and forward. He had maps and documented all his findings in journals. It's possible he stumbled upon something. A clue we could use to validate this crazy claim of secret buried treasure."

Even saying it out loud sounded ridiculous. They were chasing lore and running on coffee. Logic dictated that it was time to head back. Or maybe that was just preferable to facing his past.

Kira grabbed two water bottles from her bottomless designer purse and offered him one. “Did he ever mention the Collector, or anything resembling a stockpile of looted artifacts?”

“Not in so many words. But the man lived and breathed the outdoors, and the hunt was in his blood. It wasn’t until Theo mentioned the name Fenton that it dawned on me. My grandfather used to have a drinking buddy with the same name, and it’s not a common one. Grandpa loved a good story, so I wonder if Fenton ever said anything that might be in my grandfather’s old journals.”

Kira put her hand on his arm and gave his bicep a squeeze. “I definitely think it’s worth the drive to find out. What’s another adventure with my new partner?”

Partner. The word had a nice ring to it. Though there was a definite electric current running between them and he needed to keep his distance if he didn’t want to get shocked.

Bryce pulled onto the main road. “I just want to warn you, my father isn’t the most pleasant person around. Assuming he’s sober when he answers the door.”

“Don’t worry. I’ve had my share of people disappointing me.”

His heart cracked at the pain radiating through her voice. “I’m sure it was hard for you growing up in an orphanage.”

“There’s that. But I was in a relationship when I lived in New York. Turned out the man wasn’t who I thought he was. We were on the force together, and let’s just say that things didn’t work out between us. I’ve always had the goal of joining the Bureau, but when that happened, well, it’s one of the main reasons I hung up my detective cap to join the FBI.”

No way was Bryce leaving it at “things didn’t work out.” Not when she was finally opening up about her background and what made her tick. “Tell me what happened. We have a forty-five-minute ride, and it might get my mind off seeing my father after almost eighteen years."

She squirmed in her seat. "There's not much to say. I thought we had a good thing going. But he had a second thing going."

It took Bryce a minute to process that. "He cheated on you?"

"Yep. And I felt like such a dolt. I'm a detective and I was clueless. We were engaged, and he chose her instead of me. Some blond cheerleader—literally—barely out of college."

"I'm so sorry, Kira. That's messed up." How could people be so cruel? Granted, he hadn't known Kira long, but he didn't need time to know she deserved someone who would be her hero, her partner. Not a man who'd stomp on her trust, especially after her rough upbringing. Someone who didn't have baggage and—

"You'd think I was used to getting passed over. The orphanage taught me rejection is just a part of life, so I work around it. I adapt to my surroundings and give people what they expect. But getting involved with anyone from work? That's a mistake I won't make again."

Her comments reeked of loneliness, but what could he say? After his failed marriage, he'd written off relationships. "I get the need to protect your heart. But don't you get tired of living the life of a chameleon?" The words slipped out before he could stop himself. And then he tried to backtrack. "I just mean that I think we both have spent a lot of time trying to prove ourselves to others."

"No, it's a fair question. I do my best to work harder than anyone else to prove myself. I'm fine to play the game to get what I want."

"But what do you want?"

She didn't answer right away. "Despite all of the pretenses, I do want people to know the real me," she finally said. "I have people in my life that love me. My parents are always there for me, along with my roommates. But part of me thinks if things get tough, they may bail. And I know it's not true, but those old fears creep in at times. Relationships are fragile."

He reached over and gave her hand a quick squeeze. "I'm here. I'm listening. And you don't have to pretend with me."

The woman he'd just met had kicked open the door to his heart and was taking up residency—after he'd just reminded himself that she was off-limits.

Kira pointed at a lookout spot, and Bryce pulled into the gravel parking area that overlooked the valley below.

"This is beautiful. I can't believe you grew up around here." She craned her neck, scanning the area until her gaze finally found him. "How did you move on from your past?" Her voice was soft and inquisitive, trusting he'd mastered the art of healing the gaping wounds of a mother who abandoned him and an alcoholic father who'd neglected him.

"I started to go to church in college. My grandfather's influence, I guess. But one sermon in particular woke me up. I realized that no matter how hard I worked, I wouldn't be able to earn love and acceptance. That the only person who would love me for me was Jesus. I let go of the years of living up to my father's expectations, and peace began to replace the bitterness. I became a believer."

Where had that come from? He hadn't anticipated taking their conversation deep.

She didn't exactly roll her eyes, but he picked up on her skeptic vibe. "My adoptive parents are Christians. I've heard tons about faith, repentance, and love, but it's so hard for me to see it."

He understood, more than she knew. "The point of faith is believing without seeing. But if God hadn't stepped into my life, bitterness would have consumed me." His life would have taken a different trajectory had he given in to the victim mentality that haunted his childhood.

She pinched her lips together as if weighing her next words. "Maybe we have more in common than we first thought."

"Right, so you're also straitlaced and by the book like me?"

She laughed, and he relished the sound. When had he last laughed like that?

"I'll admit that my first impression of you might have been wrong."

Bryce feigned indignation. "What? You didn't find me irresistibly charming?"

She punched his arm. "To be fair, I met you at one a.m. in a police station while I was covered in blood. I wasn't too focused on you."

"That's fair."

"But yes," she said.

"Yes? Yes what?"

"I actually do find you charming."

His eyes dropped to her lips before he could tell them not to. Oh boy. He cleared his throat. "I like you too, Kira."

For a moment neither of them moved, then he got himself together and pulled back onto the road that would take them to Sawyer's Peak. The silence was awkward, so he picked a topic. "What's your favorite holiday?"

"Christmas. I love the lights. What's yours?"

"Thanksgiving."

Thankfully, that eased the tension, and time flew by as they chatted. Bryce turned off the single-lane paved road and exchanged it for a dirt-and-rock trail. His father was never going to pay to have the long driveway paved. He made a mental note to send someone to do it and not tell his father.

His fingers tapped out a nervous rhythm on the steering wheel, his nerves twisted into one big knot. What was Kira going to think of the run-down trailer he'd called home as a kid? Not to mention his caustic father.

The trees parted and Bryce pulled up next to his father's ancient pickup truck. Thunder rumbled in the distance. Hopefully they could make it back to DC before the rain rolled in.

"Is your father home?"

Of course his old man was home during the day. His dad hadn't worked as far back as Bryce could remember. "I think so, based on his truck being here. He hasn't held down a job in years. At one point, he had a construction job, but he hurt his back and refuses to work even though he's now able. He lives off a settlement from the jobsite and takes checks from the government. But he drinks away every penny he has." Or at least he had. He didn't see any evidence that had changed.

The grass hadn't been mowed in weeks. Mold rimmed the white siding of the mobile home. A random tire lay next to the house. He hated to imagine the condition inside. "This isn't going to be pretty, Kira."

"It's okay, Bryce, I promise." She nudged him. "I've seen autopsies before. And worked in New York City. I've got a strong stomach."

His laugh came out sounding more like a snort. "Right." He uncurled his fingers from the steering wheel. "Let's do this then."

"Are you sure the journals are here?"

"Yes. They weren't anything my father could sell, so he wasn't interested in them. I left a few boxes of my grandfather's belongings in a closet in the back bedroom. Dad will never find them because he doesn't clean. It's like this house was frozen in time. Nothing has changed since the year my mom walked out."

She looked at him with soft eyes that encouraged him to tell that story, but not now.

They opened the car doors, and Bryce could already smell something that reeked like spoiled milk. Kira scrunched her nose but said nothing.

Bryce stopped at the overgrown flower bed near the porch and pointed at the gawdy stone bunny rabbit statue that resembled a long-forgotten Easter decoration. "Some things never change. My father would hide a spare key under this." He picked it up, and sure enough, a key was stuck to the bottom of the lawn decoration with a piece of duct tape. He set it back down. What was up with the rabbit theme?

He walked up the cement steps to the front door. A television blared the theme song of some daytime game show. He knocked. The volume decreased and shuffling sounds came from within.

"What do you want?" his father barked behind the closed door, not even bothering to open it.

"It's Bryce."

The lock clicked and his father opened the door. The man's shaggy hair was now bushy gray. His stooped shoulders made him appear feeble. Bryce caught a whiff of the smell, body odor and who knew what else, through the screen. How could his father live like this?

Tears welled in Bryce's eyes. He blamed it on the pungent odor and blinked to clear his vision.

"Well, if it isn't my long-lost son." His father opened the screen door and waved Bryce and Kira in while he marched to the living room and returned to his recliner—the same one from Bryce's childhood.

"Well, don't just stand there. What do you want? Did you come for money? Because I ain't got any."

Bryce moved into the room through the path of newspapers, pizza boxes, and beer cans to the couch, and Kira followed. He wasn't going to sit on the dirty couch that was once white, now stained brown from cigarette smoke and . . . he didn't want to know. This place was a hazard and should be condemned.

"There are a few boxes of Grandpa's belongings here," he said. "I wanted to find some of his old journals."

"Now why would you want those old things?" Barely sixty years old, his father wheezed like he was gasping his last breath.

"Just nostalgia." Bryce would never mention anything to his father that might lead him to believe there was any kind of treasure.

His father pointed to Kira. "Who's this? I heard you got

divorced. I knew you'd wind up just like your old man. Divorced and broke. And now you come crawling back home—"

Kira strode over to his father's chair. "Hi, I'm Katrina. I don't think we've met before. I'm Bryce's wife."

DIVORCED? BRYCE HAD BEEN MARRIED? The man had a heartless father, a mother who had abandoned him, and now an ex-wife. She'd jumped in without a second thought, and now Bryce's father stared at her with his mouth hanging open. "You must have heard wrong. Bryce and I are happily married."

The man shook his gray head. "My mistake."

"And we didn't come here for money."

She surveyed the room, noting the piles of clothes and other debris scattered across the dingy carpet. Then she turned her attention to the man in the chair. He might seem physically frail, but he made up for it with his feisty attitude. "I know you don't know me, but I'm very interested in art history. Bryce told me so much about growing up and hiking with his grandfather. There have been great Civil War–era finds all around the area, and I was hoping to read some of his grandpa's journals to see some of the things he discovered with his metal detector."

The man swatted his hand across his face like he was shooing a fly. "Oh, that old thing? My pa used to spend hours searching around and finding nothing. Seemed like a pretty useless hobby to me."

She bit her tongue to keep from saying anything inappropriate. "I know he didn't find a lot of things that were important to you, but a few things he located had some historical significance. Mind if we take a look?"

"Whatever." Bryce's father turned the television up as if to dismiss the conversation.

Bryce wouldn't meet Kira's eyes as he surveyed the messy

room. "Pa, I thought Aunt Janice was checking on you. Has she been around lately?"

Mr. Lambert snorted. "She died a year and a half ago. Her son came by a few times. I chased him away. He was stealing from me."

Bryce walked away without a response and headed to a back room. She followed, and Bryce's dad continued to sit in his chair. What kind of life did Mr. Lambert have? No one checked on him, and he seemed to have zero friends, so . . . not much of one?

Her heart ached that Bryce had grown up in a house without love, friendships, and joy. She wanted to wrap her arms around him and let him know that she appreciated the man he'd become. Thank God he'd had his grandfather.

Maybe there was something to faith, because she couldn't fathom how Bryce hadn't let bitterness become his constant companion. He'd left, setting his life on a better trajectory. It was admirable and she was proud of him.

She followed Bryce into a bedroom and made sure to not touch anything. The bed against the far wall held a bare mattress. An end table next to that. She bit her tongue to keep from squealing at the cockroach that climbed the wall in the far corner.

Bryce dug through the closet, pulled out a box, and set it on the mattress. "I'm sorry you had to see this place. I tried to get him help. I spent my teenage years bailing him out of trouble more times than I can count. But I'll admit, I had no idea things had gotten this bad. I tried, Kira. So many times. I hired cleaners to come and he'd throw them out. I used a grocery delivery service to deliver food, but he'd refuse to take anything from me. I finally gave up. And now I feel guilty for not trying harder."

She put her hand on his shoulder. "What more could you do? He threw you out. You had no control over the situation. And maybe God is bringing you back into his life now for a reason." Had she really just attributed circumstances lining up to some sort of act of God?

Interesting. Unexpected, but interesting. Bryce might be rubbing off on her.

He nodded. "After this investigation, I need to come back and try to convince him to accept help. And find a way to forgive him." He frowned like he couldn't believe those words came out of his mouth. She couldn't either, to be honest.

"Forgiveness will be the toughest challenge of all," she said. "He's just as mean as you described."

Bryce opened the box and riffled through the contents. "These are just some of Grandpa's clothes and personal papers. Let's try another one." He moved back to the closet and pulled out the next cardboard box, placed it on the mattress, and opened the top. "Bingo. Old journals and notebooks. The Lamberts are quite the hoarders, but in this case, it's paid off."

Bryce removed the first book and flipped through it. "I knew Grandpa had these, but I've never gone through them. As far as I know, it was just times and dates of the treasures he found. Well, treasures to him." He added the journal back to the box and folded the top over. "I don't want my dad to catch wind that we're investigating buried treasure. But I do want to question him about Grandpa's connection to the Young family. I think our best bet is to take these and go through them back at the brownstone."

The sooner they left this place, the better. "Works for me." She grabbed the box while Bryce put away the other and headed back to the living room.

Bryce followed. "I'm going to call around to see if there are any organizations that cater to seniors who live alone. And figure out a way to get the man some help, whether he wants to accept it or not."

They walked through the living room. Kira marched past Mr. Lambert and headed outside to put the box in the car. He didn't even glance at her, so maybe he wouldn't complain about them taking the items from the bedroom.

After dropping the box in the back of the SUV, she returned

to the house, where Bryce was trying to get through to his father. The old man's expression made it clear he resented the intrusion—anything that pulled him away from his rigid routine of sitting in front of the TV, glued to endless reruns of 1970s game shows. "Pa, please, just listen a minute, will you?"

The man huffed but turned his attention to Bryce. "What is it?"

"Do you remember a man named Fenton Young?"

His father perked up and some of his hostility fell away. "I do. Is he in some kind of trouble with the FBI? Are you investigating him? I never liked the man. Way too secretive. I ran into him a couple of times. He hung out with my pa a lot. Riley isn't that far away."

Small-town gossip ruled Sawyer's Peak. Everyone knew everyone else's business and preyed on the failure of others. "It's nothing like that. I do remember Grandpa drinking at the bar with a man named Fenton. But you say he was secretive? How so?"

Mr. Lambert grimaced. "The Young family all worked in the town government. Fenton was mayor at one point. Generations of them worked for Riley. Except the youngest. He's a lot like you." He pointed a shaky finger at Bryce. "Always going out of his way to disappoint the family. Gotta make your own way in life. Your family isn't good enough for you."

Bryce winced but held his composure. Kira refrained from telling the older man off. Respect your elders meant something. But her patience was on its last thread.

This guy was the definition of deadbeat. And yet, she found herself feeling sorry for him. For what he'd missed by not seeing Bryce all these years. It was a huge loss for him whether he knew it or not.

"Yeah," Mr. Lambert said, "Fenton and your granddaddy used to sit at the bar and make up stories of buried treasure. They were just two old coots rambling on about art and war artifacts."

"Did you spend time with Fenton?" Kira asked. Maybe they could keep him talking without tipping their hand. The less this guy knew about their investigation, the better.

"Nah. I like to drink alone. But I would be at the bar occasionally when the two men got together to shoot the breeze. They'd just talk about their daily finds with the metal detectors."

Kira looked at Bryce for permission to take over the questioning. He nodded. It was evident his father opened up a bit more to her. "They never talked about finding anything big? Seems like a lot of work to always come up empty-handed."

"Exactly. All that searching to come home broke every night. They barely made enough money to keep the bar tab paid." He stroked his gray beard, chasing away a few stray crumbs that landed in his lap. "Except one night Fenton had too much whiskey. He claimed he was the guardian of the art world and that his father had smuggled some stolen art to West Virginia." He pointed an oddly bent thumb in Bryce's direction. "His grandpa pressed him about it and he clammed up, claiming he'd said too much. But I always wondered what the Youngs had gotten into. Probably smuggling moonshine if you want my opinion."

Excitement hummed in her veins. He didn't know it, but Fenton's drunken ramble might be the key to unraveling one of the art world's biggest mysteries. Historians had scoured the globe for the missing treasure of the Amber Room and wound up with more theories than actual evidence of its whereabouts. Assuming that the rabbit statues led to an actual treasure and weren't some local conspiracy theory. But her gut urged her to keep digging.

"Well, we don't want to intrude any longer, Mr. Lambert. It was nice to meet you."

He nodded. "I'm so glad my good-for-nothing son found a nice woman. Come back any time."

Kira bit her tongue, the tsunami of rage that welled surprising her. And while she could find compassion for him, he'd also made his choices that brought him to this point in time. Maybe if someone finally called him out on it—

Bryce must have noticed the darkness forming behind her eyes, because he looped his arm through hers and pulled her toward the door. "Thanks for seeing us, Pa. I'm going to send someone over to help you. Please don't run them off."

Mr. Lambert grunted. "Just be careful with that box. You aren't the only ones looking for your grandpa's old journals."

BRYCE FROZE. He'd been ready to bolt, thinking the day couldn't get any worse—until his father dropped that bomb. If someone had inquired about the journals, his father's safety might be in jeopardy.

He whipped around to face his father. "What do you mean?"

His father frowned. "Just that there were two Russian men knocking on my door asking about the journals. I chased them away with my shotgun. Told them I didn't own anything from my pa. That everything had been destroyed in a fire."

Of course the way the lies rolled so easily off his father's tongue, Bryce wasn't surprised the Russians believed him. And that very fact was what may have saved his life.

"What did the men look like?" Kira asked.

"Big. Dark hair. Spoke with accents. One said his name was Victor, and that he was from the historical preservation society or something like that. The other guy never said his name. But they seemed like bad news to me."

"How long ago was this, Pa?"

His father scratched his beard. "Around a few weeks ago. Can't be certain. All the days run together."

Bryce bent by the arm of his father's recliner, taking in the man's gaunt appearance. Was he sick? "Please, Pa. Stay safe. I know you can take care of yourself. But why not let someone help you with cleaning and preparing meals? I want to make sure you are taken care of."

"Oh, so now you care. You didn't care when you left and never looked back."

Bryce's fingers tightened around the arm, and he forced them to relax. "You threw me out, remember?"

"Yeah, but families fight. You were supposed to cool off, not run away forever."

He couldn't deal with the hurt that surrounded those words. Not now. Mostly because he couldn't tell if he'd truly wounded his father by leaving or if the man was once again trying to gaslight him.

Nevertheless . . . "Well, I won't run away this time. If you accept my help."

The old man nodded, which was more acknowledgment than Bryce had received in the past. He'd make sure his dad received care. Clearly the man suffered from mental and physical illnesses. And how had he not known his aunt had passed away eighteen months ago? Shame crept up beneath his collar and he raked a hand down his cheek. *Not now. Don't think about it now.*

He led the way to the car. Kira glanced around. "I wonder if someone is watching the place," she said. "We have to assume that someone knows we visited with Derek and Theo. If they're watching, they now know we visited your father. I don't like this."

"Neither do I. But I didn't see anyone follow us out of DC. I even checked for trackers on the car first." Had he not been careful enough? Bryce started the car, and once Kira closed her door his adrenaline slowed. "Did I just bring trouble to my dad's doorstep?"

Kira buckled her seat belt. "You didn't bring the trouble, but I hate to say it—it means that your grandfather was onto something. These people are connecting the dots like we are, and it led them to the journals."

Bryce made a three-point turn in his father's dirt driveway and headed back to the main road. Kira settled in for the ride back to DC and took out her iPad. "I'm emailing Turner our update."

"Perfect." The sky opened up and rain pelted the windshield. The weather would make it harder to navigate some of the passes through the mountains.

"Okay," she said. "I've emailed Turner and also looped Everly in so she can work on tracking this mysterious Victor who keeps showing up. Now, for a few calls."

"Calls?"

"Yep. I got this. You can just listen in." Kira placed calls to several organizations in the area, requesting them to check on his father. Meals on Wheels agreed to deliver food. She found a cleaning service that worked with hoarders. And while his father wouldn't be the worst they'd seen, at least they knew what to expect. Whether his dad would let them help was another matter entirely, but they'd tried. His heart swelled at Kira's kind gesture of jumping on this ASAP.

"Thank you for taking care of all the arrangements for my dad. I really appreciate it."

"Of course. Happy to do it."

"Now that I don't have to worry about him for the moment, we can focus on this Victor person and why he tried to question my father. How did this guy even know about the journals?"

"I have a feeling Theo the treasure hunter may be selling information. If he's from the area, he may have even met your grandfather in the past. Maybe he knew the journals existed. Someone suspects your grandfather found something of interest. But the journals were still there where you left them, so they obviously didn't get to them." She shifted in her seat to look at him. "Speaking of questions, why didn't you tell me you were divorced? You grilled me about my engagement but failed to mention you've been married before."

Ouch. "There's not much to tell. The marriage lasted two months. Adelaide and I met in college, and it was a whirlwind romance. We got married the day after we graduated. I was young and just wanted to be with someone. I never noticed the red flags in our relationship." Did he have to continue or would she leave the subject alone?

"Like what?"

Guess he was continuing. He gritted his teeth, then blew out a low breath. Fine. She might be the one person who could relate after her own failed relationship. "Addie had been in a bad car accident when she was a freshman. I didn't see the signs of her addiction to painkillers. When I realized what was going on, I drained our savings account to get her into rehab."

The memories danced at the forefront of his mind. Memories he'd tried to forget. "She went into rehab and promptly checked herself out. Addie left me. I would have taken care of her, gotten her through it, but she chose to leave. I tried to track her down, but six months later, she sent me divorce papers." He couldn't save her.

And just like that he found himself divorced. A carbon copy of his mother and father's failed relationship. He couldn't save them either.

Some hero he turned out to be.

A hand grasped his shoulder. "Believe me, I know the sting of betrayal. And based on meeting your father, I can see how much you've overcome. You couldn't help Addie any more than you could make your father accept your support."

"I'll take some of the blame for the failed marriage. I wanted to find someone, and I glamorized our relationship. She was beautiful, the life of the party. Unfortunately, I didn't realize she was high most of the time—and had no desire to accept responsibility or recognize she needed help."

Her hand slid down around his bicep. "It's not your fault she left."

"Well, it didn't help that I had my father's voice in my head, telling me I'd never amount to anything. But I've always regretted not doing more to find Addie, pushing harder for her to come home. I'll admit I was angry when the divorce papers finally came and signed them almost without reading them. The regrets came later."

Kira squeezed his arm. "Thank you for sharing with me. I know this sounds cliché, but I get it. I really do."

Their unspoken connection—not to mention her physical touch—shot an electrical current through him. She understood in ways most people couldn't comprehend. When she released his arm, he missed the warmth of her touch. Why was his body short-circuiting around this woman?

"My past is what drives me," he said, redirecting his brain back to the conversation and not the beautiful woman sitting next to him. "I want to be a better person than my father. I want to care for people and show love and gratitude. I'm not going to let the negativity of others shape my future." What had his pastor told him? "God created something from nothing."

"What?"

Oh. Had he said that out loud? "Nothing. It's just something my pastor in college told me, and it stuck with me. God created the earth out of nothing. Spoke it into existence. And if he has that kind of power, he can shape my life into something new from all of my past broken experiences."

She focused on her iPhone screen. Had he shared too much? Maybe she hadn't experienced the strong connection like he had. After about a minute of silence, she put the screen down and said, "I've never really thought about that perspective before. Thank you for sharing with me."

At least she hadn't shut him down. "Well, it's the only thing that's helped me destroy the lies and replace them with the truth."

The road narrowed as they headed down the mountain. The single lane had always been a dangerous spot, with small patches of gravel to allow someone to pull off for passing. But in the rain, it was even more treacherous.

A glint of metal in the rearview mirror caught his eye. It looked like a shiny new pickup truck. It was close enough that he could see the Dodge emblem on the hood. "Watch out," he said. "Another truck is on our tail. It might be a local driving on these back roads like a maniac. I'll pull over as soon as I get the chance."

A knot formed in the pit of Bryce's stomach. He heard the truck's motor revving when it should be decelerating. To the right, all he could see was rocks. To the left, he saw open sky beneath the guardrail. "There's a pull-off just a mile or so down this hill. We'll move off the road. But I don't like how this guy is bearing down on us."

Kira twisted to watch out the back window. "He's not slowing down. I think he's going to try to—"

Boom!

"Bryce!"

Kira's cry echoed while the Mercedes fishtailed. Bryce fought the steering wheel, trying to keep the car on the road. He pressed the gas and the engine responded like the dream it was. Kira held on tight to the grip above the door.

"You okay?" he asked.

"Yeah. But I'm going to have a seat belt bruise. You?"

"Same."

The truck backed off slightly, revving its engine for another hit. Bryce scanned the area for any sign of an escape route.

"Keep your foot on the gas," she said. "I'll crawl into the back and see if I can shoot out their windshield."

Before she could get the seat belt off, Bryce put his arm across her. "Don't. I'm concerned about what would happen if we crash. Because I have a feeling that we're going to wind up hitting the rocks or . . ."

No need to state the obvious. They'd be going over the side of the mountain. If they were lucky, a tree might slow their descent. If the impact didn't kill them first.

The truck rushed to within inches of Bryce's bumper, but this time tried to pass them.

"What are they doing—" But he realized too late the other vehicle's intentions.

The truck sideswiped the car, shoving it toward the rock wall on the right.

"They're trying to crush us," Kira yelled. "I can't get off a shot from my position."

Bryce pumped the brakes, but another bump from the truck sent Bryce's car careening into the rock wall. The front end folded like an accordion.

Airbags burst open.

Kira screamed from the impact.

And then, silence.

Burned rubber, smoke, and dirt stung his nose and made his eyes water. The only sounds Bryce heard were the radiator hissing and rocks and debris falling from the cliff above.

"Kira! Are you okay?"

No answer.

Glass shattered, and Bryce tried to crane his neck from his cramped position to see out the back window. The console and steering wheel had him pinned in, but he could turn enough to see a man with a ski mask and a crowbar reach through the back window and take the box containing his grandfather's journals.

"Kira?" *Oh, God, please let her be okay.* "Kira!"

Still no answer and his world was spinning. He reached up and touched his head. Something warm and sticky ran through his fingers.

Blood. No wonder he felt woozy.

Lightheadedness won out, and Bryce succumbed to the darkness.

10

KIRA'S HEAD THUMPED a steady rhythm, and it took a second to gather her awareness. And note the pain in her legs along with the rain pouring down on her, saturating her.

She shoved at the dashboard, but it wouldn't budge. Which explained why her legs hurt so much. And the windshield was gone. She stared out of the glassless front window and saw the crumpled front end. *Oh, God . . . help?*

Outside her passenger window was nothing but rock.

"This is not good," she whispered. "How—?"

Bryce!

His father's house and the journals.

The truck that shoved them off the road.

Bryce calling her name. But she hadn't been able to get her mouth to work to respond.

"Bryce?" Her voice croaked.

And now he wasn't answering. She closed her eyes to try and focus on anything but the pain pumping through her. Finally, she opened her eyes and surveyed the damage. The dashboard had crumpled around them, creating a cocoon of plastic, metal, and airbag remnants.

"Bryce! Talk to me!" She moved the airbag away from her

face to see Bryce facing her, eyes closed, and a deep red trickle of blood coursing down his pale face. His eyes fluttered. "We've got to get out of here."

But Bryce was barely conscious, and she couldn't move her legs.

Maybe it was time she took up prayer. Because there was nothing she could do to help free them from this mess.

God, if you are real, if you can hear me—

"Kira!"

She stilled. "God?" she whispered into the darkness.

"Kira!"

Wait, was someone there?

"Help!" Her mouth tasted like she'd eaten a hundred cotton balls. Had the person heard her cry?

She turned her head and spotted a man next to the driver's side of the car. He seemed familiar, but it didn't matter. She had to get Bryce out of the car, and this guy could help.

But when the man stuck his head through Bryce's paneless window, she gasped.

Ivan Sokolov.

Where had he come from?

Ivan pulled the handle, but the door wouldn't budge. He caught Kira's eyes. "I called 911, and I'll get you out of here."

"How . . . why . . ." She had so many questions, but her brain refused to form words.

"Let's just get you both to the hospital. I'll explain later."

Sirens wailed in the distance, growing closer, and soon two paramedics arrived and pulled Bryce out of the car. Had Ivan run them off the road only to rescue them? The fog in her brain lingered. But one thing was clear, she was still trapped.

"Kira, you okay?" Bryce groaned his question, and she let out a breath.

"Yeah, Bryce. I'm okay. And you are too."

Voices echoed and two more paramedics arrived. A firefighter in full gear leaned through the empty window of the driver's side door. "Hang on. We may need to cut you out of the car. Your side is crushed against the rocks."

How had she survived?

Butterflies took flight in her belly when they brought out a contraption that had two sharp saws at the end. The firefighter wasn't kidding. They were cutting her out of the vehicle with the Jaws of Life. Fabulous. But she clung to that word . . . *life*.

Thank you, God, we're both alive.

The car vibrated from the tool, then a loud grinding sound set her teeth on edge. She kept telling herself the firefighters were trained for this and she'd be fine. The seat bounced as pieces of metal gave way. She drew in a shallow breath and willed herself not to have a panic attack. Visions of being impaled by a jagged piece of metal taunted her. Would this be how she died? Trapped in a car on a mountainside, alone? No, not alone. Bryce was with her. Not in the car, but somehow she knew he was watching. Waiting for her to be pulled from the wreck. Bryce. Good-looking, straitlaced, by-the-book Bryce. She really liked him. She shouldn't, but she did.

And if this was the end for her, why was she thinking about Bryce?

Sparks flew from the grinding of metal. With one final crunch, two firemen lifted the car off Kira's legs. Blood pumped through her veins once more, and her feet prickled as they woke up.

"Can you move your legs, ma'am?"

She tried and succeeded. And wonder of wonders, she didn't think anything was broken. She'd been trapped but not crushed. Her legs ached. She was banged up and bruised but relished the sensation returning to her feet.

A paramedic helped her stand. She wobbled, and he held on to her. "I think you'll get your feeling in your legs back soon. Have a seat with your friend, and we'll get you both to the hospital to get checked out."

She stepped over the wreckage while leaning on the paramedic's arm and hobbled to the ambulance.

Bryce sat on the edge of the ambulance with his head wrapped in a bandage. She parked herself next to him.

"I'm so glad to see you," she said to Bryce.

"Not as glad as we are to see you," a paramedic said. "We almost couldn't convince him to stay put while you were being cut out of the car."

She smiled.

Bryce grabbed her hand. "That was a close call. But who called 911? This place isn't exactly a hub of activity."

"Oh, you'll be surprised. It was Ivan Sokolov."

"Why . . . how?"

She smirked. "I think those were my exact words. He must have tracked us." A paramedic handed them each a bottle of water, and she dropped Bryce's hand to take the drink.

"And we're supposed to believe he's on our side?" Bryce moved his arm and winced.

"I'm starting to believe Ivan is one of the good guys. He wasn't the one in the truck. I think that's his car there." She pointed to where a Mercedes sedan had pulled off to the side. "If he wanted to kill us, he wouldn't have rescued us. Right?"

"Good point." Bryce winced again, and a paramedic walked by at the perfect time to see the expression.

"Let's take you both to the hospital to be checked out. You two dodged a bullet. We're all shocked that you walked away from that crash."

Not a bullet. A Dodge Ram used as a weapon against them.

Kira wasn't arguing with the professionals about getting checked out. And they were stuck with a mangled car. Bryce would hear from Turner on that one. Hopefully the FBI had good insurance.

An officer rescued her designer bag from the wreckage. The inside contained glass shards, but the contents, including her phone and notebook, had survived. The officer handed Bryce his iPhone, but the spiderwebbed screen signaled its demise.

"At least *we* are in good shape," Kira said. "Your phone looks like someone dropped a bowling ball on it."

He nodded, and they rode in silence in the back of the ambulance to the hospital, where they received separate rooms. Kira's checkup confirmed her legs were going to be big-time sore, but there wasn't any permanent damage. She'd have a nice-sized bruise on her hip where the door collapsed into her. But things could have been so much worse. She headed to the waiting room to watch for Bryce.

Once there, she called Turner and gave him a rundown of the day's events. She was about to call Violet for an update when the sliding doors to the room parted. A man walked in and made a beeline for Kira.

Ivan Sokolov.

Maybe she'd finally get some answers.

He plunked down across from her in the plastic chair she wasn't sure would hold his weight. "I take it you aren't hurt too bad?" he asked.

"A few scrapes, some bruises and soreness, but I'll be good to go in no time."

"Yes, well, please accept my apologies for the incident at the gallery. I only knew I was followed, and I didn't know who you were. So sorry for hitting you with that frame."

She gave him a small smile and a nod of appreciation. "FSB?" She opted to speak Russian. The man obviously knew who she was, but it also helped them talk without anyone in the waiting room listening in.

He folded his arms and scanned the room. "Did you think you're the only one undercover?"

"Actually, yes. What's your story?"

He scrutinized her, as if assessing whether he could trust her. "The Russian government has a vested interest in recovering stolen artifacts of cultural significance. Before someone else gets to the pieces and they are lost forever."

"Who is the 'someone else'? Is the Bratva involved?"

He paused, possibly for dramatic effect or because he didn't want to have this conversation in a waiting room with nurses, patients, and visitors bustling about. Not that any of them likely spoke Russian, but one never knew.

"It's not the Bratva," he said, lowering his voice. "There is an underground organization within Russia that believes their lineage entitles them to secure certain cultural artifacts by any means necessary. I'm trying to figure out who they are and make sure we don't lose more important pieces of our history forever."

So, not the Russian mafia. Wow.

"Alex Dominik isn't innocent," he said, "but he's not the mastermind behind this. He's doing someone else's bidding. The secret society is blackmailing him."

"Blackmail?"

"Yes."

"Then who killed the security guard?"

His eyes fell. "I don't know. Someone came out after me when we stepped outside. The guard had promised me some information on Zaika, and I paid him, but he didn't deliver. That's why we argued."

"The gallery was quiet that day." Ignoring the pain it caused her, Kira stood and double-checked the sparsely populated waiting room. A row of plastic seats lined three walls of the windowless room. A man sat in one corner by himself and appeared to be asleep. Close to the entrance, a pregnant woman who looked like she might be in labor sat with a man trying to comfort her.

No one was paying any attention to them, so Kira continued. "A couple of security guards and the gallery attendant were in the area. The attendant had moved on to another group of patrons before I took off after you."

"Yes. This is the mystery."

Kira didn't buy that Ivan had no theories on who might have killed the guard, but she'd leave the topic alone for now. And she still wouldn't take his name off the suspect list.

One question burned within her, and she decided to take a risk and ask. "Who is Victor?"

The man's nostrils flared. "You need to stop this investigation now. Victor is a dangerous man. You would be wise to walk away."

Tired of the stonewalling, she faced off with the man. The pregnant couple were called back by a physician and the other man still slept. With hands on her hips, Kira stared the Russian down with narrowed eyes. "Why were you following us through the back roads in West Virginia? I find your timing impeccable."

Ivan huffed out a breath. "I wasn't following you."

"Really?" She tamped down the desire to unleash her pent-up fury and say things she might regret later. "I appreciate the mountainside rescue, but I find it very convenient that you came running the second after someone attacked us."

"I just wish I had been closer to stop that truck."

"But that doesn't answer the question of why you were there."

"Listen closely." Ivan's voice barely qualified as a whisper. "You and your partner are in this too deep. You're not safe."

"You do realize that we're trained to do this kind of stuff?"

He snorted and scowled. "I might not be able to stop the next attack. Especially if we uncover the secrets of the Collector. Believe me, these men will kill everyone who stands in their way for the fortune buried in these mountains."

Movement at the nurses' station drew her eye. Bryce was speaking with a man in blue scrubs and looked up. Then his gaze landed on Ivan and his eyes narrowed. Ivan saw Bryce and stood. He grasped Kira's hand as if he were giving a goodbye handshake, then leaned in, close to her ear.

"I wasn't following you. I was following the person following you."

BRYCE HAD ALREADY SIGNED the little iPad that would give him his freedom, so he marched toward Kira and her companion.

A little too late. Ivan moved to the exit with the speed of a cheetah and disappeared.

Bryce reached Kira and gripped her arm with a gentle hold. "What's he doing here? Are you okay?"

She ignored the first question. "I could ask the same of you." She lightly touched the bandage gracing his forehead.

"Five stitches."

"And no concussion? You were out cold."

"All the scans were clear. The doctor thinks I passed out from the loss of blood."

"We should head back to DC." She shot him a look that communicated they'd talk once they left the hospital.

Bryce lifted a brow. "In what car? Ours can't be drivable."

As if on cue, Violet Bancroft glided into the waiting area and stopped at the reception desk. Kira grinned with relief.

Violet turned when the receptionist pointed in their direction, and she caught Kira's eye. She walked over to them. "Part of me wants to be a respectable agent, but the other part wants to give you a big ole hug." The woman's Southern accent floated gently over his ears. He still had a hard time believing she was a Special Agent, but despite her sweet demeanor, the woman had proven to be a formidable agent, especially with her marksmanship skills on the shooting range.

Kira grimaced. "You know I'm not a hugger."

"Well, I guess that makes me the Special Agent that hugs." Violet wrapped her friend in an embrace, while Kira mouthed, *Help me*, over her roommate's shoulder.

Bryce snickered, but Violet glared at him. "You'd better watch your tone or I'll hug you next."

He held up his hands in surrender.

"What are you doing here, Violet?" Kira asked.

"Turner sent me to help the local agents with interviews. I've been assigned to assist with your investigation since I just closed a case. I was going to spend the night in the area, and now I'm here to pick you up." Violet ushered them outside to a black sedan waiting in the parking lot. "I booked a hotel room about twenty minutes from here and they had plenty of availability. If we stay tonight, I can drive you back tomorrow after I finish up a few interviews in the morning."

Bryce climbed into the passenger seat, while Kira slid into the back seat behind him. The second Violet started the engine, Bryce pulled down the mirror so he could see Kira's face in the back. "What did Ivan Sokolov want?"

"What?" Violet swiveled her head to scan the garage. "Ivan Sokolov was at the hospital?"

"He was. Someone is watching us. I just don't know who." Kira continued her debrief as Violet navigated out of the hospital parking garage. "Sokolov said that he was following the person watching us. But he never gave me a name."

Kira checked her phone, and Bryce powered up the burner phone Violet had brought him.

Kira said, "I need to text Everly to see if she found out anything about our friendly neighborhood treasure hunter Theo Durham."

"Sounds like a unique occupation." Violet adjusted her rearview mirror. "I've never met a professional artifact seeker."

"Definitely an interesting character," Kira said. "I think it's going to be a race to see who gets the rabbit statues first. But I get the feeling Sokolov thinks the treasure is much bigger. If the rumors of the Collector are true, we may have a mess on our hands with all the people who want to claim it first."

A memory sparked for Bryce. "I saw someone at the crash site. The guy wore all black and had a ski mask on. He smashed the back window and took my grandfather's journals. That's the last thing I remember before blacking out."

Kira sank back into her seat. "So, someone followed us and

didn't like that we picked up the journals. Your father said a man named Victor showed up and asked about them. Ivan made reference to the Collector and his hopes of finding the treasure before anyone else. Maybe the key really is in one of those journals."

Bryce rolled his shoulders to release the knots from his overtaxed muscles. "My grandfather loved to track his hunts. He had maps and notes. But he never told me he was hunting for anything of significance. There were always rumors of buried treasure, of course, but he didn't put a lot of stock in those. I wish I could remember, but I've tried so hard to block out most of my childhood memories. I don't know whether he had useful info or if it was just a log of arrowheads and Civil War coins." He kind of surprised himself by admitting that in front of Violet, but whatever. Maybe he was coming to terms with his past.

If only Bryce had initiated more conversations with his grandfather back in the day. What he wouldn't give to spend five more minutes talking with Grandpa. He shoved off the sadness and tried to focus on what they needed to do next.

Violet pulled into the parking lot of the hotel. As soon as Bryce got settled in his room, he crashed, his body aching from the accident.

The next day, after catching up on some work from the hotel, they headed back to DC, tackling the nearly five-hour drive with a few rest stops and a late lunch.

Once they arrived in DC, they stopped at Violet and Kira's apartment, where a new vehicle from the undercover unit waited for them.

Everly met them in front of the building with the keys to the sedan. "Bye, you two, be careful." She and Violet disappeared inside, and Bryce slid behind the wheel.

"You sure you don't want me to drive?" Kira asked.

"How are your legs?"

"Sore."

"I'll drive."

"Well, how's your head?"

"Sore, but I'll still drive."

A short time later, Bryce pulled the car up to the curb in front of their fake home and turned off the engine. Kira's phone beeped with a text. "It's Everly. I'll text her to call me in five minutes so I can get inside. I'll let you know what she says." She fired off the message to Everly and took it easy getting out of the car. Based on her tentative movements, the soreness had set in from the accident.

Movement from the brownstone next door caught his eye. Was that the front door opening? Bryce deliberately took his time getting out of the car so he could observe.

Sophia stepped out her front door and waved. She walked around the five-foot-tall hedges separating their houses and made a beeline for Bryce. He stood by the car as she approached.

"Brian! Welcome home. But this is not your car? You got a new one, yes?"

She stood a little too close for Bryce's tastes and rested her hand on his arm.

He pulled back a few inches and she let go. "We blew a tire on a treacherous mountain pass. It messed the Mercedes up a bit, so this is our new ride for now."

"Well, that's a relief." Sophia ran a hand through her long, straight black hair. "What were you doing in the mountains anyway?"

"I have some family close by, so I figured we should see them while we're in town." Simple answer, not far from the truth.

She glanced at the bandage on his head as if not buying his story, then took an envelope out of the pocket of her cream-colored silk slacks. "You must be a very important person. Ivan insisted we give this to you."

She handed him the envelope, and he willed his pulse to slow. If this was what he thought it was . . .

Her hand lingered a little too long on his during the handoff.

"This is an invitation to a private art auction," she said. "You and your wife might want to attend. Plenty of pieces to add to your employer's private collection."

And just like that, they were in.

He took the envelope from Sophia, but her hand never left his arm. She smiled, and he tried not to grimace.

There was nothing subtle about the woman's intentions.

11

KIRA RACED INTO THE BROWNSTONE, nearly slamming the door as she fumed about the scene she'd just witnessed. Sophia was flirting outrageously with Bryce. The man who, as far as Sophia knew, was Kira's husband.

Agent Hudson watched out the window. "That woman is definitely up to something."

Kira stood on the other side of the window, acting like some creepy stalker spying from behind the curtain. But she couldn't take her eyes off Sophia leaning toward Bryce, her hand on his arm.

"I'm going to throttle her."

"I don't blame you," Agent Hudson said.

Kira's phone trilled. Agent Hudson waved and headed toward the kitchen. Everly's name filled the screen, and Kira answered, her eyes still glued to the street in front of the house. Would Sophia ever leave? And why did Bryce just stand there? And yes, she realized she was being ridiculous.

"Hey, Everly. What's up?"

"What's going on? You sound distracted."

Everly's question brought Kira back to reality. "Sorry, Ev. I'm just watching what appears to be Sophia making a move on my supposed husband."

Everly snorted. "Well, that didn't take her long. Barely even two days."

"Maybe it's not what it looks like. I should give her the benefit of the doubt." Meanwhile, Kira's mind spun different scenarios, all of which had Sophia lying flat out on the floor. Again. Ridiculous.

"Hmm." Everly remained silent on the phone.

"Why are you hmm-ing, Everly?"

"Just that you seem pretty possessive of a man you also just met."

Kira took a few steps back from the window. The curtains fluttered back into place.

Everly was right, but Kira wasn't ready to admit it. She'd already called herself out. That was going to be good enough for now. "I'm going to go outside and rescue my husband. I'll call you back with Bryce so we can both catch up on the last few days."

Kira hung up with Everly and headed outside. "Brian! I was worried when you didn't come in. But now I see you're chatting it up with our new neighbor. Talking about art, I suppose?"

Sophia's hand dropped to her side. "Yes. I came over to extend an invitation to an art auction. I thought you might be interested in attending."

Kira placed a hand over her heart. "Of course we would love to go."

Bryce handed her the invitation and she read it. The note card in the envelope had the details of the event at District Gallery on Saturday evening along with two tickets. But anyone could score an invitation to this event. Kira had seen signs posted in the lobby.

"This sounds exclusive." It wasn't. "I love getting dressed up and spending our client's money."

Sophia smiled. "It is a great excuse to have a night out. But I need to head back to Alex before he sends the security guards out to search for me. Have a wonderful evening."

She spun on her strappy black heels and headed into her brownstone.

Once they'd headed into their unit and shut the door, Kira pounced. "What was that about? And why did we get tickets to an event anyone with a little cash can attend? The gallery has been advertising this auction all over the place. They're not selling Zaika here."

Bryce seemed a little shell-shocked. "That was definitely unexpected. I'm not sure what her end game is, but I picked up a vibe."

"Vibe?" Kira put her hands on her hips and then removed them. "She was totally hitting on you."

And why was Kira so stinking mad about it? Again.

It wasn't like they were in a real relationship. Once this assignment ended, Kira and Bryce would part ways, live in different cities, and lead separate lives.

Kira headed to the kitchen and he followed. "It's been a while since we ate," she said, "so I'm going to make a snack. Do you want to connect with Turner? We'll need to debrief and see how he wants us to handle things now that we have an official invitation to the auction." She used air quotes around "auction" and rolled her eyes.

Bryce sat at a barstool at the counter and examined the note card. "You're right. This isn't the invitation we were hoping for. It's just a fancy gala the gallery puts on to move a bunch of artwork. Nothing secret about that."

Kira handed him a bowl of ice cream and took the seat next to him at the bar. He passed her the note card, and she flipped it over. The thick cardstock held the date, time, and pertinent details of the legitimate auction. The back contained a list of items up for auction with some rules for placing a bid.

She placed the card on the counter and stared at it while taking a bite of ice cream. It didn't lie flat like it should but rather formed a raised edge in the middle. "That's weird." She picked up the card and felt around the center. "There's something else between the cardstock."

She handed the invitation to Bryce. "I feel it too," he said. "I can't believe you noticed that." He pulled out a pocketknife and made a slit in the paper, wide enough to slide his finger into the note card.

He slipped out a piece of paper, about the size of a business card. Kira leaned in for a closer inspection. Bryce held the card up to the light. "It's a faint pencil mark, but it says WR, 8th, and then it has some kind of code on the second line."

"What do you think this means?"

"I think this is our real ticket," Bryce said. "I've heard of secret auctions that take place during a legitimate auction, but they have a back room where they sell the stolen artwork. People who are into that kind of thing would know about the hidden ticket." He snapped his fingers. "I should have realized . . ." He shook his head. "Well, whatever. We have it now."

"So, this was a test."

"Probably." Bryce stood and walked to the refrigerator. He grabbed two bottles of water, then stilled. "What if that eight means the eighth item up for bid on the public bidding list is the signal—that's when a private sale starts somewhere else? Maybe in the basement or another room close by."

"Wow, you got all that from a string of numbers? I'm impressed."

A ding sounded from Bryce's laptop. "Boss wants a video chat." He sat back down and scooched his chair closer to hers. Normally, she loved her personal space. But with him—she didn't mind. He was close enough for her to catch a whiff of his aftershave. A light woodsy scent.

She ran a hand through her hair as if to displace her wayward thoughts. "At least we have good news for once. Maybe that will offset us destroying a car."

Bryce waved a finger at her. "Technically, not our fault."

"Yeah, well, I'm telling him you picked the most expensive car from the impound lot. That sporty thing was all you."

The laptop chimed again, and Bryce flipped it open. SSA Turner's face filled the screen—stern, tight with stress, and edged with anger. Then again, he always seemed to look that way. "Glad to see both of my agents are alive and well."

Kira filled him in on their latest findings and the discovery of the secret invitation.

Turner let out a breath. "I have half a mind to pull the plug on this operation. Ivan Sokolov is a wild card. We know he works for the FSB. The Russians assured us that if we helped them, they'd help us, without actually telling us what they're up to. However, doesn't mean we should trust the man."

Kira tapped her foot. The last thing she wanted was to be dismissed from her first case as a field agent. She had to see this through, close this case, and prove her worth to the Bureau.

"He did save our lives," Kira said. "I agree, he might be playing both sides. However, it doesn't appear that he's told the Dominiks who we really are. He's kept our cover secret."

Turner nodded. "I'm inclined to see this play out and let you stay in. Especially now that you might have an invitation to a secret auction. I think we need to get our hands on that statue."

Kira had wanted to do that from day one. "We could steal it from the auction."

"Not what I had in mind, Kira. However, you and Bryce are supposed to be high-rolling art buyers. What if you just make sure you have the highest bid?"

Kira's pulse thumped. "The price tag could jump into the millions if everyone wants it."

Her boss stared at her through the screen. "It's an illegal auction. They won't see a dime of our money once we raid the place, now that we know what's going down behind the scenes. Think you two can handle it without getting abducted, run off the road, or shot at?"

"We'll do our best, sir." Bryce went to say something else, but Turner had already disconnected.

"We're really going to do this," Kira said.

"It appears that way." Bryce leaned in closer to grab his drink off the counter, and his arm brushed hers.

She jumped to her feet, and to cover for her overreaction, she smacked her head. "I forgot to call Everly back. She has news and I rushed off the phone to rescue you from Sophia's evil clutches."

"Evil clutches?" Bryce laughed. "I think I can hold my own against a woman like Sophia. She's just trying to cause trouble. Probably to feel us out to see if we're legit buyers."

"By breaking up a marriage?"

"By trying to gain the upper hand. The woman is all about leverage and power. And I must have done my job by appearing to be rich and successful."

If that was the case, Kira needed to up her game. After all, she was supposed to gain Sophia's trust and learn a few of the woman's secrets.

"Do you think she's in charge?" Kira cleared the bowls and cups from the countertop and put them in the dishwasher. "Could she be the ringleader of this secret organization out to obtain stolen treasures before anyone else?"

"I'd say it's possible. I get the sense Alex is taking orders from someone else. Maybe his wife is in charge."

Kira nodded. "Ivan alluded that Alex is being blackmailed. But let's move to the living room and we can call Everly."

She headed to the living room, and Bryce set up the laptop on the coffee table in front of the sofa. The cozy two-person sofa.

So much for keeping her distance.

She sat down next to him, and within seconds, Everly's face appeared on the screen. The woman had a new hair color—jet-black with a blue streak down the right side and bangs.

"Sorry for the delay, Ev. Bryce and I wanted to see what you found out."

"The most important information I have is to not trust Sophia. I discovered more about this secret organization smuggling art and artifacts. Their leader is a woman."

"SOPHIA IS THE MASTERMIND behind this secret organization?" Bryce rubbed the stubble on his chin.

"It's a possibility," Everly said. "I just figured you'd be interested in the background of this group. I found a site on the dark web that tracks era treasures and artifacts stolen in World War II. One user was especially chatty and said the Russians have a group, led by a woman, that pays top dollar for information leading to Russian treasures. The group is specifically searching for pieces of the Amber Room. They call themselves the Amber Crown Society. Supposedly, the head of the organization is a direct descendant of Catherine the Great."

"That may explain why someone took my grandfather's journals," Bryce said. "If he'd stumbled upon any information, even a theory, as to what is buried in the mountains, it might produce a valid lead."

"Did you find anything out about our treasure hunter?" Kira asked.

"Not much," Everly said. "That guy stays off the radar. I'm doing some digging, as I think Theo Durham is an alias. Other than his business info, I don't see much about him online. At least he's not lurking on the dark web or doing online transactions. I bet his business is cash only."

Bryce had more questions than answers. "Are we dealing with two secret organizations? One called the Collector, with a family that secured art for centuries under the guise of preservation, and a separate group maintained by a Russian matriarch that wants to regain their legacy at all costs by obtaining stolen pieces?"

Everly clicked on her keyboard. "I think that's a fair assessment. I'm still doing research on the Collector. Like you, the only thing I'm finding is speculation. That someone, potentially Derek Young's grandfather, might have diverted a crate from the Nazis and shipped it back home. It makes sense if you consider Daniel Young was a high-ranking officer in the Army and worked in Germany for a time."

Bryce ran a hand through his hair. "I wonder if this Russian group sells art through the smuggling ring. Maybe they're the supplier."

"I bet that's how they've funded their operation," Kira said. "Selling off the art they don't want to fund their exploration for the pieces they desire."

Excellent theory. If only he'd seen the clues in front of his face. "I can't believe Grandpa may have had information all along." His past and present fused as if woven together by tight threads, with his family clutching decades-old secrets.

Everly froze on the screen. He went to move the mouse but realized she was in deep thought when she blinked. "I think that theory holds water. They're known to pay a lot of money for pieces, so dealers bring the art to them."

"Everly, have you ever thought about working in art crimes? You've got some excellent investigative instincts, not to mention you found information that I've been searching a long time for."

She giggled. "No, thank you. I'm only as good as the information I can track down online. Not to mention that I have zero desire to be in the field. I like behind-the-scenes work. You two are much more suited to deal with bullets and car crashes."

Everly disconnected. Kira kicked back and folded her legs under her, then winced and straightened them again but laid her head back against the cushion. "What's our plan for tomorrow?"

Bryce stifled a yawn. His shoulder and head throbbed occasionally to remind him to take it easy. "Well, I think we spend the day doing a little research. What if we make some calls and see if we can find more information about Theo the treasure hunter? I also want to see about getting my dad some permanent help."

He looked at Kira, and she was out cold, slouched against the back of the couch. Her soft auburn ringlets framed the side of her face. An ache formed in his chest. She made him want to break his no-women rule. But how would he keep her safe? He knew the dangers of this job. They were both called to put their lives on the line if need be, but if he allowed himself to fall in love with her, could he deal with that fact? It might be too late to worry about it.

He grabbed a blanket from the back of the couch and covered her. In his mind, he'd gone upstairs and crawled into bed, but the next morning he woke up on the couch. The same blanket he'd given Kira now rested in his lap. The smell of bacon and eggs drew him toward the kitchen. She had already dressed in workout gear and was ready to go with a full breakfast laid out.

"Why are you up so early?" Bryce took the steaming mug of coffee she offered.

"I gave Sophia Katrina's cell phone number the other night after dinner. She texted me at seven to ask if I wanted to join her for something called hot yoga. It sounds awful, but I told her I'd go."

"I guess you're building that friendship after all."

Kira did some fake rolling punches in the air, and he couldn't help but laugh.

"I plan to feel her out about the invitation," she said. "I want confirmation of what pieces will be up for sale. Who goes to an auction without seeing the merchandise first? Also, we need to know what the code means."

A desire to protect her burned through him. Where had that come from? "I need to go with you to make sure you don't pick up a tail. I will—"

She put a hand on his shoulder. "I can manage this. Plus, I'm sure Sophia has security everywhere she goes."

Agent Kaup walked into the kitchen and put her gym bag on the counter.

"Oh, did I fail to mention that Agent Kaup will be trailing me, taking the yoga mat right behind me and watching my back the entire day?"

He took a few steps back, his shoulder tingling from her touch. "I can live with that. Seems like you've thought this through. I'll spend the day working. Just because I'm out of the office doesn't mean the emails stop."

She rolled her eyes. "Your favorite. Checking emails." Kira strode out of the room with Agent Kaup, and Bryce prayed she'd be safe.

The day flew by with calls and emails. Every so often, he distracted himself with memories of taking Kira to see his father. She'd never said a word of judgment, just jumped in to help, but he couldn't help wondering what she really thought. And then he'd force himself to shove those thoughts aside and focus. Then find himself thinking about it again.

"Ugh." He rubbed a hand over his chin. He'd just talk to her when she got home so he could get the whole thing off his mind.

Kira returned in the evening after a late lunch with Sophia followed by shopping. She'd texted and checked in with him to let him know she was fine, but they hadn't really had a chance to reconnect all day. Bryce fended for himself for dinner. A grilled cheese sandwich. Nothing as spectacular as Kira's meals.

He sat at the dining room table with his laptop. Kira joined him, wearing a new outfit, and he blinked.

She raised a brow at him. "What?"

"Nothing. Nice outfit. Not your usual style." The zebra-print pants and black top fit Katrina's character to a T. He didn't hate it, but it wasn't Kira.

"I have to look the part, and we shopped for hours. It's exhausting being rich."

"Did you find out any useful information?"

She frowned. "Not much. She talked a lot, but it was mostly superficial. She doesn't like to talk about her family at all and flinched when I asked her if she had any kids. She said no, but something tells me she wasn't a hundred percent honest."

Interesting. "Did she say anything about the secret auction?"

Kira slid into the chair next to his. "She said you'd figure it out, because she assumes you've been to these kinds of events before. I really think the six-digit number on the back is a code to a locked room."

Despite unraveling their current mystery of the invitation, his mind refused to let go of one thing. What did Kira think of him, now that she saw where he'd come from? They'd never had a chance to debrief from their encounter with his father. Had her opinion of him changed overnight?

And why did what she thought of him matter so much?

"Bryce?"

"Oh, sorry. I'm listening, but I have something I wanted to get off my chest."

"Okay. Go for it."

"I should have said this earlier but never had the chance."

"You're killing me. What?"

"I'm really sorry you had to see my father in such bad shape. Thank you for calling around to get him some help. Had I known he'd shut himself off from society, I would have intervened sooner."

"You've been thinking about this all day, haven't you?"

He blinked. "Um—"

She placed a hand on his arm. "Don't worry about it. We'll get him someone permanent to check on him. It's hard. You aren't close geographically or relationally."

When did he become a "we"? They'd gone from strangers to partners . . . or more? The marriage was fake, but were the underlying feelings?

Kira never moved her hand. "I'm just sorry you grew up in

a neglectful environment. I was an orphan but wonder if that's better than being stuck at home with a father that doesn't care. Not that it's a competition. We each had challenging upbringings. But you are a survivor, just like me."

Their shared connection sparked to life again. She understood him and didn't judge him. He could put the worry out of his head and move on. "It made me grow up fast, that's for sure. After my mom left, he fell into a pit of depression that he never could escape." A grandfather clock softly chimed seven o'clock. But time seemed to stand still under Kira's touch. He cleared his throat. "Well, like you said, we both had challenging childhoods." And he desperately wanted to know more about hers.

Without realizing it, he swept a wayward auburn tendril away from her eyes. He snapped his hand back, regretting the intimate gesture. "I'm so glad you can relate. I have a hard time talking about it, but my past definitely shaped my desire for justice." He'd never wind up like his old man. He'd be someone.

Kira leaned closer, her hand still on his arm. "We make pretty good partners. Which is refreshing since I'm used to working alone. I could get used to this."

What was she implying? That she wanted to see more of him when the assignment was over? His brain scrambled to see outside of this moment. Did she feel the spark between them? "I—we work. I mean . . . this partnership works well between us." Why was his tongue always tied in knots around her? His mind conjured a myriad of words to describe Kira.

Beautiful. Intense. Alluring.

Dangerous.

But none of that came out. At least he hadn't called her *adequate* again.

She gave his arm a squeeze. "We work."

Wait, did he imagine that she just leaned in a fraction of an inch closer? He mirrored the subtle movement. His focus zeroed in on her lips, stained burgundy from a makeover with her new friend. His vision hazed over and he felt a little lightheaded. If they got any closer, he'd kiss her.

He reached up and caressed her cheek with his thumb. She didn't pull away. With a tilt of his head, his lips hovered over hers. His heart thumped.

The sound of a gunshot jarred him out of the most perfect moment in his life, saving him from the inevitable regret that was sure to follow.

12

THE FACT THAT KIRA had almost kissed Bryce took a back seat to the sound of a gunshot.

She'd unpack her emotional baggage later. "That was a . . ."

"Gunshot? Yes. It came from next door." Bryce was on his feet, gun in his hand, and halfway out the front door before Kira regained her senses. The back door clanged as Agent Hudson headed out to investigate. Kira palmed her own weapon and raced after Bryce.

The brownstone next door had lights blazing in every room. Alex's security team streamed in and out of the house, and a few congregated in front of their unit. They didn't have to walk far to peer over the hedges and see a man, lying still, on the front steps of the Dominik residence.

A Mercedes pulled up to the curb and parked. Ivan Sokolov stepped out. The man must have radar, because anytime there was a whiff of danger or drama, he inserted himself right into the middle of it.

Ivan spotted Kira and Bryce standing in their front yard and sauntered over as if he didn't have a care in the world.

"What happened?" he asked. "Alex called me with an emergency."

Kira decided to work with the man and tell him what she knew. Which wasn't much. "We heard what we think was a gunshot. Maybe a break-in?"

Ivan walked toward the Dominiks' residence like he owned the place. Kira shot Bryce a look, and he raised his shoulders slightly, so they followed the man until Bryce stopped short.

They stood behind the row of bushes that separated the two houses. From her vantage point, she could see a hand sticking out from under a rumpled bomber jacket. "A dead body. And that jacket seems familiar, doesn't it?"

"That explains the gunshot," Bryce whispered. "And we've definitely seen that jacket before."

Derek Young had been wearing that exact same jacket.

She pointed to the back of the brownstone. "I'll watch out front. You should back up Hudson and monitor anyone coming and going from next door."

He put his hands on his hips. "I'm not leaving you alone. At a murder scene with all these—"

"I'll be fine. I just think we need to cover our bases. Now go."

"Fine." His growl conveyed his resistance, but he headed through their unit to the back of the property.

Kira kept watch through the hedges. Ivan had disappeared. Sirens sounded in the background. She'd have to watch her cover with the police involved and fired off a text to SSA Turner asking if he'd notify the authorities of the FBI presence.

At least the action shut down her inner monologue that nagged her about getting too close to Bryce. The man wasn't looking for a relationship—he'd made that clear—and she most definitely wasn't interested in getting involved with a colleague from another state. She'd made that mistake once.

And yet, Bryce had opened up to her, sharing some of his darkest childhood trauma. If only she could reciprocate. Emotional expressions never came easy to her. It was best to move on, create something new—not rehash the past.

Her heart stirred at the dismal upbringing he had that mirrored her own. She knew what it was like to work twice as hard to prove her worth. Which was why she refused to revisit her past.

She spotted Sophia standing on the other side of the yard, away from the body.

Kira approached. "Sophia, are you all right? We heard the shot."

The woman turned, and Kira noted the mascara running rivers down her tear-stained cheeks. "It's simply awful. That man tried to break into our house. He had a gun, and the security guard had no choice but to take him down."

Why was Derek breaking into the Dominiks' place? It didn't make sense. Had he followed them back to DC?

Could Derek have been the culprit behind their collision? It didn't seem likely.

A police officer approached to take Sophia's statement. Kira wanted to listen in, but the officer walked the distraught woman back to his patrol car. It would be too obvious for her to follow.

"At least I have an alibi for this murder. I wasn't here." There was no mistaking the voice behind her. Ivan strolled up next to her. They faced the house and watched the police examine the body.

Kira stifled a groan. Against her better judgment, she needed Ivan to talk, without tipping her hand to anyone watching—or listening. "What happened? Was this a simple breaking and entering?" She had to remember to keep up her New York accent and attitude. But exhaustion started to play with her mind.

"You shouldn't be here, Katrina." Ivan's voice bellowed across the yard. "Where is your husband? I will escort you to your place where it is safe."

They walked toward the sidewalk, and Ivan lowered his voice to barely a whisper. "You stirred the hornet's nest. Someone didn't like you talking with Derek, and I suspect someone shot him and then staged it to look like a break-in. The man had become a liability and had no useful information."

"I heard a shot."

His shoulders shrugged in a *so what* manner. "I'm sure someone fired a gun. What I'm saying is that someone is cleaning house. They're eliminating everyone who might be standing in the way of the treasure. I think Derek's lawsuit got him into hot water and they dumped his body here to keep the Dominiks in line."

Who was *they*? Kira decided to tread lightly so Ivan might share more. "It's not like Derek had information. He seemed clueless as to the value of the items he donated."

Ivan swiveled his head left and right. They approached the steps that led to her front door. "He hired some high-priced lawyer, claiming rights to Zaika. A lawsuit was forthcoming. But with Derek gone . . ." He flicked his hands as if washing away the problem.

"Who has the two statues?"

He paused at her front steps. "There is an unsanctioned Russian organization running things. They aren't tied to the government, and their mission is to find lost Russian art. I've been tracking them for a long time. If anyone has the statues, it's them, and they are desperate to own the third."

The words from Fenton Young's note came to her mind.

These rabbits are the key.

"Why should I trust you? Because as far as I can tell, you're in pretty tight with the Dominiks. Who's to say you aren't after the treasure all for yourself?"

Ivan's nostrils flared and his eyes darkened. "That treasure belongs in a museum, not stuck in some underground bunker. And definitely not sold for scraps on the black market."

"Is this Russian secret society running these illegal auctions?"

His silent nod confirmed her suspicions.

"Does this group have a name?"

She assumed he wouldn't answer, but he let out a breath and faced the street. "Amber Crown Society. They've been hunting for the Amber Room for decades. Just like the Collector supposedly stole the art in the name of protection, the ACS seeks to reclaim what they believe is rightfully theirs. I think they moved in the second that rabbit statue surfaced and found the other two before anyone knew to look for them."

This matched Everly's intel. They were searching for the ACS.

He turned back to face her. "I've told you plenty and now you owe me. Go home, Kira. Don't attend the auction. The more you and *your husband* investigate, the more you'll be stepping over dead bodies to get what you want. And next time, I might not be in the area to help you out of a jam."

The man spun and walked away, as if he were some gentleman escorting a woman to safety.

But that man wore danger like a cloak.

BRYCE RUBBED A HAND over his face. What had he gotten himself into?

Not the active crime scene at the brownstones, but the almost-kiss with Kira. He struggled to tear himself away from the woman. Saved by the gunshot sounded harsh, but that's exactly what had transpired. The unwelcomed interruption had kept him from crossing the uncrossable line. He'd backtracked through the brownstone to come out through the basement door that led to the garage. A quick search and he'd head back to Kira.

Bryce wasn't sure exactly what he hoped to find. If security guards had shot an intruder, they could easily clear things up with the police by providing the gun and explaining their situation.

But things weren't adding up. He took a page out of Kira's playbook and headed for the trash cans. His goal was to see who might be coming and going from the back of the house while Kira watched the front.

He ducked behind the bins, mulling over the facts of the case while pushing out thoughts of Kira. The silky soft texture of her hair in his fingers. Those hazel eyes—although he missed her true deep brown eye color. Her soft red lips.

Get your head in the game, Lambert.

This was his case and no way would an attraction on par with a middle school crush get in his way. The wind shifted and he caught a whiff of something foul. He'd stay another few minutes, then find somewhere he could pull in a deep breath. Once the police swarmed the place, he didn't want to be found hiding in the backyard.

A scratching sound caught his attention, and he looked up from his crouching position. Someone was opening a window at the back of the Dominiks' house.

And crawling out of it.

In the shadows of night, Bryce couldn't make out features. It was definitely a thin but fit man, dressed in all black. The guy wore a knit cap low over his forehead, helping to shadow his features. The person's feet hit the ground with a soft thud, then he walked away like he was taking an evening stroll.

Should he follow or not? If the man recognized Bryce, then it would be game over for his cover. He placed a hand on his weapon.

Against his better judgment, Bryce shot off a quick text to Kira and took off in the direction the man headed. Fleeing a murder scene. While doing his best to disguise himself. Yeah. Sketchy.

Sirens echoed in the distance. Bryce walked down the driveway to the access road, where he caught sight of the man crossing the road and heading into the woods. The guy probably had a car stashed on the other side of the trees.

Red and blue lights flickered off the asphalt, but the officers hadn't made their way to the back of the units yet. On the surface, it would appear as though a security officer had shot an intruder, but the police would investigate every square inch of the neighborhood shortly. Bryce picked up his speed but hung back far enough so as to remain undetected. He maneuvered his way to the edge of the woods and dropped down to one knee as if tying his shoe and scanned the area.

Saw nothing.

Bryce proceeded deeper into the wooded area and hid in the shadows behind a thick tree trunk. Everything was quiet, but he waited.

The bark next to Bryce's head shattered, and he dove for the overgrown bushes next to the tree to take cover. Another bullet shaved leaves off the shrubs above him.

This man was shooting at him—with a suppressor attached to his weapon.

His heart hammered while he tried to locate the shooter. This was more than a security guard killing some sort of intruder. Bryce knew in his gut this guy was getting rid of anyone tied to this buried treasure. Once he got to safety, he'd message Turner. The Bureau needed to send someone to watch his father's house. If they associated those journals with his dad—or worse, had watched Bryce and Kira visit his dad's trailer—there could be more visitors to his childhood home.

He needed to move. The bushes weren't protecting him from bullets. Voices filtered through the cool night air from the front of the neighborhood. But toward the back, Bryce didn't detect any movement or noise. The man might be gone.

Or he'd doubled back.

A light flashed in his pocket. He pulled his phone out, and Kira's text popped up on the screen, asking him for a status update. He didn't want her heading his way, not with an active shooter.

Before he could fire off a reply, a twig snapped.

"Don't move." The voice rasped from behind him. "It's not very neighborly to follow someone."

Russian accent. A gun pressed into the base of his neck. Bryce, crouching near the bushes, raised his hands, still clutching his phone. "I wasn't sure who you were," he said, praying the guy's finger wouldn't twitch. "With the break-in next door, I thought I'd make sure you belonged here." This guy could shoot him, and even with police officers swarming the front of the neighborhood, could disappear before anyone showed up to investigate the shot. "I'm just protecting my home, my wife. I don't want any conflict."

The phone in his hand lit up again. If he didn't text Kira back, she'd show up and be in just as much danger as he was. Not to mention the fact that if she startled the man holding the gun to him, things might not end well.

"What do you want?" The voice was gruff, and the man pressed the gun muzzle farther into Bryce's neck. "Why are you here?"

Bryce sucked in a breath. A hundred scenarios spun through his mind, but he landed on taking the direct approach with this guy. "Treasure. I want Zaika for a private collector. He will pay top dollar for it."

Bryce couldn't see the man holding the gun against him, but he felt the flinch at his words. "And you think we have information regarding that?" the man said.

"I don't know who you are. We moved in and met the Dominiks. I had heard Alex had connections to get me into the auction. That's it. I swear."

Bryce needed to find out who this man worked for. Normal security guards didn't jump through back windows. This guy had the makings of an assassin posing as high-priced security.

"Who are you?" Bryce pivoted his head slightly to glimpse his attacker, but the pressure on the gun against his neck intensified so he stopped. "Tell me what you want and I can help you. I'm connected to some powerful people with money. I'm sure we can work something out."

Voices grew closer. The police must be moving through the

area, scouring for clues now that they'd triaged the front of the neighborhood. While only a few minutes had elapsed, Bryce's current predicament dragged on for an eternity.

"You need to stop asking questions. It will get you and that pretty wife of yours killed."

Footsteps sounded behind them and a voice called out. "Brian!"

Kira! He wanted to yell at her to stay away, but the gunman had other plans. A sharp pain radiated across the back of his head, and he hit the dirt beneath the shrubbery.

13

"BRIAN!" KIRA'S VOICE BOUNCED off the row of buildings behind theirs. She couldn't untangle the knot that had formed in the pit of her stomach. Bryce had gone out back and never returned her follow-up text.

Two officers with flashlights walked by, aiming their beams in bushes and driveways. She nodded when their lights washed over her.

"Everything okay?" the female officer asked.

"My husband went for a walk, and I wanted to make sure he was all right after what happened next door."

The officer nodded. "We're sending everyone home, so we'll find him and let him know. And you should head inside as well."

"Thank you, Officer. I will." After she found Bryce.

She checked her phone. Still no text. She headed the opposite way from the officers, toward the intersection of the road that contained another row of brownstones.

Had Bryce found something? It was unlikely that he'd wandered too far away, which added stress to Kira's already jangled nerves.

She stopped at the end of the brownstone's private drive. The wooded area across from her lent the neighborhood a peaceful charm—at least in daylight. Tonight, the trees cast shifting shadows in the glow of red-and-blue police lights, making her scrutinize every inch of the darkness.

She headed into the woods. The groan hit her ears before she saw the movement. In front of some overgrown shrubbery, someone sat up from the ground.

"Brian," she hissed, just in case it wasn't Bryce.

"Yeah, it's me."

She raced over and offered him a hand to help him up off the ground. "What happened?"

"I was in the wrong place at the wrong time, and someone ambushed me."

She ran her fingers across the back of his head and found a small bump. "It's not bleeding, so that's good."

"He didn't knock me out, just stunned me. I'm not dizzy and can walk fine." He took a few unsure steps but landed them successfully.

"There's an ambulance in front. We can get you checked out."

He shook his head and tried to hide a wince, but she caught it. "I don't want to explain how I wound up getting conked in the head with a gun," he said. "Our cover is unbelievably still intact."

They headed back to the brownstone, not saying anything. She'd get the details the second the door closed, though.

Once inside, Bryce sank into a chair at the dining room table. Kira called Turner and asked him to send a paramedic over. Turner let her know the paramedic would be dressed in a police uniform and would knock on their door, posing as an officer to ask additional questions about the incident.

Kira handed Bryce an ice pack and a bottle of water. He had to quit getting hit in the head before he suffered brain damage. "What happened?"

"I watched a man jump out the back window and take off. I decided to follow him to get a description or see where he was heading. He definitely didn't want to talk to the cops."

Kira slid into the chair next to him. "Did you get a description?"

"He was fit, but lanky. Not big and buff, but solid. And he had a heavy Russian accent. He knew we were the new neighbors. I had a split second to make a decision with a gun to my head, so I went for it and told him we would pay top dollar for Zaika."

"That's a great play. It lets them know we are serious about being here and finding the treasure. It puts us in the crosshairs, too, but makes us credible. Since they're following us, they already know we've been searching. I probably would have made the same call."

A knock at the front door sent Kira sprinting to it. A police officer greeted her and discreetly pulled out his FBI badge. "I'm Mike Metcalf. Someone needs to be checked out?"

"In here." She ushered the man to the kitchen and hovered in the background.

Ten minutes later, he met her gaze. "It's just a bump on the head. No signs of concussion or anything to worry about." The man was probably in his twenties and looked more like a wrestler than a paramedic. The police officer uniform suited him just fine.

Kira thanked him and walked him out. At least she had peace about Bryce's condition.

She returned and sat at the table with Bryce. "I didn't get the chance to fill you in on Ivan," she said. "He told me that this underground group—he called them the Amber Crown Society—is cleaning house. They're closing in on the treasure, or so they think. Derek had filed a lawsuit to stake his claim on the statue, so the ACS took him out. Anyone in their way, or who might even *get* in their way, is toast, and Ivan warned us to stop investigating or more people will die."

Bryce held the ice pack to his head. "I don't think he's sold us out yet. I really don't think Alex or Sophia know who we are."

Kira agreed. "Turner would have pulled us out if he thought

Ivan was a threat. But things should be interesting with the auction tomorrow night."

"Yeah, we should probably get some rest. It will be a busy day tomorrow." He stared at Kira, as if wanting to say something else.

Should they talk about the obvious issue, the one glaring them both in the face?

The tiny sparks of attraction had roared into an inferno, and someone needed to throw some water on it. Because if they hadn't heard a gunshot, Kira was a hundred percent sure they would have kissed.

She needed to face this head-on. "I'm sorry things got a bit . . . emotional between us earlier. It's just that I can relate to your childhood stories."

Bryce nodded. "We were just carried away for a moment." He abruptly turned the tables on her. "Would you tell me about your upbringing? What it was like being raised in an orphanage?"

Heat washed over her from her neck to her face. Not a subject she cared to share, but she'd brought it up.

She stood and moved about the kitchen, busying herself by filling a teakettle and putting it on the stove. Here she was, the risk-taker, and he was the one risking his heart by sharing with her.

Kira leaned against the bar that separated the kitchen from the dining area. Probably best to put some space between them. "It was rough. The conditions weren't the greatest, and it was so hard to make friends or have anything permanent."

The smell of mold mixed with rotting meat hit her senses like it was happening right now. But those were the smells from the kitchen at the orphanage. "We mostly ate porridges and stews. There was one room with rows of bunk beds. I claimed a top bunk." She looked away and rubbed her arms. "It was the one thing I could say belonged to me."

"I'm so sorry, Kira."

Bryce's voice was low, caring, wrapping her in warmth,

allowing her to continue. "My parents died when I was five from a car crash, and they were both only children. I had no relatives, no one to take me in. So I wound up living at the orphanage until I was ten."

Bryce whistled. "Five years is a long time."

"All the days eventually ran together, especially since the scenery never really changed. I had chores with very little play time. We had tutors, but we didn't learn much. Most of us just wished our days away, counting down the time until someone adopted us and took us out of there. Or we aged out."

The memories flooded back like a waterfall. "I had one friend. She and I were there the longest and had become permanent fixtures of the orphanage. Until a family adopted her. She never said goodbye, and that's the last time I saw her. Everyone always leaves."

The rejection stung like it had happened yesterday. "The staff allowed Cecilia time to gather what little possessions she had, and she chose to leave without saying a word to me. Told the staff it would be too hard. I get it—she probably felt guilty for being picked over me. I loved her like a sister. Apparently she didn't return the sentiment."

She pulled in a ragged breath. "And honestly, I can't blame her for what she did. After all, she found a family—that was the goal all along for both of us. But she should have talked to me. I would have been happy for her. Instead I was left alone, wondering what I'd done to have her cut me out of her life without so much as a backward glance."

Bryce moved to the bar and laid his arms across the counter, covering her hand with his. "That's a difficult place to be. Losing your parents, and then your best friend."

He didn't know all of it. The words echoed through her mind, dredging up the day she overheard a conversation between two staff members. *"Kira's never going to get adopted. They all want a blond newborn. No one wants an older kid."*

She banished the thought. Her adoptive family took her home and loved her unconditionally. The Millers gave her an example of sacrificial love. But at the time, the words had embedded deep in her heart.

No one had wanted her, even Cecilia.

"Well, you can see how much I understand what you went through all those years ago." Kira moved back, pulling away from Bryce's touch. She was losing her mind, and her heart. "I'm going to call it a night. I'm glad you're all right. Tomorrow will be another busy day."

Bryce stepped back as well. "Good night, Kira."

She raced up the stairs and headed to her bedroom. It wasn't until the door closed that she let out a breath.

If these Russians didn't kill her, this attraction between her and Bryce might.

BRYCE AVOIDED KIRA most of Saturday morning, and now it was time to get ready for the auction. The nearness of the last twenty-four hours had gotten the best of him.

Kira deserved someone who would love her without making her be something she wasn't. And now was not the time to explore how much he wanted to be that person. He needed to get his head in the mission. Tonight was going to be a big night. He'd distracted himself by spending the day scouring the internet for information on the Amber Room. The theories, the myths, the legends.

Lost in research, he hadn't realized it was almost time to leave for the art auction, and he hurried to shower and dress. He donned one of his finer suits and headed downstairs to wait in the living room for Kira.

This isn't a date. This isn't a date.

The mantra beat a steady rhythm through his mind.

He stood in front of the picture window in the living room and watched the rain drizzle. He swiped his hands across his suit pants. If this wasn't a date, then why was he so nervous around Kira?

The illegal auction would take place at the same time as the advertised event. Art connoisseurs, billionaires, aristocrats, and diplomats would converge to bid on the priceless works of art, acting like they belonged in the legitimate auction. They might even drop a few bids to keep up the ruse.

And he'd be there—right in the middle of the action. This was their big break.

Footsteps turned his attention to the stairs. Kira glided down and he forgot to breathe. This stunning woman didn't resemble the Kira he'd first met—the one with the leather jacket and a chip on her shoulder. This version of the same woman held a different kind of confidence.

Her long silky black dress flowed with each step. From the black heels to the dangling sparkly pendant that graced her neck, Kira appeared like a socialite who would blend in nicely with the art patrons. And he couldn't rip his eyes from her.

She hit the landing at the bottom of the stairs and twirled. "What do you think? Adequate?"

Heat rushed up his neck and he willed the color to dissipate. "Way more than adequate." The word *exquisite* popped into his mind and he clamped his mouth shut. "More than adequate, Katrina Beckett." He shot her a wink, and a knock at the door broke their eye contact. Bryce headed to open it. "I hope you don't mind. I hired a limo for the evening."

She clicked her tongue. "You spare no expense, especially on someone else's dime."

He offered his arm to her and escorted her out to the waiting limo driver, who was also an undercover agent. Several agents would be strategically stationed outside the gallery in case things went sideways.

Their chauffeur held the door open and ushered Kira into

the back seat, then went around to the other side to assist Bryce. They settled into the expansive seat of the limo. The driver looked through the partition separating the front from the back. "I'll close this so you can have some privacy, but I've swept this entire vehicle for listening devices and you're good. We have a car that will follow us in case there are any signs of trouble."

Bryce nodded his appreciation. He studied the fascinating woman beside him. Tonight, she was all business. Last night, he'd broken through her armor, uncovering the real Kira, only to have her walls rebuilt and reinforced today.

She got down to business, laser focused on being the version of herself that the situation called for. "Who do you think we'll be bidding against in the auction?"

"I've spent the better part of the day reviewing the high rollers of the art world. Alex will most likely be bidding on the piece on behalf of his supposed client."

"Unless Sophia and Alex are behind this secret society. Maybe there isn't a client. It might be a ruse to get in the country on a work visa."

Bryce tapped on his phone to pull up the notes he'd taken. "Good point. There are other art benefactors that may make an appearance."

Kira pulled out her phone and placed it between them on the seat, as if they needed some invisible buffer between the two of them. His suit made him hot, but the heat had more to do with the woman sitting next to him than the ambient temperature inside the car.

This is not a date.

"Let's call Everly," Kira said. "I asked her to research a few of the big art collectors and track flights and travel arrangements to see if any of them are in town. They may want to bid on Zaika, especially if it's connected to a bigger treasure."

She hit a button and Everly picked up on the first ring.

"Everly, we're in a fancy limo on our way to the art auction, and I wanted to see if you found a copy of the invitation list."

A few clicks of a keyboard and Everly spoke. "I was able to get a master invitation list from the gallery, and we can assume some of the attendees will cross over into the backdoor auction." She cleared her throat. "We have several international dignitaries flying in for this event. The legitimate auction has a lot of expensive and rare pieces being sold. Based on what you told me about the code, I think Bryce is right, and when the auctioneer announces the eighth item, that's the signal for those attending the underground auction to make haste."

Bryce sank back into the plush leather seat as she continued. "Now, you asked about the attendee list. We can't confirm that these people received invitations to the second auction, but I would suspect you might find a few of these people in attendance."

Bryce opened his notes app to jot down the info as Everly read the list. "We have Chen Liwei, a private billionaire collector from China. Some startup tech company owner. Rumored to own an original van Gogh. Next is a prince from Saudi Arabia named Samir Al-Fulan. He backs some up-and-coming artist with work for sale in the auction. But that might just be the cover Samir needs to get in."

Everly read a few more names. Most were from Italy, Spain, and some Middle Eastern countries. A few were American collectors who Bryce hadn't encountered before.

"Julianne Bishop is an American collector from New York," Everly said. "Steer clear of her, because she has the biggest potential to blow your cover. According to the information I found, she knows everyone in the art world. But it's rumored on the dark web that she's got millions of dollars of stolen art in her collection."

"Got it," Kira replied. "All of these men and women may be after Zaika. I guess we'll have to wait and see who shows up to bid in the backroom auction."

"As far as the Becketts go, Brian has a fifty-million-dollar line of credit with the auction house. We've already provided proof of the funds and set up the bank account—or so they think. All you have to do is bid."

Everly signed off and Kira disconnected the call. "At least other agents will be available for backup. We have several undercover inside along with agents stationed outside the building and even on the roof."

She stashed the phone in the world's tiniest black purse. How did she fit anything in there?

"What's the plan, Bryce?" Kira asked. "Do you want me to make a beeline for Sophia and stick with her for the evening? I do think we need to divide and conquer."

He'd had the same idea. They could observe both sides of the room if they separated. But somehow, the thought of her—in that dress—in a roomful of rich piranhas gave him heartburn. "We should stick together as much as we can. We're newlyweds, remember? But if you watch Sophia, I can keep an eye out for Ivan and a few of these other dignitaries. Sophia will stay close to Alex, so you'll be able to watch those two. I also want to cover the door to the stairwell that leads to the area behind the main room—where you found the murdered security officer. I want to keep track of who comes and goes."

DC traffic slowed their progress. The driver opened the partition between the front and back of the limo. "I've radioed the car behind us. I'm turning off the main road because of an accident."

"Thanks for the update." Bryce checked his watch. They'd built in a buffer of time, but the delay caused his mind to generate a list of all the ways this mission could go sideways. For once, more was at stake than just his mission. He had Kira's back to watch.

Or rather, his wife. Katrina Beckett. She checked her makeup in a compact mirror that she'd pulled from her magical bottomless purse. After he'd sworn off relationships, was it possible for him to open his heart and take a risk? After the mission, of course. He didn't know. And that bothered him.

"Kira, I've got your back. No matter what. Just remember that."

She smiled, a wide, genuine grin. "Thanks. I'm grateful for our partnership, even if it's a bit weird to be married day one of meeting someone. It makes for some great reality television, but I never assumed I'd be living it."

Maybe someday they could test those waters.

Brakes squealed. The hard slam knocked the wind out of him.

14

EVERY MUSCLE IN KIRA'S BODY seized at once. *Not again.*

Kira blinked, trying to clear the smoke from her field of vision. They were in the back of the crumpled limo. Something had struck them. But what?

Or who?

She unbuckled herself. "Bryce?"

"I'm okay, Kira. I'm just tangled in the seat belt. It worked, I just can't get it undone."

"I'm good too." She checked her face and head for cuts. She'd have a second bruise on her shoulder from the seat belt. The glass in the window next to Bryce had spiderweb cracks.

"What happened?" she yelled to the driver over the hissing sound from the radiator. She looked over to Bryce, who struggled against the seat belt.

No answer.

"I've got a bad feeling about this, Bryce."

She slid forward as far as possible to the partition. The front of the vehicle folded in on itself from the impact—a collision with a light post on the side of the road. It sliced the hood almost in two and crunched the front seat toward the interior of the limo. But between the smashed front seats and the airbag, she saw the man's arm. Following the arm up to the steering wheel, she saw the driver's face. And the hole in his forehead.

"Oh, no no no. Sniper took out the driver. We need to get out of here."

Bryce yanked the seat belt. "It won't budge. Do you have a knife in that purse? Might need to cut me out."

Where were the other agents who were supposed to be behind them?

She moved to help him, but something hammered the window by her head. The glass crashed around her and one arm snaked around her neck, another under the right armpit. And then she found herself sliding out the open window on her side.

"Katrina!" Bryce's voice faded. She tried to struggle, but the arm around her throat was making that difficult. Her kidnapper dragged her down the sidewalk, toward a parked car on the street.

She twisted to get a look at her abductor, but all she could see was a shadow of black and ruthless dead eyes.

"Katrina!" She could see Bryce struggling against his bonds while she fought the man who hauled her backward. A second figure stepped from the parked car. He moved fast, grabbing her legs while the first man shifted his arms around her torso, pinning her arms to her sides. The trunk popped open, and Kira had seconds before it was game over.

Kira wrenched one leg free, then drove her heel back hard. The stiletto struck flesh. The man at her legs screamed and stumbled away, giving her a brief edge. She twisted hard, nearly slipping away, but the attacker behind her clamped down again, dragging her toward the open trunk. The other assailant recovered quickly and seized her by the ankles, lifting her off the ground. She thrashed, her body suspended between them—one man gripping her torso, the other her legs—a human jump rope as they hauled her toward the waiting vehicle.

They were in a more desolate area of downtown DC—not a

soul in sight. If ever there was a time to believe in God, it was now. Because if they shoved her in the trunk, no one would ever hear from her again.

God. Help.

Her hip bumped the edge of the trunk—which might very well double as her coffin. She bucked hard once more, throwing her weight sideways, and the man behind her lost his balance and released her. She hit the ground shoulder first. Pain exploded, but she rolled with it.

Using the reprieve, she snapped her leg out, slamming her heel into the other man's shins. He staggered back with a curse. Kira kicked free and army crawled under the car.

Bryce's shiny black loafers appeared. She'd give anything for a weapon right now, but they'd left them at the brownstone, and now she wished they were better prepared for a street fight. She inched forward and watched Bryce take a swing at one of the masked men. The other assailant backed up as if he were about to bolt.

Oh no. He wasn't getting away. She needed answers.

With Bryce busy with the first guy, Kira flipped her legs around and swiped the man's legs out from under him. The goon toppled to the ground, and she scampered out from under the vehicle. Her dress didn't have pockets, and her purse was in the crumpled limo. Zip ties would have been handy, but she had nothing.

The fallen attacker stood and faced Kira, but out of the corner of her eye, she could tell Bryce was having a struggle to subdue the other guy. He'd managed to pull a gun and was inching it toward Bryce's head.

Police sirens whined in the distance. Making a split-second decision, she chose to let the other man flee. The attacker bolted while she spun to face Bryce and his opponent, locked in a struggle for control of the gun. She noted the silencer. Could this be their sniper?

Before she finished the thought, Kira jumped on the attacker's back and wrapped her arms around his throat. He growled and tried to throw her off, but she hung tight, cutting off his air. He dropped his weapon and used both hands in an attempt to dislodge her. And still, she kept her grip, squeezing.

The guy dropped to his knees while Bryce grabbed the gun. The man finally passed out and Kira released her grip. She pushed to her feet, panting, pulling in ragged breaths and straightening her dress.

She met Bryce's assessing gaze. "I'm all right, but we can't leave him on the sidewalk. If those sirens are for us, we also can't get picked up by the police or we'll never make it to the auction." She ran her fingers through her hair, praying she could return it to its sleek style, and took a look at her dress.

The bottom had a small tear in the fabric, but the black satin hid the dirt well. She brushed off the sand and grit as best she could. Looked like they'd be adding a few new bruises to the ones they'd collected from the previous crash. But at least neither of them had sustained serious injuries.

The sound of a motor caught Kira's attention, and a sedan stopped next to the wrecked limo. Another navigated around the two vehicles to pull up next to them.

Violet.

"How did you—"

"Get in. Talk later."

Kira hurried to grab her phone and purse from the back seat of the crumpled limo. Her heart stopped at the sight of the fallen agent. A family would get the worst news of their lives tonight. These bad guys needed to pay, and Kira would make sure everyone connected with this case was rounded up.

With a glance back at the agents dealing with the scene behind them, she and Bryce hopped into the back seat of the sedan. Violet merged into the traffic on the main road that had backed up due to the prior accident.

"Thanks for the rescue, Vi," Kira said. "But how did you know we were in trouble?"

"I was following the vehicle tailing you. We were only a few cars away, but we were in a gridlock because of that accident. It took us a few minutes to navigate our way through the congestion."

Adrenaline evaporated, and Kira's nerves settled. "Are the police investigating the accident?"

"I placed a call to 911 as a concerned citizen witnessing the accident." Of course, Violet had the details under control. "But Turner is already working with local law enforcement. He assigned me to make sure you get to the gallery. This is our last chance to stop the art thieves. After tonight, he feels like the trail will go cold again."

Bryce nodded. "This is our only shot to get in. If we don't show up, we'll never get another invitation. We still have our cover. They attacked Brian and Katrina, so our presence at the auction is not welcomed. Maybe they don't like the competition of someone else bidding on the statue."

His words left no room for debate. They were doing this. Not that Kira would consider giving up. In this moment, she realized how important closing this case was for Bryce.

"But I'm not leaving your side," he told her. "We can't trust anyone and have to have each other's backs."

She took the compact out of her purse, giving her hands something to do. Bryce's compassion about her safety always seemed to catch her off guard and she had no idea why. It had been a long time since someone had her back. What she wouldn't do for a gun in her tiny purse, but security screening would be tight. They weren't getting any weapons or recording devices in.

Except one.

Bryce adjusted his deep red bow tie. "I'm hoping this works."

Kira caught Violet's eye in the mirror. "Our team installed a camera in the bow's knot," she said. "It looks like a pin to hold the knot in place. Once Bryce activates it, if he straightens his tie, it'll snap a picture. It has no signal, just a tiny flash drive to store about twenty images. We'll use it to capture a few faces for us to run facial recognition software later."

"I love it."

Violet turned down the road that led to the gallery. The scenery changed. Shops and tourists filled the streets, unlike the sparse, run-down area they'd just left.

"At least we'll have something," Bryce said. "I don't trust this place. They'll have jammers for sure."

"Or a small EMP," Violet added. "They could have an electromagnetic pulse device that fries electronics upon entry into the building. Small enough to destroy anything in the area but not cause harm outside."

Bryce squinted. "I hadn't thought of that." He touched the edge of his bow tie. "But this doesn't have extensive capacity or emit any frequencies. It's all we can use that's untraceable, so it has to work."

And if it didn't, they'd figure out something else. Kira had no idea what, but . . . they would. They drove a few more miles in stop-and-go traffic, and Violet pulled up to the curb in front of the art gallery. Bryce jumped out and raced around the back of the car to open the door for Kira. He offered his arm to her, and she stepped out. Her long black dress swirled around her ankles as they walked up the steps.

Reporters lined both sides of the street to get a peek inside. Several up-and-coming artists had their work up for sale, and a few rare paintings had made it onto the auction's docket.

This felt like a Hollywood red-carpet event. They ducked media cameras and worked their way through the crowd to get to the lobby's glass doors.

Kira's pulse spiked in anticipation of the things to come, despite more aches and pains popping up. No new wounds might be visible, but the soreness was a real thing. The audacity of art thieves to auction art right out the back door while legitimate bidders purchased art the legal way burned her sense of justice in every way possible.

A tuxedo-clad man opened the door and ushered them inside the lobby. The circular room contained lines of people in front of metal detectors, X-ray machines, and guards with wands. "We knew security would be over the top," Kira whispered. "But TSA has nothing on these people."

"Tell me about it."

They joined one of the two lines on either side of the room. People filled the space with a sea of black dresses and suits. Very little color, but very expensive outfits. Kira flattened out her dress, praying her tussle with the bad guys hadn't done any discernible damage.

"Ticket please," a deep voice asked the people in front of them.

Kira stared at the man. He hadn't seen her yet. But he might remember her.

The last time she was in the gallery, Vince Palmer, the gallery attendant, had shown her around. And here he was, standing in front of them collecting tickets. Would he remember her as the one who had found a body in the back stairwell?

This could blow their cover wide open.

KIRA'S SUDDEN DEATH GRIP on his arm alerted Bryce that something was wrong.

Bryce handed the tickets to the gentleman while Kira tucked her head against his arm, letting her hair fall around her face.

Okay, she didn't want to be seen by the guy taking the tickets. The words Gallery Attendant on the name tag rang a bell.

Kira had been to this gallery, and he recalled her testimony the night at the police station. She'd spoken with an attendant in the Zaika display. She was afraid he would recognize her.

The man scrutinized the tickets like he was inspecting an actual piece of art. Once he looked them up and down, he smiled and handed the tickets back. "Please step through the metal detectors. We don't allow cell phones or electronics of any kind, so you can place them in Faraday bags that we provide and pick them up on the way out."

Bryce placed his keys, wallet, and phone in the conveyor belt tray and held his breath going through the detector on the off-hand chance his bow tie–hidden camera set the thing off. But he passed through with no flashing lights or sirens. Same for Kira and her tray.

They headed to a table after retrieving their items. A coat check was in place for outerwear, as well as all electronics and cell phones. No photography or any kind of recording device was allowed inside. The woman working the table provided them with bags for the phones, and then a number to claim their belongings when they were ready to leave.

It didn't matter. The phones had no ties to the FBI and had been wiped clean of any information about their real identities. They contained a few doctored photos of his and Kira's "honeymoon" along with generic texts and contacts.

He shot a look at Kira. She'd fixed herself up nicely after the attack, but Bryce noted the faint bruising around her wrists where the man had grabbed her.

A security guard opened the door to the main room. Kira gasped. "This place is beautiful," she whispered, her arm woven through his. "Last time I was here the space had separate rooms with walls."

The area had round tables and seats with space for well over a hundred people. Chandeliers dripping with crystals cast a shimmer of light across the room. A buffet of hors d'oeuvres on the left side of the room smelled amazing. Rows of puff pastries, desserts, and sweets lined another wall.

The other side of the room displayed the paintings and sculptures that were up for bid. Artists stood by the pieces, engaging patrons and answering questions. Bryce picked a table and pulled out Kira's seat for her. "There are seventy-two pieces up for sale." He passed her the brochure that listed the items and the descriptions.

"They spared no expense for this event." She glanced around. "Hopefully we can find Sophia and Alex."

A server appeared behind them and took their drink order. Even the drinks had themes tied to the various artists, like a mango-flavored cocktail inspired by artist Juan Ortega. His painting *Mosaic Memories* would command a pretty penny tonight.

Once the waiter departed, Kira whispered, "We still don't know the exact location of the back room. I'm hoping to spot Sophia and just ask. They have to offer some kind of preview of the pieces. Who risks their reputation on an illegal art auction without seeing the merchandise first?"

It took a few minutes of searching, but Kira finally spotted Sophia and sent her a subtle wave.

Sophia crossed the room on six-inch heels, her stride effortless, weightless. The layered black dress whispered around her legs as she walked. Heads turned, eyes followed. And the confidence in her step said she was well aware of the effect she had. And she loved it.

"Brian and Katrina," Sophia said. "I'm so glad you could make it to the auction. May we join you? Alex is somewhere around here, probably doing the math on how much we can spend on some of these rarer pieces."

Kira waved a hand over the empty chairs. "Please."

Bryce listened to Sophia and Kira chat about their outfit designers. They still had half an hour before the real auction started, and the background music of the three-piece ensemble was now drowned out by muffled voices as the room filled up.

But he heard Kira ask about seeing the items up for bid in

the secret auction beforehand. She indicated that Bryce's employer was a very motivated buyer, but she wanted a sneak peek first. Sophia whispered something in Kira's ear, and she nodded. "We're going to the ladies' room," Kira said and kissed Bryce on the cheek. He had no idea what that was code for. Did she mean for him to follow?

He stood as the two women headed to a door at the back of the room by the buffet tables.

On the one hand, Kira could take care of herself. But on the other hand, his gut said not to let her out of his sight, even for a second.

He traced the path the women took and stepped into a hallway that ran beside the main room. Kira vanished into the ladies' room, followed by Sophia. Bryce looked at his watch and tapped his foot, just to indicate to everyone who might be walking by that he was impatiently waiting for his wife to come out.

When the ladies didn't return, real impatience—along with some worry—rose with each tap of his foot. He should have insisted Sophia show *him* where the secret auction was to be held. Now that he thought about it, it might have been more believable coming from him, but Kira wanted to play the friendship card.

Another watch check showed five minutes had passed. To enter and possibly look like a creep? Or stay outside and risk Kira's life?

Movement at the end of the hallway caught his eye. Two people stepped into the dimly lit hall from a room at the end. One was the gallery attendant who had taken the tickets. The other woman looked familiar, but he couldn't place her. He adjusted his tie to snap a picture of both of their faces, then turned to study the mural painted on the hallway wall. They walked by, holding hands. He folded his arms and checked his watch once more.

Time's up, Kira.

He'd go after her even if it meant embarrassing himself, assuming he were mistaken. He grabbed the brass handle to the women's room door and ducked in. Then listened. Silence. Now the disquiet stirring in him swelled to epic proportions. He should hear *something*. The restroom had its own mini waiting room with a couch, chairs, and mirrors. He rounded the corner and noted three stalls on one wall and a row of elegant sinks lining the other.

But no Kira or Sophia.

Had Sophia abducted Kira? Was she in trouble? He kicked himself for letting her out of his sight. The room didn't have any windows since it sat in the building's interior. They couldn't have gone far.

So . . . where did they go?

Lights flickered, signaling the auction would begin shortly and that patrons should find their seats.

An elderly woman with beehive hair and a dress that had to be an original from the 1950s pushed through the door and squeaked when she saw him standing there.

He held up his hands. "I'm so sorry, ma'am. I got lost and went in the wrong restroom. I've never been here before and wasn't paying attention."

Her shocked expression faded, and she laughed. "Of course. It happens."

He left, wishing he could have finished searching the stalls. No doubt there was a hidden exit that led to a back room.

Maybe he needed to take his seat and wait at the table for Kira to return. A hand clamped over his shoulder, and he spun to see Theo Durham, the treasure hunter.

"Good to see you again, Brian." The hand moved from Bryce's shoulder to slap him on the back.

"Hey there. I was just waiting on my wife. I thought she went to the restroom, but I haven't seen her come out yet."

Theo sneered. "I'm sure she won't want to miss the auction. Seems like there will be a fury of bidding on a little rabbit statue."

So Theo knew about the secret auction? Interesting. The man leaned against the wall. He was dressed as if he were going to a rodeo versus a fancy ball. Theo looked Bryce up and down, as though he questioned Bryce's right to show up in an art gallery. "You know, it's not too late for us to work together on this thing."

Bryce smirked. "My employer is spending a lot of money to get what he wants. I think we're good."

"Suit yourself." Theo kicked off the wall and walked away. Then paused and turned back to Bryce. "But I have something you want. Something way more valuable than a stupid rabbit statue."

Bryce folded his arms. "Yeah? What's that?"

"Those journals you took from that old man in Sawyer's Peak. I don't know how you knew about them, but I know who took them from you."

15

SOPHIA LOVED TO SHOW OFF, and Kira wasn't surprised the woman had jumped at the chance to showcase the pieces in the illicit auction. She had taken her to the women's restroom and straight to a high-back couch. She slid the couch to the left, revealing a keypad.

"I knew that was a secret code on the invitation," Kira whispered.

The woman's smile widened. "Our husbands both have employers who will spare no expense on the finer things. But I'm not supposed to let you in here, so just keep quiet."

A hidden panel popped open when Kira entered the numbers she had memorized from the invitation. She stepped into what looked like a long supply closet, but at one end a set of stairs descended into darkness below.

"The men's room also has a door so as not to draw much attention," Sophia said.

Kira considered a thousand different scenarios that could happen and almost all of them involved her death. But she nodded and headed down the stairs, praying Bryce would figure out where she was—or that Alex would bring him. The last step opened up into a room that looked like an old wine cellar.

At least she wasn't claustrophobic. The rectangular space had several chairs lined up on one side. The opposite side contained display cases with pieces behind locked glass panels.

Three items.

Sophia's voice whispered behind Kira, as if the narrator of a documentary. "We have an original Degas lost during World War II. But our curator tracked it down."

Our curator? Confirmation Sophia and Alex were in on the smuggling ring.

And that they bought Kira and Bryce's cover.

"The next is a Rembrandt, also stolen during the war. Now here, ready to be added to someone's private collection."

Kira stared at the painting behind the glass panel secured to the wall.

Then she moved to Zaika. The statue rested in the same glass box as the first day she'd laid eyes on it. With the same security lock on the outside that flashed a red light every fifteen seconds. She'd counted.

Sophia slid next to Kira. "Don't get your hopes up on this one. Alex and I will be bidding for this."

"Really? Why the interest?"

Sophia gave her a dismissive wave. "Let's just say we have a personal interest in this piece. And that gallery owner has had this piece locked up tighter than a Russian prison. This is the closest I've been able to get to the statue. But enough about that." Sophia waved her hand in front of her face for dramatic effect. "Are you ever going to tell me more about Brian's employer? Maybe next time, we can do business on a direct basis. The gallery owner collects pieces like these, and Alex helps with the financial arrangements. But Alex can help broker private deals."

Everly had given Bryce's employer a fake profile, but Kira wanted to string Sophia along a little bit longer. "If all goes well tonight, I'll facilitate an introduction."

Kira acted like she had the power in her relationship with

Bryce, and admiration showed on Sophia's face. The woman fingered her gold necklace that hung over her low-cut dress. "Perfect. Alex and I are always looking for new clients. But it's almost time for the real auction, and I'm sure your husband's employer might like some of those items as well."

Of course, purchasing the real items and creating a transaction would mask any black-market purchases. If anyone questioned transfers of money to the auction house, someone could point to the real art purchases.

Kira followed Sophia up the stairs and back into the ladies' room. Upon exit, Kira nearly bumped into Bryce talking with . . . Theo?

Sophia disappeared down the hallway.

"Oh no. Were you waiting for me long?" she said to Bryce while slipping her arm around his waist.

He shot her a look that communicated desperation—and relief. "There you are. I was beginning to think I was going to have to come find you."

"All is well. Theo, would you excuse us? I don't want to miss the beginning of the auction since there are a few pieces I will be bidding on."

"Right." The man had a slow Southern drawl that gave the word an extra syllable. "I'm moseying to the auction myself." He sauntered down the hall.

"What happened?" Bryce leaned close to her ear as they walked to the auction room. The gallery had moved walls from their exhibit areas to create an open area with tables and a stage. "You vanished. I thought something bad happened and then Theo cornered me. He knows who has the journals. I spent ten minutes trying to get him to tell me who, but he wouldn't budge. He wants cash, of course."

"Of course. Well, we'll have to worry about that later. Let's take our seats." Now she really wanted to see the journals. "There's a hidden door behind the couch in both bathrooms. I know where the secret auction is."

Bryce pulled out Kira's chair, and she sat. Sophia and Alex were nowhere to be seen. She also hadn't spotted Ivan, but she knew the man wouldn't be far. He'd never miss the auction for anything, and she suspected he might even bid just to keep anyone else from getting Zaika.

One of the gallery staff members, an older gentleman who looked to be in his nineties, rose and kicked off the night's activities with a warm welcome and motivational speech. His flashy suit and gold rings suggested he'd done well for himself. "It's our duty to protect the artwork that has been passed down from generations before us. Please be prepared to spend. A lot. Thank you and let's get started."

Laughter sounded around the room.

Could his money come from the illegal auctions? They still didn't know who the top person behind the illicit sales was, just that Alex assisted with procurement.

With the opening lot announced, the painting by Ortega, the auctioneer slipped into the familiar breathless rhythm of the trade. "Bidding will start at $1,000."

People leaned forward, ready for the bidding to get intense. Kira swept her gaze over the room. No doubt a good many of the attendees had come for the drama.

Ortega had become a hit after drug dealers used his paintings to smuggle drugs into the United States. He had talent for sure, but it was his shady past that seemed to attract buyers as well.

In a room of about a hundred and fifty people, Kira estimated that half raised their numbered paddles to bid. At some point, she'd have to show interest and make some bids, but she definitely didn't want to win any of these items. She flipped the paper paddle over in her hand. Number 82.

She had one prize. Zaika.

What would be the odds of her and Bryce winning the auction? That treasure hunter would bid, along with several others. And probably Ivan. She scanned the room but still didn't see the Russian spy.

The flurry of bidding continued, with people dropping out in proportion to the increase in cost. At $20,000, it came down to just two bidders—an Asian man with gray hair and glasses with circular rims, and a Saudi Arabian sheikh with a full headdress and attire.

"Way too much for me to bid," Kira said, looking at Bryce, who feigned interest in the action to discreetly snap a few pictures.

The final bidding war ended with the sheikh paying $28,950 for the Ortega painting. These people threw money around like confetti in a ticker-tape parade. Disposable and all for show.

Another bidding war began between an older woman and the same Asian man. Bryce continued his subtle scan of the audience while Kira kept an eye out for the Dominiks, but they never resurfaced.

When the item up for bid hit number seven, Kira nodded her head toward the door. She wanted a front row seat at the backroom auction. She excused herself from the table, stating she needed the restroom. The others at their table ignored her.

Once in the hallway that ran along the main room, she waited for Bryce, who followed thirty seconds later.

"Sophia told me there are only nine invitations to the secret auction," she said. "But I want to get there early. We don't want to be caught lingering in the hallways since security is so tight."

Bryce looked up and down the deserted corridor. "We should be good."

They linked arms and headed for the restrooms. Kira was about to push the door open when another door creaked and a man stepped out at the end of the hallway. He headed right toward them, and her heart froze.

The gallery attendant. The man who might remember her from her visit to the gallery.

Not good.

She reached up and wrapped her arms around Bryce's neck. "Just go with it," she murmured and drew him toward her. She kissed him and sandwiched them against the wall, with her face away from the man walking past them.

And then reality faded as Bryce's lips covered hers. Time stood still and she sank into the kiss. It was a good kiss. An unbelievable kiss, sending an electrical pulse through every nerve ending. He tangled his hand through her hair. She wrapped her arms around his neck and pulled him closer.

She heard a *tsk-tsk* sound and then retreating footsteps as the attendant headed toward the gala.

The kiss lasted longer than it needed to, but she didn't want to let go.

"I think he's gone," Bryce said, moving his lips away from hers.

Oh, right. Her scrambled brain tried to reboot and she took a step back. "I just wanted to be sure he left." Bryce was wearing her lipstick, and she used her index finger to wipe his lips. He stared at her, eyes wide, but let her finish. "That's better. Don't need to announce to the world that we were making out in the hallway."

She willed her knees not to buckle as she opened the door to the restroom. Bryce headed to the men's room, and she made sure the area was empty before entering the code. The door opened and she met Bryce in the secret room between the two bathrooms.

Her heart skipped a beat when he shot her a smile and grabbed her hand to help her down the stairs.

Making out with Bryce Lambert. Whew. Actually, Katrina Beckett had just made out with her husband in the hallway. Not Kira. Not Bryce.

The whole thing was a sham. The relationship. The kiss. This was just her playing a role, nothing more.

We are Katrina and Brian Beckett. This is all pretend.

She drilled that mantra into her head until it stuck.

Too bad Kira's heart wasn't buying any of it.

SO THAT JUST HAPPENED.

Bryce tried to shake the tingle from his lips and the heat from his face. That kiss might have been a stunt to keep the gallery attendant from spotting Kira, but now he just wanted more.

More kissing. More Kira.

He willed his sanity to return so he could focus.

At the bottom of the stairs, he reached for the gun he hadn't brought. No weapons. Only his hidden camera that could take a few more pictures. Bryce prayed for protection as they emerged into the hidden chamber, which was more like a cave than a place of business. The objects up for the black-market auction lined one side of the room, with chairs set up for the bidders.

The room already had six people in it—five too many for Bryce's tastes. Alex and Sophia were in one corner of the room by the chairs, talking with the sheikh who had placed bids in the upstairs auction. A different Asian man sat, making notes on a notepad. That must be Chen Liwei, the name Everly mentioned as a potential buyer. Making the sheikh most likely Samir Al-Fulan or someone who worked for him.

Footsteps pounded down the stairs, and Bryce turned to see Theo the treasure hunter enter the space. "Last chance, Beckett," the man said, spreading his arms out wide with some sort of invitation to join him. "You can work with me, for a price, and I can get you what you are looking for."

Bryce shook his head, and Theo sat down next to the Chinese private collector.

Bryce leaned over and whispered in Kira's ear. "Where did Theo get the money to bid? They verify bank accounts and make sure the bidders are good for it."

She shrugged and mouthed, *No idea.*

Bryce and Kira stood by the wall next to the only entryway. He didn't relish getting trapped in this coffin-like room full of piranhas, waiting to tear each other limb from limb over who could pay the most money for a hunk of rock.

An elderly yet regal woman descended the stairs.

"Julianne Bishop," Kira whispered in his ear. Her nearness sent an electrical current racing through his body.

He had to get his head in the game.

A man Bryce was not familiar with entered the room and walked up to a small lectern in front of the chairs, next to the three items up for bid. "I'm Davis Steadman, owner of the gallery."

Bryce's eye twitched. He'd heard that name before.

Davis Steadman was on the FBI watchlist. They'd tied this guy to the art smuggling ring. But no one had any hard evidence to put him away.

Until today.

He and Kira took seats in the front row and Steadman continued. "Today, we have three items up for bid. Whatever your amount due is, we will add to the price of your legitimate bid for the paintings upstairs. Auction items 25, 32, and 41 will need to go for the amount you bid on one of these items. We've planted a few bidders to help bid you up."

Bryce bit his lip to keep from smiling. So this was how they got away with the laundered funds. They bid on "real" pieces to pay for the priceless works. The owner came out even and laundered the money by auctioning three fake paintings upstairs whose "real" value rivaled the illegal sales. Any auditor might wonder why a particular painting had a jacked-up value but would be hard-pressed to track it to an illegal sale.

Genius.

But just how much would Zaika go for?

The stairs groaned once more. Bryce looked over his shoulder. Ivan entered the room and took the remaining seat behind him. He nudged Kira. "Don't look now, but Ivan just got here. Let the games begin," he said, then adjusted his bow tie to capture the gallery owner's face.

Davis stood beside the first of three items. "This evening's collection consists of three pieces that were thought to be lost during World War II, and the gallery has recently come into possession of these fine works of art. First up for bid is an original Degas piece that was last seen in 1940, *Five Dancing Women*."

Bryce hadn't seen the items like Kira had, and the shock of sitting in the presence of this painting rocked him to the core. *Five Dancing Women* was about to be sold and removed from history entirely.

The second this ugly affair ended, Bryce would rush outside and call the agents to swarm the place. He had men on standby who could put the gallery on lockdown. Maybe they could recover the pieces and catch the buyers before they left the building.

The sheikh and the older woman locked eyes and volleyed bids back and forth like a tennis match, mesmerizing the onlookers.

The price tag hit one million dollars and climbed. Bryce held his breath at the intensity of the bidding but also at the potential loss of history. Anger bubbled at the private collectors who bought stolen paintings to sit on their shelves or hang on their walls for their own enjoyment. The thought made him sick. Not so much that he had a problem with people owning nice things—his problem came when they thought they were entitled to something that was supposed to belong to anyone who wanted to see it.

He put aside his personal feelings by the time the elderly woman paid ten million dollars for the simple brown and green painting of ballerinas dancing. What a shame. The piece should be in a museum for all to enjoy. And it would be if he had anything to say about it.

Then there was the Rembrandt. Another stolen painting that was about to be ripped from the history books forever. Bidding began between the sheikh and the Chinese private art collector, but it only went for twelve million dollars.

Only.

Kira scooted to the edge of her seat, and he reached over and squeezed her hand. Probably didn't need to do that, but he was the doting husband, right? They'd agreed that Kira would bid while he snapped pictures of the participants.

"Now, for our most prestigious piece in today's auction. Zaika is a fine piece of history and a rare find. The bidding will start at three million dollars."

A flurry of paddles rose in the air. Bryce took inventory while Kira bid. So far, Sophia, Theo, Ivan, the old lady, the sheikh, and the wealthy art collector were all in the race. The bids crept higher.

Five million.

Six million. The sheikh dropped out.

Eight million. The elderly lady called it quits.

Ten million. Kira stayed strong, her bidding paddle never wavering.

Twenty million. Ivan's paddle fell to his side.

Twenty-five million. Sophia's hand stopped raising.

It was down to Kira and Theo. He obviously had someone's financial backing. Kira kept bidding, with a steely look in her eyes and a fire in her spirit.

But Theo kept pace and bid fifty million dollars.

Kira looked at Bryce, as if to ask how long she should keep bidding. Bryce's attention snagged on Ivan. The man's eyes were wide, bouncing between Theo and Kira. As if he suspected something bad was about to happen.

Bryce put his hand on her arm. She raised her brow but let her paddle fall in her lap.

And just like that, it was over. Davis declared Theo the winner. Theo rose from his chair and Davis unlocked the secure box that contained Zaika. The treasure hunter grabbed a pair of gloves next to the display case, put them on, and reached into the glass enclosure to lift out his prize.

A sizzle zipped through the room, plunging them into darkness. Screams from upstairs echoed through the building. Chairs scraped and clattered to the floor above them.

Bryce couldn't see anything, but he grabbed Kira's hand. There was a scuffle in front of them. Another scream. Footsteps stomped down the stairs, and Bryce heard the distinct sound of a muffled pop. Like a bullet leaving a silencer.

He threw himself on top of Kira and took her to the floor. Someone—likely the gunman—fled up the stairs with thundering footsteps.

A minute later Davis pulled out a phone and shone a light around the room.

Zaika was gone.

And Theo's lifeless body lay crumpled on the ground.

16

KIRA TRIED TO SUCK IN A BREATH, but Bryce had her pinned on the floor. "Let me up." She pushed on his shoulder.

The hum of generators kicked in, and the lights returned, exposing the chaos of the room. Bryce rolled off her and stood, offering her a hand so she could get up. She hurried to Theo and pressed fingers against his neck. Nothing.

Sophia let out a loud wail. "What happened? Who did this? We were supposed to get that statue."

Kira had to believe Sophia knew exactly what was going on. The statue was gone and Theo was dead.

Davis began boxing up the other two pieces of art. "Everyone clear out. We'll keep the auction going upstairs. This was just a small power outage, nothing more." The gallery owner ignored Theo's lifeless body and raced up the stairs with a painting under each arm.

Apparently it was every man for himself now. The sheikh and other patrons had already vanished. And where was Ivan? "Let's go," Bryce whispered. He grabbed her hand and pulled her toward the stairs. She willed her legs to move.

They passed three security guards in discussion about how to dispose of Theo's body. "Take him out the back," one of the men said. "No one will know."

Kira bit back the bile in her throat, wishing she could arrest them all. Someone stole Zaika and killed Theo. How had she and Bryce not seen this coming?

They both ducked out of the women's restroom after agreeing to stick together. They couldn't afford to be separated now. In the dimly lit hallway, they were able to slip out unnoticed. A few people were gathered in small groups, talking in hushed whispers, probably trying to get the inside scoop on what was happening. Kira and Bryce cut through the auction room toward the front of the gallery. The generators lit the area, and dazed patrons stared at the auctioneer, who was apparently trying to determine if he should continue with the auction. But the FBI had begun locking down the entire building, sending some into panic mode. One affluent man shouted at an agent, claiming to be an attorney and his rights were being violated.

"Let's get out of here while we can." Bryce looped his arm in Kira's and led her to the main entrance where they obtained their cell phones.

A few guests were stopped at the main exit by agents. Bryce and Kira weaved through the crowds to an agent Kira knew. He nodded and let them duck out the exit door.

Kira texted SSA Turner an update as they moved down the front stairs of the gallery to the street. By the time they made their way out of the crowds, Violet had pulled up to the curb. "Glad I stuck close by. What happened?"

"Fill you in in a sec." She needed to catch her breath.

Her phone buzzed in her hand as they got in the car. SSA Turner's name popped up on the screen and she answered. Before the man could speak, Kira jumped in rapid-fire. "Send the teams into the restrooms. There's a false wall behind the couch, leading to a secret room with stairs. The invitation contains the code to access the door. You should have a copy of it. Theo

Durham was shot and killed. They also have an original Degas and Rembrandt in the illegal auction, which they will probably try to smuggle out of the building. Davis Steadman is behind this. The owner is a flight risk."

Flashing blue-and-white lights surrounded the building while Violet drove them in the opposite direction. Kira's heart still pounded. "What just happened?" She looked at Bryce. "How did Theo have that kind of money? Who killed him? Where is the statue?" She didn't really expect answers but wanted the questions out there.

Bryce ran a hand through his hair and blew out a breath. "I only have theories."

Kira called Everly. "Everly, where did Theo get the cash to bid like that?"

She put the phone on speaker and heard the clack of keyboard keys. "I think I found his alias on the dark web." Everly whistled. "Evidently Theo was leading quite the double life. He changed his name and scrubbed himself from the internet. It took me a while, but I uncovered that his real name is—or was—Henry Theodore, a billionaire tech mogul and art collector. I think he caught wind of the treasure. But he had the cash. I'm following the money trail. I'm also checking the areas around Sawyer's Peak, Riley, and Copper Creek to see if I can find out where he might have been staying. I'll keep you updated."

Everly hung up and Kira sank back in the seat, her adrenaline spike crashing. She turned to Bryce. "I'm glad you made me stop bidding. They would have tried to take me out instead."

"It started to feel less like an auction and more like an ambush. And Ivan picked up on the vibe as well."

Her mind replayed the auction scene like a movie on loop. The lights cutting off. Theo's lifeless eyes and the bullet wound in his temple. The missing statue.

And how close she'd come to death. In the dark, that shot could have hit any of them. Had God intervened and protected them? Maybe it was time she put her trust in something more than herself.

She rubbed her hands together to steady her nerves. "What now?"

No sooner had she spoken than her phone buzzed with an incoming message. "Everly says, 'He has a house in the area under Theo Durham, but Henry Theodore is listed as the owner of an old motel on the outskirts of Copper Creek. It's no longer open. Closed about a year ago. You might try there.'" She tipped her phone for Bryce to read the message.

"Let's dig into Henry Theodore," he said. "Maybe we can get to the motel before anyone else. He claimed he knew where the journals were. It's entirely possible he took them."

Kira nodded. "Good point. I'm not sleeping anytime soon. I vote road trip in the middle of the night to scope the place out."

Violet parked in front of their brownstone and pointed at the sedan.

"Thanks for the ride, Vi. Again." Kira coughed in an effort to regain her composure a bit. She wasn't about to break down now, but Vi's presence meant the world to her—like the sister she'd longed for as a child. "I appreciate you stepping in when you did earlier."

Violet turned in the seat to face Kira. "I've always got your back, but this case isn't a walk in the park. Be safe."

Kira nodded, her eyes misting at Violet's genuine concern. Her friends had her back, no matter what. Violet parked the car, got out, and opened the door for Kira.

"Stay safe." Violet wrapped Kira in a tight embrace the second her feet hit the ground. For once, Kira didn't mind. "And watch out for that hunk over there," she whispered. "You think I don't see the way he looks at you? Please. He's absolutely smitten. I mean, you look smoking hot in my dress."

Her roommate spun on her heels before Kira could protest and slid back into her car. Had Bryce heard that exchange? Heat crept up her neck, and she appreciated the dark of night to cover the effects of what that man was doing to her heart.

"Meet you at the front door in ten minutes?" she asked him.

"Perfect."

They headed inside, and once they were changed into more comfortable clothes, they climbed back in the car with Bryce at the wheel to head to West Virginia again.

"I'm not sure what we'll find at Theo's place," he said, "but he was playing everyone." He turned on his blinker to merge onto the interstate. "What if he's the one who followed us and rammed us off the road? He could have taken the journals and then sold them."

Kira pointed the heating vents toward herself and got comfortable for the ride to West Virginia. "What I don't understand is how you knew when to stop bidding."

Bryce checked the rearview mirror. "Call it a God thing. I saw the look on Ivan's face and knew something was wrong. I hate to say gut reaction, but that's what it was."

"God's protection?" Where was God when she'd needed him in the past? Silent and stoic. Definitely not guiding by inspirational feelings or whatever. "We had similar upbringings. I'm surprised you rely on faith so much."

"Well, what do you rely on?"

The answer escaped her. It had always been her against the world. "I guess I trust myself. But after tonight and being so close to that bullet, it got me thinking that God did protect me."

"We're all fallible. Doesn't it get tiring trying to do everything on your own? If you don't have help, you risk having to work hard to keep up appearances. You'll spend your life trying to please everyone else. At some point, something will break."

The words pierced her heart. "I learned at an early age it was easier just to be what others wanted. I could get what I wanted by meeting expectations."

"What happened?" He reached across the console and gave her hand a squeeze before returning his to the wheel.

The intensity of their kiss flashed before her eyes and heat seared up her neck. At least it was dark and he couldn't see. Only the fact that he'd shared his own tragic upbringing loosened her tongue.

"I was ten, and still in the orphanage," she said. "I told you about my friend who got adopted and left me there. But I overheard the orphanage staff talking about how hard it would be for me to be adopted. That's the last thing a kid needs to hear." Kira shifted in the seat, the memory scorching her like it had happened yesterday. "I happened to be outside the office door when someone was talking with the headmaster of the orphanage. They almost pitied me and said it would be highly unlikely I'd ever get adopted because I wasn't a blond newborn. No one wanted a dark-haired ten-year-old. They'd given up hope of finding me a family. They weren't even searching anymore."

"Oh, Kira. That's awful. I can't imagine how that shaped your worldview after that. I'm so glad the Millers stepped in."

Her heart skipped a beat at the mention of her adoptive parents. They'd never treated her as anything other than their daughter. But the damage had been done. Kira still fought the feelings that she wasn't enough. She had to work hard to be accepted.

Love came with strings attached. Families only wanted a newborn. Her boyfriend wanted a young, perky *blond* cheerleader.

What did God expect her to be? "I just got used to being what everyone expected me to be. And it's bleeding into my job. We need to solve this case so I can be the best Special Agent. Because everyone will walk away if I lose. I can't let the team down."

"I think you know that's not true."

"In my head. It's my heart that's having trouble with it."

Bryce glanced her way. "That's where the power of God's love comes into play. We can't earn it. And he meets us exactly where we are. No pretenses. God sees the real us."

The theory sounded great. Too bad she'd spent her life living up to everyone else's expectations. She didn't think she knew how to stop performing.

BRYCE'S HEART WRENCHED for the woman sitting next to him. The beautiful woman who'd had her own heart stomped on so many times that she couldn't fathom a love that would accept her as is. "Kira, there is nothing wrong with you. You *are* enough. You've just had bad experiences. But that doesn't dictate your future or who you are."

The words rang in his ears. Didn't he want to make something of himself to show his hometown that they were wrong about him? That someone from some small backwoods Appalachian mountain town could turn his life around?

Kira didn't say anything, and he didn't want to push her. But part of him wanted to stop the car and wrap her in his arms to comfort her. Her silence communicated years of pain from being left behind, forgotten.

They drove in silence until they were close to Sawyer's Peak. Kira navigated with the map on her phone and the address Everly had provided.

"It should be up here on the right," she said. The map dinged, confirming their arrival.

Bryce pulled into the parking lot of the sketchiest motel he'd ever seen. It was definitely old and falling apart. "Yikes" was all he could say. "Power's still on." The sign in the front advertised color TVs in every room. The *v* in vacancy was missing.

"I'm surprised they didn't murder Theo here." Kira stood back and looked over the place. Then pointed to the second-floor row of rooms with the doors facing the parking lot. "There's a light coming from that room. The only room that seems to have any light at all. Wanna check there first?"

"Let's go."

They found a stairwell that smelled like garbage and walked up the steps. There was a half-eaten hamburger in the breezeway, and ants worked on devouring it.

"We don't have a key," he reminded Kira. "What's the plan when we get to the—"

The door hung open, falling off the hinges, the Do Not Disturb sign clinging for dear life to the handle.

"That answers my question. It looks like the place has been ransacked. We'll clear the room in case the burglars are still here."

Kira nodded and pulled out her weapon. He stood on the other side of the door and did the same. They entered, and he turned on an additional light, trying not to gag at the smell. It didn't take long to clear the room and bathroom. To-go containers with rotting leftovers sat in a trash bin. "So, not great at housekeeping, was he?"

Kira lowered her weapon. "Something isn't right. Why was he here? He's from this area and we have an address for his house. Why would he stay in such a shady place? Let alone own it?"

"Maybe he needed to get off the grid. Find a place where the Russians couldn't track him. I'm assuming this made a great place to hide. It took Everly a while to find this place, and she's good at what she does."

Kira holstered her weapon and slid her hands into a pair of gloves. Bryce did the same. "I've got the bathroom," he said.

"You can have it. I've got under the beds and the drawers."

Bryce breathed through his mouth. The bathroom was nasty, and the last thing he needed to do was touch anything, even with gloves on. They had probable cause to enter, but once they called it in, it wouldn't be long before the police and FBI swarmed the place.

He stared at his reflection in the mirror. Was the gray around his temples more pronounced or did the dim bulb cast shadows? No doubt this case had aged him.

Nothing in the bathroom seemed out of place. Just decades' worth of dust on the floorboards, peeling paint, and a whole lot of grossness. But . . . a new full-length mirror covered the space between the sink and the toilet.

"Kira."

She poked her head in the cramped space. "I'm not coming in there. No thank you. What is that smell?"

"The whole place stinks, but why is there a brand-new mirror in an ancient motel room? See?" He pointed to the silver scroll on the sides. "It's fancy and ecompletely out of place."

She squinted her eyes and surveyed the area. "Some drunk guy probably smashed it in a fit of rage and they had to replace it?"

"Sure, but they'd buy something cheap, wouldn't they? This looks like a fairly expensive mirror. And why put a full-length here? It should be a smaller mirror over the sink. I think Theo did this."

He felt around the sides and then popped it off the wall. Only it didn't come off the wall. It swung open.

"A secret door?" Kira's eyes widened and excitement flickered. "It's worth risking disease to check that out."

Bryce stepped over the ledge of the thin rectangular opening and shone his phone light around until he spotted a string dangling from the ceiling. He pulled. The single bulb illuminated a space that was roughly seven by seven.

Kira followed. "Whoa."

A marker board took up one full wall, loaded with pictures, notes, and maps. On one side of the board, Theo had a timeline, and on the other, it looked like a genealogy. Of the Young family.

"Yeah. Whoa is right." He snapped pictures of the board. Then moved to the other wall and got the Post-it notes and more photos, connected by yarn.

"Theo—aka Henry—has been at this awhile. He must have become convinced that the treasure was real and made himself a lair while he searched the area for clues." Bryce stopped short at the papers tacked to one wall. He pointed and Kira moved closer. "That's my grandfather's handwriting. Well, now we know Theo was the one to take the journals. And he made copies before selling them."

Kira took out her phone and snapped close-ups of the journal. "The pages have hand-drawn maps, with *X*'s and dates. Your grandfather was definitely looking for something. But did he find it?"

Bryce's mind spun. The whole time, his own grandfather had been so close to uncovering a treasure, and the man hadn't even known the extent of his find. "Let's take as many pictures as we can and get out of here. I'll call this in and have the scene processed."

Bryce stepped into the main room to contact the Pittsburgh Field Office, which oversaw most of West Virginia. They could assign some agents from the resident agencies in the state to open an investigation. He returned to the secret space and continued documenting as much as he could alongside Kira. They took pictures and videos of Theo's hidden chamber.

When they exited, Bryce moved the mirror back in place. They headed outside to the breezeway, where Kira called her SSA to report their findings. The FBI would arrive soon to secure the place before anyone else arrived and figured out that Theo had been hiding a secret room. The man had constructed a puzzle and was only missing a few pieces. Maybe Bryce and Kira could figure out the location of the Young family's hidden bunker.

About twenty minutes later, a car arrived with two agents who would secure the crime scene. "Let's go to that diner we passed right off the highway," Bryce said to Kira after filling in the agents on what they'd found. "It was open twenty-four hours and we can look at the photos and regroup before heading back."

Kira followed him, and they drove off in their sedan, leaving the sketchy motel in the dust. "I need ten showers to get rid of the motel room ick, but that place was a gold mine."

"I just wish I'd seen it sooner. Did my grandfather even understand the magnitude of what he was looking for? He could have been killed over all of this. But he died of a heart attack."

"I think your grandfather wanted proof before making claims about the treasure. He probably knew who he could trust. It's possible he told no one what he was doing."

"I still miss the man every day."

Without Grandpa and his college roommate, he could have turned out just like his old man. He shuddered. They pulled into the all-night diner and a waitress named Bonnie greeted them. "Your table is ready. Your friend is already here."

He stopped short and stared at the middle-aged woman with a beehive of red hair piled on her head. "We're not with anyone else—"

A man waved to him from a booth in the back corner.

Ivan Sokolov. Their old friend—or nemesis. Bryce wasn't sure which one it was.

17

AT 3:15 IN THE MORNING, in the middle of nowhere West Virginia, Kira's brain couldn't compute how Ivan Sokolov had found them. But there he was, sipping coffee and scarfing down a plate of bacon, eggs, and hash browns like he was on vacation. "Sit, sit," the man said with his mouth full, gesturing to the open booth seat. Kira looked at Bryce, who narrowed his gaze.

She still didn't trust the man one hundred percent. She slid across the green plastic seat to make room for Bryce. The waitress brought out plates of food and poured coffee without asking.

"How did you know we'd be here?" Kira watched Ivan take a sip from his mug. "You ordered food for us."

Not that she was complaining. The aroma of extra crispy bacon and seasoned potatoes hit her nose. She dug in while Bryce sat back with his poker face firmly in place.

Ivan wiped his mouth with a paper napkin. "I made an assumption. I was correct. What did you find out?"

"Theo had a secret hideout," Kira said. "Inside the wall of a run-down motel." What was the point in hiding it?

Ivan's head swiveled around the room as if someone might be eavesdropping. Dark circles ringed his eyes. He seemed to be feeling the pinch of no sleep as well. He leaned across the table.

"I've proposed an official joint venture between the FBI and the FSB on this case. Your boss, Jeremiah Turner, should be reaching out with the details. No sense putting it off. I think we need each other to stop the art smuggling ring and allow Russia to recover pieces of her history."

Kira texted Turner to confirm that the joint venture was approved. This guy liked to name drop, and Kira wasn't taking his word for it.

A return text lit her screen. Turner had been in contact with Ivan and would fill them in on the details soon.

"Did the Dominiks get picked up when the Feds raided the art gallery?" Kira asked. They hadn't had time to check on this little tidbit.

Ivan smiled. "This is why I like you Americans. You had agents posted all around the place. They picked up the key players trying to sneak out the back door. But for the sake of your undercover operation, your team opted to let Alex and Sophia slip out the back."

"And the Degas? The Rembrandt?" Bryce finally picked up a fork and stabbed at the eggs Ivan had ordered.

Ivan's grin grew wider. "Congratulations, Agent Lambert. I think your case is closed. Davis was picked up by the FBI—caught red-handed with both. The man behind the illegal auction house will spend a long time behind bars. The smuggling ring lost its head. I'm sure they'll regroup and start over, but for now, you've stopped them from looting and money laundering."

"So who has the journals?" Bryce still had an I'm-not-trusting-you look etched across his face. But Kira knew the man was rejoicing on the inside. His hard work had paid off.

Now if only they could close down this Amber Crown Society, all their cases would be wrapped up with a tidy bow.

The waitress came to the table and refilled the coffee mugs. Ivan sat back and the plastic squeaked at his movement. "As much as it pains me to say this, I still don't know the identity of Alexandr's client. He won't tell me."

Kira stifled a yawn. She had to keep going and took several big sips of coffee. They were finally getting somewhere with Ivan, and he seemed chatty. As long as he kept talking, she'd hammer him with questions. "Do you think Sophia is involved?"

Ivan stroked his chin. The salt-and-pepper beard, neatly trimmed, gave the man a sophisticated look, which probably helped him infiltrate the Dominiks. "Oh, you've heard the rumor that the head of the Amber Crown Society is a woman. I thought for a while that it might be Sophia, but she pretty much says and does everything Alex tells her to. She's in it for his money and status. I don't think she's behind the smuggling ring or the murders."

"Did you figure out who's behind the murdered security guard at the gallery?"

"Another mystery. I met with the security guard because he was supposed to hook us up with access to the statue. I was paying him to make me a copy of his key card. The man pled for more time, so I agreed to come back later in the week. I left out the back. When I heard footsteps, I realized someone had followed. Hadn't suspected it to be Kira."

Ivan tilted his head as if recalling a memory. "The ACS scoured the area for anyone connected to the Youngs. I think your grandfather must have been a legend in the town when it came to treasure hunting, and they paid your father a visit. I don't believe he was on their radar, though."

"It was someone named Victor." Kira cast a concerned glance at Bryce. "Is Mr. Lambert safe? What if they return?"

Bryce's face paled. He must have come to the same conclusion.

Ivan stared at Bryce. "If I were you, I'd get your father out of town until this blows over. I can't say if he's a target, but if these journals prove to have any useful information, the ACS may show up looking for more."

She wasn't about to admit this, but the information in the

journals could provide these terrorists with everything they needed to search for the missing treasure.

Bonnie stopped by their table to refill Kira's coffee and put down their check, then moved on. "You didn't say who has the journals. Theo obviously had money to bid as high as he did. I'm assuming he sold the journals to the Society."

Ivan steepled his fingers together. "That's my theory. Theo followed you after you met with him the other day, and he was the one that ran you off the road and stole the journals. I'd been tailing him, not you, that day. I just wish I had figured out what he was up to sooner so I could have warned you."

Kira wanted to keep Ivan talking, and herself so that she'd stay awake. "Who killed Theo?"

Ivan's eyes scanned the room, as if to catch an eavesdropper. "The ACS has an assassin. It's most likely the same man that killed the security guard and Derek."

One question lingered and Kira decided to go for it. "Who has the rabbit statue?"

"I do."

THE LACK OF SLEEP had caught up to Bryce. Had he heard Ivan correctly?

"*You* stole the rabbit statue?" Bryce blinked, trying to clear his head.

Ivan smiled. "I saw an opportunity. They were going to steal the statue. I got there first."

"Where are the other two bunny statues?" Kira asked. His partner must have had half a dozen cups of coffee, but not a muscle twitched in her body as she stared Ivan down.

Could they trust this man, even if the FBI had fully vetted him? Ivan could be a double agent, playing both sides to gain access to a treasure worth a fortune. Then again, why admit he had the statue if the latter was the case?

All the unanswered questions were giving him a migraine. He rubbed his temples.

Ivan finally broke the staring contest between the two of them. "I believe the Society has the other two."

"And why is it so important to have all three?"

Ivan leaned forward in his seat and looked each of them in the eyes. "I'll tell you, but you have to promise to work with me and tell me what you know."

They both nodded, but Bryce wasn't giving up that they had pictures of the journal pages. The maps could potentially lead them right to the underground bunker. And the idea that Ivan might be a double agent burrowed deeper into the rational part of his brain, the part that was still awake and functioning.

"We'll tell you where Theo's secret lair is." Bryce didn't care. The FBI had contained the scene and Ivan would be his boss's problem. They needed Ivan's information now.

"That's fair. Although I'm sure your people are already dismantling the hideout." Ivan folded his arms. "Fenton Young was eccentric, no doubt. The guy was a big conspiracy theorist and thought everyone was out to get him. When his father passed, he inherited the art bunker and responsibility for keeping the secret. We believe there is a bunker that contains lost art from as far back as the Civil War. Fenton's father was in the Army during World War II and saw the devastation the Nazis created to the art community. He took an opportunity to redirect one of the twenty-seven crates full of priceless artifacts and had it shipped back home. I guess he switched the labels and no one caught him. All the other crates disappeared or were destroyed. But as the legend states, one escaped—and it contained artifacts from the Amber Room."

Bryce's pulse thrummed with a new wave of energy. In his

lifetime, he never imagined being part of such a find as a missing crate containing pieces of the infamous Amber Room.

Kira also hung on Ivan's every word.

"Apparently Fenton started to lose his mind," Ivan said. "Lots of isolation and paranoia will do that to a man. He refused to trust Derek and had no one to pass along the responsibility for keeping the bunker safe. So he devised a code. While the statues may have been part of the treasure from that crate, the Society thinks the statues are clues to the location of the treasure."

Based on the note Derek had shown them, this theory might be a reality.

"He probably meant for his son to figure it out, not to sell all his belongings in an estate sale," Kira said, "but Derek was so bitter toward his father that he packed up all his father's belongings without realizing what he had. Fenton had left clues, but they were ignored. So . . . the three statues together lead to the treasure room. Wonder how."

Bryce swallowed the lump in his throat. But for the grace of God, he could have wound up like Derek Young had, bitter and resentful, operating out of a place of anger over forgiveness. How much had he missed by clinging to bitterness and resentment? His own father couldn't fend for himself, and while he hadn't known how bad it had gotten, Bryce had avoided dealing with the situation all these years. Despite how badly the man had treated him, Bryce believed in forgiveness, grace, and the power to change that all came from his relationship with Jesus.

He ran a hand through his hair and refocused. "So without all three statues, the secret can't be unlocked."

"Correct."

Bryce wrote down the information for the motel on a napkin and slid it to Ivan. "Theo owns the place. We discovered his real identity. Billionaire Henry Theodore."

Ivan let out a low whistle.

Bryce continued. "The mirror in the bathroom leads to a secret room with all of Theo's research and notes. Have you had a recent tetanus shot? The place should have been condemned ten years ago."

Ivan threw several twenties on the table. "I'm going to check out this motel. I'll be in touch." Amid the bills, Bryce saw a business card and snatched it up, sticking it in his pocket in case they needed to call Ivan.

Kira slumped down in the plastic diner booth seat. "What should we do now?"

Bryce checked his watch. "It's 4:20 a.m. I'm going to call the local police department to put someone on watch duty at my dad's house. I don't like the idea that these smugglers might think my dad knows more than he does. We passed a decent-looking hotel just outside of Copper Creek. Let's get rooms and some rest. First thing this morning I'd like to convince my father to move to a hotel until this is all over. Hopefully he won't put up too much of a fight."

Kira yawned. "Sounds like a plan."

They headed to the hotel and checked into adjoining rooms. He didn't want Kira far from him. But as soon as his head hit the pillow, he was out cold.

An alarm woke him up. The digital clock flashed 9:00 a.m. He groaned but rolled out of bed and called the officer on duty to make sure there hadn't been any trouble at his father's house. The officer indicated it had been a quiet morning. Bryce's heart returned to a normal pace when he heard Kira moving around next door.

A quick shower reenergized him and he was ready within minutes. Kira knocked at the door and, at his invitation, poked her head in. "I'm ready to go when you are."

"All set."

When they checked out, Bryce extended his room—which was under a third assumed name—and prepaid for another week in cash, with the goal of having his father move in.

They left the hotel and drove over to his father's place. "I have no idea how we're going to convince my father to leave the house."

The word escaped his lips so naturally. *We*.

He loved being part of a team with Kira. The thought of heading back to his sparsely decorated one-bedroom apartment in Richmond held less and less appeal the more time he spent with her.

Would she want to see him after this adventure ended? She'd probably be given a new partner and a chance to live her dream of working in the field.

But what would he do once the case was solved? The search for the smuggling ring had consumed his life the past five years. What was next?

Bryce waved at the officer parked in front of his father's place. Hopefully his dad didn't notice the extra pair of eyes on the house. He turned into the pothole-ridden dirt drive, which meant his musings about the future would have to wait. The car bounced and shuddered all the way up to the trailer.

When they approached the rickety steps leading to the front door, a voice shouted, "Come in," over the volume of the television.

The door wasn't locked. That wasn't like his father.

"Dad, why isn't the door locked?" Bryce asked as they stepped over trash on the floor.

The man swatted his hand in the direction of the police car. "I saw that officer stationed out in front of the house and figured you had something to do with it."

Bryce knelt next to his father's ancient armchair. "Okay, I'm working a case and it's taken a dangerous turn. I'd like for you to leave the house for a little while. The Russian man, Victor, is a bad dude, and I don't like having you here alone. It will only be for a little while."

"Psh. Always working on some case. Everything is always your next big break. I've lived here for fifty years and nothing bad has happened. You just be on your way. Go solve your case. You've left me alone before. You can do it again."

The man's caustic attitude could cut through steel and felt like a battle he'd never win. "Dad, it's not true. I've always cared about you. But you cut me off. Told me to leave. I'd like to make amends. We still have time. I just need you to stay at a hotel for a week so I know you're safe. I've already paid for it. Please."

His father turned his gaze to Kira, who stood by the doorway with her arms folded across her chest. She listened but didn't intervene.

His father nodded to Bryce. "Who is she really? She's not your wife. Phil from the post office said that you were divorced. Said Addie left you. I guess you couldn't hack it as a husband after all and had to lie about it."

Bryce's blood boiled. Small-town gossip never ended. And who was Phil from the post office? In that moment, the memories of his seventeen-year-old self flooded back. His father's words rang in his ears as he'd walked away from the trailer with all his worldly possessions in one box. He'd been accepted to college, and his dad threw a fit when he found the acceptance letter hidden in Bryce's pillowcase. He'd left his own letter for Bryce, one that Bryce found when he'd unpacked that one flimsy container in his dorm room.

You'll come crawling back one day. You think you can get out, make it on your own? Leave. Now. But never forget that you're no better than me. My blood runs through your veins. You're destined for failure.

18

KIRA BIT DOWN on her tongue so hard she tasted blood.

Everything within her screamed for her to intervene, but that wasn't her place. Not yet.

Bryce could handle the man. This was his battle. One that she had a feeling he had to win in order to truly heal.

"I'm not leaving. You can't make me." Mr. Lambert sounded like a petulant five-year-old throwing a tantrum.

And while she kept her mouth shut, the pain of his father's words rattled through her as if he'd hurled the insults directly at Kira.

Bryce stood and nodded to Kira. "He's not moving. Let's go. I'll ask if an agent or local police can continue to watch the place."

An inner voice pumped a steady anthem through her head. *Don't intervene. Don't intervene.*

Bryce's father studied Kira. "Don't say I didn't warn you about this one."

Oh, she was intervening.

Bryce stormed out of the trailer, the door slamming so hard the walls rattled and the crooked picture above the sofa crashed to the floor.

Kira moved to stand next to the old man in the chair. She had plenty to say, but to be respectful, she let the man have it . . . in Russian. "You are a sorry excuse for a father. Your words have caused your son so much pain and suffering when all he's ever done is take care of you, worry about your well-being."

The man's eyes widened at the inflection of her tone. Russian was a harsh language for most Americans. He didn't understand the words, but her meaning was clear through the tone.

She carried on, telling him exactly what she thought of him, holding nothing back. With her hands on her hips, she let her Russian words fly off her tongue. "You will leave this house. He needs to solve this case without worrying about you. And we will have someone come in and clean the place from top to bottom. All your son wants is to restore a relationship with you, and you need to work on accepting grace and forgiveness. It's not something you can earn or that you deserve."

A memory flashed with a phrase her adoptive mother told her a thousand times. *"God wants us to come as we are."*

Maybe she needed a lesson in extending grace to herself.

Mr. Lambert sat in the old chair with wide eyes. She hadn't threatened him, but with her Russian accent, he might have misconstrued her intentions.

Oh well.

She switched to English and softened her voice. "Your son wants a relationship with his father. To do the right thing. Is that too much to ask?"

He blinked. "He's the one who—"

"No more excuses. No more blame. It's time to move forward. Your son is extending grace to you. Please come with us. He's trying to protect you, because despite the past, he loves you."

He wriggled under her stare. She stepped back and watched the man's resolution fade.

Finally, he heaved a sigh. "Oh, all right. If you insist." The man shuffled to a back bedroom and within a minute had a duffel bag stuffed with who knew what.

She opened the front door, and he marched out. Bryce stood by the car, talking on his cell phone. He lowered the phone from his ear to watch his father emerge with his packed bag. Mr. Lambert opened the back door of the sedan, tossed his bag across the seat, and crawled in.

Bryce gaped at Kira. “What happened?”

Kira held her hands up. “We just had a conversation, and he had a change of heart.”

Mr. Lambert piped up from the background. “Your girlfriend threatened me.”

Kira laughed. “Did I now?”

“Well, if I could understand what you said, I’d know it was a threat.” The man crossed his arms and sulked.

Bryce glanced at Kira, and she feigned innocence. “I don’t know what he’s talking about. Do you have a key to the door?”

He pulled it from his pocket, and she hurried to lock the door and placed the key under the ceramic bunny. And smirked. Of course it was a bunny.

She returned to the car and hopped in the front seat. They dropped Mr. Lambert off at the hotel in Copper Creek, making sure he had everything he needed. The place had a dining room, and Bryce left additional cash with the front desk so his dad could have meals there if he wished. But he gave strict orders to not allow him to use the money for alcohol. Then he offered the front desk clerk a hefty tip for his troubles.

They headed back to Theo’s motel to see if there were any new leads in the investigation.

Bryce glanced at Kira. “Thanks for helping with my father. I don’t know what you said, but I’m glad you were able to get him to leave.”

“I told him the truth. In angry Russian. But he got the message.”

He chuckled. “I’m sure he thought you were going to kill him just by looking at him. You can be fierce when you want to be.”

She shook her head. "And maybe someday your father will see you for who you really are, not through his own selfish lens."

Kira pulled out her phone to review the pictures she'd taken of the journal pages. A new email message notification popped up from SSA Turner.

She opened her inbox and read the contents. It contained the pictures from Bryce's hidden camera.

She flipped through each face like she was playing a game of Clue. The sheikh in the auction room. The elderly lady in the secret auction room. A couple in the hallway.

"Wait. Who's this?" She zoomed in on the picture.

Bryce didn't take his eyes off the road. "Describe who you're asking about."

"The photo shows two people emerging from a back room, close to the bathrooms. The man is Vince Palmer, the gallery attendant. He has his arm around a woman in an intimate gesture. She looks familiar."

"I'm not sure," he said. "I couldn't place her, but I remember seeing her."

She zoomed in on the woman's face. "I think that's Natalia, Sophia's maid."

She held up the phone, and he took a quick glance. "Ah, I should have recognized her after she busted me snooping. But she appears different all dressed up. Elegant. Like she belongs there."

"Maybe she's seeing Vince."

"It looks like the man has a bandage on his hand." She zoomed in on him. "He does have gauze wrapped around his palm."

Kira remembered the gallery attendant, but it looked like he'd ditched the thick glasses. She'd pegged his age at around forty, although his thin face and dark eyes made him appear older than he probably was.

"Could he have been one of the men who attacked us?" Kira asked.

Bryce tapped the steering wheel as in thought. "When you first met this Vince guy at the gallery, what did he sound like?"

"He was very dry, with a monotone voice, but it was kind of nasally. No accent that I can remember."

"The guy that climbed out of the Dominiks' window and then got the jump on me after Derek was murdered was a thin but strong man. And he had an irritatingly nasal voice with a distinct Russian accent."

She texted Everly to check on the gallery attendant. "Vince is in the perfect position to hide in the shadows and keep an eye on the statue. It's possible the Society had the man pose as an attendant at the gallery to keep watch."

"It makes sense. And he was there when the guard was murdered."

So . . . had they just figured out who murdered the security guard? She remembered Ivan's comment about the ACS having an assassin.

Bryce adjusted the rearview mirror. "If we agree with that theory, this means the gallery attendant—Vince—might be responsible for killing both the security guard and Derek. Maybe even Theo. I mean, we saw Vince at the art auction."

"I'll send our theories to Turner," Kira said. "We're onto something. I can feel it. We just need some hard evidence to tie it all together."

They stopped for some burgers, and Kira got back to work when they hit the road again. She sipped her half lemonade, half unsweetened iced tea. No sweet tea for this Russian-born woman. She'd never get used to that Southern tradition.

She pulled up the photos she'd taken of the maps from the journals. There were four hand-drawn pages. "I'm assuming these are of places he searched for the treasure. The first page has two mountains and then a valley. Some rocks or boulders maybe. And I think the circles represent towns in the area." She pulled up a map of the area, squinting to make sense of what she was seeing. It wasn't clear at first glance. It would probably be helpful to print the pages and study them side by side to match the geography against a real map. Each sheet looked similar, but laid out side by side, they might form a more cohesive picture of a specific section of the mountains.

"Did your grandfather write in code?" She studied the *X* marks the man had drawn in various spots along the maps. "I can't tell if the *X*'s are where he tried and failed or if he found something in those spots."

"He liked a good mystery, but I never read his journals to know. I'll study it with you when we get back."

Bryce's phone buzzed with an unknown number. Kira picked it up and put it on speakerphone since Bryce was driving.

"Brian? It's Sophia."

Kira held the phone between Bryce and herself. She switched to her New York accent. "Darling, it's Katrina. Are you all right? We were so worried about you."

The woman paused. "I didn't know what had happened to you and Brian. You never came home last night." Sophia's voice sounded raspy and stressed.

"We headed out of town until the heat cooled off a little. Are you okay? If you and Alex are in trouble, Brian and I can head home right now."

"We need help. I—I need to know if you took Zaika."

"No. We might participate in an illegal auction, but rest assured we would never steal."

Sophia groaned. "Someone kidnapped our maid, Natalia, and they're holding her hostage. They've threatened to kill her if we don't return the statue."

BRYCE'S STOMACH CLENCHED.

"Where are you?" Kira asked. "We can come to you."

"No. They want us to meet them somewhere. We're waiting

for a text on the location—but it's somewhere in West Virginia, so Alex and I are driving that way. They told us we have three hours or they'll . . . they'll kill her." Her voice trailed off into a sob.

"Sophia, we can help. Once they tell you where to meet, we can figure out a plan to get Natalia back."

"But without the statue, it's no use. We don't have it." The woman wailed.

Bryce pulled off the road so he could focus on the call.

"We can help," Kira said again, trying to keep the woman talking. "Once you find out the meeting spot, let us know. Brian and I are in West Virginia and will wait here."

Sophia sniffed. "I'll . . . I'll call you when we're closer."

Kira disconnected the call and faced Bryce. "What should we do? I can call Turner and at least get the FBI mobilized."

She fired off a text, and Bryce fished the card out of his pocket. "I have Ivan's card he left on the table. And we know he has the statue. We should let him know. Maybe he'll make a trade."

"Doubtful but worth a shot. We don't want someone caught in the crossfire."

Something didn't sit well with Bryce. Wasn't Natalia with the gallery attendant, who they presumed was a member of the Amber Crown Society? The pair looked rather cozy, and he hadn't sensed that she was in danger. But maybe the attendant had used her to get close to the Dominiks so he could keep an eye on them? They were the most likely ones to win the auction and walk away with Zaika. He had no proof, of course, but it was an idea.

Kira dialed Ivan, but Bryce spoke. "Ivan, we need to meet. According to Sophia, someone took Natalia hostage. They are demanding the return of Zaika or they'll kill her."

Ivan sucked in a harsh breath. "That's not good. I know they'll make good on their threat. In fact, she might already be dead."

Bryce clenched the wheel.

"What do you know about the gallery attendant?" Kira asked.

"We have a picture of him at last night's event coming out of a back room looking very cozy with Natalia. Could he be part of the Society?"

Ivan remained quiet for a few seconds. "His name is Vince Palmer. He's Russian but has been in this country since birth, so he's a citizen. He's led a quiet life, making a living in the art community."

"But . . ." Bryce figured there was more to the story.

"His background is clean. Too sterile. Like someone created a backstory for the man. But there is nothing out there tying him to the Society, or anything for that matter."

Bryce didn't like the sound of that. "Do you want to meet us at the diner while we wait for Sophia and Alex to contact us?"

Ivan grunted. "I'll be there." The line disconnected.

Kira stashed the phone in her pink go bag. At least they'd had the foresight to bring an overnight bag. Who knew when they'd get back to the house? She'd claimed she needed it for all her snacks.

They headed back to the diner near Sawyer's Peak that had become their default home base for this operation. Bonnie greeted them, still working, although her attitude was a lot less chipper than earlier. How many hours had the woman been on her feet?

They snagged the same booth in the back corner. Bryce wanted a plan before Ivan came and dictated one. "Any thoughts, Kira?" He watched her. She had ordered more coffee and, despite their lack of proper rest, looked refreshed and ready to go. The woman's ability to adapt to any situation continued to impress him.

She sighed. "I'm not convinced Ivan has the statue or that he's not playing both sides."

"Right, and on our own, I'm not sure how we can help Natalia without blowing our cover. Calling in for a raid seems like our only option."

The front door opened, and Ivan strode in, followed by another man.

Kira moved into the booth next to Bryce and the two men slid in across from them.

"Hi, I'm Special Agent Jordan Bailey. I've been assigned by our field office to go undercover as Levi Solinger to try and negotiate the release of the hostage."

The agent with dark hair and brown eyes appeared to be around her age, thirty-three. She'd heard of him and his impressive résumé with the Bureau, and it was good to have him on board.

The waitress returned with a coffee carafe for the table and extra mugs. She asked for orders, and everyone but Bailey took a pass.

"How are we going to intervene to rescue Natalia?" Bryce asked once the waitress left. "Is there a plan in the works, one that won't blow everyone's cover?"

Ivan stroked his salt-and-pepper beard. "I've turned over the rabbit statue to the FBI for safekeeping." He nodded at Bailey. "But we think we should set up an exchange. The statue for the woman's release."

This caught Kira's attention and she perked up. "Then they'll be one step closer to the treasure. We can't let them have that much power."

Ivan leaned across the table, looking both ways for anyone who might be in earshot. "Not if we can get to the treasure first."

"And how do you propose we do that?" Kira asked.

Bailey shot Ivan an irritated look. "One thing at a time. Ivan will inform the Society that he's blackmailed Solinger—me—into giving up the statue in exchange for Natalia. Apparently Ivan has some serious dirt on me that could put me away for life if the information is leaked to the authorities. So, I begrudgingly agreed to attend the meeting and hand over the statue. We'll have FBI agents on surveillance around the property, and if necessary, they'll step in."

Ivan cleared his throat. "And if anyone is suspicious as to why

I would go to so much trouble to free Alex's maid, I'm going to announce that she's secretly my daughter. I got her a job in Alex's house to get her out of Russia and help her become an American citizen."

"What about me?" Kira asked with an edge in her tone.

Ivan glanced between Agent Bailey and Bryce, as if they had a secret and he would let them decide who should be the one to tell her.

"Sophia is trying to get you out of the picture," Ivan said. "She told Alex that you were the one who called the police and FBI to the art gallery. She's been planting seeds of doubt about your loyalties. Alex thinks you have the statue."

"And you didn't bother to defend me?"

Ivan grunted. "I have nothing to do with protecting your cover. However, Sophia isn't pointing a finger at Brian. And we can use that to our advantage. If Brian and Levi cut a deal with the Dominiks, this helps us get closer to the Society. Alex may finally reveal his secrets and give us the identities of the members of ACS."

Red rose from Kira's neck and flickered across her face. "So, I'm cut out of this operation, just like that?"

Agent Bailey steepled his fingers in front of him. "I'm not sure. From what I understand, it looks like Sophia has been playing you. And Ivan suspects she's trying to move in on your man." His head bobbed toward Bryce, and his stomach churned. Of course Sophia would make up rumors to drive a wedge between them.

Ivan shifted in the booth seat, plastic squeaking beneath him. "Alex told me that the Society thinks Kira is a distraction." He looked at Kira. "Your aggressive bidding at the auction didn't help."

"Your cover is still intact," Bailey said, "but it might be better for Bryce and me to go in alone, with Ivan, to negotiate for the release of Natalia. However, I'll defer to you and Bryce on this since I'm coming in new to your undercover assignment."

She stared at Bryce, her eyes pleading with him to keep her in the game. If she were to be cut out of the operation—

His thoughts shifted gear. If she stayed behind, he wouldn't have to worry about her getting caught in the crossfire. There was a confirmed target on her back. Sure, the woman was more than capable of defending herself. But the way she'd captured his attention—and his heart—he might be better off if he knew she wasn't in direct danger.

Don't do it. Don't do it. Don't—

"Kira, I may need to play this out alone," he found himself saying. Everything within him wanted to keep Kira safe . . . even if it meant sidelining her. "If I have Sophia's attention, we have the power to—"

The waitress chose that moment to bring Agent Bailey's order, which silenced Bryce.

But the look on Kira's face told him everything. He'd just ended their partnership.

And maybe any potential relationship going forward.

19

BRYCE HAD JUST CUT HER OUT of the mission. She'd worked so hard to get here, and now she'd watch the action go down from the sidelines?

Not going to happen. She'd earned her status as a Special Agent. They couldn't just remove her from her first assignment. Well, technically, they could. Bailey would be calling the shots. But she didn't have to smile and accept it. "My cover is still intact. I'm still an asset. I can—"

At Ivan's and Agent Bailey's unblinking stares, she stopped protesting. It made her appear weak. She dropped her gaze and ordered her seething fury to cool.

A worthless effort.

She'd trusted Bryce. Done everything by the book. And look where it got her.

Left out in the cold. Abandoned yet again because she wasn't enough.

Bryce touched her hand. "Kira, I just think—"

"No. That's fine. I understand." She removed her hand and crossed her arms. "Sophia sold me out to get to you. Might as well see how that plays out."

Bryce's eyes pleaded with her to understand. "This protects

your cover. They won't think you stole Zaika if I lead them to believe I acted independently and gave the statue to Levi."

She plastered a smile on her face. "Sounds like a winning plan."

Meanwhile, the gold digger Sophia would get everything she wanted. The statue and Katrina's husband.

Kira's fake husband. Why was Sophia's scheming such a gut punch to Kira? The woman was a criminal. This wasn't personal. She and Bryce didn't have a real relationship. Personal or professional, apparently. She'd weather this like she always did. Alone and with her walls intact. She shot him her coldest stare and tightened her lips.

Agent Bailey scrutinized her and Bryce, as if he might have to jump in and referee an argument. But Kira wouldn't pitch a fit. She'd be the team player, the agent who stepped aside so the operation could continue. It was the right thing to do, of course. She knew that.

What stung the most was that Bryce didn't stand up and fight for her to stay.

"Kira," Bryce said. "You've done an amazing job with this assignment. If it weren't for your translation, we wouldn't be here. I just think we can play this Sophia angle and shut this case down so we can all go home knowing this treasure doesn't fall into the wrong hands. It has nothing to do with your ability to get the job done."

"I understand." And she should understand that this wasn't personal. Any Special Agent knew circumstances changed in an instant when on assignment, and she needed to think about what was best for her team. Along with recovering a hostage. Time to put aside her past baggage. The only person at the table telling her she wasn't good enough for the mission was herself.

Kira took a deep breath and did something she hadn't done in forever.

She prayed. Asked God to remove the lies that she wasn't

enough. Prayed for the success of the mission and God's protection.

Agent Bailey studied her as she shut down her negative thoughts. "Kira, I want you hiding in the surrounding areas with the other agents, on standby. You've got sharp instincts, and I want you listening while we go in. We may need your input and translation ability. You know the players and we'll need your expertise."

She nodded. She would work hard, even if it was from the outskirts. Her mind cleared, and her focus returned with double sharpness. They'd rescue Natalia and find those statues.

They discussed the plan details. Ivan started dictating the mission again, and Bailey—despite the occasional subtle eye roll—allowed the man to lead. For now.

"I will bring Levi and Brian to the meeting and force them to give up the statue. We will trade Zaika for the woman's freedom."

"Of course, we'll be on comms and the FBI will surround the place for protection, then tail the bad guys from the scene to track down the other two statues," Bailey said, turning to his hefty-sized lunch of eggs, bacon, and a mountain of tater tots. "I love this place. My wife never lets me eat bacon."

Ivan went outside to make the call.

Under the table Bryce placed a hand on hers, presumably so Agent Bailey couldn't see. "Kira, you know I'm only agreeing to this because it's the most likely path to stop the bad guys, right? If Sophia has it in for you and you're there, it could jeopardize everything."

"I understand. Really, I do." And she meant it. Sure, she needed to process some hurt feelings, but a sense of peace had replaced her initial anger. She squeezed his hand but didn't let go. "I want what's best for the team. And who knows? Because I'm so close to this case, I might be better serving the team by observing and listening in."

Her fingers tingled from his touch. Were the sparks real, or just a temporary by-product of their whirlwind fake marriage?

That kiss in the gallery hallway made the fake seem oh so real. For her anyway.

Ivan returned and sat back down next to Agent Bailey. Bryce moved his hand and the moment was gone.

"Alex communicated our request to the kidnappers," Ivan said, "and they have agreed to let us meet with the statue. They will trade. We might finally find out who is behind the Amber Crown Society."

For their plan to work, Kira needed to disappear.

She locked eyes with Bryce, her confidence rising. "I'll take the sedan and find a place to lie low until the meeting. Bryce can go with you two. Just text me where the meeting is happening." She grabbed Bryce's keys off the table before anyone protested and headed for the sedan in the parking lot.

A friendly face waited at her escape vehicle.

"Violet? What are you doing here?"

"SSA Turner wants me to partner with you temporarily. My active cases can wait a bit. This just took priority. Hopefully this will be all over soon and we'll recover the statues. And maybe find some ancient rare treasure."

Kira's phone buzzed. She glanced at the message, then waved the device at Violet. "They sent the meeting location. We can go find a spot to stake out the area."

Violet nodded. Kira tossed Violet the keys and jumped in the passenger seat.

"Where are we headed?" Violet asked. The engine turned over, and Kira researched the address on the map. She cranked up the heater full blast and longed for her heavier jacket. The temperatures had cooled with the elevation.

Violet noticed. "I tossed my coat in the back seat. Feel free to use it."

Kira looked. "That's your favorite one. I'm honored."

"And you're one of my favorite people. Put the coat on."

Kira did so, then buckled up. She read off the address. "Looks like the middle of nowhere." She tilted the phone so Violet could see the screen and double-tapped the map to home in on the satellite image. The grainy picture revealed a house or shack of some kind, with lots of land surrounding it.

And trees, rocks, and no roads.

"It's going to be hard to surround the place," Kira said. It was the only structure within miles, meaning they couldn't just drive up and park outside. Security would be tight and would see anyone approach.

"We'll have to go in on foot." Violet took out her phone. "Of course, they'll have their people surrounding it as well, so our perimeter will probably be wider. I'll contact the agent in charge of the raid on my sat phone and find out what area they want us to cover."

Kira nodded, but her focus wasn't on the perimeter of the meeting spot but on what would happen inside.

Violet backed out of the parking lot and headed toward their destination. "How are you doing with being asked to sit on the sidelines?"

"I'm fine."

"Liar."

Kira shifted in her seat and glanced up from her iPhone. "Okay. It stinks. I'm a good agent. I just haven't had the opportunity to prove myself yet. But I decided to let go. I prayed, and I understand the reasoning behind it. It's still disappointing, though."

Violet smiled and playfully punched Kira's arm. "That's my girl. This isn't about you needing to prove yourself. This is about what's best for the mission."

"I know. You don't have to preach."

"I'm not. Okay, maybe a little. But you graduated from the Basic Field Training Course. That's not an easy task. A few people in our class didn't make it to graduation. What if by working the perimeter, you're in the exact spot you need to be in? Maybe things go sideways inside and you're the one to save the day. God might have other plans, and you could miss something doing it all on your own. But whether you're in the field or on the sidelines, it's not what you do that matters. It's who you are."

Isn't that what Bryce had told her? He'd called her a chameleon, always changing her personality to fit any and all situations. Trying to earn her status and reputation.

Kira let out a long breath. Fatigue hit her, not from the lack of sleep—although that was part of it. She'd grown tired of always performing, striving to meet everyone's expectations. "You know what? Bryce liked me for, well, me. I didn't have to pretend to be someone else when I was with him. Which is why it was such a blow when he agreed that I should sit this one out. But I'm trying not to take it personally. It's not all about me."

"He didn't cast you off, and you're still on the team. Maybe not in the role you want. But believe me, I can tell by the way the man looks at you, he's not brushing you off anytime soon." Violet's phone vibrated with a text. "I have the location where the agents are setting up and the coordinates of where they want us. It's about four miles from the property and then it's on foot from there." She headed in the direction the GPS indicated.

Kira bounced Violet's words around in her head. She could still help, add value to the mission, even if it wasn't the way she envisioned it. She pulled out her phone and examined the photos of Bryce's grandfather's journals again while Violet drove. Grandpa Lambert's hand-drawn maps needed a legend. There were *X*'s all over the place, as if he'd searched them and came up empty-handed.

But didn't *X* usually mark the spot?

"I can't tell if Bryce's grandfather searched these spots and ruled them out or what. And if he did search, if he found the treasure, which one marks that? Of course, he may not have found it, but . . . ugh. I asked Bryce, but he didn't know either."

She thought he'd found something, though. Why go to all the trouble to conceal what he knew if there was nothing to hide?

She flipped through the four photos that formed a complete map, looking at each one by one. Theo had them lined up on the wall, but with the photos, it broke the map into four pieces. There were mountains in the background, circles that might be rocks or boulders, trees, water—like a river or stream. "This place could be anywhere," she muttered. "And we're out of time. If the Society gets all three statues and they have the journals, they'll figure the location out before we do."

The ride to their designated spot took about forty-five minutes, and Kira memorized the pictures. She studied them from every angle, upside down, and sideways until they were firmly planted in her memory. If she saw the place in person, she'd recognize it.

Violet turned down a dirt road and found a place to pull off and park the car, out of sight from the main road. They'd hike through the woods from there, until they reached a place where they could observe the house with high-powered binoculars.

Kira zoomed in on the X marks while Violet checked her service weapon. Within the four pages, there were twelve *X*'s. She rotated her phone, checking the various positions of the hand-drawn *X*'s. Some were near water, near rocks, and a few by crudely sketched trees.

She enlarged the photo to the highest magnification and then she saw it. Each *X* had a tiny dot in the center. She flipped through the other pictures. All *X*'s had one pin-prick dot next to the cross mark in the *X*.

All except one. That *X* had three minuscule dots.

Violet got out of the car and grabbed a backpack from the back seat. "I'm going to walk over to that clearing so I can test our comms and check in with the team. I don't want the trees to disrupt the signal. I'll check yours too."

Kira noted where Violet pointed. "Sounds good. I'll join you in a second. I just want to finish reviewing these maps."

She stared at the image on her phone. Had Bryce's grandfather found something at this location? What if he put a dot each time he went to the site? Bryce said he kept handwritten notes of every site he visited. So, had he visited this particular location three times? Maybe? Or had he found three things there? Was she onto something?

She never would have noticed the dots without the ability to enlarge the images.

Violet was right. The drive had given her time to think and study the map. She couldn't wait to tell Bryce. They had to find and search this location.

She jumped out of the car to look for Violet.

A crack hissed through the air, and Kira dove for the ground.

Before she could grab her gun, a hand yanked her up and a damp rag covered her mouth.

THE LOOK OF DISAPPOINTMENT in Kira's eyes haunted him. They were supposed to be partners, and Bryce had cut her from the team. A move that he knew would hurt her. He hoped in time she'd come to realize it was the best decision for the plan, not because he thought she couldn't handle herself. She could. She'd proven it over and over.

He sat in the passenger seat next to Bailey, watching the West Virginia mountain scenery fly by.

He'd miss having Kira at his side, but he'd done what he thought would keep her safe. The fact that it was the best thing for the mission was just a bonus. The Society saw her as a threat. He couldn't save his father. He couldn't even stop his ex-wife from leaving. But he'd die trying to protect Kira. No doubt in his mind.

"Comm check," Bailey said. "We're here."

Here wasn't a very descriptive term for the place. More like middle of nowhere. Forest surrounded the area on all sides of the expansive field. They'd taken a dirt pathway to get to the house. At least he knew Bureau snipers hid in the trees—along with the gun-toting bad guys, he could only assume.

Bryce said a quick prayer for the operation and for Kira's safety as they sat in the car, staring at the dilapidated wood building. It looked like a one-room house, long abandoned and in massive need of repair.

"Who do the Dominiks work for?" Bailey asked. "We know Alex worked for Steadman with the illegal auctions. He helped the man launder money. But is he also taking orders from the Amber Crown Society? We still don't know who is in charge of the organization, other than it might be a woman."

"Anything is possible. But I don't think Alex knows everything. He seems to take orders from someone else. And I don't like the fact that we're sitting ducks out here. Where is Ivan and everyone else?"

No sooner had the words left his mouth than two cars pulled in next to theirs. Ivan jumped out of one car, and Sophia and Alex emerged from the second one. Bryce noticed that Alex didn't have his security team with him. Why wouldn't he bring his hired gun Peter?

Bryce and Bailey stepped out of the sedan. The cool air sent a chill down his spine, but it might be the thought of stepping foot into the abandoned building that had his nerves working overtime.

Three men with guns walked out of the house and approached. Bryce didn't recognize any of them. The burly bearded man with a tattoo running up his thick neck patted down Bryce. The other guy—younger, taller, and skinnier than the first, but just as rough looking—gave Ivan and Bailey a thorough search. Interesting that they didn't pat down Alex and Sophia. More confirmation that they were in way too deep. The third man stood at the door, with a rifle in his hands. The man had weight-lifter muscles, a buzz cut, and a scar above his right eye.

Alex glared at Bryce. "Let's get this over with. I can't believe you betrayed me and took the statue. After I took a risk and got you that invitation to the auction."

Sophia matched Alex's hard stare. "And I just want to get Natalia back."

Ignoring Sophia, Bryce assumed an arrogant attitude and could only pray it was authentic. Kira was the actress. Not him. "That auction was going sideways to our purposes and you know it. I couldn't let Mr. Solinger down."

Bailey sported an expensive suit, looking like he'd just stepped off the cover of a fashion magazine. Tall, lean, but muscular. He folded his arms across his wide chest, ratcheting up his intimidation factor. "Someone please tell me why I had to fly across the country and drive to this barren wasteland?" His eyes shot invisible laser beams at Alex, and even Bryce wanted to flinch.

Alex matched Bailey's hard glare. "I don't even know who you are."

The guard at the door waved his rifle, indicating they should enter the dilapidated house. They all pivoted their view to the front door that had rusted bolts and was hanging on by broken hinges.

Bryce stomped his feet, shaking the dust from his fancy shoes. "We're only doing this so an innocent woman doesn't die. I might take part in illicit art auctions, but I'm no murderer."

Ivan grunted. "You're doing this to protect your boss's reputation. He doesn't want the information I have to be leaked online."

Bailey strode to the back of the sedan and popped the trunk open. He removed a bag and returned to the group still staring at the house. "Let's go get this over with." He marched forward, and Ivan fell in step behind him. Bryce and Alex followed.

Alex's face was pale and his hands were shaking. Fear? Where was his arrogance? His confidence? Did he really care about his maid that much? Maybe the guy wasn't completely heartless after all.

Sophia grabbed Bryce's arm and pulled him aside, while the other men continued to the house. She leaned toward him to whisper. "You have to believe me. I'm not complicit in the Society's affairs. I don't even know who they are."

Bryce shook off her hand. "I don't believe that. You've been doing their bidding this whole time. I can't imagine you don't know who you are working for."

"Don't try to double-cross these men. You won't win. I didn't. Your wife certainly won't come out of this alive. They want her dead."

Rage seethed. "Katrina had nothing to do with this. I took advantage of the blackout and stole the statue. Solinger is paying us a hefty price."

One of the gunmen grunted for them to move, and Sophia stomped toward the door of the house. "Just don't say I didn't warn you."

Bryce stepped onto the stairs with the splintered boards and rusty nails. The three guards brought up the rear. He followed Sophia and moved through the front entrance into the main room of the house and stopped short.

Natalia was tied to a chair. And gagged. A man in a ski mask pointed a gun at her temple. She wriggled and tried to scream, but the cloth shoved in her mouth and tied around her head muted most sound. The fear in her eyes begged him to do something.

"The statue." The man swung the gun from Natalia to Bryce and then Bailey. "Put it on the fireplace mantel."

Bailey's face hardened. "Release your hostage. I want her to walk out of the cabin before I give you what you want."

"You don't call the shots."

Bailey took out the statue from the satchel on his shoulder and held it in front of him. "Let her go. Now."

The man returned the gun to Natalia and pulled the trigger. The woman slumped over in the chair, blood streaming down her face.

Sophia's scream pierced the air. Bryce flinched and looked away from Natalia's lifeless body.

Game over. With that one shot, the situation flipped. Outside the cabin, the FBI was now prepping for a raid instead of a surveillance op.

The masked man pointed the gun at Bailey. "Now, you have something I want and I will be taking it."

The man's lean but muscular frame seemed familiar. However, it was the gun with the silencer that filled in the blanks for him.

The gallery attendant. Vince Palmer. The assassin. The same man he'd encountered in the woods behind the brownstone. But hadn't he and Natalia looked cozy at the gallery? Had Vince used the housekeeper to get close to the Dominiks?

Bryce stepped forward. "We know who you are, Vince. You can stop pretending and take the mask off."

To Bryce's surprise, the man did. "You know nothing. My name is Victor Baranov. And here is where your journey ends, Brian Beckett."

Ivan flinched but covered it with a cough. Good to know the Russians hadn't figured out Bryce's real identity.

Victor stared Bailey down. "Give. Me. The. Statue."

"No way. The deal is off," Bailey said, shoving the statue back in his bag.

Bryce's pulse spiked. One wrong move and this room would turn into a kill box.

At Victor's nod, the body builder with the buzz cut grabbed Sophia and shoved her toward the window, gun raised to her temple. Sophia shrieked and cringed away from the weapon.

"Something's wrong," the man said and swung his gaze to Victor. "We need to get out of here."

Bryce didn't know what set the man off, but if they didn't do something soon, Sophia was dead. He could see it in the guy's shifty eyes.

"Maybe killing her will compel you to be more cooperative." Victor nodded to the man holding Sophia. "Do it."

The front door exploded inward, splinters spraying the floor. A flash-bang erupted—light, noise, concussive force swallowing the room.

"FBI! Drop your weapons!"

Sophia and Alex bolted out the front door, with Ivan on their heels. Bryce and Bailey hit the floor. Gunfire rang out—short, controlled bursts from outside as the SWAT team engaged.

The Russians staggered back, spraying wild rounds that shattered glass and tore into drywall.

Bryce started to crawl to Bailey when the icy press of steel touched his neck.

"Don't move," Victor hissed. "Or you're dead."

Bryce raised his hands slowly, just high enough to catch Bailey's attention. But Bailey lay motionless on the floor. No blood. His chest rose and fell ever so slightly. Pretending to be unconscious? Bryce's pulse hammered as the firefight raged around them.

One of the gunmen ripped the bag from Bailey's shoulder and tossed it to Victor.

Bryce slowly stood but didn't dare turn his head to face his captor. "What do you want?"

"You."

Victor shoved Bryce toward the doorway of what used to be the kitchen area of the house. At least Bailey wasn't wounded, but he had no weapon to stop Victor.

How far could Victor get with agents surrounding them?

Another shove and Bryce held out his hands to keep from toppling over. He grasped the edge of the doorframe to the kitchen, but the wood piece came off in his hand.

"Move," the gruff voice said. A bullet whizzed by Bryce's head and exploded in the wall next to him. He moved into the ancient kitchen, complete with a stove from the early 1900s. This place was a historical gem, except for all the fresh bullet holes. The three other gunmen continued to return fire out a broken kitchen window.

Did these guys really think they were getting away?

Bryce stared at the doorway at the end of the galley-style kitchen. Victor shoved him forward, and he grabbed the rail to keep from plunging down the dark, very unstable-looking wood stairs.

Oh. These guys really *were* going to get away.

The FBI hadn't had time to do a full reconnaissance on the area. If they had, they'd have noted the underground tunnel leading away from the house. Or maybe this area wasn't even on anyone's radar. Who knew how long this place had been there.

This house had been picked because of the escape tunnel.

Bryce crept down the not-so-stable stairs until he hit the rock-and-dirt floor of the hidden passageway. His captor aimed the beam of a flashlight into the area, and Bryce had to duck to fit. Roots and dirt covered the ceiling, and he could reach out and touch the walls on either side.

He inhaled a mouthful of dry dust and coughed. Why did these people want Brian Beckett? They'd left Levi Solinger, the billionaire, on the floor.

He crawled through the underground cavern, thoughts on Kira even as the sound of bullets hitting the walls from upstairs reached him. Had Kira rushed in with the other agents? *Please keep her safe, God.*

"Faster, faster" came a nasally voice from behind them. The three other gunmen were right on their tail. He prayed the FBI knew about this secret tunnel—or at least could find it fast.

Up ahead, streams of light poked through the dirt and earth. They approached a door, and the guard with the meaty arms pushed past him and shoved it open. Bryce blinked at the bright light.

He ascended the steps and followed the man out into a wooded area. Echoes of voices and the occasional gunfire rang out in the distance. But there was no one around.

"What now?" Bryce asked. He had no weapon, and it was now four against one.

Headlights cut through the trees, casting shadows from the thick foliage at the perimeter of the property before coming into view. Was Kira out there somewhere watching this go down? She might be his only hope in having the FBI pinpoint his location.

The men marched him toward the approaching vehicle. Ice pulsated through his veins. If he left with his captors, he'd disappear forever. Just like the treasure room would if these men got ahold of it.

A gun pressed into his back and forced Bryce to move to the back of the car.

No. Not the trunk. Not the—

The trunk popped open and inside was a body, bound and gagged.

His heart stopped.

Kira!

20

THE BRIGHT LIGHT HURT Kira's already thumping head. She tried to reach up and shield her shut eyes, when she realized her hands were bound in front of her with duct tape.

Where . . . what . . . how? She couldn't even form coherent thoughts. *Think!* She remembered hitting the ground at the sound of gunfire.

She attempted to feel around, but the duct tape on her hands and legs prevented her from any wide movements. The surface beneath her scratched her skin.

Carpet?

Something thudded and slammed into her. She finally opened her eyes and squinted.

A body? Was it Violet?

The screechy sound of duct tape being unrolled meant they were binding the person who now lay next to her. It was a man in a suit, who had what looked like brown hair. The lighting wasn't great even with the lid open.

The trunk slammed shut, plunging her into darkness again.

"Kira?"

The voice brought tears to her eyes as he removed the gag from her mouth.

"Bryce! What happened?"

He shifted his position and reached over to grab her bound hands with his. She took comfort in his touch.

"It was a total ambush," he said. "Three gunmen and the art gallery attendant, whose real name is Victor Baranov, outmaneuvered us. Victor shot Natalia and demanded the statue. The next thing I know, I'm being shoved through an underground tunnel. They want me alive, apparently."

"Someone must have followed Violet and me. She'd left the car to get into position, and I was so absorbed in studying your grandfather's map that I didn't notice anyone behind us. Do you know if she's okay?"

"I didn't see Violet, but I don't think they want her. I'm a valuable target because they have the journal but probably have no idea what the notes mean. They'll want me to decipher my grandfather's writing."

"Well, I figured a few things out, so we have a bargaining chip at least. But if these men killed Natalia in cold blood, they won't leave witnesses alive. We're expendable once they locate the fortune. Hopefully Violet made it to safety."

The car jostled, and Bryce bumped into her. "I think we're not on pavement anymore," Kira said, missing Bryce's touch when their hands fell apart.

A hard bounce and Kira whacked her head on the side. Bryce covered her with his bound arms in an effort to steady both of them.

Steady. A perfect description for the man. Bryce's presence, his no-nonsense attitude, his stoic countenance and occasional subtle humor, all added up to a sense of security that she hadn't felt in—well, her entire life. Even when the Millers had adopted her, she continued to struggle with the notion that she had to be exactly what they wanted her to be or they might take her back to Russia. That her dream home with parents hung by a thread, based on her performance. Of course, the Millers never set any of these expectations, but Kira couldn't destroy old childhood lies to see that truth.

But with Bryce, things were different. She could be herself and he didn't judge her for that. Of course, they might die soon, and any life-altering conclusions about herself didn't matter if they couldn't get free. "Thank you," she whispered.

"For what? I should apologize to you. I didn't want to cut you off the team like that. We're partners, and I know how much my actions hurt."

"I'm not upset about that. I'm thankful that you understand the why. That you allow me to be myself and don't judge me. You are the one person I don't have to perform for."

She could feel his thumping heartbeat against her cheek. "You told me God wants us to come as we are," she said. "That we don't have to try and fix ourselves first. I think you're right. God is the only way I'll ever find peace. I don't have to perform for him. I'm done trying to please everyone."

Tears stung her eyes, and she tried to wipe them on the scratchy carpet without success. She had an entire seven-piece luggage set of emotional baggage to unpack after this ordeal was over. Assuming she lived to do so. But for now things started to settle in her heart—the one place she'd refused anyone access.

Including God.

She sucked in a breath. "Okay, emotional Hallmark movie moment over. What's the plan to get us out of here?"

He groaned when he tried to shift positions. "We'll have to wait for them to open the trunk. I'm not getting anywhere trying to find a sharp edge in here that can cut through this duct tape."

Kira snuggled against Bryce, and he put his bound hands over her head and around her shoulders in a half hug.

After what seemed like an eternity but was probably a few minutes, the car lurched to a stop. Muted voices filtered into the trunk from the outside.

"I guess it's showtime." Bryce untangled his arms.

Kira tried to move herself into a position where she might kick someone once the trunk lid opened, but who was she kidding? With her feet bound, she'd never get enough force behind any type of kick.

The trunk lid creaked open, and two hard faces stared at her and Bryce. Rifles pointed at them, then hands yanked them out and half carried, half dragged them to the front of the car.

Victor stood in the headlights of the vehicle, one hand on the hood and the other on his weapon. Another car pulled up, and Peter, Alex's head of security, stepped out.

"Guess we know who followed me," Kira whispered. The guy must be playing both sides, assuming Alex wasn't part of the Amber Crown Society.

Kira surveyed her surroundings. Nothing but shadows and trees. Night had fallen, and they were as off-grid as they could get. She shivered, thankful they hadn't taken Violet's coat. Or Violet. It seemed they wanted her and spared Violet. Hopefully her roommate wasn't hurt.

The dirt road continued on, but Victor had made himself a parking spot in the one patch of grass that wasn't covered in foliage.

And the temperature continued to drop. She snuggled her chin deeper into the collar of the coat and wished for Bryce's arms around her.

"Let's get down to business, shall we?" Victor's Russian accent was now pronounced. "You two will lead me to the treasure."

He waved two flashlights over the hood of the car, which was covered in papers.

And Grandpa Lambert's journals.

"Well, we're going to need our legs and hands free for that," Kira said. "Where are we going to run to? We're in the middle of nowhere."

Victor pointed at the burly Russian guard with the snake tattoo running up his neck. "Boris, undo their bonds." He turned to the other gunman, the younger guy with a mean scowl. "Rolan, keep that gun trained on these two. Shoot them if they so much as flinch." Both men complied.

Another man emerged from the car and stood by Peter, his gun also trained on Kira and Bryce. This guy had a buzz cut and muscular arms.

Free hands and feet created an opportunity to fight back if given the chance, but Kira didn't have a plan. With five against two, the odds weren't in their favor. Besides, she had no idea where they were. She assumed the dark shape looming over them that blocked the moonlight was a mountain.

At least Bryce was there. She grasped his cold hand and looked down at the documents. Victor passed them flashlights.

"These are the original journals," Bryce whispered. "I thought I'd never see them again." He touched the soft cover of a notebook.

"Get started. Find the location." Victor's commanding voice sent shudders down Kira's spine. How much should she reveal? This was their only bargaining chip.

"Do you have a real map by any chance?" Kira asked.

Victor stuck his hand in the bag slung across his chest and pulled out a folded map of the area. He handed it to her and lingered. A little too close. No way could she work while this man hovered.

"Can you give us a few minutes to review these? Brian hasn't even seen the journals, since someone ran us off the road and stole them."

When he took a few steps back, Kira opened the journal to the pages with the hand-drawn map. Then she picked up the real map. "I didn't realize they still made these," she muttered, unfolding the accordion-shaped paper and spreading it over the car hood.

She studied the pages in the journal and pointed to the *X* she'd noted earlier. Bryce leaned in closer to examine it. What if she was wrong? But she lined up the water marks that Grandpa Lambert had drawn and matched it up on the physical map.

"Crystal Lake," she murmured.

"Yeah." Bryce leaned closer to the map. "Here's Crystal Mountain with the lake next to it."

The *X* with three dots rested between them, in front of what looked like a boulder.

"But why here?" Bryce asked, keeping his voice low since Victor was within earshot.

"Three dots in the center of the *X*."

"Wait, the dots." He tapped the map. "Yeah. I remember now. Grandpa would put an *X* over the areas he checked, then some sort of tally mark for areas he'd revisit."

"This spot has three. I suspect he found something."

Victor inserted himself between Bryce and Kira. "What did you find?"

If she gave Victor the information, they were expendable. If she picked the wrong location, they were dead.

Bryce made the decision for her. "Based on this *X*, I believe my grandfather found something at this location."

Victor ripped the map from his hand. "Let's go." He used his satellite phone to make a call. She translated the Russian in her head and heard him give the caller the exact GPS coordinates for the spot on the map. Then he requested reinforcements.

Victor shoved them into the back seat of the sedan. Boris jumped in the passenger seat, and they took off. Peter, Rolan, and the nameless third lackey raced to Peter's vehicle to follow.

Whoever was on the other end of the call also knew about the location.

And they'd just given up their only bargaining chip.

BRYCE TRIED TO THINK of a way out of this, but with five armed men and the fact that they were in the middle of nowhere, the options of escape diminished with each step he took. They'd reached the point where they had to approach on foot and now walked along the edge of the lakeshore toward the rock face of the mountain. Shadows flickered under his flashlight beam as he lit the dirt and rocky path in front of him.

No tourists would dare to camp here. Even experienced hikers wouldn't venture this far out into the wilderness. There was such a thing as being too far off the grid. The nearest convenience store or gas station was at least thirty miles away. The only sounds were shuffling feet kicking up the dirt, leaves, and rocks as they trudged forward. Boris and Peter led the pack, followed by Bryce and Kira. Victor and the other two armed men were right on their heels.

Kira stumbled on a root and Bryce reached out to steady her. The gunman with thick arms and a buzz cut prodded her with his gun to keep her moving ahead. Bryce had heard someone call the guy Nick earlier.

Bryce tried to get a good view of what was around them, but it was too dark outside the light cast by the flashlights. "Are you a member of the Amber Crown Society, Victor?" he asked.

The man grunted. "It is our mission to return the Amber Room to its rightful owners. The bloodline of Catherine the Great."

Interesting. So this wasn't the work of the Russian mafia or any government-sanctioned group. The ACS wanted the treasure for themselves, based on a connection to their history.

Just like the Collector who hid the art to keep it safe.

"Did you kill Derek?"

Another snort. "He got too greedy. Sent a private investigator after us and threatened a lawsuit to claim that he rightfully owned the statues."

"Is Sophia in the Society?" Everly had thought that a woman was in charge.

"Of course not. She and Alex were a means to an end. They just helped us get access to the statues."

"Did you kill Theo?" Kira's voice held notes of fatigue.

No answer.

Victor sighed. "Theo became a liability," he finally said. "No more questions."

Bryce scanned the darkness, hoping for any signs of life. As Victor shone his flashlight around the area in front of them, Bryce caught a glint of something in a clearing off to their left side.

"Katrina," he whispered. "Check out the area over there." He pointed his light to reveal some kind of metal structure. The area had no trees or shrubbery around, indicating someone must have cleared the land.

"What is that?" Kira said while she ran her light up the side of the tall, man-made structure. Rust-colored crossbeams created almost a ladder effect, reaching high up over the tree line.

"It looks like a windmill," Victor said and trudged toward the source. The gunmen at their back never moved.

In the clearing next to a shadowy pile of tall boulders stacked up near the mountain's base, their lights uncovered a windmill—that appeared to be working. Wide silver turbines at the top spun lazily in the still air.

"Now why would someone put this here if they weren't protecting something?" Victor kept his light on the object.

He was right. Someone was generating power in the middle of nowhere, which meant they were close.

Kira moved toward the stacked rocks. She climbed and examined the area with the flashlight. Bryce followed, keeping one eye on the ever-watching gunmen. If they could get a few feet away, maybe they could run.

She shone her light at a crack in the rocks. When she clicked off her flashlight, flickers of light still shone from behind the rocks.

"I see light." Bryce edged across the rocks and loose stone shifted beneath his boots. A dark gap yawned between the boulders, shadows pressed close around it—except for that faint shimmer bleeding through. Light.

Victor hovered, scraping Bryce's nerves. He'd like to knock the man flat on his back, but the other gunmen kept him in check. Peter had backtracked, probably making sure they weren't followed. At least that was one less goon to worry about.

"It's an entryway." Victor pointed his gun at Kira. "You go through."

Bryce went with her, even though Victor spoke to Kira. No way was she leaving his sight.

They squeezed between the rocks, which opened up into what appeared to be a wide hallway. "Wait, these are stairs." Kira's voice echoed off the rock walls. "Someone carved stone steps that lead into a cave." From the outside, no one would ever notice. They proceeded down the ten steps that rounded like a medieval spiral staircase with stone walls.

His grandfather had been so close to this place and yet missed the entrance. The craftsmanship was impressive. But none of that would matter if this cave became their coffin.

The end of the stairs opened into an atrium of sorts. It was definitely a cave, but the area had a smooth stone floor—and lights?

Lightbulbs shone from two lanterns that hung on the rock wall. Victor shoved Bryce to the side to inspect. "This entire place is wired for electricity."

Bryce circled the area and touched the wall made of gray stones. The two lanterns hung on either side of the wall, as if announcing the presence of a door or entryway. He ran his hand along the surface but found nothing. "These rocks were used to build this wall. Why light the area if there isn't an entrance?"

Kira took three steps back. "Don't touch anything. There could be booby traps. If they hid information in the statues about finding the entrance, then they wanted their secrets well kept."

Vince scoffed at her. "Please. Fenton was a moron."

Bryce saw no outline of a door, or anything that might suggest a hidden panel. The two lamps indicated something more was here. But what?

He tried to keep an eye on everyone in the enclosed area. Peter hadn't returned, and the three guards flanked the one entryway. Victor circled the area, inspecting the wall.

Kira continued to study the area, taking small steps and examining every crevice. She finally stopped, sighed, and turned to their captor. "What do we do now, Victor? We don't know where the treasure is."

"You are going to figure it out, Kira. You and your *husband*. You're both highly dedicated federal agents so get to work."

Bryce's heart pumped ice through his veins. Victor knew the truth. "How did you find out?"

Victor grunted. "It took us a while. Your agents did a nice job with those fake profiles online. But information is always for sale, and we found out William Lambert had a son—in the FBI. It didn't take us long to figure out both of your identities from there with our connections. You think you're the only ones with expert hackers on your payroll? But as of now, you work for the Society."

Bryce made a mental note to track down that leak in their organization. "Right. And why should we help you?"

Rustling came from outside the cave. And voices? Great. Victor had called for reinforcements. He wouldn't keep Bryce and Kira alive past their usefulness.

Two new guards entered the room—increasing the firepower to five armed fighters. They dragged two people into the area with them. Alex and Sophia.

"The Dominiks will die in three minutes if you don't get me access to the treasure room." Victor's voice echoed around them. "You weren't willing to let Natalia die, so I'm sure you will want to rescue your neighbors by finding the door."

Bryce inched his way to place himself between Kira and Victor. "We need the statues. You're going to kill us all anyway. Give us the statues and we'll figure out how to get in." Or stall until backup arrived.

Please, God, let backup find us.

Victor shrugged the bag off his shoulder and held it out to Bryce. He took it, never breaking eye contact.

Sophia whimpered, and the guard shoved her to the ground. Alex wrestled free from his captor and knelt by his wife. "We did everything you asked. Where is our son?"

Bryce's eyes bounced to Alex. The man trembled from cold—or rage? "Your son?" he asked.

"They kidnapped our ten-year-old son right out of his bedroom one night." Alex's voice cracked. "Forced us to come to the United States and collect the statues. They won't release him until they have the treasure."

One of the new armed guards shoved Alex to the floor. "Enough talking." The sound of a gun cocking brought Bryce's attention back to the bag in his hand.

The statues.

He lifted each figure out of the bag and placed them on top of the flat rock next to him. The little bunnies stared back at him. It was hard to believe these ugly little statues had cost people their lives.

All three were reunited. The ACS had found the lost ones. Each statue was the same shape and size. While the original Zaika had two long ears sticking straight up, the new rabbits had shorter ears, each with a different length.

But now what?

Kira shoved the flashlight into her pocket to inspect the area and ran her fingers along the smooth stone. Bryce didn't see a seam or any indication that the wall would open.

Victor moved next to Bryce and placed the gun against his head. "Where is the treasure room, Kira? Open the door or your *husband* dies."

21

KIRA NEEDED TO BUY TIME.

Not only did she need to figure out where Fenton had hidden an ancient treasure room, she still held out hope that the FBI might rescue them.

"The rabbits are the key," she said. Kira picked up one of the statues and thought of the history she held in her hand. But only for a second, because Bryce's life depended on her figuring out a way to the treasure.

Victor grabbed another statue. "What do you mean?"

"Fenton told his son that the rabbits were the key."

While the guards kept their weapons trained on the Dominiks and the rest of them, Kira searched the wall and stones for anything that resembled a keyhole. Victor joined her, which meant the gun wasn't trained on Bryce for the moment.

She ran her hand over the surface of the wall. All the stones were solid, not moving when she pressed on them.

Except one.

She hated that Victor might get to the treasure first. But if she didn't share her find, this cave would double as a mass grave for the four of them. "Found something." She pulled the loose stone out of the wall. The man aimed his flashlight into the rectangular opening.

"Keyholes," Kira said.

Three copper disks contained two holes each in the exact shape of the rabbit ears. "The ears have grooves on them. I think they fit into this mechanism."

Victor hovered so close she could smell his breath. She lined up Zaika with the deeper set of holes, and the ears slid into place. The base and body of the statue stuck out, looking almost like a doorknob or handle. She used the statue to rotate the dial and heard a faint click.

What in the Indiana Jones was going on? Fenton and his family had created an elaborate system for protecting their art.

And then never told anyone about it.

Victor added the other two statues and turned the dials.

They waited.

Victor pointed his finger in Kira's face. "If this is some kind of trick—"

Kira held her breath and prayed.

A pop sounded, then a creak.

And then a rumble.

The wall between the two lanterns rolled to the right like a sliding glass door to reveal a tunnel. She looked at Bryce. Her eyes had to be as wide as his. Several people called Fenton eccentric. And this proved it.

"The Collector upgraded his game over the years. That was pretty high tech." Kira peered through the opening but saw only darkness. Should they enter or insist on the release of hostages first? Did she and Bryce have any bargaining power?

And did the FBI know where they were?

Victor took charge. "I'm going in and taking Kira and Sophia. You men won't do anything to jeopardize the lives of the women you love."

Love?

Although Kira had met Bryce mere days ago, she could see herself falling for him. If she hadn't already. But did he feel the same? She could only pray she lived to find out.

"No." Bryce stood and faced the man. "Take me."

Victor raised his gun and fired. Someone screamed. Bryce grabbed his shoulder. Blood seeped through his fingers. Kira clamped a hand over her mouth.

No. No. No. Please, Lord, don't let Bryce die. Not when we just found each other.

She raced toward Bryce, but an arm caught her and dragged her to the tunnel. Victor shoved her through the opening. She stumbled and fell to the ground, landing on her hip. Pain flared.

Using his flashlight, Victor found a button on the inside wall. He pressed it and lights illuminated a pathway. Then, at Victor's nod, a gunman handed Sophia off to him, and he pulled her into the passageway as Kira rose to her feet. He pressed another button, and the wall started to slide back into place.

"No!" Kira attempted to race through the closing entryway. Victor shoved Sophia toward her. Sophia fell, blocking her way, and the wall closed with a thud, trapping the three of them on one side.

"Get up," Victor said to Sophia, who sat on the ground sobbing.

Kira wanted to join her on the floor and cry. Instead, she stuffed her feelings into a mental compartment and forced herself to focus on staying alive. And helping Sophia do the same.

She pulled the sniffling woman to her feet. "Stop crying," Kira said, keeping her voice soft. "It won't help get us out of this." If Victor heard her, he didn't bother responding. The place had lights embedded into the wall on one side that gave them just enough light to see. A tunnel, carved into the mountain, lay straight ahead of them. Kira pulled out the mini Maglite and shone its powerful beam around the area. At least Victor had let her keep it. Too bad it wasn't big enough to make an effective weapon.

Sophia whimpered, and Kira found her heart had softened a bit toward the woman. Someone had kidnapped her son. The Society had blackmailed them into doing their dirty work. While Alex may have been involved in the smuggling ring, no one deserved to have their child stolen in the middle of the night.

"Move," Victor yelled from behind them. He hung back, planning to let them take the brunt of any booby traps.

Kira and Sophia pushed forward through the stone corridor. The eccentric Young family had taken it upon themselves to preserve art from war, but they hadn't made it easy for anyone to find.

"I'm so sorry." Sophia sniffled. "They made me be a distraction to your husband. They planned on taking pictures of him and me and blackmailing him. Before they knew who he really was. But I guess he's not really your husband."

The words stung, but Kira had no idea why. She and Bryce weren't married—that was true. But the last reaction she expected to that statement was sadness. She shook it off. "I'm sorry they took your son. I'll do my best to help bring him back. I have resources." She checked over her shoulder. Victor was shining his flashlight along the walls.

"Look out!" Sophia pulled Kira to an abrupt halt.

Kira stared down and gasped. One more step and she would have fallen into a black hole. She shuddered and swallowed a surge of nausea. "Thank you," she whispered.

Victor waved his light around a cavern. The light never reached the top or the bottom.

The tunnel ended. Below them was inky blackness.

She pulled a bottle of hand sanitizer from her pocket and tossed it into the hole, waiting for a splash or thunk when it hit the bottom. But all she heard was her own ragged breaths. More nausea churned. The cavern was deep. Even with her flashlight and the ambient lighting from the cave's wind-powered lights, the only thing she could see was darkness. No shapes or shadows.

Just emptiness.

A splash of water hit her face and she wiped her brow and listened. The faint sound of water reached her from . . . somewhere. But she couldn't see the source.

Victor shoved her aside. "Where is it? Where is the treasure?"

She needed to keep her distance from him, but the ledge wasn't big. If Victor got mad, she and Sophia might wind up knocked into the abyss. His desperation came through in his frantic movements. She needed to keep him from becoming unhinged with a gun.

"There has to be something here," Kira said, keeping her voice soothing, praying she kept her terror hidden. "Otherwise why protect it with complicated keys?" She continued to explore the cavern, passing her light over every surface. The lamps ended in the tunnel, and it was hard to make out anything in the dark cave.

Finally, a glimmer reflected back. She focused the light in the area. The ledge extended along the rock wall, and she saw the outline of something to her left, hanging across the chasm. "There," she said. "What's that?"

Victor hovered next to her as they stared at the most unstable-looking bridge that connected one side of the cavern to the other.

With nothing underneath it but darkness.

Victor stopped, turned, and nodded at Kira, then at the ancient structure. Her hand trembled and she tightened her grip on the flashlight. She knew what was coming.

Victor was going to force her to go across that death trap.

The bridge had single wood panels for steps, about a foot wide with another foot-wide gap between each board. The thick brown rope holding the boards in place appeared to be sturdy, but the bridge swayed even with no air circulating through the cavern. Bolts anchored the ropes to the cave wall on either end.

"This must lead to the treasure room," Victor said, eyeing the rickety contraption. "There must be another door on the other side. I think there is a ledge like this one on the other side as well."

With both flashlights aimed at the bridge, she counted twenty steps across.

Kira aimed her light in the area at the end of the rope bridge. If she squinted, she could see the faint outline of a doorway in the rugged rock. Or was it her imagination? Either way, her stomach sank at the prospect of crossing that thing.

As if reading her mind, Victor aimed his gun at her. "You're going to cross and find out for us."

BRYCE SUCKED IN A DEEP BREATH. Fire shot through his shoulder, reminding him he was alive. His mission came back to him with crystal clarity. Save Kira.

Pain sliced through his arm. His head pounded. "Ow."

"Hold still," a voice said. "I'm trying to bandage you up. The bullet nicked you, so I'm trying to stop the blood. But you hit your head when you fell. Our captors are standing guard at the entrance, but at least they left us alone for a few minutes."

Memories pierced through the fog in his mind. They were in a cave, in the middle of nowhere. Armed men. A buried treasure. And he thought he'd heard a scream.

"Kira!" He sat up and regretted it.

"Hold still." Alex was on the ground with him, wrapping his shoulder with material torn from the man's own shirt.

"So now I'm supposed to believe you are one of the good guys?" He squinted at Alex, who had flecks of blood in his beard. Bryce's blood.

The man sighed, the sound echoing in the locked chamber room of the cave. "I've done some bad things and worked for some very bad people. I hired Ivan to help me find my son. He was going to steal the statues to give us a bargaining chip. It's my fault." The man's voice broke. "I should never have started working for Victor. But the money was good. I had never met the man until the auction. I had always taken calls from a woman."

Alex applied pressure on the wound and Bryce winced. "Thank you, Alex."

He nodded. "I'm going to need you alive to help me get Sophia back. I'm relieved you are FBI and not a criminal art dealer."

Alex helped Bryce to his feet, and he braced against the wall for support until his head stopped spinning.

Alex pointed to the rock wall. "The door closed behind Victor, Kira, and Sophia. One of the men—Peter, my supposed security guard—took one of the statues. I think the rest of the men are waiting for more people to arrive, now that they may be close to finding the treasure room."

Bryce studied Alex. "They had their own men as your security?"

He nodded. "We were prisoners in our home. They watched our every move. But I never suspected Peter."

"We've got to get that statue back," Bryce said. He was going after Kira.

He swayed and went to his knees to keep from falling. Alex put his hand on Bryce's good shoulder and gave him a gentle shove to go the rest of the way to the ground. "You'll be more useful if the guard thinks you are still out cold. Maybe you can get the jump on him."

Footsteps and voices filtered through the cave. Bryce had to admit that Alex's plan made sense. Kira needed him, and this might be his best bet for getting the statue back. He lay on the ground with his arm over his eyes, attempting to look like he was unconscious.

Heavy boots stomped into the area, kicking up dirt and pebbles from the stone floor of the entryway to the cave. A boot connected with his ribs and rocked him, and Bryce bit his cheek to keep from wincing.

"Has this guy been out the whole time?" a gravelly voice asked.

It was Peter.

"Yes," Alex replied. "I bandaged his wound. No sense in letting the guy bleed to death. But he never regained consciousness."

Bryce dared to open his eyes into slits. Thick, black work boots clunked to the center of the room and joined a newcomer. The person was covered head to toe in a black cloak, a creepy druid look from ancient times. Fitting for their current situation that resembled an Indiana Jones movie. Only Bryce was no Indy and he needed a plan.

Alex gasped but said nothing. He clearly recognized the new person.

"So what are we waiting for?" the feminine voice asked.

This had to be the woman in charge.

Bryce wasn't daring any movement to try and peek at her face. But the voice stilled him. Why did she sound so familiar?

More shuffling of feet echoed through the chamber. Bryce dared to tilt his head up.

Boris and Rolan flanked the entrance to the cave with rifles slung over their shoulders. The two new gunmen had disappeared, presumably stationed outside. Looked like the Society had plenty of reinforcements on the inside and outside.

He prayed for a miracle.

Nick paced at the wall that contained the secret passageway. "We need the key, Peter."

Peter's thick boots clomped to the control panel, and Bryce watched him pull the missing statue from the deep pocket of his tactical pants.

Bryce's mind spun out different plans of attack. He had to stop them from entering the corridor, because it meant Kira would have more adversaries to contend with. Currently, he and Alex were trapped with four gunmen—the original three and Peter. They also had to contend with Victor and this druid woman. He'd worry about the number of gunmen outside when he made his way to freedom—which seemed like a dream at this point.

Peter inserted the missing rabbit key and turned the base. Bryce used this distraction to his advantage and looked at Alex, who nodded and mouthed, *Go time.*

Bryce heard a pop, and the door rumbled open. He had to get to the opening.

Alex whacked Boris in the face with his forearm, sending the man reeling in pain. Blood poured from the most likely broken nose. But Rolan kicked Alex in the stomach, and he fell to his knees.

Bryce swung his legs and connected with Nick's knees. The man hit the ground and Bryce flipped over, caught the guy in a choke hold until he passed out. He grabbed the pistol, stood, and found himself staring down the barrel of Peter's gun.

"Not so fast." Peter sneered. Bryce froze and watched the woman in black robes duck through the moving rock wall as it was closing. Hydraulics hissed as it sealed into place. Peter had given the woman just enough time to disappear through the entrance.

And now Bryce stared at the closed rock wall.

Kira. He *had* to save her. But first he and Alex had to contend with Peter and Rolan.

"Drop your weapon." Peter glared at Bryce, who matched his stare.

Bryce wasn't giving up so easily. But when Alex flinched from the gun pressed into his neck, Bryce tossed the gun to the side and held up his hands.

Peter may have won the round, but he'd not win the prize.

A gunshot echoed in the distance. Was that the good guys coming to the rescue or just more of Victor's reinforcements? It was all the distraction Bryce needed. He threw himself to the side and rammed into Rolan, knocking him away from Alex.

Peter ran to the rock wall and grabbed two of the statues from the keyhole, then raced for the mouth of the cave. Was the man crazy enough to make a run for it with the statues?

Rolan was scrappy, fit, and younger than Bryce. The guy managed to stay on his feet and retaliated with a kick to Bryce's already sore side. Stars danced in front of his eyes, but he gritted his teeth and dove for the gun with his uninjured arm. Before he could grab it, Rolan gave him another hard kick in the side. Those boots must be made of metal, and Bryce's body screamed in protest. He looked up and saw Rolan swinging his leg for another kick to Bryce's gut, but the man stopped.

Alex had jumped on Rolan's back and wrapped his arms around the guard's thick neck. Rolan stumbled backward, smashing Alex into the rocks, but he didn't let go until Rolan had dropped to his knees, gasping for breath.

Another loud blast rocked the area and the ground trembled. Rolan collapsed to the ground and Alex stood.

"Thanks, man," Bryce said, and Alex offered a hand to help him stand. "You saved my life."

"We may have more trouble. I hear noises outside. They must have called in more reinforcements. And Peter ran with two of the statues. Coward."

"Freeze! FBI! We have the place surrounded!"

Bryce grinned. "Not bad guys, Alex. The good guys." He called out, "All clear inside."

"Until they arrest me for all my work with the art smugglers." Alex's face paled and he put a hand on Bryce's shoulder. "Please, I have only one request. I don't care what happens to me. Please rescue Sophia. And my son."

Alex's fierce eyes indicated he was ready to continue the fight. Desperation to save one's child could do that for a person.

Agents swarmed the cave. Violet entered and made a beeline for Bryce. Other agents took care of the three on the ground.

"Not bad work for just you," Violet said, surveying the cave.

"Alex helped me. But how did you find us?"

"Ahh. My roommates make fun of me for putting AirTags on everything. I remembered Kira grabbed my coat before she was kidnapped, so I was able to trace her location. It took some time to get a team in place, but we made it just in time by the looks of it. But where is Kira?" The stress in Violet's face matched his own.

Bryce pointed to the solid rock wall. "She's behind this secret door. The statues are the keys to open it. Did you see Peter outside?"

Violet's face paled at the realization this wasn't over. "An agent shot a gunman before we had the place surrounded. But he couldn't have gotten far."

Not good. "Peter stole two of the statues and ran. We have to get that door open. Kira needs us. We have to find Peter."

22

THE SMELL OF DAMP EARTH made Kira's nose itch, and the idea of stepping onto a rickety wooden bridge crossing a bottomless cavern sent her pulse through the roof. She'd managed to stall up to this point by getting on her knees and testing the first few steps with her hands, then tugging on the ropes. But now Victor was losing patience, and she was going to have to cross.

At least she didn't have a fear of heights. Much. Crossing the bridge over the pitch-black yawning hole might change that.

Victor jabbed the gun into Sophia's temple, eliciting a cry from the woman. The only option for Kira was across the cavern. Maybe if she got to the other side first, she could find something to use as a weapon, or lock herself in another room until help arrived.

"Don't give this pig what he wants," Sophia shouted.

Victor slapped Sophia, and she fell to the ground. He pointed his pistol at Kira and nodded to the bridge. "Go."

"Don't yell at me if you want me to do this," she said. She moved toward the rocks behind her and ran her hand along the jagged surface. If only she could find . . .

"Lights." She pressed the button, and lights built into the rocks shone along the ledge that led to the bridge. Enough so she could see the rickety, old rope bridge swinging slightly in the draft of the cave. It also turned on a light across the cavern, so she could see the destination, which was another tunnel.

There had to be an easier way to access the treasure room—a back door? Some kind of service entrance? A low hum from the other side of the bottomless pit caught her attention. There had to be power running through the entire cave. The art needed to be kept cool, otherwise the humidity would destroy it.

So why did it have to be this bridge?

Kira pocketed her flashlight, stood at the base of the bridge, and prayed. It would take a miracle for her to get across this. She thought of Bryce and it fortified her courage. Every step she took would mean she was that much closer to seeing him again.

She tried to block the gruesome scenarios swirling in her mind—most of which had her free-falling into the abyss below. Once she committed to a step, she'd have to go for it. No way to test it.

Kira put her full weight on the first plank and held her breath. The wood creaked but held.

She exhaled and settled her wrists on the ropes, one on each side, then twisted her arms so the rope was wrapped tight over the thick coat sleeves. She gave a hard tug on each rope and they held. The coat protected her skin, but it was going to be slow going the way she had planned to do this. Sucking in a deep breath, she kicked out a leg and aimed for the next step. Her foot connected with it, and it disintegrated.

She fell through the plank, but the ropes kept her from tumbling into the abyss below. Sophia's scream bounced off the walls. Pain ripped through Kira's shoulders, and she gasped, choking on her own screams.

She finally caught her breath, prayers winging heavenward while she dangled over the deep, dark pit. *Don't look down, don't look down, don't look . . .* The lights along the cave wall gave enough illumination to see the bridge, but below it was pitch black.

Fire continued to burn its path through both shoulders, and her arms trembled from hanging over the abyss. The ropes dug tighter around her arms but held.

Kira swung her leg up. Tremors raced up and down her arms, and the rope bit into her palms, but she held on for dear life.

Her foot connected with the step. Metal clanked from the impact. She pulled the step closer with her heel and managed to get her other leg up. Then she rewrapped her arms in the ropes so she could shimmy until she was seated on the next plank as if it were a swing.

The board was solid, reinforced with a steel plate under the wood.

She sat for a minute to catch her breath and give her arms and legs a chance to stop shaking.

And she figured it out. This was how the Youngs walked across. There was a pattern, with reinforced steps. These men loved their codes and patterns.

She stood. A crack sounded and a bullet whizzed by her head. Kira ducked. "What are you doing? Stop!"

Over her shoulder, she caught a glimpse of Sophia lunging for Victor's gun. She must have knocked his arm for the shot to go wild. A sharp cry tore from Sophia's throat in Russian as she drove punches and kicks at the man. She'd exchanged her rich trophy wife image for that of a battle-weary warrior taking her last stand. She obviously had some training when it came to fighting and had no doubt taken the big man by surprise. He threw up his arms to block, but Sophia's heel connected hard, knocking the weapon free from Victor's grasp.

"Sophia! No!" Kira didn't know whether to go backward or forward, so she leaned forward and rewrapped her arms, taking every other step until she was standing in the middle of the bridge.

Sophia had managed to get the gun and now turned it on Victor, who stood with wide eyes and hands up. "Where's my son!"

Victor growled and made a quick move to take the gun back.

The shot echoed off the rock walls. Victor stumbled backward, hand to his chest, with blood seeping through his fingers. His foot hit the edge of the ledge and he stumbled into the pit.

"No!" Sophia's cries mingled with Victor's. And then Victor's ended. Abruptly. Sophia's continued.

"Sophia! Stop! Please! It's going to be okay!"

Kira huffed out a breath. At least now she didn't have to worry about Victor shooting her in the back. But that wasn't the outcome she'd wanted. Death was never the goal, no matter how much evil she faced.

Sophia wept. "Now I won't know where he was keeping my son. I didn't mean to shoot him." She wailed and covered her face.

"It was self-defense, Sophia. He was coming after the gun and probably would have killed you if you hadn't fired. We'll find your son. Please."

Sophia's sobs turned to sniffles. "How?"

"I don't know, but I can't think about it here. Go get some help. Please. It's just you and me back here now, and we need to find Bryce."

Kira made the choice to keep going. She was inching closer to the other side anyway. She took every other plank again, searching for the reinforced ones. It was still a big leap between rungs, and she continually had to rewrap her arms in the ropes, but every second board held with the metal plate underneath, and she made it to the other side.

She fell onto the stone ledge with tears in her eyes. She looked back over the chasm at Sophia, who still stood with the gun at her side.

"Sophia, go get help."

The woman glared at Kira. "No. I'm coming with you. I want to see this treasure that people are dying for—the reason they took my son."

Kira weighed her options. Victor's reinforcements may have

already worked their way into the tunnel, so sending Sophia for help might get her into more trouble. It made sense to keep the woman with her. Strength in numbers and all that. "Okay. Just take every other wooden step, starting with the first one. They alternate with reinforced metal, so they'll hold."

Sophia tucked the gun and flashlight into her waistband, then started across the bridge, taking tentative steps and clinging to the ropes. Once Sophia reached solid ground, they both breathed a little easier, and Kira was finally able to survey their surroundings, thankful for the flashlight Sophia had brought. Hers had fallen out of her pocket and into the abyss when she stepped on the loose plank.

The rock wall loomed ahead of them, but they found the tunnel similar to the one they'd used to enter the cavern. They walked for a few minutes, following the stone-walled hallway, and approached another room. Smaller this time and they had to stoop as the ceiling dropped to five feet in height. They searched the face of the rocks for any kind of keypad or entryway.

"What do we do?" Sophia whispered. "This can't be it."

"Let me see your flashlight. I think I see something."

Sophia handed it over, and Kira aimed the beam into a hole in the side of the rock. "It's too dark to really see anything, but . . ." She took a deep breath. "Please don't let there be creepies or crawlies in there," she whispered. "Or bats. Or anything else." Then she slid her hand into the hole. She squeezed her eyes shut and felt around until her hand touched something solid. And metal. "I think I found it."

"What?"

"Some kind of lever." One way to find out. Kira pulled up.

The rock wall groaned. If she'd just started an avalanche, they'd both be dead.

Not an avalanche. The wall in front of them separated like elevator doors.

Kira eyed Sophia, and the woman shrugged and said, "After you."

Of course. Kira always had to go first.

She stepped through the opening and felt the wall until she found a light switch. Kira nearly stopped breathing at the sight before her. Electric lights lit the room that was carved out in the rock, with high ceilings and wall-to-wall shelves.

"I—I can't believe this exists." Sophia spun around. "There is a century's worth of missing art. And very well preserved."

Cool air flowed through Kira's hair, and she found the source near the ceiling. They'd built an air-conditioned room in the side of the mountain to keep the art in mint condition. Kira moved deeper into the room. The place resembled an art gallery, with paintings and sculptures set up as if on display. Each painting had a light to show it off, and there were even a few chairs spread around the area. Paintings hung on stands on either side of the room, and the walls of the cave shone with amber glitter. A gallery for the enjoyment of one.

"It's the missing crate from the Amber Room." Sophia gaped at the ornate wall. "The jewels. The wall sconces. They're all original pieces."

Two panels—rectangles five feet high and four feet wide—hung on a fake white wall. Made entirely of amber, they shimmered in the lights. Jewels ran up and down each side, along with intricate designs carved into the panels. Mirrors added to the brilliance of the piece.

Sophia stepped to the left, taking in every inch of the twenty-by-ten room. "We can't let the Society find this place." Then she stopped and looked at Kira. "We can use this as leverage to get my son back."

"I think you're getting ahead of yourself. We have no way out and one gun to defend ourselves from anyone who followed us in."

Sophia reached out to touch some of the amber stones from the piece, attempting to break a stone off. "I have to get my son back. They'll make a trade. They blackmailed my husband, so they understand the language of money. I can give them what they want."

Kira placed a hand over Sophia's. "If *The Goonies* movie taught us anything, it's that booby traps are everywhere. Don't touch. We don't know what we're up against. These men protected this art for centuries, so what's to keep them from having a trip wire to blow up the entire cave?"

The woman hesitated. "Then what do you suggest?"

Kira had convinced her. That was shocking.

But the question hung in the air between them. How were they going to get out of this? If only Kira had a way to communicate with the FBI and see what was happening on the other side of the mountain. And Bryce . . .

Did he survive the shooting? She'd been desperately trying not to think about him so she could focus on staying alive, but now the thought intruded, and she whispered a silent prayer to the one who knew.

She ran a hand through her hair, shaking out a layer of dust. "Maybe we should head back over the bridge. We need to find Alex and Bryce."

"You're not going anywhere."

Kira spun. A woman with her face hidden in a black cloak stood in the entryway.

She knocked back the hood on her cloak, and Sophia gasped.

Kira stared. "Natalia? But you're dead."

BRYCE RESISTED THE URGE to pound on the rock wall that housed the secret door. It had been over twenty minutes since he'd last seen Kira. She'd crossed the threshold into a spooky cave with no backup and no weapons. The place was probably crawling with booby traps.

Agents worked around the cave, collecting evidence.

"How are we going to get her back, Violet? Without the keys, we can't open this door."

Violet put a hand on his good shoulder, the one that didn't throb with every heartbeat. "Kira is strong. She'll make it. And we've got an engineer on the way to see if he can get this rock wall open."

FBI agents had swarmed the area and rounded up all the gunmen who'd arrived to defend the Society's interest in the bunker.

An agent escorted Alex out of the cave to wait while they searched for Sophia. Alex mouthed, *Find them*, to Bryce, and he nodded.

He paced in front of the invisible door. "Who is the woman in the cloak?"

"What woman?" Violet radioed another agent to ask the status, but the man had no information. "I didn't see anyone when I came in, but I did make a beeline for you since you needed help."

Bryce ran a hand through his hair. "There was a woman. And now Kira's trapped, with the good guys on this side and the bad guys on the other. She's outnumbered."

"There has to be another way into the tunnel." Violet began investigating the rock wall, shining her flashlight into every crevice. "They couldn't just use some funky key combination and not have another way in. These men were smart. What if there's a back entrance or something?"

Bryce followed her lead, but they came up empty-handed. And the clock was still ticking. "It's no use. They took the keys and we don't have time to search the cave for a back entrance."

"God, please open this door," he murmured.

Nothing happened.

"Argh!" He slammed a fist on it, and it shuddered. And shifted? He hit it again. Then again. A pop rang out, followed by a creak, and the ground rumbled.

Violet squinted at Bryce. "Did you just pray the door would open and then—"

The door slid open.

"Apparently I did." Still confused, Bryce stared at the wide-open entryway. Then examined the key holes. The locks were old and his pounding on the door had shifted the mechanisms. Maybe? He laughed. *Go God.* Wait until Kira heard this story. *Please, God, let me tell her this story.*

Violet's eyebrows shot up. "Should we go in? I'm concerned it's a trap."

She had a point. Why had the door suddenly opened without the key? He didn't want to take the credit from God, but . . .

Ivan entered the cave. "Well, don't just stand there. Let's go."

Bryce didn't know what to think of Ivan. "I'm so glad you're on our side. How did you get it open?"

"I walked the perimeter while your agents rounded up the Society guards. I found an override switch built into an electrical box in the side of the mountain. They've got a generator somewhere. I heard it humming. But no time to talk. We need to find Kira and Sophia."

So, God had still opened the door. He'd just used Ivan to do it.

Violet took a second gun out of her ankle holster and handed it to Bryce. They followed Ivan through the entryway and into a long, dimly lit stone tunnel.

"What are we up against, Ivan?" Bryce asked, sandwiched between Ivan and Violet. They kept a slow and steady pace.

"I saw the woman in the cloak arrive. It looks like the leader of the Society was a woman after all. Natalia, Alex's maid."

"What?" Bryce frowned. "But she's dead. We saw her get shot."

"Yeah, only she's here. She must have had it all planned to fake her death and disappear with the treasure. It was definitely her, and Alex confirmed it when I spoke to him just now."

In all of their efforts to survive, Bryce hadn't considered the ramifications of finding the long-lost treasure room and what it would mean.

Money. Power.

Death.

"My team has done some research," Ivan said. "The ACS has ties to terrorism. They believe that because of their heritage, they should be the ruling class of Russia and have been supplying weapons to Russian enemies. If they get the treasure, the group will have enough money to fund a war. Against Russia."

They walked in silence until Ivan stopped short.

"What's wrong? Is it a booby trap?" Who knew the extent the Young family would go to in order to protect the treasure.

Then Bryce saw it. The flashlight beams lit the ground a few feet in front of them and then nothing. Two lanterns hung on one wall. The rest—inky blackness.

"What is that over there?" Violet asked and shifted her light to the left. A wooden rope bridge swayed over the black chasm. On the other side of the black hole, Bryce could make out a faint light, but other than that, it was just more of the same—rocks and darkness.

"That must be the way to the treasure room," Bryce said and started for the bridge. He inspected the bolts that attached the ropes to the cave walls.

Violet moved behind him. "I can't see the bottom."

One of the wooden planks was missing. Had someone fallen into the abyss? He shuddered at the thought. *God, please. Not Kira. Not anyone.*

"What's the plan?" Ivan said, keeping his voice low. "We're powerless if they catch us on the bridge. I say we ambush them on the way out. This way we have some semblance of control."

"But in the meantime they could kill Kira and Sophia—assuming they're still alive. You and I both know they want to get rid of everyone standing in the way of the treasure."

Ivan grunted. "Still, I don't like leaving the entrance unprotected, even if the FBI has the place surrounded. Any of Victor's men could slip in. I'm going to make sure we weren't followed, and I can let other agents know we need some backup in here."

A minute after Ivan left, voices rang out from across the chasm.

Were they too late?

They retreated to the tunnel to stay out of sight. Bryce didn't like hiding but conceded it might be the best course of action at the moment.

I'm coming for you, Kira. I promise. You're not on your own.

23

KIRA NEEDED TO DEFUSE this situation. Fast.

Sophia continued to face off with the maid, who was supposed to be dead. The woman had screamed at Natalia, despite the fact Natalia held a gun.

"You kidnapped my son," Sophia said, heaving great lungfuls of air. "You used my husband and destroyed our lives."

Sophia still had Victor's gun, but would she use it?

"I did what I had to do to preserve my family's legacy." Natalia stared Sophia down.

"I'm Russian too. Why would you turn against your own people? You stole my child!"

The woman laughed, a low chuckle that sent a shiver up Kira's spine. Natalia spoke in Russian. "You're too trusting, Sophia."

Defiance spread across Sophia's face. "I saw you get shot," she said. "They killed you right in front of me. Blood poured out of your head."

Natalia gave a small smile. "We were close to the treasure and I needed to disappear. The FBI can't come after me if I'm dead. No one will suspect that I'm in charge of the Amber Crown Society. Meanwhile, this treasure belongs to my family. This is our legacy, stolen from us. And I will take it back."

Kira's mind spun, trying to put the pieces together—and keep Natalia talking until she had a solid plan to get them out of this. "So you blackmailed the Dominiks into tracking down the treasure for you, all while working for them, watching their every move?"

Nothing like hiding in plain sight.

"I was a maid. Invisible. But had access to many conversations and no one was the wiser. My only regret was not figuring out that your husband was really an FBI agent. I caught him snooping around but bought the billionaire art buyer act."

From the look on Sophia's face, she had no idea her enemy had been under her nose the entire time.

Natalia glared at Kira. "You pulled a fast one on us. But don't worry, we'll take care of you and that precious *husband* of yours."

Kira's breath hitched. If Natalia had Bryce on her radar when it came time to clean up, that meant he was still alive.

Sophia sniffed. "Why, Natalia? Why would you kidnap an innocent child?"

The woman scoffed. "We needed a reason to legally be here in the United States. And Alex was involved with the art auctions here, so we knew he could get us access to the statues."

"But what do you hope to gain from this?" Kira asked. "It's not like you can get all this treasure out of the country."

"The Amber Room belongs to me. The rest can be sold, but I will inherit what is rightfully mine." Natalia scanned the room, admiring the beauty of what lay before them. "Where is Victor?" The lust in her eyes turned to fear. "I don't see my husband. He came with you, no?"

Things just went from impossibly bad to apocalyptic in one second. Natalia was about to find out that her *husband* had died, swallowed up by a black cavern.

Kira stared at Sophia and silently willed her not to confess to shooting Victor.

Sophia stepped forward, brandishing Victor's gun.

Don't say it. Just don't say it.

"I killed him. Just like I'll end you. Tell me where my son is."

Natalia pulled the trigger. Twice. The deafening booms sent Kira to the floor. She rolled looking for cover and saw Sophia clutching her stomach.

"Sophia! No!" Kira covered her head and waited while the mountain groaned and pebbles and dust fell around them. The rocking stopped, but the sound of rocks shifting spiked her pulse even more.

She hurried to check on Sophia, keeping one eye on Natalia. She'd ducked as well and was still on her knees, weapon clutched in her hand. Would the next bullet be for Kira? Sophia had a weak pulse and blood seeped through the woman's expensive blouse. Kira took off Violet's jacket and wrapped Sophia's stomach with the coat to stop the bleeding. She wiggled Victor's gun out from under Sophia's hip and stuck it in her waistband.

Natalia had distracted herself with all the shiny jewels. So Kira did the only thing she could think of.

She ran. If she could get across the cavern, she could get Sophia help.

God, please let Sophia live. Too many people have died because of greed. She deserves to be reunited with her son.

Kira stopped at the edge of the bridge. It was now or never. She moved across the planks, two by two, wrapping her arms in the ropes again. But if she went fast enough, maybe she could make it before—

"Stop right there."

Kira halted. She wrapped her hands around the rope railing and turned her head to see Natalia pointing a gun at her back.

Just great. Kira took two more steps, every other plank. Now she hovered in the dead center of the bridge and turned to face off with the crazy woman brandishing a gun.

"You killed Victor." The woman stepped onto the bridge, following Kira's steps. "He knew you were trouble from day one when he killed that security guard in the gallery. He should have killed you when he had the chance."

Kira whipped out the gun from her waistband and aimed it at Natalia. The two stood out in the wide open and faced off. Nothing underneath them except a rickety plank and some rope. And a big black hole.

They stared at each other. Kira could take the shot, but between the stress and the dim lighting, accuracy would be the issue. The last thing she wanted to do was have a shot trigger a rock slide. But Natalia wouldn't hesitate to fire. She'd already shot Sophia.

Natalia stood and glared, the dim lights casting shadows over her contorted face. But Kira couldn't turn to move or the woman would most certainly shoot her in the back.

The bridge lurched. Kira tightened her death grip on the rope in her left hand, the gun still trained on Natalia in her right hand. She searched for the source of the jolt and spotted it.

The rock wall had two spots on either side of the chasm that anchored the ropes in place. When Sophia had lunged at Victor, the gun had fired and the shot whizzed past Kira's head. And now she knew where the bullet had landed.

In the anchor securing the bridge to the rock.

She looked at the end of the rope railing. One of the two anchor bolts had dislodged from the stone wall. The other strained under the weight. It wouldn't hold much longer. Natalia noticed it too and backtracked toward solid ground.

"Run, Kira!"

She turned to see a shadowy figure at the edge of the bridge. She'd recognize that voice anywhere.

Bryce.

Kira plunged forward, desperate to reach Bryce, taking the planks two by two. She continued her process of wrapping her hands in the rope but picked up the pace. With a quick glance over her shoulder, she noticed Natalia was almost to the other side—closest to the treasure. But no treasure compared to Bryce.

She was eight planks from the end. Four more steps and she'd make it to solid ground. Bryce stood at the edge, arms out, ready to help her. Violet stood at his side.

A snap sent a jolt through her spine, and the bridge collapsed, sending Kira free-falling.

"KIRA!" BRYCE LUNGED for Kira's hand, but she slipped through his fingers. "No! Kira!"

He stood at the edge of the chasm and peered into the abyss, heart pounding, breath suspended.

Violet leaned over the side and pointed. "There. The bridge now looks like a ladder, and she's holding on to the side."

Kira clung to the rope, her feet dangling in the air. But she held on and swung her legs toward the rock wall. Her foot connected to a solid plank below her and she managed to get her other foot onto the step. It supported her weight, but her arms began to visibly tremble from the exertion.

He and Violet each grabbed a rope and pulled, but the bridge wouldn't budge from the weight. Bryce hit the ground and extended his good arm to help drag Kira up. "Untangle one arm. I'll help you up."

"We need to get help for Sophia." Kira's face strained from clinging to the rope ladder. She just needed to climb about four feet before he could grasp her hand.

Where was Ivan with that backup?

Bryce felt something on his back and noticed Violet holding him steady while he reached down. "Climb, Kira."

She gripped the rope, but the bridge jiggled. She looked up at Bryce. "What was that?"

And then he saw it. A hand coming out of the abyss. Natalia

had somehow hung on and was climbing the ladder, now a few feet below Kira.

Kira's feet connected with the wooden step, but she bypassed it for the one above it.

C'mon, Kira. Just a few more feet.

Natalia kept coming for Kira, rage marring her once beautiful youthful face. The woman caught up and dug her dagger-like nails into Kira's leg. Kira kicked the woman away, trying to shake her off.

Natalia hung on and tried to drag Kira down.

Bryce reached out as far as he could and Kira reached up. Their fingers missed each other by mere inches. Just one more step and he'd be able to pull her up. His other shoulder smarted, but he pushed through the pain.

One of Kira's hands fell from the rope. She flailed to get her hand back on the rope, but Natalia continued to pull.

A gun fired, and Natalia screamed. The woman let go of Kira's leg and fell backward. And then she disappeared. They didn't even hear her hit the bottom of the cavern.

Kira locked eyes with Bryce, her breaths coming in short pants. He glanced across the gap. Even in the dim lights installed in the rocks, he could make out that Sophia stood with a gun in one hand and the other hand pressed into her bleeding stomach. He prayed there was another entrance to this place, because Sophia collapsed to the ground.

"Take it slow," Bryce said to Kira. "Sophia shot Natalia. You're safe now." Well, safe from being shot. "Just a few more feet and we'll pull you up."

She grunted and repositioned her arms higher, clutching the rope. But her arms quaked, and Bryce could tell her strength was sapped. "I can't reach," she gasped. "I'm not sure I can pull myself up any farther."

"Kira, I believe in you. You're one of the strongest people I've ever met. You're so close. Please, darling, try."

Just one more wooden rung and he'd have her.

"Don't look behind you, Kira. Keep your eyes on me."

She stared at Bryce, her face sparking a ferocity he'd never seen in her before. One of sheer determination. She pulled her foot up, skipping a step, he assumed, to save time.

"They reinforced every other step with metal," she said, as if reading his mind.

"Just keep climbing, Kira. You're doing great."

With another groan, she dragged herself up to that next step. This time, when she reached out her hand, Bryce caught it. He lifted her up, and Violet reached over to grasp Kira's other hand. Together they hauled her up and she rolled onto the ledge. Violet let go of both of them, and Bryce stood, pulling Kira up and into his arms, away from the chasm.

She gasped and pulled in several ragged breaths, and he just held her. Finally, she looked up. "Thanks for the rescue, partner—"

He cut her off with a kiss. She wrapped her arms around his neck and melted into him. He loved Kira and wasn't wasting another second.

She kissed him back with the same intensity. He ran his hand through her auburn locks.

Now that she was in his arms, he was never letting go.

The moment was perfect, until footsteps echoed through the tunnel and Violet cleared her throat. "Could you two maybe take that outside? We've still got a lot of work to do now that you've uncovered a secret treasure."

Pulling his lips from hers, Bryce saw two agents appear at the tunnel's entrance, taking in the scene.

"Sophia!" Kira tore herself away from Bryce's grip, and his arms instantly ached for her. They both looked across the pit. Sophia managed to stand again, then clutched her stomach and stumbled backward.

"We'll get help, Sophia. We're coming back for you."

The agents stayed behind as the three of them raced out of the cave through the tunnel. Bryce wasn't prepared for the quick lighting change when he stepped outside. He used his hands to shield his eyes from the harsh glare of the portable lights the FBI had stationed all around the entrance. The area must have been lit for a mile.

"Over here," a voice called.

They rushed toward Agent Bailey, who looked up from reviewing a map with several other agents. "I'm so glad to see all of you," he said. "You had me worried there when the place started rumbling—"

"We need to find another way in to get to Sophia," Bryce said.

"My wife!" Alex called out and ran over to them. "Where is Sophia?"

Bryce put his hand on the man's shoulder. "She's trapped right now, on the other side of the cave, and we couldn't get to her. Natalia shot her, but she saved Kira's life by shooting Natalia."

"The treasure room has climate control," Kira said. "The Youngs had wind power to generate electricity for the cave. There has to be another way in, a mechanical room, or something other than one entrance. I can't imagine they crossed that stupid bridge each time they wanted to get to the place."

"Of course! They must have a back door." Ivan took over the map Agent Bailey had been reviewing. "Here." He stabbed the map with his finger. "That's the most logical spot in the mountain to have a secondary entrance—or exit."

Agent Bailey barked orders for some agents to check it out.

Ivan turned to Bryce. "My work here is finished. Thanks to you and Kira, we've stopped the smuggling ring, taken down a secret organization that threatened Russian national security, and recovered priceless treasures."

"National security threat?" Kira asked.

Ivan nodded. "The Society claimed to be about preserving art and maintaining culture, but they have ties to a militant organization. We believe they were funding a terrorist group that threatened both the US and Russia. They've been profiting off the sale of antiquities for years and turning cash into weapons. We stopped the treasure from disappearing and found the statues Peter tried to run off with. He'd hidden them behind a tree, and one of your agents found them. So all three statues will be reunited and preserved."

"What about Alex and Sophia's son?" Kira asked. "Has he been found?"

Ivan's eyes fell to the ground. "Not yet. I've been tracking their son, and I believe he's being held in DC by a Russian couple who are members of the ACS. Your friends at the FBI should be raiding the place as we speak."

He moved to talk with Agent Bailey, and Kira and Bryce debriefed with another agent, telling their version of the events. After about twenty minutes, whoops and hollers erupted from the agents and law enforcement officers who had descended around the mountain. Two paramedics carried Sophia through the forest and over to a makeshift medic tent. Alex went running.

"I guess they found your back door, Ivan," Kira said. "Information that would have been helpful before I had to cross that bridge of death."

Ivan chuckled. "I heard what sounded like a generator, I just couldn't see it. So glad your team found a way to get Sophia—and the art—out."

"What will happen to all the art? I'm sure different countries will want their artifacts back, and lots of people will claim ownership."

Ivan frowned. "I'm sure you are right. But Russia is willing to share custody of the pieces with the US until claims are reviewed. We want the world to enjoy these pieces, now that they've been found."

"We're just glad you were on our side for this mission." Bryce's vision blurred, and had he slurred those last few words?

Kira put her hand on Bryce's arm. "You don't look so good. Someone should check out that wound."

As if to prove her point, his legs gave out from underneath him. Maybe it was the adrenaline crashing, but the throbbing pain under his makeshift bandage told a different story.

Ivan held him up, careful not to bump his wounded shoulder.

Kira walked with them over to the tent and flagged down a paramedic. They lowered Bryce onto a chair.

The man said, "The wound looks a bit rough. I recommend we airlift you to the hospital so they can make sure you don't have an infection from the bullet wound. It might be a scrape, but we need to get you cleaned up. We will want to check you for a concussion as well."

"I'll go." No need to argue. The adrenaline had subsided along with the danger, and the wound throbbed in time with his beating heart.

The medic nodded. "I'll give you a shot for the pain. Hopefully this will help."

Kira squeezed his hand as the paramedic jabbed him in the upper arm. Whatever meds were in that vial kicked in, and he started to feel good.

A little too good. He sat in the camping chair and his eyes grew heavy.

But his mouth worked double time. "I told you I'd be there for you, Kira. We're partners. Forever."

His words sounded garbled, so he hoped they had come out in the right order for Kira to decipher.

"You're on drugs," she said.

"No, I'm in love. With you. In case I hadn't made that clear."

She kissed him on the top of his head. "I love you too."

He watched Kira. The woman probably looked worse than she felt. Blood and dirt streaked her face, and her normally wavy hair was in disarray. But she was still standing.

And still as beautiful as ever.

The FBI would never let them work out of the same office. Yet the career he loved and had made the center of his universe suddenly seemed . . . less appealing. He couldn't imagine living miles away from her. And her career with the FBI was just beginning.

Whatever happened to him, all he knew was that he wanted Kira to be a part of his life.

After he took a quick nap.

24

BRYCE'S HEAVY EYELIDS drifted open as rhythmic beeps lulled him out of a deep sleep. A fluorescent light blinded him, but objects slowly came into his field of vision.

"Where . . . where am I?" His parched throat barely let out a whisper.

"You're in the hospital," a man's voice said. "I'm Dr. Sullivan. You just had surgery on your shoulder from the gunshot wound. We're still amazed at how long you stayed on your feet with that wound, but surgery went well, and you should heal nicely within the next few weeks. And more good news—you don't have a concussion."

"Kira?"

The doctor with silver hair and thick black-rimmed glasses smiled. "You have a few people in the waiting room. They refused to leave until you were out of surgery. I'll let visitors in, but only one at a time."

The memories resurfaced. The cave. Finding the treasure room—which, sadly, he never saw. And Kira, fighting for her life on the edge of a cliff.

They were safe now. The case would be closed. Life could get back to normal.

But did he want normal? He wasn't sure and that shocked him. The man who craved structure and security now wanted something . . . more.

A knock at the door spiked his pulse as indicated by the faster blip of the machine. All he wanted to do was see Kira.

"Come in." His hoarse voice croaked.

Too bad his father shuffled in. Not Kira.

And then it clicked. His father had come to see him in the hospital.

Talk about abnormal. "Pa?"

His father sat next to Bryce in a bedside chair. Bryce hadn't seen him willingly go anywhere in years. In the hospital lighting, he appeared frail, with saggy skin and bushy gray eyebrows. Not the intimidating force Bryce remembered from his childhood.

"Son, I'm glad to see you awake." His dad met his gaze, then looked at the ground. "I was worried that we might lose you when I heard about the shooting and the surgery."

"Why are you here?" Bryce's father hadn't shown any interest in him for fifteen years. Why now?

The old man shifted in his chair. "I've been a fool. It took hearing you were in the hospital for me to get off my high horse and say the things I should have expressed a long time ago."

Tears filled his father's eyes and Bryce lost his breath. He'd never seen his old man get emotional about anything.

"Son, I'm sorry for being a cranky old coot. You tried to reach out all of those years ago, but I was too stubborn. Had to do things my way. And, well, I wanted to say that I'm sorry for ruining a relationship with you."

He got up to leave, obviously not used to sharing such an emotional burden. Bryce reached over and grabbed the old man's hand. "I forgive you."

Pa's eyes glistened, and his shoulders shook. "I don't deserve it."

"It's grace. We all need it." His throat ached from both the surgery and his emotions. But he wanted to know more. "What changed?"

His father winked. "Oh, your *wife* made this old curmudgeon realize that while I never throw anything away—I mean, you never know when you might need it again—I had trashed the most important thing in my life. A relationship with my son."

Bryce smiled, although coming out of the effects of the anesthesia, he wasn't sure his face was working properly. "Stay in touch."

His father smiled, a sight Bryce had rarely seen. "Did Pa really find buried treasures? After all those years with the metal detector, I can't believe he stumbled on something big."

Bryce nodded, his head protesting the motion. "He was so close."

"You're just like him, Bryce. The man was tenacious but kind. You remind me of your grandpa."

Bryce blinked back the tears forming under his drowsy eyelids. That compliment erased the years of mean things his father had said. "Thanks, Pa."

His father dropped his hand and cleared his throat. "Well, I've taken too much time. There's someone else who's been pacing the waiting room floor wanting to see you, so I should let her in." He moved to the door, but turned back. "Oh, and I know I'm not in the position of offering you advice, but don't let this one go. She's something special." And he left.

"Oh, I'm never letting her go," he muttered.

Another knock and Kira entered without waiting for a response. She rushed to his bedside. "I'm so glad to see you awake." Her smile lit up the drab, sterile room. Bryce hoped she didn't notice the uptick in beeping sounds, because his heart rate had just kicked up a notch thanks to her presence.

He motioned for her to sit, and she pulled the chair closer. Her hand grasped his through the bedrail. "Details, please," he said. His head wanted to know everything even though his body screamed for rest.

"Sophia had surgery, and the doctors are hopeful there isn't permanent damage from being shot in the gut. The FBI arrested Alex in connection to the art smuggling ring. He's asking for leniency. Seems he'd been keeping copies of Davis Steadman's books. Davis had been purchasing small and struggling art galleries—through legitimate transactions—but then running illegal auctions through his verified businesses. And Alex, as his attorney who arranged all the legal—and illegal—business ventures, had access to the proof necessary to put away Steadman for a long time."

"What about their son?" Bryce chose as few words as possible. His throat was on fire.

Kira handed him a cup of water and helped him sip through a straw. "The FBI raided the home of Victor's sister-in-law. She and her husband had been taking care"—she made air quotes—"of Isaac. Olivia Baranov claims her husband was in the United States to place an orphan up for adoption and didn't know about Isaac's abduction. Not sure anyone is buying her story. Victor's brother seems pretty deep in the ACS affairs. And that's about it."

Now that the case had wrapped up, Bryce couldn't help thinking about the future. The thought of his one-bedroom apartment—far from Kira—had no appeal.

His eyelids drooped. If only he could stay awake, have the conversation he and Kira desperately needed to have.

"What next?" he managed.

She sighed and ran a hand through his hair. "Next is rest for you. Heal. We've got plenty of time to discuss the future."

"Don't leave."

She squeezed his hand. "I'm not going anywhere, partner. We're in this together."

Bryce drifted off to sleep. The heaviness of the past few days melted into peace.

Two Weeks Later

KIRA SCANNED THE CROWDED RESTAURANT looking for her roommates. She'd chosen the patio of her favorite Mexican restaurant, despite the cool temperatures. Where were Violet and Everly?

She checked her watch again. One fifteen. Kira had finally accepted Violet's invitation to attend church. Now she understood why Violet attended every Sunday. The vibe and authentic community gave her a sense of connection. She'd definitely go back.

But it wasn't like her roommates to be late to lunch. She held a four-person table while people stood in line waiting to get in. This place didn't mess around when it came to tacos and enchiladas.

She texted Violet. No response.

No response seemed to be the theme of her life these days. After Bryce had left the hospital, she'd hardly had any contact with him. Sure, things got busy for her—with a new case and a new partner.

But he couldn't just disappear from her life. Not after all they'd gone through. Not after their declarations of love. She needed him.

She thought he needed her too.

But what if he decided pursuing a long-distance relationship wasn't worth it? She'd refused to call and text him endlessly and allowed him space to make the next move.

She pulled up her last text to him.

When can we meet up in person? I miss you.

The only response had been *We'll meet in person soon. I promise.*

Two days had passed. That was all. No plans made, no calls or texts. Just a *See you soon, pal* generic message.

Had she read their relationship wrong? Absolutely not.

She tossed the phone onto the table, and it jangled the silverware. "I should have known better," she mumbled.

Their relationship had started in a time of crisis. They'd forged a connection based on their circumstances. But with her newfound trust in God, she refused to concede to the thoughts that told her Bryce had left her because she wasn't enough.

She wouldn't allow herself to go there ever again, and replaced the lies with truth.

The waitress stopped at her table. "Can I get you anything?"

"I'd like to order some chips and queso, please."

The woman nodded and scurried off with a bin of used dishes she'd confiscated from an empty table.

Kira might as well drown her feelings with cheese dip.

Her phone vibrated with a text from Violet. "Finally."

Everly and I won't be joining you today. But we've got a surprise for you. Just look up.

Up? She raised her gaze. At the wood beams on the outdoor patio ceiling?

And then she spotted him.

Bryce.

Her heart thudded a faster beat. He strode down the sidewalk toward her. His jeans and well-fitting sweater made him look more like that famous soccer player than the overly serious FBI agent specializing in art crimes.

Bryce opened the patio gate and stood in front of her table. "Is this seat taken?"

She smiled. "Apparently my conniving roommates aren't going to show up today."

He laughed, a sound that melted away some of the doubts

about their relationship. He sat down in the chair next to her and threw her a mischievous wink. "What can I say? Everyone has their price, and Violet and Everly's is chocolates from the finest DC chocolatier."

Kira crossed her arms. She wasn't letting him off the hook that easily. "You could have texted back."

He sighed. The waitress came back with the chips and queso, and Kira noted her sudden interest in Bryce. The woman was a little too flirty while taking their orders. She returned in seconds with three bowls of salsa and a drink he hadn't ordered.

Kira bit back a smile. "Do you ever get tired of all the attention from women?"

"All I want is the attention from one woman. And I did text you back. I said we'd talk in person. I'm not having a relationship with a phone. But the last few days have been a whirlwind."

"Right. One vague text with no information. Way to make me overthink everything."

He shot her a contrite look, and she laughed. "I heard you have desk duty," she said. "I know what it's like to be sidelined with an injury. I'm pretty sure that's how we met."

He chuckled. "I needed a few days to get my head together. You know I'm a man who plays by the rules, but this mission had me throwing the rulebook right out the window. So I had to figure a few things out."

She leaned in over her plate. Maybe he had some clarity on things, and she didn't want to miss a word. "Like what?"

He steepled his hands in front of his chin. "We should discuss what we're going to do now that we're not actual partners on the job. And we're not married anymore. I'm not dealing well with not seeing you."

"Same. I kind of like having you around. Someone to cook for."

"Well, I do love to eat. But we're partners whether we work together or not." He sat back in his chair, appearing calm and comfortable, despite this deep talk he was having. This was so not like the straitlaced, hyper-organized, serious Bryce that she'd met that night in the police precinct.

"I want to run a few things by you. Make sure you agree with some decisions I'm thinking about making."

He wanted her opinion? About his future?

No. Their future. He was laying the building blocks for a future that included her. She just needed to keep her heart from melting into a puddle on the floor.

Let the man talk, Kira.

"First of all, I'm thinking about hanging up my hat with the FBI."

She gaped, then snapped her lips shut. "What?" Okay. Not what she was expecting.

"I love being a Special Agent, but my life had been so wrapped up in the art smuggling case. I think it's time I pursue another career. Maybe a job that might bring me to DC."

Definitely not where she thought things would go. He was giving up his life to be with her. She couldn't let that happen. "B-but—"

He put up his hand. "This has nothing to do with you. You're not making me move or change. This is what I want."

Wow, it's like he could read her mind. All she could do was smile. "Continue with your master plan."

"I used to work for a small private gallery and I loved it—getting to procure pieces and help with the restoration process."

He pulled out a folder from the satchel she hadn't noticed him carrying. Maybe her focus had lingered a little too long on how good he looked in that sweater. She took the beige file and flipped through it.

"There's an art gallery for sale in DC. It's in an up-and-coming area. I want to buy it. I've spent the last few days figuring out my finances, trying to convince my landlord to break my lease. The place has an apartment above it where I can live. It has two bedrooms, and my father said he'd even come visit. He's also allowing me to move him to an independent living facility where he can get meals and help when he needs it."

"I'm so glad your father has come around. But you won't be in the FBI. And you're a great agent."

"If I'm not in the FBI, we can date. If I live in the same city as you, we can date. If I'm not working eighty-hour weeks, throwing myself into a case—"

"We can date." He'd removed all obstacles to enable them to have a relationship.

He reached over and took her hand, raising it to kiss her knuckles. "That is, if you want to date me. Kira, I love you. And I want us to be together. But you take things at your own pace. I don't want you to rush—"

"I'm all in. I decided that the moment I met you. I'm in love with you, and all that comes with it. You accept me for who I am. I want to see where this partnership will take us."

The waitress set the food in front of them and raced off. He glanced at the mountain of tacos, rice, and beans she'd ordered. "I'm assuming that wherever life takes us, it will involve an excessive amount of foods smothered in cheese?"

She stifled a giggle. "It most certainly will."

AUTHOR'S NOTE

I am so appreciative of all the readers who went on this adventure with Kira and Bryce. The idea for the story is loosely based on real events. The Amber Room is a real piece of art and history—a room fully decorated with intricately carved amber panels, jewels, and mirrors that actually existed. The art was gifted to Russia in the early 1700s and eventually was displayed in the palace of Catherine the Great. Then during World War II, it was dismantled by the Nazi forces and transported to Germany. But this is where the mystery begins (and my story idea).

No one really knows what happened to the Amber Room.

Historians are confident that the panels were dismantled and boxed into approximately twenty-seven crates. The crates arrived in a German city on the Baltic Sea (Konigsberg). From here, the theories run wild. Many historians believe the treasure was destroyed during bombings of Konigsberg. Or maybe it's hidden in underground mines in Germany or Poland. Could the Russians have recovered it and never told anyone? One of the more plausible speculations is that the crates were put onto ships that were sunk during Soviet attacks. So far, nothing has surfaced from the wreckage. Although less likely, some believe the Amber

Room may have been divided into smaller pieces and sold on the black market, possibly coming to America by a private collector.

As a suspense writer, I love a good unsolved mystery, and this one is epic and potentially worth half a billion dollars. My mind spun out a list of what-ifs: What if a piece of the treasure came to America? What if someone recognized its value and rescued one of the crates to preserve history from being destroyed? And what if a Russian secret society believed they were the rightful owners of a cultural artifact that the Germans stole from their ancestors?

While the rabbit statues were created for the story effect, imagine if even just a fragment of the Amber Room resurfaced now. There'd be lots of people and countries involved in establishing provenance as to who owns the rare find. Please take this story as my own (very fictional) theory about the mystery of a real missing treasure. And let's chat about your speculations! I'd love to hear from you.

—Kelly

Read on for a *sneak peek*
at the next book in the

FBI NEW RECRUITS
SERIES

Available October 2027

1

IF NOTE-TAKING WERE an Olympic sport, FBI Special Agent Violet Bancroft would have three gold medals by now. Witness number seven sat across from her at the café table. He'd recounted the details of his story, which consisted of "I saw someone running away from the convenience store wearing a black hoodie. He had his back to me. It was black. The hoodie. I don't know about the guy."

A detailed description of the man's back. Fabulous.

She jotted *dead end* in her notebook and slapped it shut. Maybe someday she'd use a recorder, but she found people clammed up if you set a device in front of them. And she liked to keep witnesses on their toes.

Jeremy Dyson sipped his steaming cup of coffee and smiled. Ten seconds into the interview, Violet knew the guy had nothing to offer, but she proceeded with more questions because every detail mattered. Maybe he'd noticed something that she could piece together with what the other eyewitnesses had given her. Doubtful, but she'd try.

He puffed up bigger than the thick winter jacket draped over the back of his chair. "Of course I thought about chasing the perpetrator."

"Of course," Violet murmured. "Anything else you can tell me?"

"The dude was tall."

Awesome.

The case had ties to organized crime, which was why the FBI was investigating a chain of convenience store robberies. But the shine of being a Special Agent had dulled when most of her life consisted of paperwork and interviews. Not that she minded the basic tasks, but she was ready for her first big break.

Dyson leaned back in the wooden chair, hands gripped around the oversized mug. Red spread across his cheeks and his dark eyes flickered with interest. "You know, I might remember more later. Let's meet up for dinner. There's a great place by the harbor—"

"I'm so sorry." She cut the man off before he went any further. "But you're a witness, which means I'm not allowed to go out with you. Wouldn't want to compromise the investigation." Violet tucked a wayward lock of her curly blond hair behind her ear. Time to pull the plug on this interview and move on to the next.

"You have the most beautiful blue eyes I've ever seen. Most FBI agents don't look like fashion models. Once you catch the bad guy, let's say we—"

Her phone buzzed with an incoming text. She pulled the device from her pocket. "This might be an emergency. Official government business. I've got to take it. But thank you for your cooperation. Another agent will be in touch if we need additional information."

She stood to leave, and Jeremy called out to her. "Could I at least get your number?"

Emergency, she mouthed over her shoulder and made a beeline for the café exit. She glanced at the phone and saw the text from her friend Kira Miller.

Dinner tonight?

Okay, not so much an emergency, but a lifeline to make her escape.

Violet wrapped her gray blazer around her and walked to her car parked on the street. Early November dropped hints of a chilly winter today. While she typed a quick response to Kira, her phone vibrated with an incoming call.

Her boss's name filled the screen. Supervisory Special Agent Jeremiah Turner. She answered. "Yes sir?"

"I have an urgent situation developing right now, and you are the closest agent," he said in lieu of a greeting. "I'm pulling you from your current case and reassigning you to a murder investigation of a federal judge. There's a witness I need you to interview."

Her "emergency" had become a reality.

"Brindleman and two other agents are on the way to back you up," he said. "I'm emailing you information on the deceased."

"On my way, sir." She disconnected the call, put the car in Drive, and pulled onto the street, heading to the address Turner provided, about ten minutes away.

Her first murder investigation. Maybe she could shirk her rookie status with this new assignment. Even if she had been chosen by being "the closest agent." Right place at the right time.

"Call Kira." The voice command prompted her phone to dial her roommate.

"Dinner plans may have to wait," Violet said. "I'm on my way to a crime scene. Someone killed a federal judge."

"Wow." Kira was also a Special Agent with the FBI. Sometimes their cases intersected, but at least Violet could share details with her friend. "That's big."

Violet merged onto the highway. "Yeah, I hate the circumstances, but it came at the right time. My last interview was a bust. The guy had no information. And then he hit on me." She rolled her eyes.

Kira laughed. "I can feel your eye roll through the phone. It's not every day a guy gets questioned by a former Miss America contestant."

"Oh, please. Those days are behind me. I'm more than just makeup and a pretty smile."

"Yeah, and if he knew your shooting record, he'd run like the rest of them. But maybe you should have said yes. You never know."

Violet shook her head. "Not interested. I've been down that road before. I was engaged once, remember? It didn't end so well." A chill ran up her spine, not from the cold, but from the memory of leaving her fiancé the night before their wedding. Not her finest moment.

Kira's sigh filled the car. "You had your reasons. And you aren't that same girl from seven years ago. There has to be someone that can keep up with you and love you for the woman you've become."

"Great. You fall in love with a fantastic man, and now you dispense relationship advice like a fairy godmother. You've got it bad."

Kira giggled. A sound so out of character for the bike-loving non-girlie girl that Violet raised a brow. "Bryce is something special," Kira said.

"In case you can't hear it, I'm rolling my eyes again at you."

"Of course you are."

Violet pulled off at her exit. "I'm almost there. Gotta run."

She disconnected to focus on where she was going. After a few turns, an affluent neighborhood sprawled before her. Despite the nip in the air, the tree-lined streets still showcased an array of fall colors—red, yellow, and orange leaves danced in the light breeze, unaware that death was just around the corner.

The conversation with Kira had dredged up memories Violet rarely let surface. Like her failed engagement. Something had shattered inside her the night she'd left Atlanta, for good.

The first domino had fallen, causing her life to crash down all around her.

But now at age twenty-six, the grown-up version of herself made smarter choices. She'd joined the FBI after graduating from college with a master's in criminal justice and never looked back. This was what she was meant to do.

Had she run out on the marriage her family had expected and let everyone down? Sure. Was she still running away seven years later? Maybe.

The emotional baggage of guilt never lightened with time. Which is why she tried not to think about it. She parked on the street in front of the three-story house and pulled up her email on her phone. Police lights and crime scene tape robbed the tranquil neighborhood of its midmorning serenity. Neighbors huddled in their yards, phones out, craning their necks every time the front door to the home opened.

Federal judge Jillian Hawkins, age fifty-eight, lived here, according to the information Turner sent. Divorced. Lived alone, while her two children resided in other states. Someone had discovered her stabbed to death in her bed this morning and had called 911.

Violet prayed for wisdom and stepped out of the car.

Brindleman's car pulled to the curb behind hers, and she waited for him. Together they followed the sidewalk to the crime scene and flashed their badges at the nearest officer.

Violet had worked with the old-timer on a few cases. "Aren't you a bit out of your element, Brindleman?"

Joe Brindleman prided himself on staying out of the action and even referred to himself as the king of paperwork. Despite his gruff demeanor and by-the-book attitude, the man had been a legendary agent, putting away some tough criminals. Now he was close to retirement age at fifty-six.

He snorted. "I might say the same thing about you, rookie. How did you spring a murder case?"

Geography. But she wouldn't mention that. "What? My talents as an investigator speak for themselves."

He crossed his arms over his ample midsection. He was fit for duty, but barely. "I heard Turner has you running down witness statements all day. My kind of assignment."

Great. She now had a reputation for desk work? Not exactly how she saw her career taking shape.

"Whatever." Another eye roll. She'd have to watch her facial expressions to avoid predictable habits. Not to mention it wasn't professional, and she had a job to do. "Let's get to it."

Brindleman lifted the crime scene tape, and she ducked under. They checked the bushes and windows around the house, looking for any signs of forced entry, but found nothing. Three stairs led to the front door, where the medical examiner met them.

"I'm Leland McAvoy. Let me show you what we've got." The man was in his thirties and spoke with a hint of a British accent.

Just inside the entrance, Violet and Brindleman slid plastic booties over their shoes. Violet had on heels today—not the best footwear for trudging through a crime scene, but it was this or the sneakers from her gym bag in the trunk. Her outfit consisted of a pink blouse and a gray-striped pencil skirt.

They followed the medical examiner through the ornate living room and up a staircase. A heaviness hung in the air, and Violet's heartbeat increased with each step she took. The stairs opened into a hallway where bloodstained footprints trailed through the ivory carpet and a handprint smeared blood on the wall.

Violet pointed to the blood and the ME nodded. "The suspect ran out of the room when he discovered the body. He headed into the study allegedly looking for a phone."

"Wait. Suspect? I heard a man called 911." Most suspects didn't take time to dial the police and report their own crime. Not that it couldn't happen, of course, but still . . .

McAvoy shrugged. "I assumed he's a suspect. You'll need to talk to him. He's claiming amnesia. Apparently he woke up next to the dead judge and has no idea how he got here. His story sounds fishy to me."

She glanced at Brindleman, whose face mirrored her own skepticism. They followed the ME to the master bedroom, and Violet asked, "Where is the suspect—I mean, witness—now?" Innocent until proven guilty still meant something, right? But she agreed, the statement *did* sound fabricated.

"Downstairs in the kitchen, waiting for transport."

Violet itched to question the witness. She'd check out the crime scene first, but her interview skills were ready to get the truth out of their witness and see if they needed to move him into the suspect category.

McAvoy cracked open the door and Violet froze. From her vantage point, all she saw was blood. Brindleman put a hand on her shoulder, which oddly helped stabilize her.

They entered the room only a few steps, so as not to disturb so much as a carpet fiber. A woman lay sprawled across a bed. The dark red quilt had once been white. A knife protruded from her chest.

Violet cleared her throat. "How long ago was she stabbed?" She refused to look away from the body.

Brindleman's eyes committed to one side of the room, and she took in every detail to the left—a habit from when they worked together during Violet's probationary period as a new Special Agent. A flash from a camera startled her, and she noted the ME's assistant snapping pictures from the head of the bed.

The woman's ash-colored hair was spread around her and across the pillows. But the blood spatters indicated she put up a mean struggle. The wall, the headboard, and her nightgown glistened with blood droplets reminiscent of a low-budget slasher film.

"This is Judge Jillian Hawkins," the ME said. "I can't be official on her time of death until I perform an autopsy, but I believe it was within the past three to four hours."

Two other forensic agents arrived and began collecting evidence. One swabbed the victim's fingernails, the other used a black light to highlight and photograph the blood spatters.

"Looks like we're freed up to talk to our only witness, who happens to be the suspect," Brindleman said, heading for the door. His face was gray, and she took comfort that he was fighting the same queasiness that churned in her own gut.

A police officer, the first on the scene, escorted them downstairs to the kitchen. "I arrived and found the witness covered in blood, standing near the victim," he said. "According to his statement, the witness woke up and discovered the judge dead. He then moved down the hall to the study to search for a phone. Apparently there wasn't one in the bedroom. Once he found the victim's cell phone, he rushed back to the bedroom and used her face to unlock it. But he claims to have no memory of how he got here and has no ties to the victim. Allegedly."

They walked downstairs toward the living room. A hallway led to the kitchen in the back of the house.

"What's the witness's name?" Brindleman asked.

"The guy's name is Noah Kingston. From Atlanta, Georgia."

Violet stopped.

Could there be another Noah Kingston from Atlanta in this world? Because there was no way this was *her* Noah Kingston.

The officer also stopped and turned to watch Violet. She stood statue still in the middle of the hallway, unable to breathe.

"What is it, Bancroft?" Brindleman studied her. "I know you just saw a dead body, but what's spooking you worse than that?"

Words. Why wouldn't her brain connect? "I'm sorry. Did you say Noah Kingston?"

The officer flipped his notebook open and double-checked. "Yeah. Noah Kingston. He currently resides in Atlanta and has no idea what he's doing in DC."

Her stomach churned and bile rose in her throat. She covered her mouth, afraid she might vomit. *This isn't happening.*

After several deep breaths, she rallied and found the two men still staring at her. "I'm okay. Sorry." She cleared her throat and marched into the kitchen. This had to be a mistake. She needed to see for herself . . .

A man sat at a table with his forearms resting on his thighs and his head ducked low against his chest. But she'd know that curly sandy-brown hair anywhere.

"Noah?" she whispered.

He looked up, his brown eyes flickering with recognition.

This was her Noah. The man she'd left the night before their wedding.

The man who was the prime witness in the murder of a federal judge.

And possibly the main suspect in her death.

ACKNOWLEDGMENTS

I am so blessed to be able to write books that readers enjoy. God has gifted me with an amazing writing community. Even during difficult times, other authors have been supportive and given me the encouragement to keep going. I want to thank my family and friends for all their love and support—I know I didn't have a lot of free time while trying to make deadlines. I also want to thank Lynette Eason. Collaborating on this series with you has been an amazing experience. It's been such a joy to work with you! To the team of editors at Revell, thank you for following along with a convoluted story and helping shape it into an amazing adventure. Also, I echo Lynette's thanks to Dru Wells. She spent considerable time with the manuscript and lent her expertise to help get the technical components right about FBI processes and procedures. (I hope I did it justice!) And thanks to every reader who has read my books, signed up for my author newsletter, or offered encouraging words to me. Each review you leave and every email you send makes my day.

—Kelly

LYNETTE EASON is the *New York Times* and *USA Today* bestselling and award-winning author of *Twilight Tactics* and *Deadly Charade*. She has written many thrilling romantic suspense series, including Lake City Heroes, Extreme Measures, Danger Never Sleeps, Blue Justice, Women of Justice, Deadly Reunions, Hidden Identity, and Elite Guardians. Learn more at LynetteEason.com.

KELLY UNDERWOOD's debut novel involved working with Lynette Eason as her mentor and lead author. *Defending Honor*, part of the Elite Guardians series, earned third place in the Selah Awards and was a finalist in the Carol Awards. Learn more at KellyUnderwoodAuthor.com.

Sign up for Lynette Eason's newsletter to stay in touch on new books, giveaways, and events.

LYNETTEEASON.COM

Lynette Eason | LynetteEason | LynetteEason